ONE LAW

Chronicles of the Reclamation: Book Two

Brandon J. LeBlanc

Edited by Clairmont Publishing
Formatted by Erika Russell
Cover designed by GetCovers
Published by Jackson Auto Publishing

Trigger Warning

To the Reader:
Chronicles of the Reclamation Book Two: One Law presents a dystopian world where law and order are scarce, leading to instances of profanity, violence—both implied and explicit—and themes of abuse, including neglect and abandonment. These elements are integral to the story's narrative and have been included thoughtfully rather than for gratuitous shock value. However, I understand that such content may not be suitable for all readers. If you anticipate difficulty with any of these themes, I respect your decision to forgo this book.

Parents and Educators:
As an English teacher, I believe *One Law* is appropriate for most high school readers aged 14 and up. However, it's essential to consider the aforementioned warning before recommending it to your children or students. While these themes may be unsettling, they also present opportunities for meaningful discussions. Ultimately, the decision rests with you, the parent or educator, in guiding your young readers appropriately.

For Mrs. Davis

Epilogue

Appendices

Prologue: The Reclaiming of Haven

Wednesday, 30 October, AD 2564
Haven
Brother Simon

Brother Simon closed his eyes and let the sweet smoke enter him through the woven fiber mask and into his nostrils.

Into his soul.

The Catholic Forty formed two semi-circles outside of the open gate of the Village of Haven. The sun had set in the west, behind them. Twilight had given way to dusk, and the shadows of the cloaked Brothers and Syballine lengthened before vanishing into the dark.

But not for long.

"The Darkness is the closing of the door. But the door will open again."

Brother Raël recited the mantra as the last rays of the western sun extinguished beneath the horizon of tall trees and rolling mountains. If their timing was correct, the new light wouldn't rise until forty minutes past sunset.

Forty was the most important number to the Ansati. Simon recalled the frequency of the number in his studies. Whole tribes traveled in exile for forty years. The flood waters had receded after forty days. Therefore, the numbering of the Catholic council would also be forty.

Yet tonight, they numbered forty-one.

Simon's eyes shifted to his right. Syballine Sister Esparánza held the hourglass in her right palm, but it was too dark, even in the light of the full moon, to see the slow stream of sand granules seeping through the narrow neck into the bottom chamber. Esparánza's eyes met his only for an instant. Both returned their attention to the village beyond the open gate.

The Reclaiming Ritual required that the village be emptied of its culture, its history, and its inhabitants by sunset for a full twenty-four hours. Indeed, every second was needed for Simon to lead the light bringers through the empty streets. He knew the village well. It had been his home for many years. Simon instructed the light bringers to disperse the incense strategically, keeping aware of the direction of the evening breeze. Horses and wagons had moved through the streets as quietly as a funeral procession. In a sense, it was a funeral procession.

The final pass through Haven was meant to check every building one last time. Simon's work had begun in earnest months ago, when it had become apparent that a Reclaiming was necessary. In those earliest days, the village folk were completely unaware of his work. When it became clear that he could no longer purge the village without drawing the suspicion of the residents, he had called upon Mayor Harp. He was a good man. He deserved to know.

When it was no longer a secret, people began to panic. Some fled. Some took their own lives, choosing to take their destiny into their own hands. Some pulled their blankets over their heads at night and never woke up the next morning.

The Darkness tonight was a blanket, and Haven would not awaken tomorrow.

The grains of sand trickled on in Esparánza's hourglass. Simon heard the crackling sound begin deep in the heart of the empty village. The light of the moon rose higher and shone brighter. At a glance, it appeared as if there were about ten minutes left in the timekeeper. He closed his eyes again as the Catholic Forty began to hum.

Simon didn't know what had made him stop at one particular house. It was small, occupied no more than a family of three. He had already been through it, removing a small cache of photo albums and personal effects. The Regazzo family had been poor, so it hadn't taken him much time to select what he would bring before closing the door behind him. A stroke of red paint above the door would be a sign for the light bringers that this home had been cleared but was not suitable for lighting. That would have required the full *crux ansata* to be painted. That was one Ansati legend that was entirely true. The rest were all *Reaper* tales.

Something had drawn him to the dead house. As though he were being drawn closer by a magnet, Simon had approached the building and opened the door wide. Behind him in the village, the motion of the wagon wheels and horse hooves were the only sounds he had heard. But something wasn't right.

Only after he had stepped inside and shut the door had he realized he'd left far too early the first time.

Esparánza held the hourglass gently as the final grains slid through the narrow way.

Brother Raël removed his hood. "Sister, is it finished?"

"Yes."

Raël raised his hand to signal the pipers to prepare. But Haven wasn't ready yet. The Light had not yet risen, though the smoke heralding its imminent rising hung on the air, rendering the light of the moon opaque in the mist. Simon couldn't remember the Light ever being late before.

And then it occurred to him.

Forty-one.

Sure enough, after a painful, hanging minute, the first licks of orange and yellow danced above the roof tops and the crackling intensified. He turned to the Syballine Sister once again. She smiled as the light of Haven's burning glowed in her beautiful, deep brown eyes. The Brothers followed Raël in removing their hoods as he closed his hand tight. The pipers exhaled a long, discordant wail into the smoky, autumn night sky, and the Light stretched upward, engulfing the village one building at a time.

"The Light pours over us, always…"

The Catholic Forty echoed Brother Raël's call as the pipers played a mournful melody that could have been heard in the surrounding villages. Simon rested his hands on the shoulders of the forty-first observer. The boy had been hiding in a pantry when Simon had softly called into the Regazzo house. Trembling, the orphaned boy tumbled onto the floor, clutching his knees close to his chest at the sight of the robed and hooded intruder. The boy had shaken his head at first, when Simon offered his hand. But when he drew down his mask and pulled back the hood, he recognized Simon from among the villagers. When the men had come to take the surviving children away, he must have been left behind. The poor Regazzo boy could have been in his new home by now, far away in a coastal hamlet in the loving arms of his new adoptive guardians. Le_Renard had promised a home for every child. Instead, he was left here to see what no child should ever have to see.

The death of his world. He was far too young to understand its rebirth.

"No one goes unnoticed, Andreas. Neither by ghosts, nor men."

The boy stood tense in the glow of the burning village, now fully consumed by the flames. Simon wasn't sure if the beads of water on his cheek were perspiration or tears. He couldn't tell if the boy understood that he was spared the red hand that had taken his parents and so many others. Or if he wished he hadn't been spared. They had much to talk about on the long trip back to Moab.

"We *Reclaim* you, son."

Chronicles of the Reclamation: Book Two

One Law

I: The Lion

All Created Things

Wednesday, 24 May AD 2572
The Library of Moab
Brother Andreas

The rungs of the wooden ladder creaked beneath Andreas's forty-kilogram frame. He was average weight, Brother Simon assured him. Maybe for another time, when food was richer and generations of altered genetics reduced the stature of twelve-year-old boys. He was always hungry, even if he never went without a full nutritious meal. Ansati farming needed no enhanced fertilizers or growth enhancement sciences. Andreas still remembered the sweeter foods in Haven, grown and traded up and down the Hudson. He still remembered much of his early years. Before the inferno consumed his home. Before it consumed him. Looking down from the seventh rung, his hands trembled in their grip as his head swirled from the height.

"Breathe, Andreas." From a plush, burgundy-upholstered chaise, Brother Simon coached him. "Close your eyes and breathe, son."

Closing his eyes made no difference. It never did when a red episode came on. Still, Andreas couldn't argue with the technique. The wave always subsided, whether he slowed his breathing and his heart rate or not. But with the exercise, he would stay in a red state far longer—sometimes enough to induce fever. He looked through the ladder rungs, only three from the top where the ladder met the archive shelving on track wheels. The spines of the volumes, deep browns and trimmed in gold, offered him nothing. Millions of titles lined the library stacks, from as high as four stories, row after row in claustrophobic corridors. None revealed their wisdom freely. Some were in languages no one in the order could interpret. *What value do they have if no one understands them?*

Smug book spines lined with what appeared to be Latin titles glared back at him. Andreas narrowed his brow, as if he were in a stand-off against a centuries-old textbook. Drawing full lungs of musty archive air, he closed his eyes, cursing his adversary as the red crept over him. He would burn them one day. All of them. He knew a thing or two about fire.

His hands tightened, blood vessels bursting in his fingertips from the pressure. The only way he was falling was with the ladder itself. It would shatter on the tiled floor at Simon's sandaled feet, but Andreas would not break. The shards of the ladder would be fuel for the final fire. And everything around him, deep crimson and radiant in its combustion, would go up in white-hot flame.

When Andreas imagined the Light pouring over all, it was always this way. And when the red subsided, it left him with hollow terror.

"Have you passed through?"

Andreas opened his eyes. *Lex Romana Burgundionum.* The title on the spine spoke to him, now that his episode had ended. Precisely the volume Brother Simon had sent him to retrieve. The episode had ended. He inhaled through his nostrils.

"I have passed through, Brother," Andreas responded once he was able to enunciate the words without stuttering. "How long? I counted thirty seconds."

Andreas heard Simon stand from his chair. One of the legs scraped the tile; the felt padding must have dislodged against a seam. Keeping a grip of the rung with his left hand, Andreas plucked the book with his right, tucking it into his leather satchel slung over his shoulder, as though he were harvesting apples. With as much confidence as walking a straight line on a level surface, he descended the final six rungs, stepping onto the library floor face to face with his mentor.

Simon's eyes always looked the same as that first time, when he opened the cupboard and a burst of light caused the boy to squint.

There was always a wash of light surrounding him. His eyes were patient, pathetic. His smile had grown wrinkled and hidden beneath a graying beard. But the expression remained. Andreas still couldn't translate it.

"I counted one hundred twenty-two seconds."

It was still a shorter episode. Andreas frowned. There was so much work yet to do. He handed Simon the book. On the front cover, a reproduced painting of a bearded man in robes could have been any of the Catholic Forty, even Brother Raël.

"Thank you." Simon received the book in hands patched with faint scars and spots. He set it on the study table. "But I think it's time we took a trip. The stories of *Gundubad* and *Sigismund* have waited patiently for millenia—a few more days won't hurt."

"Where are we going?"

Simon nodded his head, and that was all he needed do. Andreas's eyes brightened for the first time in memory.

Brother Simon and Andreas left at once. Sheol awaited.

Three full days by horse and cart, and the pair had passed through the seam, that invisible barrier that kept most from wandering too close to the Ansati city of Moab. The tall structures that formed the city core were long in their rear view, dipped beneath the rolling hills, seemingly drawn lower with each sunset. Two more days of travel in healthier lands, safe in their overnight camp from a perimeter of *crux ansata* symbols hung on trees, Andreas slept peacefully beneath the stars. He had no red episodes since the library. They were indeed rare in the wilderness. Pancha, Simon's mare, appeared to be more comfortable in nature as well. Simon always looked relaxed.

Lush woodlands gave way to sparser hardwoods over rockier terrain. It became clear that Pancha wouldn't be able to navigate the rocks much longer. Simon guided her into an open quarry surrounded by high walls of carved out stone, growing in with tall grass and shrubs.

"Pancha will have plenty to eat here," Simon explained as he slung a travel sack over his shoulder. He kept his hood over his head every second they were outside Moab's borders. Andreas did the same. "There is a spring. The same spring we're seeking, actually."

He had been unaware they were looking for a spring. Their leather canteens were full. Andreas followed as Simon crawled over boulders and bluffs, leaving his mare and cart in the quarry for who knows how long. Few knew where to find Sheol. Fewer knew what it was.

It was mid-afternoon, and the sun had melted away the clouds. As though on cue, Simon exclaimed. "Ah, here it is!" He beckoned Andreas with a lively wave before disappearing behind a sandstone ledge. Once he had caught up, Andreas glared down into a misshapen crevice framed with broken black and grey timbers. Simon's voice echoed from beyond the shadow of the opening.

"Lamps alight, son. The journey is now afoot."

Once past the threshold of the half-collapsed mine shaft opening, Andreas followed Simon down a steady declining grade, through humidity and earthen funk deeper and deeper underground. Colonies of bats huddled together by the tens of thousands, indifferent to the lamp light that passed beneath them. Rodents scurried and water droplets echoed all around them. After what felt like half a day, Simon approached a wall instead of continuing down the wide mine shaft. Lifting his lamp to eye-level, he felt the damp lichen-layered stone before nodding an answer to a question he hadn't asked.

"This is it." The Ansati Brother shifted his light to reveal an opening too narrow for even a fifty kilogram twelve-year-old to pass through. Simon set the lamp on the ground and leaned into the right side of the crevice. With a sturdy shove, it creaked and gave way, opening into a hidden tunnel that would have been near impossible to discover without prior knowledge or a dozen pairs of eyes searching. Andreas wondered how Pancha was managing back in the quarry. As Simon disappeared into the new passage, he almost wished he could have been back with the horse and cart.

"Come, Andreas. Keep your lamp level and follow close. We have some ways to go before we camp for the night."

Camp? How far is Sheol?

His inner chronometer already unreliable, Andreas gave up guessing how long they had hiked, or how far they had traveled. The air was thicker, harsher. There were fewer animals, and even lichens and mosses didn't grow this deep in the earth's crust. Simon must have sensed Andreas's apprehension.

"Sister Mora tells me you have been researching beyond your scriptural studies."

There were no secrets in the library. If Andreas tried to sneak into the sections that contained literature the Forty deemed beyond his grasp, the Syballine Sisters and researchers would report it back to the council.

"I've been diligent with my study, Brother." He wasn't lying. Andreas didn't mind reading old texts like some of the initiates. Every time he conquered a new volume, it was a victory over the ancients who had written them. Andreas hoped Simon would allow the deflection.

And for a time, he did. "Mora is indeed impressed by your study. Especially your effort to learn more about your episodes."

"There is plenty to read." Andreas stumbled on a loose rock, shaking the lamp light.

"Maybe share a line or two?"

Andreas gulped. He had a way of memorizing that the Brothers and Syballine Sisters envied. "There is one that I found comforting: *'The Light doesn't burden a soul beyond what it can bear.'*"

"Yes, that is a fine passage. *Qur'an*, if I'm not mistaken. 2:286." Simon was rarely mistaken when it came to sacred text. Andreas once believed that his mentor had memorized all of them. "But you misspoke. *'Allah* does not burden a soul beyond that which it can bear.' We must always be mindful of the original authorship, son."

"Of course. But isn't *The Light* the same as *Allah*?" There were hundreds of words Andreas took to mean the same. He never once meant any disrespect.

"Perhaps. But if you were face to face with the author, or the scribe who put those words to parchment all those years ago—*they* would have felt different. So, we honour *them* by keeping their observance."

Except they're dead. Long dead.

"That is a wise passage. I think it applies especially to you, Andreas." Simon had once told a younger, thinner, and more timid Andreas that he was stronger than most. That he had overcome tremendous obstacles in his short life. That he was a survivor.

The Light only gave what he could take. No more.

"But still, you are searching for… more." Simon had not forgotten his first question. "Mora says you have been asking about the Ossuary. May I ask you why?"

He had been dreading this conversation. Andreas stopped, setting his lamp on a jagged splinter of preserved, petrified timber. "Part of me feels empty, Brother. It always has. I realized one day that I remember nothing of my family. Of Haven. What my mother and father looked like. It's as though they were only a dream."

Simon set his lamp next to the other, doubling their shared light. They had emerged into a widening of the tunnel. "When the time is right, we can open your family's plot. But often it's a deeply emotional experience. And I worry about your—

"My episodes." Andreas finished Simon's thought. "I found another passage that makes a lot of sense to me, Brother. *'All created things are grief and pain.'*"

Simon sat, a troubled expression exposing the lines on his face in the lamps' shadow. "*Dhammapada*, Chapter twenty. But, you are missing the rest of the verse… 278, if I'm not mistaken."

You are never mistaken, Brother Simon.

"'*He who knows and sees this becomes passive in pain; this is the way that leads to purity.*'" Simon recited the rest of the verse on point. "Do you believe that everything is pain, Andreas?"

The red inside of him shifted. Andreas breathed and closed his eyes.

"I don't know if it is for everyone. But it is for me."

Simon rested a hand on his shoulder. "I wish it wasn't so… I wish it wasn't so."

Andreas silently counted to thirty and opened his eyes. "I'm tired. How much longer?"

"We'll stay the night here." Simon didn't answer the question, but he unpacked their bedrolls from his bag. "Sheol is a real place. But I think a part of you is already there, son."

Sunday, 3 June AD 2590
Moab
Brother Andreas

The fireplace heat was stifling, but Andreas wasn't sure he could contain the simmering red deep in his abdomen. It always broiled there first, like a knot that wound itself tighter somewhere behind his stomach. The red episode nested like a rotten egg in an abandoned nest. He chose to sit in a rigid wooden chair instead of the soft cushions of the divan. The Syballine Sister sat on the end closest to the fire, her veil obscuring her to the point she was faceless. It was an early warning sign that an episode was under way. The features of the face faded first.

"They tell us that Sheol *is* a real place. That one day, when we're ready, we will all visit it someday. And that when we see it, we will understand everything. *Who are the Ansati? What is our purpose?* The moment our sand-grained eyes open, the Light will fill us with all the wisdom that's been festering inside us." He took a sip of bitter tea from an earthen mug the Syballine Sister had offered him. Her matching mug, lumpy and uneven before the clay hardened in the kiln, sat on the small table between them. The old woman listed gently, left then right, as if she were fighting off sleep. Her breath drew the veil in and out with a soft wheeze. She didn't interrupt.

"But what they choose not to tell us is that the answers *aren't* within us. They're not in a stinking, rotten hole in the earth. They're not swelling in a big ball of hot gas in the sky. No, Sister. They are *here*. In Moab. In our Library, in our Ossuary. And that's why Sister Mora had to tell the Forty." Andreas swished the tea around the rim, droplets spilling over and running down onto his hands. The red was doing the same in his abdomen, burning the back of his throat like pyroclastic splashes.

The Sister groaned. The skin of her arms hung like wrinkled canvas, spotted and veined. She trembled, expending more energy to keep from toppling over.

"Brother Simon told me my whole life that there are no secrets. All we need to know is there for the reading. And I read, Sister. I asked the questions, and instead of answers, I was given directions—which stack, which row, which volume. But one day, I asked the wrong questions."

The episode flourished, out of his core into his extremities, seeping like an injection of pesticides. Tips of his fingers, under his toenails, from every pore. He smiled.

"Can you feel it, Sister? I know you can feel it. I learned in Sheol not to fight it."

The old woman huffed, drawing the veil to her cracked lips, until her breath soaked the lace with speckles of blood.

"I can't really blame you. It's in our nature to leave our loved ones behind. To leave them naked, in the wilderness, where the only shelter is the Light. It's our way."

Andreas gulped the last mouthful of tea and looked at the earthen mug, tilting it so he could read the bottom. His name was frozen for all time in the pottery, scratched with a small stick by a six-year-old's shaking hands. He had suffered an episode the day he fired the mugs, made under the Syballine Sister's careful supervision. He remembered sad eyes, not hidden under a veil, but reddened with a longing he couldn't understand. That he still didn't understand.

It's too late.

"Know, Sister, that I will not leave you. I know, now, why you left your son behind. Why Mora tried to keep me from learning the truth. No, Sister Hazel, I will not leave you."

The old woman twitched, then erupted into violent spasms, nearly toppling into the fire. She fought with the same determination as her son. Andreas admired that quality.

Syballine Sister Hazel heaved forward, then back into the cushions. Andreas sat next to her, inspecting her earthen mug. She had drunk half of it, enough to administer the dose. He draped an arm over her shoulder, steadying her body as the last curls of fire consumed her from within. Andreas inhaled, his episode subsiding despite a circuitous warmth coursing through his body. *It is complete, now.*

"I will not leave you to die." The old woman breathed her last, steam whistled from the breached pressure from her lungs. "I wouldn't miss it for the world."

The Key

Lunes, 16 abril NE 267
Eastern Lake Region
Lieutenant-Colonel Paolo Desantos

The directions Mr. Allen had encrypted for him weren't difficult for Paolo to decipher. *Follow the scratches, south to north. On the southern shore of the eastern-most of the lakes. Past the sleeping lions by the river. Five north and three east. With a hollow step, the young lion's den is here.* Paolo didn't have anything that could instantly point him on the trail to the Junquer shop. There were no eyes in the sky that could aim a signal and spread open a digital map on a screen small enough to fit in his hand. As far as he knew, at least. According to the Allen agent he had met after his return from the Chapel of St. Jude, the next best thing was tucked away in an underground lair perilously close to the eastern Lake Region sprawls. When his back was still freshly scourged and red from the healing salve, and the red behind his eyes still burned, the first step in his new plan depended on the acquisition of something that could accomplish what he needed to execute it.

Paolo's handheld was sophisticated compared to the general-issue devices the rank and file received. They could fulfill the everyman's daily tasks: computations, quick messaging, banking, even a calendar to keep all Motherlanders organized and efficient.

Paolo Desantos was no everyman. And his ambitions required so much more than that.

Follow the scratches, south to north. That was easy enough. The long, slender lakes that lay parallel to each other, like fingers outstretched, lay before him in the lowlands beyond the mountains. The trails were easy to follow. Paolo had led several incursions into the townships and settlements north of Motherland at Eminence De Léon's behest. Raw metals for the armoury. Livestock and crops. Human labour in the form of captives. Whatever was left, the Reapers could have as they saw fit. When they were through, the ashes of a former village were all that remained.

Paolo squinted in the noon-day sun, tilting the handheld screen to read the clues. He would have to pass between two of the narrow lakes. Which two, the message didn't say. It didn't matter. The rest of the code gave it away.

The *young lion's den* referred to a city of old, long deconstructed and rendered by the elite who built the domes centuries ago. Anything east of the falls were reclaimed by the progenitors of New Inland, his father once told him. Beyond the great falls, the sprawl lands were gobbled up by the machines of the young, burgeoning Hyacynthe. The cities and towns of old were long gone. No digital fingerprints to trace. But, on rolls of yellowed paper, in libraries that survived the Reclamation, old names lived still, in fancy fonts on coloured splotches. It didn't take Paolo long to determine which former city was associated with "young lions".

At the greatest of the lakes, that looked from above like scratches upon the earth from the right hand of a god, he would need to travel between the thumb and index, where the land was low, before turning west. Travel was easy between the finger lakes; scattered settlers had established trails any off-road vehicle could navigate with little discomfort. His Motherland military-issue rover rumbled and gurgled through the high grasses and low shrubs, as foxes and deer scurried, and birds wheeled overhead. People would be watching, Paolo knew. They would be as inconspicuous as bobcats or coyotes—curious about the noisy interloper in their lands, but wise enough not to approach it.

Paolo's rifle rested on the passenger seat, entangled in its shoulder strap. They were wise not to approach him.

The sleeping lions by the river. That was easy to decipher once he knew which former city he was seeking. The old map indicated an old cemetery that provided the eternal resting place for the "lions" who once occupied the area. Paolo scoffed at the metaphor. Lions don't sleep. If they did, they would be vulnerable to the cowardly species crouching in the bushes, the bobcats, the coyotes. Opportunists just waiting for the lions to lose their focus.

The former city left few clues to its imperial past. The uneven earth that sprouted trees once boasted of artificial structures. Concrete and steel once reached into the sky, black-topped flat streets traced between them where luxury vehicles cruised the avenues and the homeless fed pigeons from their park benches. Where street buskers and food vendors exchanged their wares for money. But that was several lifetimes ago. The pigeons had to feed themselves, now. Paolo wondered if they were happier for it.

Past the former cemetery, indicated in the present day by massive open pits the Reapers left when they harvested the sleeping "lions" beneath the surface, Paolo retrieved the folded paper map and narrowed his gaze on the grid of thin lines that were once a suburb. Five streets north, and three east, and there would be an access point. But once he arrived at the ordinal point, the real hunt was on.

Paolo stood at the intersection of the fifth and third streets, which were no longer black-topped. With a careful examination, he was able to notice that different species of trees grew where once the roads laid. Taller, wiser trees now occupied the blocks of old tenements. Tall grasses stretched high, without any telltale signs of passage in the form of flattened footsteps. The Junquer likely had multiple entrances to his underground lair. It made sense that the Allens gave Paolo instructions to a rarely used one. The Junquer trusted the Allens—but not their clients. Allen diplomacy could only do so much, so Paolo accepted the instructions, sparse as they were.

Now, the search begins…

Narrowing his eyes, he scanned the topography of the old city block. The streets were long overgrown with tall grasses and shrubs. However, with careful examination, anyone with or without prior knowledge could figure out that small, circular patches of shorter grass were clues to what lay beneath.

Reaching into his knapsack, Paolo retrieved a collapsible metal rod. He thrusted it into the topsoil and the needle point struck a hard surface. It could have been a rock. To be sure, Paolo jabbed again, this time feeling the reverberation of metal on metal.

Manhole covers were all over the ruined streets of Allentown. The iron disks that once covered sewer entrances in Motherland had long been removed and smelted. Paolo had learned over his years in the wild lands that surrounded his city that hundreds of thousands of access ports to endless labyrinths beneath the ground dotted the continent in all directions. Some were occupied, like those beneath his feet. Others were long abandoned. How many pairs of eyes had adjusted over generations to life without natural sunlight?

Were they any different from the New Inland elite? Were they any better?

Kneeling in the grass, Paolo dug his gloved fingers into the shallow soil that had accumulated over the manhole cover. Tracing a circle, he curled his fingertips into the narrow crease until he found a space wide enough to grip. It took every ounce of his upper body strength to budge the cover, but he needed his metal rod to pry it free. An acrid smell wafted from the darkness below as he rolled the cover aside. As if he rang a doorbell, a light ignited in the depths.

The Junquer was home.

Lowering himself down the shaft by way of a rusted, thin-runged ladder, Paolo descended into the faint light that had been turned on to guide him into the sanctuary. As his feet touched down onto the tunnel floor, he turned to the corridor illuminated with faint lights. The tunnels beneath Allentown hummed with electricity. These were as quiet as tombs. Paolo swallowed and followed the light.

After nearly twenty minutes and as many twists and turns, he arrived at a double door, guarded by a mounted camera and a square, black speaker. Before Paolo could utter a word, the speaker crackled.

"Name."

Paolo looked up at the single eye lens above the door. "Desantos."

"Business."

"The key."

Mr. Allen had instructed him to use "the key" as the password. In a sense, that was what he was hoping to buy. *A key.*

The door mechanism clicked. Paolo grasped the handle and turned, and the doors opened. No sooner did they part, then the space beyond emitted a familiar electrical hum, intermittently broken by crackles. The light was brighter, but it dimmed with every crackling surge in power. A mixture of burned metal and polymers was strong enough to draw tears to the corners of his eyes.

"Your reputation p-p-precedes you, Desantos."

The shop was long and narrow with a low ceiling, hung with long bunches of conduit cables stapled irregularly. Piles of formless, twisted scraps of metal, coils of wires, fragments of transistors and motors, and parts Paolo couldn't identify lined the sides of the room, as many as several feet from the unseen walls. At the far recess of the room, a work bench occupied the rear wall, the gaunt frame of an old or diseased man hunched beneath a carefully angled pot light. The whole place smelled diseased. Paolo inhaled deeply through his nostrils to acclimatize them to the stench. It didn't help.

"Please, keep your boots on. And don't mind the smell. I'm told it's strong to n-n-new visitors."

Paolo had no intention of taking anything off in this place. He cursed himself for not bringing a breathing mask.

"You are the Junquer."

The man didn't answer. As his sight focused in the artificial light, Paolo spotted a set of thin drawers suitable for small screws or fasteners. Tools of unrecognizable shapes hung from the peg-board perpendicular to the work surface. Wires snaked around him, connecting to diagnostic boxes with meters and needles. Mounted vice grips and hanging, circular magnifying lenses completed the scene of the most shambled workshop Paolo had ever seen. The disorganization was causing him indirect anxiety.

"I do not wish to offend you."

The man twitched and reached a grease-stained hand to the bandages that encircled his head like a melted crown. He gargled deep from his throat in a vain attempt to clear his passageway. Reaching beneath the work surface, he pulled a stained plastic jug to his mouth, gulping back the contents as they leaked around the mouth.

"You don't offend me, young lion."

The man returned the water jug and wiped his mouth with the back of his left sleeve. He turned to face his guest. Paolo winced. The man's face appeared as if it had been stitched together from multiple others, with the seams long faded but the patches still visible. Long tufts of grey hair hung in uneven lengths and patches from his chin. Mr. Allen had even warned him of the Junquer's unsavory appearance. Nothing could have prepared him for this.

"Your *name*… That's a d-d-different matter." When he stuttered, the Junquer's teeth clattered behind his cracked lips. "It carries far. And it does you d-d-disservice."

"You are familiar with my name."

The Junquer's thin smile twisted like a length of copper wire. "Few in these lands are not. Indeed, the Allens were very convincing, young lion. Otherwise, you would not be here."

"Pleasantries aside, I am assured you have what I am seeking?" Countless hours of research, bargaining, price arranging, and travel had better pay off.

The old man swiveled his stool back to his workstation. Paolo approached him in careful, measured steps.

"That's close enough, Desantos. I've been taking my medicine, but I wouldn't want to make you s-s-sick."

The Junquer swiveled back, holding a device that looked like an oversized handheld that was half-constructed. Paolo squinted at the silicon-based processor chips and minute, soldered bits. Beyond that, only a handheld-sized swipe screen offered any outer protection for the open innards of the device.

"I was told it was ready." Paolo tried to withhold his disdain at the half-finished chunk of electronics. "The Allens paid you the full sum—"

"I don't recall specifications for your k-k-key to look… pretty."

Pretty wasn't required. But *finished*, that would have been nice.

"Rest assured, Desantos. Your key is fully functional. If you want all the whistles and b-b-bells to work when you need them to, you need sufficient airflow. Cover it if you like, but if it fails you because of overheating, don't say I d-d-didn't warn you."

For the amount Paolo had paid through the Allen Consortium, the whistles and bells had better work.

"And I suppose I will need a training course to use it?" Paolo was a quick learner. But figuring it all out in the wild, that might prove cumbersome.

"Like most handhelds, the best way to learn is to just… try it out."

The Junquer offered the device. Paolo hesitated to take it, likening the action to reaching into a latrine. "Please, give it a t-t-try." The old man's arms were cratered with pockmarks and scars, some fresh and leaking. Paolo was careful to touch only the device as he took it into his palms.

Gazing at the touch screen, he pressed his right thumb and the screen flashed to life with a soft, bluish hue.

<Identity: Confirmed. Null>

"Null?"

The Junquer laughed until he coughed. "I told you. Your name carries far. If you wish to program a different one, you can access your settings. I didn't have another for you, so N-N-Null it is, unless you see fit to change it."

Null.

It had a certain anonymity to it. Paolo Desantos wasn't used to that. But he could learn.

Monday, 18 June AC 0245
Southwest of Allentown
Ian Null

As much as Paolo was eager to learn, Ian Null was just as happy to forget. The handheld had lived up to his expectations. With the Junquer's inauspicious-looking device, he had been able to manipulate situations in real time which no ordinary man would have been able to do. Locate power sources and trigger locks. Transfer large sums of money. Track long-lost locations.

Start over.

Null followed the directions on the screen of his jumble of silicon and wires, winding through a valley nestled between two foothills. The path wound like a cracked whip, meandering in wide swooshes through lush greens in full, early summer bloom. Eventually it led him to a plateau situated on his southwestern horizon. Null's rucksack irritated the scar tissue on his back, and he shifted the weight of the pack onto his shoulder blade. When he stopped for the night, he would have to redistribute the softer goods to cushion his ammunition and other supplies from digging into those memories from his former life.

The sun was dipping in the western sky over the deep-green canopied foothills and Null had traveled, by his own estimation, two wide arcs with no signs of any permanent settlements. He couldn't decide which was worse—villages with many sets of discerning eyes that could remember the stranger with the rucksack passing through, or the chance encounter with loners like himself, direction-less, with nothing but time on their hands. It would take several of them to best Ian Null if they ever sought to try. Assuming the assailants were fit and healthy.

Null wondered how many outsiders had more in common with the Junquer. Swaddled in soiled or rotten fabrics, skin blotched and with oozing sores and half-healed scabs, allergic to clean air and unfiltered sunlight. The thought of it turned his stomach. It could have been the diseases. Maybe the stench. Most likely the manner in which they parted ways.

If anyone finds me in such a state, I hope they show me the same mercy…

Null dropped his rucksack and pulled out the Junquer's handiwork, and aimed it further along the curvature of the valley. A light flashed and the blue screen scrolled through pixels before a map route emerged. There were once several small towns in his path, but none offered any network of underground passages, either from sewers or subways. This close to New Inland, it was certain that most of the old-world city structures were long-reclaimed.

Tonight, I'll be sleeping under the stars.

There was work to do. Once a lean-to was erected, and food and water were sourced, Null would need to set the perimeter sensor application to vibrate before he shut his eyes. He wouldn't need the key to wake him. A lifetime of rigid training ensured that his internal alarm would go off before sunrise. By the time the first rays of the morning sun crept over the hills from the east, Ian Null would be long gone.

How to Reappear

Monday, 21 May AC 0245
Jackson Homestead, Spruce Grove
Phil Fox

Huh! I could have sworn we got rid of those old, holey, moth-ridden rags years ago. Imagine—first bloody shower at the old homestead in who knows *how* long—and the first towel I grab has to be this old thing!"

Phil looked away from the old man for fear the towel fall off his waist. The "Sly Fox" had more than a few extra pounds since the last time they'd spoken. "And just what do *you* think is old, holey, and moth-ridden?"

Le_Renard cocked his head, the towel-fluffed wisps of grey hair drooping as though a static-electric current had evaporated. "Watch it, son. I'm not moth-ridden."

Phil rolled his eyes. "Could have fooled me."

The old man rolled his shoulder blades. "You don't get chewed up by moths if you're always on the move. Besides—you're the one who's been sitting still too long, wouldn't you say?" Le_Renard motioned as though he was about to yank the towel away, but instead grinned that insufferable grin Phil hated all those years ago. He remembered the last time they'd seen each other, the year, date, right down to the hour. Since then, he hadn't left New Inland, let alone visited the Jackson Homestead. After a few years had passed, responsibility had been replaced by guilt as the reason he chose not to return. From the first time they had spoken inside the cluttered service bay of Jackson Auto through the final departure, father and son had covered a lot of ground. Amends were at least attempted, if not entirely made. A voice inside convinced Phil that it wasn't worth it to risk another trip.

"You're right, of course." Phil turned to the fireplace while his father retreated back into the bedrooms. Le_Renard didn't stop talking, but he did raise his voice as if he were hollering over the wind on the strait.

"Huh! Of course! Father knows best, or so I'm told, anyway!" From the clattering and clunking, Phil deduced his father was rifling through the heavy, wooden dresser for clean clothes. Choice curse words confirmed his theory. "…moths even ate my drawers! Where's the god-damned humanity!"

Phil couldn't help but laugh, imagining the old man holding up a thread-bare pair of boxer shorts, porous as swiss cheese, splaying apart as he pulled them over his plump backside. "If you need any help, 'fraid to say you're on your own back there!"

Le_Renard bellowed and emerged dressed in fashionably-dated pants and button-down shirt, tails untucked. "There's plenty of work to do that don't involve dressing me. You hungry?"

As soon as he'd heard the word, Phil's stomach curled. "I didn't think you'd been here long enough to make supper."

"Make supper? Huh! I wanted to order food from the Rex, but according to Pretty Boy they've been shuttered for years. At least he stocked up the cupboards when I radioed in."

The "pretty boy", Albert, had already greeted Phil when he'd sailed into the estuary. Phil couldn't imagine anyone being able to sneak up on Le_Renard like that. Years—decades on the run from all manner of pursuers, he had perfected the art of disappearance. The most important step, he'd once confessed to a much younger and naive Phil, was to learn how to reappear.

In the lateness of the day, Phil and his father settled on canned goods and preserves rather than prepare a meal from scratch. There would be plenty of time for that. Small-mouth bass and pickerel should be running by now. Guarantee, the old man would want to put out on the strait for mackerel at some point. As long as they cut and split the wood to season it for next year. And it hadn't escaped him that the shingles were starting to grow moss in the low-canopy shade. He was actually looking forward to all of it. *A quick supper tonight works for me.*

Phil reclined into the lumpy cushions, his belt loosened as he soaked in the warmth of the smoldering fire. Across from him, in a reclining plush armchair, Le_Renard extended his bare feet, soles cracked and dry, wrinkling his toes as he clasped his hands behind his head.

"Those canned meals, they're great in a pinch. But they're way better than the standard Kayewati meal plan, *lemmetellya.*" Phil couldn't help but smile. The old man's idiosyncrasies had served him well over the years. He could diffuse tense situations with his dialect and expressions alone. Bernard Schiff had once told him as much. A different pang in his abdomen reminded him of his late uncle.

"So what brings you home?" *Best to just rip the bandage off.*

'I could ask you the same, my boy. Let me guess, though—work's been a bitch. And you came alone. Left Kendall all by her pretty self back in that stuffy office. You still have that old barometer on the wall?"

The steering wheel-shaped ornament was still tucked inside his knapsack. "Brought it with me—figured it might be useful."

"Smart. The sea's been active—low pressure for this time of year, 'specially north of Bermude."

"And Miss Kendall is perfectly happy to have the office to herself." Phil imagined her scowl as if she'd heard Le_Renard say it. "She sends her best." It was a lie. In truth, he hadn't spoken with her since the magna-rail ride from New Inland to the harbour. He hadn't spoken to anyone, apart from seadogs and wharf hands. At some point, he'd have to charge up his handheld, link to Albert's tower in Gasperro, and check his messages. *Sixty days,* he'd told Kendall, Reekan, Marribel. If it took fifty-nine of them for him to find the wherewithal, so be it.

"Smart girl, Kendall. Best decision you ever made, to hire that one. Good help—*that's* hard to find. Huh." Le_Renard breathed his last huff with half the emphasis. It meant something was on his mind. Whatever it was, Phil knew that the old man—*his* old man—would select the precise moment to share it. Just like reappearing out of thin air.

Greenthumb

Wednesday, 20 June AC 0245
The Hanging Gardens
DHC Chair Jennings Marribel

Jennings Marribel couldn't remember if the air and sun on the outside world resembled the controlled atmosphere of the Hanging Gardens. She knew that the air was different on the fourth tiered level that was home to the private plots. The breeze was swift but thinner, somehow, and the sun was sharper for its proximity to the mirrors that controlled the rays. The sun was scheduled to dampen, to simulate natural cloud cover. Jennings paid a premium for extra light refractors. While most of her plants were endemic to the continent, some of her more delicate import varieties demanded more specific care. She smiled at the thought that nearly a quarter of her chosen flora would not survive on the outside without her care.

The mayor of Heartsburg was comforted by the fact that she could set her climate to cater to the species she had chosen. Her garden contained a mix of species protected and preserved by horticulturists in all of the continental domes. Woodland iris in wispy clumps waved over a bed of rock cress. Culver's root crowned her flower bed, nearly a meter in height capered with lilac-coloured flowers that would yield to yellow in a few short months. She was annoyed that the regulations prevented her from growing wild ginger, although she found solace in the fact that the public gardens, maintained by AgriCorps, hosted a number of her favourites that she couldn't legally grow on her own.

The flowers were her favourites, a kaleidoscope of colour that bloomed in carefully timed intervals, all at her deft design. While she didn't miss the outside climate, getting dirty on her hands and knees suited Jennings fine. Her synthetic straw hat blocked the refracted rays while she dug about in the rich, nutrient-enhanced soil. The knees of her khaki gardening pants were stained black and damp; a streak of ashen grey swathed across her cheek as she wiped her brow, accidentally smeared by her dot-textured work glove.

A soft mist began to waft over her flowers, almost in time to the soft, electronic music that she believed would help her flowers bloom wider, smell sweeter, and reach higher. The music lilted along, and Jennings's ear caught a sequence of notes that were out of place. She'd heard the soundtrack countless times in a loop and could recite every note by heart. Jarred by the realization that the soft electronic alarm tone from her handheld was intruding on the mood music, she sighed. Removing her gloves and wiping the perspiration on the sides of her thighs, she pulled her device from her knapsack.

The signal that was summoning her was not what she had expected.

Incoming: 1436h Greenthumb

Jennings swallowed before taking a sip from her bottled water. *Greenthumb* was her own contact name. That it was being used by the caller indicated an incoming call from the Allens.

"Pardon the interruption, Chair Marribel," drawled the emanating voice. "I understand it is an ideal, partly-cloudy day for your plot?"

"A little balmy, but I'll survive." Jennings countered the thinly veiled message with her trademark sarcasm. "I'm hoping for sunnier days to come."

"Indeed," Mr. Allen replied. "I'm sure that you will be able to adjust your mirrors to your new acquisitions' needs. The rainforests of Sumatra are very particular, of course."

Aquisitions. "I hear it's lovely there this time of year. I'm not expecting any delays, *Mr. Greenthumb?*"

"Our channel is secure, Jennings. You can speak freely, as long as you are alone in your plot, of course."

She sighed to herself, hoping Mr. Allen didn't pick up on her relief. The Allens played hardball. Jennings Marribel wrote the rules for it. "Can I assume this isn't about my plot?"

The Allen agent's emotionless face nodded on her screen. "I'm afraid not. Consider this a courtesy call. There have been happenings within Allentown that will be of grave concern for your council."

This time, Jennings didn't try to hide her disdain. "Give me a moment," she answered as she removed the woven-fibered wide-brim hat from her sweat-soaked hairline. Another mouthful of water that tasted like the container she drank it from, and she sat back on her ankles, braced for whatever the Allen had to say.

"Recently, violence has struck our peaceful city. There have been not one, but two separate incidents that have our organization stretched thin."

"I'm sorry to hear, Mr. Allen." Jennings didn't entirely mean it. The Allen Consortium facilitated all manner of illegal trade, in defiance of the Hyacynthe embargo, even with the Kayewati. Slow business in Allentown wasn't the worst news she could hear.

"Many lives were lost."

"My condolences." She wasn't completely heartless.

"Would those condolences be as sincere if I were to tell you they were almost entirely of Motherland origin?"

Jennings gritted her teeth. Motherland. *Reekan…*

"It's him, isn't it?" She almost bit her tongue.

"If by him you are referring to Steven Reekan, then yes, our incident involves your colleague, by some degree."

"*By some degree?* He knows damn well he's not supposed to be there!" Jennings tried her best to keep her anger to a minimal volume. No one was in her immediate vicinity, but the plot was grown high and wide. It wasn't unreasonable to imagine unwelcome ears camouflaged in the greenery.

"Madame Chair, I regret to tell you, but Mayor Reekan and most of his executive are unaccounted for at this time."

The news sent her emotions into a tailspin. She disliked him. Deeply. She dreaded the day that a sitting Mayor Reekan would assume Chair of the DHC after her term ended, as per the cycle of succession.

Heartsburg yielded to Capston. If only Phil Fox were still at the helm of Capston's mayoralty. But then again, maybe he would be the one lost in Allentown.

No, he wouldn't. Because Phil Fox wasn't an idiot and he actually followed the laws... "Go on, Mr. Allen."

"Mayor Reekan entered into an agreement with the consortium to conduct an investigation, the terms and details of which are confidential. That should come as no surprise, Madame Chair—all five cities have interests within our boundaries, as I know you are aware."

That reminder stung a bit. Of course, Heartsburg and the other three cities had eyes inside the ruined city. The difference was that four of five New Inland cities weren't causing a ruckus.

"An explosion took place by means of a land drone in the south end of the city, near a building we had leased to Capston. When we attempted to contact Reekan and his command team, we were met with silence. It was at that time we dispatched our personnel to investigate. Luckily, we were able to rescue Lieutenant Shore and Commander Gry. They are receiving medical care as we speak.

"However, we were unable to locate Mayor Reekan and Major Wall. Several sections of the catacombs caved under the explosion, and we fear the worst."

Jennings had met Major Wall once before. Phil Fox was still mayor, and he had introduced her to the young upstart within Reekan's corps while the chief of security had laughed loudly at his own jokes. She presented herself as mightier than her physical stature would have suggested. Jennings liked her.

"Have the Allens been able to determine why Reekan was targeted?"

"At first glance, it would be logical that the Motherland presence within our city is responsible." Jennings could fill in the blanks. Reekan was indeed present in Allentown to persue his theory that Motherland was somehow responsible for the attacks in Capston. She'd heard all of this before.

"However, the detonation of a massive explosive device on Motherland's position *after* the fact renders that conclusion questionable. It was that second explosion that resulted in the most casualties. The death toll is still climbing, but I can say with certainty that many of the remains can only be identified by forensic examination."

Jennings's eyes widened. An explosion of that magnitude would have left a crater in a city that already looked like a post-apocalyptic nightmare. She imagined the acrid smoke mixing with the morning fog, itching her eyes and clogging her lungs. Jennings Marribel had witnessed fires like this; even though it was a lifetime ago, the smell never left her nostrils.

"If Reekan is in any way responsible—"

"I trust your council will use the information I'm presenting you in a manner you deem appropriate. It is not of concern to the consortium how you resolve your internal affairs. But Jennings, we do not believe Mayor Reekan was responsible. Indeed, we hold out hope that he will yet be found alive."

Jennings donned her hat again and propped the handheld so Mr. Allen could watch as she returned to her plants. Her tiger lilies needed more fresh soil and water. The overcast light could use a little more sun.

"Thank you for informing me," Jennings said without looking at the screen. "I will be contacting Captain Ling in Capston this afternoon."

"We have contacted Captain Ling. She will be expecting to hear from you, I expect. It isn't my place, Jennings, but might I suggest you engage her with… humility?"

"You can appreciate that I would not offer you advice on how to deal with your colleagues, Mr. Allen. But your point is taken. I have no issue with Ling."

"Of course. Capable officer, very professional. She has been placed in an unenviable position. In our experience, dealing with Jason Holt has not always been simple."

Jason Holt? What's that about? "Is that all?"

Jennings stood and wiped her brow. Mr. Allen would be staring at her feet and shins. She wasn't concerned so long as he could hear her. "As for our prior agreement," she almost whispered. "Should I be concerned?"

The agent didn't reply. *Damn protocol. He needs to see the whites of the eyes.* She picked up the handheld, making direct eye contact with the image on the screen. "*Madame Greenthumb*, our contract is unchanged. You have nothing to fear."

The shift to her alias indicated the business was concluded. "I'm glad to hear that."

"Autumn is approaching quickly. I trust you will be placing another order soon?"

She looked over her plot. Her white trilliums were beginning to fade with the season. The adjacent plot was in the midst of change; the hostas were being removed for a fresh, more colourful addition. She ignored his question.

"My lady slipper orchids, they are expected any day now," she breathed. "Has there been any change?" As long as *Greenthumb* received the shipment, *Chair Marribel* would stay clear of any illegal importing. Whether Reekan came back from the dead, or Captain Ling assumed the Chair, Jennings very much looked forward to retirement, and less scrutiny that the office of Chair attracted.

The Allen agent smiled. She hated that it made her feel defeated. "Wild harvest orchids are very delicate cargo. They will arrive on schedule. Might I suggest some Sumatran succulents to accentuate your orchids?"

Speak the Words

Viernes, 15 abril, NE 237
Chapel of St. Jude
Tirel Desantos

As a boy, Tirel didn't understand why the suspended lanterns in the Chapel of St. Jude were unlit during the services. It had something to do with waiting in the dark before stepping outside into the light. Why suffer in darkness when you could as easily turn on the lights, he once asked his mother. Hazel had no answer. In the eighteen years since he last saw her, the answer remained elusive.

At his command, the Ansati left the hanging lanterns on, but the chapel was still too dim. The sanctuary could just as easily have been lifted from the dreams that still haunted him when he closed his eyes. The wooden benches were designed to keep worshipers' backs straight and attentive, eyes focused on the raised stage area with the wooden altar. The vaulted ceiling overhead could have reached all the way to the afterlife. If there was such a thing.

Between the raised level of the altar and the pews, Tirel stared at the wooden box resting atop a carefully arranged pile of wooden branches, stripped naked of their flaked bark and woven, allowing for their natural bending to entwine. The *palo santo* stock, true to custom, had been harvested from Karina's *spiritus arbor*. Grown in a carefully tended orchard, she had planted the seed of her spirit tree as a young girl upon her affirmation. She'd always told Tirel she felt at peace while she sat beneath its branches. The Ansati officiant understood the significance of the *spiritus arbor* to Motherland faithful. Draped in their traditional hooded cloaks, the older man stood behind the altar and lit the four candles required for the funeral. Behind him, four more druids hid inside their cloaks, only present to witness the proceedings and to serve as pallbearers after the benediction. Seated to the officiant's right, an Ansati woman, replete in her full-length gown and face draped by a grey veil, crossed her hands in her lap. She didn't move at all. She could just as well have been a statue.

"Shall we begin?" The officiant spoke softly, but his words hit Tirel like a blow to the head.

The words weren't coming. A gentle tug on his sleeve broke Tirel from his catatonic daze.

"Father?"

Tirel couldn't look Paolo in his blue-grey eyes without seeing Karina in them. He would have given his own eyes to have his wife sitting next to him and their four-year old son, instead of lying in a sealed coffin on top of a pile of dead branches. He answered without looking at him.

"I'm ready." Swallowing dry, he sat straight against the vertical back rest of the pew. Paolo's tiny fingers crept upon his own to clasp hands. At first, he didn't open his hand to accept them. But the boy was so strong, Tirel was in awe of his son's character. Here lay his mother, gone far too soon, and his first concern was for his father's wellbeing. Truly, Karina would remain alive so long as Paolo was by his side. He opened his palm and cupped his son's hand, skin so soft it almost felt like it wasn't there.

The Ansati officiant nodded as he began the recitation:

"Dies iræ, dies illa
Solvet sæclum in favilla..."

The words of all nineteen stanzas of the incantation washed throughout the chapel, any hint of sharpness absorbing into the walls or disappearing high above the lanterns. Beneath the hood, the Brother of the Catholic Forty closed his eyes as the notes rose and fell in mourning. Her hands still clasped, the Syballine Sister trembled beneath her veil, indicating that she was indeed human beneath the fabric drapes. As the last notes faded away, the officiant struck a long, spindly wooden matchstick and a flame burst to life. With a soft touch, he dipped the flame to the wick of each of the four candles. They stood side by side in the brass candelabra, each wisping upward.

"Which one is mine, father?"

That voice, so mighty for Paolo's age, seemed meek and muted in his whisper. Tirel didn't answer. The boy squeezed his hand. Tirel couldn't summon the strength to acknowledge his son by squeezing back. The Brother at the altar, hood drawn down to his upper lip, allowed only a shadowy glimpse of his carefully trimmed beard. He mouthed a few words of silent prayer before raising his voice once again in the dead language of the Ansati ceremony.

"Quod superius, sicut inferius. Vivet in aeternum, sicut illa, non morietur in aeternum. Lumen effudit super eam semper, et in latitudine oceanus et latitudinem oculum…"

The Ansati Brothers and the Syballine repeated the prayer. Tirel felt his hand squeezed a little tighter.

"Father."

Tirel sighed to himself. "Which is what, Paolo?"

The boy stared straight ahead at the four wax pillars, their flames reaching for the impossible heights of the chapel ceiling.

"Which candle is mine?"

Tirel didn't think of them that way. Even as a small boy, he had viewed them as merely instruments in a nonsensical ceremony. He had sat afraid in the dark, praying the lights would flicker on at once, saving him from the emptiness within the absence of light in the chapel. The acoustics had allowed him to hear everything, from his mother's soft breath beside him to the rustle of the altar servers' robes somewhere in the chasm before him. He found no comfort there. And as an adult, that discomfort remained.

"Which one do you think is yours, Paolo?"

The boy glanced across the host of candidates, their light bathing the raised dais that housed the altar and the assorted instruments of liturgy.

"There." Paolo raised his voice. "It's that one, second from the right."

Tirel followed his son's gaze to the candelabra, the four candle lights unwavering as the chorus continued.

"No. I don't think so. I don't believe *any* candle is yours, son." To acknowledge the symbolism of each candle representing the entirety of a life was to also acknowledge that each flame would inevitably burn to the bottom. Unless it was snuffed before its time. He didn't accept either option. Paolo's light would shine for a very long time. Tirel prayed he would never live to see it extinguish.

The service continued. The officiant continued to deliver his sermon in that same dead language. Neither Tirel nor Paolo understood the words. Still, through the strong voice of the priest upon the dais, both father and son understood their intent.

Jueves, 21 junio NE 267
Chapel of St. Jude
Colonel Tirel Desantos

The smell was dizzying. It took four full jerry cans to sufficiently douse the sanctuary, starting with the oak doors, around the cracked and partially crumbled stained-glass windows. Kaleidoscopic light danced over the remaining artifacts hanging loose and disjointed from the walls around the perimeter, in a gradual arc to the altar. Fourteen visual depictions of an obsolete prophet resigned to his impending doom. Tirel couldn't help laughing at the irony. A fuel container sloshed its contents on the raised table that housed a candelabra of four.

The red rage, born of his grief, had subsided the moment he stepped inside the chapel of Jude. His eyes narrowed. His pulse diminished. He breathed rhythmically, counting the seconds between each breath, like the doctors had told him all those years ago. Tirel wasn't permitted to attend Luther's funeral. Karina's service had been held in the sacred grounds of the Motherland spirit tree grove, and he had had to keep a brave face in front of Eminence De Léon and the Council of Regents.

And Paolo. He was only a boy, too young to understand.

Who could ever understand such a devastating loss?

Tirel stumbled down the steps of the chancel and sat in the first pew. Just like all those times he had returned to wait for his own mother to come back. She never did. *And neither will my boy.* The last jerry can gushed its contents all around him in rivers on the seat and to the floor. He tossed the hollow container to the aisle, its echo in the expanse of the sanctuary.

"You knew, didn't you, Mother? The end, it was always going to be here."

Fumbling in his coat pocket, he pulled out a silver-capped butane briquette. With the flick of his thumb, a spark ignited into flame, quivering in gentle breeze blowing in through the cracked windows. "I wanted them to burn it to the ground, you know, just like the rest of Jude. And I *should* have."

The flame danced as a rush of wind blew in from behind the altar, in this home for ghosts who never appeared.

"And you let De Léon convince you *not* to burn it down. He was pulling your strings from the very beginning." A voice from the deepest recess of the sacristy wafted on the breeze, as potent as the petrol fumes. The timbre of the words pierced Tirel from ear to ear. He knew the voice. He wanted to believe it.

"*My son?* It can't be!"

"It *can* be, if only you make it so. Say the words and make it *real.*"

Behind the celebrant's chair, the rustling of fabric along the floorboards dragged like heavy canvas or a burial shroud. Tirel's eyes watered.

"You've come back to me!"

Out of the shadow, a hooded figure emerged, sitting in the high-backed throne the priests of old used to preside over the congregation. "Of course, I have. You didn't think you'd sent me away forever, surely!"

That voice. It distorted with every poisoned word it spoke. Tirel capped the briquette and gritted his teeth.

"You. You are not Paolo."

The man laughed. "I should hope not. I would be dead!" He threw the hood back. "And as you can see, Colonel, I am very much alive."

The last person he expected to see was also the last person he wanted to see. "Even the Kayewati wouldn't keep you, Andreas!"

"*Couldn't* keep me. Aren't you going to ask about my vacation?"

The setting sun poured its waning rays through the windows onto the mad druid. Tirel gazed at the outline of Andreas, slouched in the chair. He looked like hell. Days, maybe weeks of beard stubble streaked with red lines. Slashes and tears across his mud and blood-stained robe. He looked like he could have crawled out from under a crumbled building. Tirel twiddled the briquette between his forefingers and thumb.

"Why are you here?"

"Because you're so predictable, Colonel. Where else would I find you?" Andreas gazed down over the altar at the unadorned and unfinished pine box placed upon the arrangement of dried tinder branches. "I would think Paolo's *spiritus arbor* branches are still too wet to burn as they should."

Tirel drew his attention back to the small pyre he'd built at the foot of the altar. He'd shorn the spirit tree branches himself, peeling off the outer layer of bark, exposing the still-living greenness beneath. When Captain Alvara had told him of Paolo's death, it had been as though he had been flayed alive. With every stroke of the knife, Tirel felt it piercing his own skin, so that even a gentle breeze stung with every whisper.

He raised the briquette. "When I set the fire, it will hardly matter." He'd doused enough petrol that fresh timber would dry and combust regardless.

"I see what you're doing. Set one last fire and finish everything. Paolo, Jude, yourself. And *me*—you couldn't ask for better closure!"

Tirel flicked the lid of the briquette open. "Leave if you want, Andreas. I'm through with you either way."

Andreas burst into a laughter, doubling him over in spasms. "You aren't finished with me! You aren't finished with anything!"

Tirel dragged his thumb over the flint wheel, sparking the briquette to life. "I'm finished when I decide. And I can take you with me."

"Yes! And then all three of us will mingle together here, with the spirit wood, and the rotten floorboards—all of it reduced to powdered carbon. And all of it will blow away upon the wind, and there will be no memory of us! No memory of Paolo."

The flame heated the flint to the point that he couldn't feel the pain on his thumbprint anymore. "I have nothing left!"

"And that's why you have *everything* to gain!"

Tirel's thumb blackened and his hand vibrated. He stared into the depths of Andreas's yellow and red-streaked eyes. His pupils were wide and black. He didn't blink.

"Your enemies, they haven't won anything unless you allow them to. All your life, Colonel, you controlled your destiny. Luther, Karina, De Léon. Paolo—your own flesh and blood—you built him, you shaped him. And you sent him to his death. Whether in Allentown or New Inland, you knew his fate. That he would die for your ideals, eventually."

"You will burn with me, Reaper!"

"You've already sent me to the ninth circle of hell. If you could only see what lies beneath the earth—so many dead by the deeds of New Inland. Believe me—I've seen the underworld, and it's not for me! *It's not for us!*"

"I can't bring him back, Andreas!"

"But you can fulfill him."

A flash of pain shot from his thumb up his arm. "What do I do?"

Andreas smiled and sat back on the chair. "You remove everything standing between you and your goal. Reekan. Marribel. De Léon."

Tirel unleashed a guttural howl. Through the flame, past the dead candelabra, the silhouette of Andreas was bathed in the ring of light dancing in his hand. He could have sworn Paolo was staring back at him, broken, but not beaten. Andreas was only a vessel.

"Speak the words. *Make me real, Colonel.*"

"Guide me, *my son.*" Tirel closed the briquette and tossed it to the floor. Without the flame, the chapel of St. Jude wouldn't burn yet. The fire in Andreas's eyes was a different kind.

"Use your assets in DefCorps. Remind Reekan that we are still alive."

Tirel looked one last time at Paolo's coffin and the spirit wood pyre. His charred remains were useless now.

"Dies iræ, dies illa; solvet sæclum in favilla." The day of wrath; that day will dissolve the world in ashes. Tirel spoke the words, just as he did the day of Karina's funeral.

Exodus

Friday, 22 June AC 0245
Holt Tower, Capston
Captain Ender Ling

Sometimes it pays to be a night owl. Ender Ling thrived on minimal sleep—four or five hours was often enough, at least for a seven day shift rotation. Holt Tower never truly slept, of course. Even on the 93rd level, leased out to Capston security, personnel buzzed along the corridors while Jason Holt's rich guests slept soundly on the floors below. She envied them. Behind their sleeping eyelids, the elite of Capston and the other New Inland cities didn't worry for a second about the terror that occurred outside of the tallest spire. They all slept well in the solace of Mayor Reekan's security and the distraction of Jason Holt's hedonistic facility.

Captain Ling kept the lights off in the back of the cube-shaped transport. At 0200 hours, she alone woke the Sheppard brothers. No one else knew the plan. Reekan and the rest of his senior command were in Allentown sniffing out leads on the terrorist attacks of the last several months. Her attempts to contact both Steven and Shore went unanswered. That deep in the field—especially without permission from the Domestic High Council—Ender understood the need for silence. Still, a situation had arisen, and the powers that be had left her to make the decisions.

Holt ran out of patience. Lorrie Sheppard had burned away what little good will there was left. She needed to get the Sheppards to Ap-Oz.

Now.

It took some convincing for Robbie and Lorrie to stow inside a cargo crate. Cadlen, the youngest, was still half asleep. She suspected he'd fallen back asleep no sooner than the crate was fastened shut. It's only temporary, she'd assured Robbie, the oldest of the three brothers and their legal guardian. It made complete sense for the human cargo to leave the 93rd level incognito. Once in the streets of Capston, their exodus was as nondescript as any moving vehicle whisking through the artificial night.

The shuttle sped along the elevated causeway past the ruins of the devastated Sheppard Family Inn. Through the deep tint of the passenger-side window, Ender saw the shadowy silhouette of the still-standing rear quarter of the building. There were no windows in the cargo hold. The brothers didn't need to see their home in ruins. They'd already seen the footage when it had been hacked into Holt's closed-circuit system. Unfortunately, they'd also seen uncensored footage of Clara Connelly climbing into her hot tub before she had realized she was being broadcast on screens throughout the tower. Ender didn't like the woman. She was loud, pompous, and arrogant. Still, she had been violated by the hacker who exposed her naked body to the world.

She had a beautiful body, Ender had to admit. But her curves weren't enough to cover for her personality.

There was enough room for Clara, her husband Charles, and their son Warren in the back of the cargo shuttle. The plan was to move all six to Ap-Oz at the same time. Clara had taken issue with the move, of course. It had something to do with guaranteed safety in a fortified base south of New Inland, exposed to the outside world entirely too close to the Red Line. Ender knew it was all about being separated from Jason Holt and his riches. And Jason Holt agreed with her. The Sheppards had to go now, but the Connellys could stay until Steven came back with the case solved.

It meant more planning and paperwork for Captain Ling. But at least the Sheppard absence would mean less bitching in her ear.

Captain Ender Ling strode across the dimly lit docking bay as though she had chosen to ignore the personnel buzzing about. At 0230 hours, she didn't have to ignore many. The Capston helipad and hangar were not scheduled for any departures until 0615—a shift change for Capstonian personnel in the Defense Corps stationed outside of New Inland's massive entrance maw. The Tan-Ro-47 aircraft was large enough to move two dozen bodies or a significant payload of cargo. Capston purchased six of them from Hyacynthe, long before the embargo crippled their trade. Ender did not enjoy flying, but the space offered by the Tan-Ro helicopter lent a sense of security. She preferred not to know the altitude.

The cargo hold of the light-tan painted transport was agape. Ender came to a halt and watched the technician load a secured transport crate into the black opening, its teeth squealing along the metal floor as it retracted, leaving the crate alone in the shadows. Lorrie would probably complain about the rough treatment once he was freed from the cube to walk about the hold. He had the audacity to ask her for breakfast. His protests were the last sounds she heard from the Sheppards as she fastened the latch. Silence had never before been so golden.

"Captain." Francis Ferrer stepped through the cockpit hatch and stepped out of the darkness. "I'm not sure if I should say good morning or good night!"

Ender blinked her narrow eyes. They were still grainy from too few hours of sleep. "How about 'greetings'? No reason to think it's 'good' until you're touched down." She had to remind herself not to utter the name of the Tan-Ro's destination. No human ears were listening, at least not in person. But whoever was responsible for hacking into Holt Tower could do the same at the helipad with half the effort and expense. Even the technicians loading the Sheppard-filled crate weren't aware of its contents. Lorrie could have yelled until his throat was dry and they wouldn't have heard. Ferrer would have been Reekan's choice had he been present to make the decision about who would fly the Sheppards to Ap-Oz.

Where are you, Steven? Twenty-four hours had fully elapsed since their last contact. If anything bad had happened, she would have received a secure-line message from the Allens. With both Gry and Reekan on the ground in Allentown, Ender half expected it.

Ferrer smiled. "Fair enough! The lodgings won't be as comfy, but the overtime pay is enough to let me live with it!"

"I'm sure you'll get by." Ender was finished with small talk. "You have clearance for lift off when you're ready." The bay was open; a brisk breeze filled the bay and ruffled her short hair. The outside wind a full kilometer from the ground was cold enough to dry her skin and crack her thin lips. A soak in the hot tub after her morning workout was very appealing.

Ferrer didn't answer, only raising his fingers to his temple in salute before the technicians slid the cargo door clattering to a close. In the early morning emptiness, Ender imagined it could have been heard clear to Ap-Oz.

The engine hummed to life, its nuclear-celled power coursing through the electronics throughout the craft as the twin rotary blades thrummed an increasing pitch before phasing into a blur. The Tan-Ro-47 lifted off the platform, hovering, before lurching toward the open bay into the midnight-blue outside sky. Ender wasn't close enough to the edge to see if the sky was lit with stars or if clouds left it a matte black. She didn't miss the stars enough, anyway. The helicopter rushed forward, and her hair settled as the rush of the rotary wind subsided. Only the blinking tail light left any indication that anything was happening at the Capstonian helipad in the dead of night.

Ender's pocket buzzed as the tail light blinked out of view and the bay doors groaned shut. She sighed. If it was Reekan finally getting around to touch base, he was going to have to live with her decision. *They're on their way, and I'm not opening the Sheppard crate unless I have a sedative for Lorrie...*

Her heart sank when she saw the incoming message code.

The Allens.

The silence in the bay was suffocating. Ender needed to get back inside the city before reading the bad news. At least Ferrer and the Sheppards were on their way.

No Man's Land

Friday, 22 June AC 0245
Deep Underground, Allentown
Steven Reekan

Steven Reekan knew that he and Major Wall could survive on the meager, powdered rations and wall condensation for upwards of a week—ten days at best. The pair were fortunate that the stocked rations in their bomb shelter were infused with nutrients necessary for an extended stay. The water tasted like rust, but Kenzy reminded him that it was better than drinking their own urine. Or going thirsty. The last water tests she had done before her handheld completely died had indicated that the humidity they collected was safe enough to drink. There was no guarantee that it would remain as such.

The Mayor of Capston loosened the bandages on his slowly healing right hand, allowing for air to circulate over the suffocated skin. After a few moments, he wrapped them, tight enough to keep the wound clean, but slack enough to let the blood circulate. Kenzy glared at him from her fold-out chair in the corner, prepared to rebuke him for loosening them in the first place.

"It feels a lot better today, Major," Steven lied. The sutures itched like crazy, and the redness hadn't gone down by any amount. They were out of medicine from their own packs, and what little pills Kenzy found in the kitchenette were long past their due date.

"Well, that's good. But don't get any ideas—you still need treatment for that. Save your energy."

As though taunting him, Kenzy stood and stretched her hands to the ceiling before her routine of pre-workout warm-ups. She sat on an old blanket she was using as a mat, reaching the length of her left leg until her hand cupped her foot. Steven winced. He couldn't remember ever feeling as nimble in his life.

"Don't worry. I can only walk laps around this room so much before the scenery gets boring." Kenzy allowed him to stand, stretch his limbs, and walk. Anything that involved using his hands was off limits. Major Mother Hen ran a tight coop.

The Major shifted legs, hooking the other so her foot was against her thigh and repeated her stretches. Kenzy's hair, shorn close along the back and sides, flopped over her eyes as she bowed, reaching her right hand out and over her foot. After a series of unnatural poses, she stood, adjusted her sleeveless shirt and wiped her brow.

"I'd offer you a drink, but you know." Kenzy smiled. Steven rolled his eyes.

"It's been five days, and no one has checked in on us. Talk about rude service."

"Six, if you count the day the tunnels collapsed." Kenzy still suffered the echoed effects of her concussion when she had dragged Steven away from the imminent collapse of their tunnel. It had taken everything he had to follow her through the winding ventilation ducts, away from the rising gas levels to the bomb shelter where the air tested safe. Only then did Steven surrender to his exhaustion. He couldn't remember a time in his life that he'd slept for two full days.

This whole damned adventure was full of firsts.

"At some point, we're going to have to make a decision." Steven stood from the cot and ran his healthy left hand through his hair. "Infection won't matter if we starve to death down here."

Kenzy sighed. "We can't go back the way we came—the gas levels are too high. I've tried to loosen that top hatch until my palms almost blistered. It's not budging. All we can do is hope the Allens find us."

"Then maybe we need to start making more noise!" Steven hollered; his voice muted by the closeness of the chamber walls.

Kenzy covered her ears. "Quit it! Besides, these shelters were designed to block out sound." She knew her history. Allentown had endured almost two decades of attack, from several fronts. Steven knew that his skeletal bunkmate was probably some innocent civilian caught in the crossfire of warring factions. Allentown was no man's land for bigger, stronger neighbours. The poor soul whose remains occupied the cot before they arrived was probably confused and scared. Steven could relate.

"How many of these units do you think they built under the city?"

Kenzy shrugged her shoulders. "Hard to say. They likely didn't expect to be flattened by the Federation *and* the Resistors for more than twenty years."

"True. They would have had some time to prepare, given how the Resistors were moving into the area. The Alleghenies to the west kept the push moving south and east. Allentown should have just picked a side."

Kenzy walked to the kitchenette and reached for two more packets of dried powder rations. In the first five days, they had chosen the ones at the back of the cupboard with no wrinkles or streaks on the brown paper package. All that remained were the damaged, wrinkled ones. They still contained the only source of nutrition in the place. Kenzy tossed a stroganoff packet to Steven.

"And what side would you have chosen, Steven? Assuming you wouldn't have known then what you do now?"

Interesting question. "You mean not knowing the Federation won? That they would finish building New Inland without any more local opposition?" He couldn't imagine a scenario where he would have supported the coalition of the resisting cities after all the atrocities they had committed. Chemical attacks. Child soldiers. Human shields. These were tactics used by unsophisticated, desperate excuses for soldiers. Motherland today was little better.

Kenzy tore open her packet. "Sometimes, I wonder. The Resistors fought dirty, no question. But what if they had no choice *but* to fight dirty?"

"But you have to be careful, Major. Apply that logic to Motherland and you're practically excusing them for what they've done." Steven grimaced at the ration packet before begrudgingly ripping it open and letting the powdered chunks fall onto his tongue.

"I know. And in the middle of it all, a city that just wanted to be left alone paid the price."

Steven's throat was too parched to answer. His mind drifted to the Sheppard siblings. They were Allentown, caught between the depraved vengeance of Motherland and Capston, guilty of merely existing.

Kenzy coughed. "One thing for sure, these things don't taste any better. I think mine was stale."

"Stale? No kidding! The damned things are, what? Two hundred years old? I'm amazed they held up this well at all, considering…"

Steven started to do the math in his head. The Allentown Siege lasted for almost twenty-five years, give or take, on and off. It had begun while New Inland was still under construction, that he knew for sure. But when did it *end?*

"If I learned anything from history in secondary school, it's that the siege continued for a few years after New Inland was officially covered. We calculate our years from when the highest point of the dome was closed. *Anno Coniuctionis 0245*— 'in the year of construction, 245 years'".

"So, you're saying we've been eating some really old shit!" Kenzy wiped her lip and laughed.

Steven straightened out the paper packet in his hand, reading the name of the meal and its list of ingredients in faded black print. There was one more piece of information on the bottom corner that was of greater concern.

"What year does your packet say, Kenzy?"

The Major wrinkled her brow as she scanned the packet. "It looks like it says 2540—that's weird, it's like our year now but with rearranged digits."

Steven reached out his bandaged hand. "Let me see it." Kenzy placed the wrapper in his hand. With his free fingertips, he brought it close to his eyes. Sure enough the date was exactly as she had read, but there were no identifying letters.

"This isn't a New Inland date, of course, because Allentown still follows the old-world calendar. 2540… I need something to write with."

There was nothing to write with, of course. And their handhelds were dead. Steven focused on his mental math, shushing Kenzy when she tried to ask what he was talking about.

"If I'm right, 2540 in Allentown years works out to 0195 in New Inland years. *AC 0195*. So that makes these rations—"

"Fifty years old!" Kenzy's eyes widened. "Steven, these supplies have been *restocked!*"

Which meant that the Allens restocked their bomb shelters since the war. Someone had been inside this room since the Siege. The skeleton had belonged either to a refuge-seeker from the initial conflict or had found their way inside since. Steven lunged for the waste basket and sorted through the disposed wrappers. The dates were all older, even the print design was different.

"Our roommate here must have dated back to the Siege. But when the Allens restocked, they just left him here."

"But Steven, this means the Allens know where all their bomb shelters are!"

Steven's heart rate jumped at the realization. "And if they don't find us in the rubble, they might figure we found one—which we did!"

Kenzy cupped her hands around her mouth and hollered. Steven put his bandaged hand on her shoulder.

"Save your voice, Major. We can let them know we're here, but we have to be smarter." Panning around the shelter, he spied a small metal toolbox beneath the cupboard. Inside, a rusted wrench caught his eye.

"We need to find the conduit pipes. They would reach up to the sublevels and tunnels. If we can send along a vibration, someone might detect it."

Kenzy sprang into action. She felt her hands along the metal walls, rapping her knuckles every few centimeters until she heard a hollow clang. "Here, can we get behind this panel?"

Steven gripped the wrench in his good hand and swung it at the wall. After a few hard strokes, the dented panel began to buckle. But the small tool wasn't going to be enough. He turned to the cot. Whoever the poor soul was lying in a heap of old bones, he was going to help them escape.

"Sorry old friend, but I need to borrow this!" Steven grabbed one of the femurs between both hands, feeling the sutures beneath his bandaged hand stretch. Kenzy was about to protest when Steven pummeled the panel with the thigh bone like a battering ram. Chips of bone splintered before the metal caved and a small rupture appeared. Setting the bone on the cot with care, Steven used his wrench to pry open a small hole. Behind the panel, he spied a cylindrical pipe running vertically.

"If there's any chance the Allens will hear us, it's through this."

Kenzy nodded to his bandaged hand. Red was seeping to the surface. "Let me take it from here, Mister Mayor. I told you to take care of that hand."

Sheppard in a Box

Saturday, 23 June AC 0245
Capston Air Hangar, New Inland
Lorrie Sheppard

There was nothing the captain could say to convince Lorrie to take a sedative before voluntarily allowing himself to be sealed inside a cargo crate. His mother hadn't been able to make him eat his green vegetables. Robbie couldn't make him clean up his room—when he still had a room. This floppy-haired army bitch wasn't going to force him to ingest anything. If she offered him his favourite dish, damn sure she'd be tasting it first.

Once inside, Lorrie crouched as close to the lid as possible. Robbie told him to sit down and just let the process happen. "Process? That's all this is to you? More like kidnapping…"

In the pitch darkness, he didn't have to see Cadlen to know what he looked like. He would nestle into the corner, legs criss-crossed as if he were sitting on the couch in the Sheppard Family Inn lobby—when there was still a Sheppard Family Inn. Without the benefit of sight, Cadlen would be deprived of both sight and speech, even if the mutism was selective. As the crate rose on the prongs of the forklift, and vibrated with the motion, Lorrie heard everything with more clarity. He wondered if Cadlen's hearing was amplified that much more.

One thing Lorrie could accept was the captain's order for complete silence. As the Sheppard human cargo was moved across the bay of the landing platform, Captain Ling's reminder that they were no longer in Capston, but in a space where personnel from all five cities worked, rang in Lorrie's ears. If they weren't safe enough inside Holt Tower, they were certainly no safer on the outside. It sounded like flawed logic to Lorrie. More cities should mean more security. It's not like they were out in the woods, with none at all. And how safe was "Ap-Oz", anyway?

That wasn't even a New Inland holding. All this was nonsense.

And to top it all off, they were promised that Crystal would be joining them there. As the crate lid was sealed shut, Lorrie hadn't time to ask if that Laurent guy sealed her in a wooden box. In truth, he hadn't come up with the snarky comment until it was too late.

He could ask Crystal when he saw her, he supposed. But that would mean he'd have to actually talk to her. And he had a lot more to ask about than that.

Voices of security guards muffled as the box of Sheppards rose, glided, turned, and finally came to rest. A large sliding door creaked and slammed, and a new vibration buzzed enough to make Lorrie's skin itchy. What his eyes couldn't see, his inner eardrum registered as the equilibrium of the entire Tan-Ro helicopter lifted, rocking as the twin blades leveled it out. He had seen the craft before. The day his mother had taken him up to the Hanging Gardens, a beige-coloured craft that looked like a broken pill with tiered blades on its roof touched down just across from the public gardens. Medical emergency, passers-by muttered at the time. He was too young to understand what that involved, and nothing was ever mentioned of it again, as though it just came and went. He'd never thought of it again until the captain explained what they were going to be traveling in from New Inland to the super-secret fortress in the southern mountains.

Once the helicopter lifted off the platform, the buzzing softened and the hairs on his arms settled. Even though the cabin was pressure sealed, Lorrie had a feeling that the craft had passed outside of New Inland as though the wind from the outside were blowing through him, chilling his bones. No one spoke. Robbie could have been asleep for all he knew. It wouldn't have surprised him. Robbie had just accepted *everything*—from keeping the Inn running, to staying inside Holt Tower, to being packed up and mailed to a foreign land. He'd accepted the fact his sister and closest sibling had left him to raise the younger brothers. To keep his parents' ghosts inside and customers outside.

To accept their deaths at all.

Cadlen seemed to have accepted that Robbie was in charge, that he would take care of them, that their father was still living through the eldest son like a hereditary king. But Lorrie wasn't so convinced, even back then. In the months following Robert Sheppard's passing, Lorrie watched Robbie try his best to emulate their father—strict with chores, spare on warmth. Their father had been less severe before Julia Sheppard had fallen ill. In one of her letters, Crystal reminded him how devastated their father had been when she died. That he was only focusing on the hurt. That Lorrie was, too.

Wise words from a woman who couldn't even stick around.

In the darkness, Lorrie heard a heavier body shuffle across the floor to Cadlen's corner. Despite the dark, he imagined Robbie draping an arm across his little brother's shoulder, his thick hair rustling against his shoulder. For a second, Lorrie considered retreating back with his brothers. What did he expect he could do, anyway? Burst out of the crate in mid-flight?

And then what? Commandeer the cockpit? Land the Tan-Ro in some open field, live off the land?

The last time he took the bull by the horns, he'd managed to piss off Jason Holt to the point they were kicked out of the tower. His rash, knee-jerk reaction had caused a major incident. So what if Clara Connelly was screwing Holt? If Lorrie had kept his temper simmered and his sarcasm beneath his tongue, maybe they'd have been able to work it out, find a compromise—at least until Mayor Reekan was back.

The Tan-Ro's twin rotors thrummed. The pressure in his ears contracted as though invisible fingers were pressing into his eardrums.

Lorrie might have sentenced himself and his brothers to their deaths.

Feet shuffled outside the fastened lid of the crate. Lorrie's regret dissipated and he crouched on the balls of his feet, as though he were about to launch himself as soon as the music stopped.

First One Out

Saturday, 23 June AC 0245
255 km SSW of New Inland
Lorrie Sheppard

Lorrie couldn't decide whether to chastise Captain Ferrer for waiting so long to let them out of the cargo crate or for taking his eyes off the steering wheel in mid-flight. Or pedals, or joystick—whatever he called it. Automatic shuttles, he could understand. Automatic piloting of an aircraft, thousands of meters in the air, not so much. In the neon-blue light of the fuselage, the captain's smile looked fake. Even wearing big-muff headphones, his hair was styled perfectly and his eyes sparkled. Lorrie was about to tell him as much before Robbie pulled his shoulder.

"Remember, Lor, the man is flying us in the dead of night. Let's show some gratitude."

"Right. Maybe we'll give him a discount on his next stay at the inn."

Ferrer feigned laughter. "Young fellow is right, I should be up front!"

Is this guy kidding? He's like a goddamned gameshow host…

Cadlen crawled out of the crate and stretched as though he'd just woke up from hibernation. His thick hair was twisted and matted. All he needed were pyjamas.

"Listen, Lorrie. Not everyone wearing a uniform is a jerk. Besides, he could have just left us in the box."

Robbie had a point. "Fine."

The next two hours passed without incident, save for the impossible pressure that had built up behind Lorrie's eardrums. Ferrer had returned to give a cursory instruction on how to put on and deploy the safety devices in the event they had to abandon the aircraft. Why in hell would we ever abandon craft, Lorrie asked. The captain just grinned like an idiot and said something like he hoped that never happens. Lorrie's eyes rolled almost all the way around.

Still, the evacuation devices impressed him. While falling from the sky didn't offer the best odds of survival, these rubber things gave them somewhat of a chance. Strapped to the back like a parachute, once you released the ripcord, an inflatable sphere bloomed out and surrounded the entire body. An air pump kept pressure inside, and rather than lose your breath while plummeting, the interior of the rubber ball regulated oxygen. A proper parachute would later deploy to soften the landing. Remember to only pull the cord after you jump, Ferrer had told them. No shit, Lorrie had retorted.

Lorrie couldn't tell if the sun was coming up because the small windows of the fuselage were tinted black, one-way opaque. Cadlen had chosen to stay inside the box. There wasn't much else to see or do, and his art supplies were packed away. Robbie paced, occasionally peeking up front to talk to Ferrer. Lorrie just leaned against the wall with the evacuation bubble packs. If anything happened, he'd be the first out the hatch.

It was as if just thinking about it made it happen.

A blast rocked the aircraft, listing it violently from side to side. Cadlen tumbled out of the crate. Robbie, seated on the bench opposite the side hatch doors, rolled onto the metal cargo hold floor. Lorrie smashed his forehead into the plexiglass window. He wasn't sure if the flash of light was a concussion from the blow or an explosion.

"Ferrer! What's happening?" Robbie hollered as a squealing noise whined, increasing in pitch from the cockpit. The captain didn't answer. Lorrie smelled the smoke of melting or burning electronics. He tightened his eyes and opened them again as his head spun.

"Cadlen! Lorrie! We have to get out!" Robbie had clambered up to the cockpit only to rush back. The aircraft wavered and dipped. It wouldn't be long before it flipped completely upside-down. Lorrie's vision stayed fuzzy, no matter how hard he tried to focus. He heard his older brother call his name again but he couldn't answer. He sensed a commotion, bodies buzzing around him, before two hands pulled him in close as a whoosh of freezing air gusted into the fuselage. His feet lifted off the floor.

The deployment of the rubber sphere encased both Lorrie and Robbie, squeezing them impossibly tight as it constricted them in a space designed for only one adult body. Lorrie grimaced as the stubble of his brother's unshaven cheek grated against his own, his elbow jammed under his rib cage, sucking the breath from his chest as the balloon sealed shut with a thick suctioning pop.

Just like Ferrer had said, the air pump kicked on. The pressure in Lorrie's ears popped hard enough he was sure they were bleeding. His stomach rolled as the rubber bubble free-fell. The parachute deployed, jerking the two Sheppard brothers and causing Robbie's knee to squash Lorrie's groin. At that point, he'd have rather stayed on the aircraft.

Lorrie tried to gasp but without any breath he gritted his teeth, biting the inside of his cheek as the bubble rolled like a rubber ball. As the motion began to slow, the bubble splashed and bobbed, water sloshing around on the outside.

Of all the odds, they'd landed on water. It was probably their best possible outcome, short of actually making it to Ap-Oz intact.

The inflatable escape device kept them above water. With such a tight constriction and his breath suppressed by the pressure of his brother against him, Lorrie began to contort his torso, finding life in his extremities as he tried to instinctively free himself.

He knew Robbie was imploring him to stop squirming, but the words were muffled. As he moved his hands, he fingered the shape of a handle. Hoping to use it for a grip, he reached, feeling Robbie's elbow push harder under his lower rib.

A sudden rush of air and the relaxation of pressure allowed the brothers to stretch apart while the flotation device deflated. Robbie screamed.

"Not that one! The other one!"

The rubber flattened into a flimsy drapery that alone would not be sufficient to keep the two brothers afloat. The coldness jolted Lorrie like an electric pulse. Robbie grabbed him again by the shoulders, although this time he was facing him.

"Swim just like you were in the pool." Robbie waved his arms outward as he instinctively began to tread water. Once Lorrie did the same, he let go. Their eyes met for the first time since before the explosion.

Lorrie was uncomfortable looking into his brother's eyes. All that tough talk about jumping out first, and all he could do was smash his head into the window and stumble around. Peering over his brother bobbing in the surf, he tried to find the wreckage of the aircraft. Daylight was breaking…

Cadlen!

"Cadlen!" Lorrie's voice echoed across the water. He repeated it several times before Robbie finally caught his attention. He motioned behind.

Lorrie swiveled his head as he twisted his body, a stitch growing under his rib cage. Between the brown-grey line of what looked like a shoreline in the distance and the two brothers kicking in the water bobbed a pale-orange ball. The bubble began to deflate into a horseshoe shape around Cadlen's head and shoulders, keeping him safely above the water.

First one out, little brother. Well done.

"If you pulled the *other* handle, like I was trying to say, we could have been in that!"

Lorrie grimaced. "I wasn't trying to burst the bubble, I just wanted your elbow out of my ribs, and your cheese-grater face away from mine—"

His complaints were hushed by a small wake clipping his open mouth, water that tasted like marsh muck sucking into his air passage. Realizing Lorrie was in distress, Robbie scissor-kicked as he grasped his soaked shirt, tugging him as he made for the shoreline. Ahead, Cadlen had spotted them trying to catch up, and was kicking in his rubber horseshoe to meet them. They could at least hold onto the flotation device, the three of them then able to steer it ashore, as far from the center of the wide lake as possible.

As the three brothers found enough footing to walk the rest of the way, Cadlen pulled the second handle and the device shrunk flat. Discarding it in the surf, the youngest Sheppard strode to the tall grass before coming to rest on solid ground among high, glistening reeds. Lorrie couldn't help but marvel at his tenacity. And as always, without uttering a word.

Lorrie stumbled up the bank of the spongy, slick lake shore before collapsing on a grassy knoll, a deep suctioning sound squirting from beneath his body as he sank into the moss and algae. His pulse throbbed at an uncomfortable rate, unable to calm despite the comfort of his position. He squinted as Robbie's shadow loomed over him, wider than he was accustomed.

"Come on, Lorrie," he panted. "Not far to go, we just have to get to the trees."

"For crying out loud… give me a few minutes to catch my breath, already," Lorrie wheezed. "What's the hurry, anyway?"

Robbie grabbed his muddied left arm and pulled, causing Lorrie to slip in the muck leaving a glistening, slick bare patch. "The hurry? Whatever caused that to happen—what if someone's looking for us?"

Lorrie hoisted himself up onto his backside and glared out over the lake. There was no smoke, no wake—no clue that anything had so much as flown past, let alone plunged into the deep. They had plummeted out of the sky and landed in a kilometers-wide lake, lined as far as he could see with tall trees in all directions. In the early morning light, the surface rippled gently.

"*Looking* for us? We fell from the sky, right? Who would have *survived* that?"

Robbie let his arm go, wiping the muck on his pant leg. "Well, turns out we *did* survive it, right? But if it was me, I'd want to be sure the job was finished…"

He slogged off toward Cadlen, already near the tree line, leaving Lorrie in his muck hole. As Robbie's sucking steps faded, Lorrie lifted himself up, his entire back heavy with mud nearly weighing him down. As his brother's reasoning sank in, he suddenly became very tall in a very wide-open expanse. Whoever, or whatever, caused the aircraft to crash could probably track them just as well.

His heart rate increased again as he followed his brothers into the cover of the short-growth bog brush.

The Seventh Pier

Sunday, 27 May AC 0245
Jackson Homestead, Spruce Grove
Phil Fox

You gotta remember: for every ounce you're casting out there, you'll want about ten pounds test. Can't waste the line—this stuff comes from Kayewat, and we can't just drive up there and buy some more!"

The guest bedroom had become a makeshift tackle storage for generations of Jackson fishing gear. Younger Phil had likened it to an abandoned museum, like something found in the abandoned coastal towns along the North Atlantic seaboard from the Hudson to Forks Bay. On the neatly-made bed, more than a dozen rods with eyelets and handgrips splayed in a web like a dropped handful of straight pasta noodles. The room smelled like a museum, of must and old, dried wood. Pictures in unmatching frames clung to the walls, faded from their original colour palette to dim blues and whites. Phil had stared at the most prominent picture. "Six generations ago, or maybe seven? Jackson Auto was booming back then. The rod your great-great-something Grandpa's holding—it's here somewhere. Hard to tell with the faded colours though. Huh!"

It was hard to tell if the figures in the photograph were people, or just ghosts. In the oldest photo albums that had survived the fire were dark grey strips of film that when held up to a light source showed silver-grey reversals of images of photos taken lifetimes ago. With the right tools and techniques, coloured replicas could be brought back to life. When he'd asked Uncle Schiff about it, Bernard couldn't think of anyone within a day's ride by buggy that could do it. Phil wondered if the negatives for any of the faded pictures on the wall survived.

"So, it's mackerel tomorrow morning?" Phil sat on a dusty bear hide rug, wooden crates agape, and spilling rigging and tangled spools of crystalline fishing wire. He gripped and unopened a spool of 30 lb test line. It was much more appealing to just unwrap it and start fresh, rather than untangling the partial spools in his lap.

"Yessir! And don't open that thirty-pounder—we'll need forty out at the pier."

Le_Renard hunched over a wooden desk with small drawers and a wide light angled over the surface. The set of tools his father used to wind feathers and strings onto curved hooks looked like nothing any other tradesperson would use in New Inland. Spools feeding threads up hollow tubes, pliers that needed to be pinched to open small, flat tweezers, and needles with springs and jutting arms—all employed to make lures realistic enough for strait fish species to bite. The viscous lacquer that held it all together smelled of rendered polymers, and without an open window, gave Phil a headache. The old man inhaled the glue fumes with apparent nostalgia.

"Ah, smell that! Better than rotten whale carcass! Huh!"

"I wouldn't know." Phil wrinkled his nose and set aside the unspoiled spool. 40 lb test. There had to be a partial of it somewhere…

"You aren't missing anything, my boy. You get smell-blind to it, true. But leave Kayewat for even a day—it's like starting all over again." Le_Renard squinted at the hook on the thin vice-grip. Dipping the fancy needle into the lacquer, he dabbed a small drop on the black head of the artificial minnow. It would dry like glass overnight. It would be waterproof come morning light when it was affixed onto the forty-wire and cast into the drink.

There wasn't, however, enough lacquer in the known world that would keep the two fishermen dry. Phil didn't mind being wet. It was the brisk wind along the strait that would chill him by degrees, and the sun didn't shine on their spot on the pier. Luckily the woodbox in the living room was full of seasoned, dry hardwood. The fireplace would greet them upon their return like an embrace of sunlight. After another twenty minutes of untangling the opened spool, Phil selected from the pile a long bamboo rod that had proved seaworthy all those years before when they first dropped lines together in the open water of the strait. Wind the forty-line onto the reel, double check the tackle box, then hit the sack. Those had been Le_Renard's words all those years ago, and when he uttered them again verbatim, the old man's voice had grown deeper, more strained, but still lined with enthusiasm.

Since the FTR buggy was still on the hoist in Jackson Auto, Albert was kind enough to taxi Phil and Le_Renard along the south shore to the wharf at the far-eastern reach of the peninsula. Moored for winter in a dry-dock far enough ashore to escape the whipping wind and surf, a sturdy power boat primed on first try, and the rotary blades of the motor thrumbled in the water, frothing white bubbles as the pair climbed aboard. Phil carried a fake-leather sock containing his bamboo rod and reel and his father's sleeker fiberglass model. The old man carried the tackle and the lunch box.

Nosing into the strait, Le_Renard perched on the rear bench and maneuvered the steering handle as the craft whined, increasing speed and chopping over the crisp wakes of the shallows. The boat oscillated in more rolling ups and downs as the surf rose in the deeper water. Phil knelt on the floor of the boat, resting his backside on the bow seat, squinting into the salty air. As they approached, the pier swelled into view. The closer they came, the more clearly the broken arc of the strait-spanning pier emerged. There were at least six similar pillars dotting the line that once connected the mainland to Ebbequit Island, remaining defiant against the moving water and ice floes, decades, maybe even a century since it was last a fixed link. It was the second span, Uncle Schiff had once explained. The first was long gone, but much of the original concrete piers and platforms had been reclaimed either by Hyacynthe or other local communes and villages. What remained of the second was much hardier material—polymer-infused, like the ancient Romans who used volcanic ash in their aqueducts. Regardless, the piers that remained had squatted long enough to become part of the local ecosystem.

Not unlike the Jackson family in Gasperro. The Homestead was a seventh pier.

Mooring the craft on an embedded, rusty eye-hook, Phil crouched, gripping the gunnels as he crept onto the barnacled concrete. Le_Renard followed close behind, almost nudging Phil into the turbulent strait water as he clambered ahead. Listing almost sixty degrees, the stubborn pier slope had been carved into a level platform decades ago. Phil ducked while the old man heaved the tackle from the boat to their fishing spot. Once aboard the pier, the wind slowed from the break caused by the high concrete pillar. Le_Renard angled toward a flat, corroded steel trapdoor locked shut with a padlock the size of his fist.

"Now where's that key… Hope I didn't forget it! Huh!" The old man patted his outer pockets in an attempt at humour. Phil wasn't laughing. He slung the wicker tackle box, and his father snagged it by the hanging strap. Fishing the key from one of the outer compartments, Le_Renard snorted and unlatched the door. From inside, he retrieved two collapsible chairs. After assembling the rods, Phil with his bamboo and his father with his fiberglass, the pair rigged up their forty-pound test reels and baited their hooks with Le_Renard's freshly tied lures. Phil cast his line outward toward the open sea while the old man aimed toward the island, its reddish shores forming the horizon. Within minutes, Phil's line twitched and bowed.

"How about that! Ten years, and I still have it!" Phil chided as he applied torque to his rod, slowly cranking against the action on the end of his hook. "Any action over there?"

"Patience, my boy! That old rubber boot on your line won't fight you too much!" Le_Renard wound in his reel and drew the pole back over his shoulder in a wide arc.

"Watch it, old man—you almost hooked me in the cheek, remember?"

"And I told you then not to stand so close, right? Whoa, there! Now we're cookin'!" The old man bellowed as his line tautened, then carved against the surf as his quarry tugged on the lure. Phil narrowed his eyes and bore down on his reel, hauling in hard as his bamboo pole arced to the point of nearly snapping. The old bamboo rod had survived the fire because it had been stored with the rest of the old gear in the shed, not in the actual house. Le_Renard always opted for the newer gear. Not everything that's old can stand up to modern innovation, he had once declared. Phil wondered if the old fart actually heard his own words.

Both fishermen dialed into their respective battles. Phil hauled in one last pull and felt the catch give way, as though it were resigning. Behind him, Le_Renard coaxed his prey as he slowly reeled in his line, darting back and forth with less and less vigor.

"Almost done, feller. Almost…" The old man dipped the tip of the rod almost to the surface as he drew the mackerel out of the surf, twisting and wriggling enough to knock anyone off balance on a slippery pier in the middle of the strait. Phil reeled in his own catch. To his dismay, the mound of olive-grey seaweed hung with disappointment on the bent lure, dripping as it swung inward into his grasp. The slimy, air-pocketed noodles smelled of sea salt but reeked of hubris.

"Haha! Looks like we'll have a side of dulse with our mackerel tonight!"

"Yeah, yeah. And you said it was an old rubber boot…"

Retirement

Monday, 28 May AC 0245
Jackson Homestead, Spruce Grove
Phil Fox

Fishing mackerel was only the first week. From the Jackson pier, Phil and his father hauled in submerged ropes, kept afloat with red balloon-shaped bobbers, with trapezoidal-shaped traps filled with lobsters. Few fishermen risked the open water of the strait to fish for the insectoid mollusks. Pirates from as far east as the Avalon, south to the Hudson, and even from the far coast up to Baffin converged on the shallow waters of the strait. They had no qualms confronting fishermen, and even less taking their catch. Le_Renard's pier was a fortress, at least to the other fishers. Any closer than *my* buoys, and they'll know they're too close, the old man once boasted. More than once, Phil saw his father raise the rifle sighting to his eye and fire off a warning over the interlopers' bows. Either the old man was a poor shot, or he was more generous than he'd ever let on.

After a week of gathering a king's ransom of shellfish and mackerel, Phil and Le_Renard finally took their first break since he'd arrived at the Homestead. The first three days were largely uneventful, both on the water and on the pier. It usually took about three days for Phil to tire of Le_Renard's particularities, from winding the line this way and casting it that way, to complaining about the high cost of kerosene. By the third day, every gasping "huh" made him want to pitch the old man into the surf. Let the lobsters pick his bones.

Phil sliced vegetables with a knife so old the blade was curved on the sharp side. The juices leaked off cutting boards onto the stained wood-topped countertop. He inhaled the boiled-off steam of a rich, seasoned broth simmering on the cast-iron stove. Carrots and potatoes would complement the mix of lobster and scallops that would complete the hearty chowder.

"Stir that, will ya?" Le_Renard hollered from the study. "That cream base'll stick to the bottom faster than barnacles on the bow!"

"You could help a little, you know." Phil stirred the pot in more ways than one.

"I have plenty of work to catch up on! And besides, you make a better chowder than me! Huh!"

Phil grimaced at the retort. "Yeah, yeah. Work. That's what we'll call it."

"If I don't certify those Rust bonds, you won't be eating seafood and other Spruce Grove comforts, my boy. No, you'll have to eat the Pretty Boy's cooking!"

No sooner had the old man said the words when the front door slammed shut. "Very funny, *Emmanuel*!" Albert strode into the kitchen, eyebrows cocked. "If you rather feel more at home, I can have the harbour master save some chum for you instead!"

The thought of rotting fish overrode the rich scent of seafood chowder in Phil's nostrils. Kayewati didn't actually eat rotten fish. The food had to be safe, or the entire domed sanctuary would have died off before they could even finish construction. To an outsider, the cuisine of the frozen far-north was an acquired taste at best, and toxic to an unaccustomed belly at worst. *With his money, he probably imported comfort food, anyway.*

"Let me guess, 'paperwork'?" Albert leaned against the door frame just as he did the gib crane on the wharf a week earlier. "If he really wants to help out with that, I have years' worth back at the office he can help me out with sometime."

"Jackson finances have been in capable hands." Le_Renard waltzed out of the study and joined the cousins in the kitchen. "In fact, you've been so good at cutting maintenance costs, I can almost afford the nuke cell!"

"Funny you mention maintenance. I have a trailer full of roofing out front."

Le_Renard's eyes widened. "Well there, now—you did find some asphalt shingles?" He'd been complaining about the scarcity of the old-fashioned cheap kind that were leaking too much water and hosting too much moss on the roof. Phil rested the cutting board against the rim of the pot and plowed the cut veggies into the broth.

"About that." Albert shifted his weight to the other foot. "I know you wanted to go cheaper on those shingles. But they're not as cheap to import as you remember. Now—

"Hold on, there. You *didn't* buy the sheet metal, right?"

Phil retrieved the cleaned and portioned seafood mix from the fridge. Any distraction from the exchange between his father and cousin was welcome.

"We went over this, *Emmanuel*. The sheet metal lasts longer, and we only need to import it from the Avalon, not Arctica!"

Emmanuel. Phil wasn't used to Le_Renard's original name. The one he was assigned at birth, long before he was forced to receive the Kayewati stamp and change it to something more unconventional. More unsavoury.

"But I'm telling you, *Mr. Schiff*—the metal roofing—"

"Leaks at the rivets, you've told me a hundred times." Albert tossed his curly hair. "So I went with something *else*. Polymer-infused roofing—no rivet holes!"

Le_Renard dipped a ladle into the broth and burned his lips taking a sip. "Delicious, my boy! Like I said, you make a mean chowder! Huh!"

Phil took the utensil from him before he dipped it back in the stew. "And you can wait like the rest of us, *Emmanuel.*"

"Don't be utterin' my name in vain, now!" The old man retreated to a chair at the table. After some more bickering about the extra cost for the new-fangled rubbery roofing, Phil served up three deep soup bowls with the milky soup. After a more cautious attempt, Le_Renard stopped mumbling as he polished off his first serving, helping himself to a second by dipping the bowl directly into the pot.

"I told you not to do that!" Phil scolded. "You're not in Kayewat!"

As soon as he said it, he knew it was too much. Le_Renard glowered and took his bowl into the study, like a small boy taking his ball and going home. Albert shrugged.

"Don't worry about him. He's just pouting." Albert slurped the last spoonful of his chowder and wiped his lip with the cloth napkin. "Not used to people telling him what to do. Retirement's going to be a hard adjustment."

Retirement. Huh, indeed.

Albert dropped his spoon into the bowl and brought it to the washing bin. "He's been like that since he came back. Any mention of Kayewat at all and he shuts right down. But he'll come around—you can't keep a smart-ass quiet forever!"

The door to the study remained ajar, at least. If he was *really* in a mood, he'd have closed it and slid the bolt lock. He was probably processing Albert's roofing purchase. He may or may not ever acknowledge that it was the right decision—roofing can't last forever, but if the rubber-based polymer sheets came as advertised, they'd at least last Le_Renard's natural life. Phil might not even have to replace them before the Homestead deed passed from his old, dying hands. *To whom, exactly…*

Phil washed the dishes and Albert dried them with a threadbare tea towel. The pair retreated into the living room, where the fire had simmered into glowing embers. Seasoned, dry hardwood burst into flame after only a few moments and the cousins sank into the cushions of two big armchairs facing each other.

"If you don't mind me staying the night, I can help you with the roofing," Albert said, loosening the belt-rope of his trousers. "With an extra set of hands, we can have it done by suppertime. The new stuff goes on really easily."

"You did good, Albert." Le_Renard emerged from the study and flopped onto the sofa adjacent to both big chairs, facing the fireplace. He swung both legs up onto the empty cushions and released a wheezing sigh. It wasn't lost on Phil that his father had called his cousin by his real name. It was a subtle admission of wrongdoing on his part. The pouting was over.

"Glad I could help. And you were right—the rivets would leak, since we can't easily get petroleum sealant anymore."

The trio sat for a moment in silence, enjoying the warmth of the fire and the fullness of their stomachs.

"No reaction, my boy?"

"I took some anties just in case," Phil answered. "But no, nothing. I must finally be a villager!"

"Huh! You're as real as they come. The merchants were impressed with our catch, that's for sure!" Le_Renard let Phil negotiate the earnings of their week's catch. Inland communities were more than happy to trade fresh vegetables for seafood. Most had neither the skills nor the equipment to go out on the water. Even if they did, it was a lawless frontier out there. Not unlike Kayewat.

Sooner or later, the old man will tell me what's happened…

Albert stood and stretched his arms to the rafters. "So, breakfast at five, and up the ladder for six?"

A Teacup in Space

Tuesday, 29 May AC 0245
Jackson Homestead, Spruce Grove
Phil Fox

Phil woke to the crackling of bacon strips frying in the kitchen, and the fragrance of sweet tea. If they couldn't afford petroleum sealant, there's no way they could import java. He sighed. Kendall would have had a hot cup on his desk in a temperature-sealed tumbler. Already, the Homestead was reminding him of the world he'd fled barely two weeks ago. And that was the point.

6 am became 7 am. Le_Renard was predictably late waking up. The old man skipped the bacon but devoured two over-easy eggs and a slice of dry toast. Outside, he clapped the wooden ladder against the north side of the Homestead, and with one step splintered the first rung. "Huh!" he guffawed as Albert cupped his face with an open palm. He had an aluminum ladder back in Gasperro, but that would take some time. Phil offered to stay behind to ensure Le_Renard didn't go inside for a nap. Besides, there was plenty of preparation work that could be done while Albert looped back into town.

It was almost 9 am before the replacement ladder was in service and the trio scaled the roof. The trip back to Gasperro turned out to be a blessing. While back in the village, Albert stopped by the wharf. The harbour master, after a hearty laugh at Le_Renard's misfortune, recommended a motorized jib to haul the new roofing up the two stories. It ran on petrol, but a quick stop at Jackson Auto and one jerry can later, and Albert had solved two problems in one trip. Phil's back didn't feel as weary in advance of the job.

The motorized pulley and arm took all three to unload from Albert's trailer, and a petty argument between him and Le_Renard to set it up. Once the engine coughed to life, spitting grey smoke and gargling its fuel lines free, Albert used the arm hook to hoist the entire bundle off the mossy earth and raise it up to the eaves. Phil and his father leaned hard into the pitch of the roof, and the payload came to rest on a bare patch of roof that had been easily peeled away. All told, the borrowed crane saved them about half the time they'd lost.

A brief pause for sandwiches and ale and a few hours later, the team had managed to peel off the brittle, rotten roof coverings. They flaked in peppery, soggy chunks, too viscous to sweep and too tedious to shovel. It was Le_Renard who came up with the idea to push them with the snow rake off the roof onto Albert's trailer. Work smarter, not harder, the old man boasted. Phil was impressed. Once in a while, the old man demonstrated his cleverness. *It's probably why he's still alive.*

True to Albert's claim, though, the new roofing installed easily. Bundled, they weighed a ton. Peeled apart, however, the individual sheets were pliable and light. Le_Renard needed convincing that they would provide adequate protection. Once the first two layers were fastened into place, locking airtight row by row, he acquiesced. Phil figured that his compliance was more likely based on the ease of laying them than whether they would actually work. "This is the last roofing job for this old fella," he muttered as they fitted the final row over the peak. "If they need to be fixed, you can hire some locals, pretty boy!"

The early evening sun crept westward, and the trio paused to salute it with a round of ales. There was enough chowder leftover that no one had to prepare any new food. Phil agreed to accompany Albert to the pit in the morning to dump the old shingles. The jib wasn't urgently needed back at the Gasperro landing, so Albert suggested they use it to finish any roofing needed at Jackson Auto. The metal roofing on the old service station roof leaked around the rivets, fueling Le_Renard's dislike of the product. There may not be any sealant, but perhaps they could purchase some polymer caulking when they ventured up the coast later in the week.

Phil found himself in front of the fire a second night in a row, sipping an herbal tea while his father and cousin reclined in their own chaises. Le_Renard gripped a mahogany-hued smoking pipe in his teeth as sweet smoke curled throughout the living room. As though fate were reassuring the old skeptic, rain pattered outside. It was quieter on the new roofing. Albert insisted on bringing Le_Renard up into the attic eaves to prove that the leaks were properly sealed. An evening puff indicated that the old man was satisfied.

"Well, that's one job I'm happy to see the other side of, huh!" Le_Renard crossed his ankles on the sofa. "Now, if there's nothing else that needs to be done around here, maybe we can finally sail up shore."

"You two can sail to the Avalon if you like. I've got everything locked down here." Albert smiled. "With the roof fixed, we're secure on all sides now!"

Phil gazed into the dancing flames behind the mesh screen of the hearth. It was all about security in the Jackson Homestead. In Spruce Grove. In Gasperro. In a small settlement nestled within a bay, as anonymous as the dozens of others dotting the coast, amidst the lush forests this side of the radiation seams, on the island across the strait, or along the peninsula by the ocean. For anyone who wasn't a known and wanted criminal, it would have been enough to be a teacup floating among a billion space rocks, as Le_Renard once described it. As far as anyone knew, there was no teacup out there at all. But what *if* someone finally found it? Anything short of a zero-possibility was enough to keep their guard. Whether it was a leak in the roof or a blip on the red eye radar. As soon as you take your eye off it, you're as good as gone. Le_Renard had told young Phil that all those years ago. And he'd grown to believe it.

"You know, you'll sail past Burnside on your way…" Albert left that hanging on the pipe-smoky air. Phil felt his stomach tighten.

"When we get back, I promise. I'll stop and pay my respects."

Le_Renard coughed. "That's right. And I'll come with you. Been too long."

Albert didn't press the issue. Phil avoided his cousin's eyes. There was no way he could have left Capston when Bernard Schiff had taken a turn for the worse. The cancer had dogged his uncle as long as Phil had known him. It was well known what cancer did to a body. New Inland had long claimed that the outside world carried far more medical risk than red tide. Sure, nuclear medicine had come a long way. Treating radiation was much easier than it was even a few generations before. But informative clips about the ravaging effects of cancer on the skin, in the organs, throughout the lymph nodes—it was enough to keep most people safe inside. The thought of his uncle shriveling up as an unseen disease consumed him from the very fabric of his cells terrified him. Red tide had caused his mother to lose her energy, but cancer— you could watch that disintegrate the body in horrific detail.

Still, he could have been braver. Kendall said she'd support him whatever he felt was best, but he knew she would have come up with a creative excuse if he had chosen to leave, to see Uncle Schiff one last time. If nothing else, to support Albert. Bernard Schiff was Albert's adoptive father, just as Lucas and Elsa Fox were his own adoptive parents.

If Albert had felt slighted, he'd never shown it. *Albert's a better man than me.*

Le_Renard sparked a tiny flame into the bowl of his pipe and sucked in, brightening the glow of the dried leaf as he exhaled through his nostrils. He coughed again. "I have the Rust bonds all signed off, and the cargo's all loaded on the sloop. All that for one lousy nuke-cell!"

"Yes, and you can finally finish the FTE. Then what will you do?" Phil's comment was laced with a bitter sarcasm. The FTE buggy was a lifelong project—more important at one time to the old man than meeting his biological son. It was the only reason Jackson Auto remained open. The reason why he got so bent out of shape when the metal roofing leaked. A project that he could hide behind to forget about Kayewat, about the business schemes and the wrongs done.

To forget that he'd pawned off his son to the sister of his business associate, to raise in a faraway dome in the dry badlands, a place as diametrically opposite to the Spruce Grove as you could get.

"I suppose I'll take 'er for a drive." Le_Renard inhaled from the pipe and gazed into the fire. Phil supposed he would do just that. Maybe he'd drive out of his life again. Phil Fox had long-ago forgiven his biological father. The reason for that lied in Burnside-on-the-hill. But every so often, those old feelings resurfaced. Outside, the rain fell on a defiant, polymer-sealed roof. For now, the teacup was safe in its orbit.

Red Tears

AD 2560
The Ossuary, Moab
Andreas

Even if he closed his eyes, Andreas could not avoid the scrutiny of his witnesses. They gazed down upon him from all sides, row upon row, from the floor to the high-arced ceiling. Three hundred sixty degrees. The accumulation of all wisdom, casting judgment on a ten-year-old boy. It was unfair. It was cruel.

"Breathe, like we practiced." From out of his view, Brother Simon encouraged him with a calmness Andreas never understood. The candle plate dipped in his trembling hand. The brass was polished to a shine, a standard chore for an initiate of his age. He walked in measured steps—not so quickly as to trip on his robe, and not so fast as to stumble and risk setting the entire chamber on fire. The mere thought of an inferno in this sacred place churned his abdomen. The image of Haven aflame while the Catholic Forty in their hoods and heavy cloaks recited from the sacred Ansati text never left for long. Every time he dragged the phosphorous head of a match across a coarse lighting strip, the smells and sights of the burning town triggered the red episode to begin.

Andreas inhaled and held the breath as he took a step. The tapered candle held atop its wick a flame in the shape of an orange tear drop. He didn't know if his own teardrops were red or blue.

"You're doing fine, son. No one here is judging you."

Lies.

Everyone here was judging him. Past and present. Syballine Sister

Mora sat across the table, the *palla* scarf draped over her head, holding the face veil in place. She rested her folded hands on the surface, piles of volumes standing guard over the open tome in front of her. The evening had grown dim. Andreas had delivered the Light many times. But this time, a red episode chose to interrupt the task. Never before had it occurred while he was holding the flame.

You should never have trusted me to carry the flame…

At the table, Andreas looked away from the dancing Light. All around him, the gallery of watchers stared, silent as death and every bit as final. Side by side, they melted from earthen browns and greens into deep crimson and burgundy. The ladders on wheels became rib cages. Mora turned into a statue of salt and her books corpses strewn about her. And in his hands, Andreas held a chalice filled to the brim with blood instead of a copper plate. It spilled over the lip and burned his skin like acid with every drop.

It would be so easy to just let it go. Let it fall and consume everything. Everyone…

He tightened his shut eyes, snuffing the red into blackness with all the strength he could summon. A voice pierced the dark.

"Well done, Andreas."

Light burst as he opened his eyes. The candle plate rested on the table, and the corpses were once again books. Mora blinked behind her lace veil and smiled. All around him, the stacks of books remained silent, no longer in human form. Human souls dwelt within them, of course. But Brother Simon was right. None of them passed any judgment. The red episode was over. Andreas allowed himself to inhale. No smoke, no decay.

"I was confused… I didn't think I could do it…" His eyes itched and pain welled behind his temples.

"When the red overtook you, what did you see?"

"People—so many people—all looking at me. All waiting for me to fail. And Sister Mora, she was a statue. And there were bodies…"

Andreas knew he could trust Brother Simon and Sister Mora. But he couldn't turn off the shame he always felt when these moments happened. Simon stepped up alongside him and draped an arm around his slender shoulders.

"When you see these things, you're seeing Sheol," said Simon. Mora nodded in agreement.

"What is *Sheol*?"

"It's not a *what*, it's a *where*."

"It's a real place?" Andreas had read the word before in his study of sacred texts, though he couldn't remember which one. None of the others in the order ever spoke of it, to his knowledge.

"It is. And one day, when you're ready, I will take you there."

Andreas shook Simon's arm off his shoulders. "Why? Why would I ever want to go to such an awful place, Brother Simon?"

Mora stood and circled the table. She held Andreas against her soft robe. The Syballine Sister smelled of lilac. It calmed him.

"When you are ready, you'll know."

Andreas thought a tear might stain her *stola* dress. Blue, red—anything. Nothing.

"How will I know, Mora?"

"You'll know when you instead ask why you hadn't been brought there sooner."

Holy Water

Sunday, 30 May AD 2572
Route to Sheol
Brother Andreas

After four days and nights below ground, winding through tunnels and caverns, Andreas began to worry that their lamps would extinguish. The Ansati used power cells that could last for weeks—but that was on the outside, where natural light allowed lamps to be turned off during daylight hours. Where there was no source of light to exploit, Andreas and Simon needed to keep them on for most of the day, albeit dimmed as low as possible so as to be able to see their way.

"Do you worry that the lamp will die? How could we ever find our way out?" Andreas moved in step behind Brother Simon as though he were his shadow. A shadow that couldn't exist in such a place.

"It could die. And I used to worry, but not anymore. I've made this journey many times, you see."

No. I can't see anything.

"Not much further."

Andreas dismissed the assurance as condescension. In less than an hour, however, the pair descended through a steel-beamed opening into a wide grotto. The rush of fast-moving water brought with it a coolness of air. Andreas breathed deeply. Simon raised the lamp and turned the dial to increase its luminosity.

The grotto glistened, sparkles from rock crystals embedded in the walls and ceiling, glittering like a kaleidoscope whenever Simon moved the light. The rushing water rippled with streaks of deep green.

"Don't drink from this water, Andreas. From now on, we must only drink from our own supply." No sooner did Simon utter the words that Andreas craved a mouthful.

"It's a river... underground."

"The *Acheron*. Legend says it is one of the great rivers of the underworld, that it flows to all parts of the world. In the *Suda*, it is written that this is a river of healing. We can preserve our lamp light by following it. One more day, and we'll arrive."

That final day along the narrow, rocky banks of the Acheron slowed as though they had turned an hourglass with limitless sand. Some sections were impossibly tight. They had to crawl at times, holes wearing through the knees of his trousers as Andreas crawled on all fours in near pitch darkness, only the dim glow of Simon's lamp ahead of him.

As the tunnel expanded and they could stand up straight, Simon turned, holding the lamp chin-high. Andreas looked into his stern eyes.

"We are about to enter *Sheol*. No matter what, you must breathe."

Andreas nodded, and Simon returned the gesture, turning ahead and slowly brightening the lamp light. The blackness gave way to a greyish-green hue. The Acheron had slowed to a calmness that mirrored the lamp light in distorted waves all around the open chamber, to a ceiling higher than the Library of Moab.

And just like the Library, it was lined on all sides, as far as he could focus his eyes, with human bones. Not orderly, in rows, or sorted by types. Twisted skeletons—skulls, arms, ribs, and legs, down to the fingers and toes. By the hundreds. Thousands. Tens of thousands.

Andreas lost his breath as though the Acheron had sucked it from his chest. He spun around, his eyes seeing the same in every direction. As a young boy, his red episodes had caused him to hallucinate that the stacks and stacks of books on the library shelves were each human remains. He watched them disintegrate until only the skeletal remains were left to stare at him. The red would wash over him like a lava flow, until it had passed and he woke from the spontaneous nightmare. Andreas closed his eyes, pressing his fingers so hard he thought they might burst. But when he opened them, nothing had changed. The stacks and stacks of tangled bones were still there. The Acheron was still.

"Remember. Breathe."

In a flash of panic, Andreas turned to run. A sharp crunch beneath his feet stopped him in his tracks. Looking down, he lifted his foot off a splintered femur. Faster than it had ever before, the red inside him roiled, expanding out of his gut until his whole body shook. A geyser of vomit erupted before he could cover his mouth, spilling through his fingers. With a blink of his eyes, Andreas saw tens of thousands of skeletons reanimate, stirring and twisting as muscle tissue, blood, and skin stretched over their frames. The bodies writhed, naked and stained with the reversal of decay. Brother Simon stood fast, unchanged in the lamp light.

Help me! Andreas screamed in red, but the words never came from his mouth. The entire cavern was seething like a dead body covered in maggots. There was no way out. Except...

The Acheron.

Wild-eyed and suffocating, Andreas hurled himself toward the still water of the green river. He heard Simon begging him to stop, but the voice was muffled so much it sounded like a memory echo. Stumbling over loose bones and rocks, he waded three strides into the river and plunged beneath its surface.

Don't drink the water, Andreas. No matter what.

His clothing shrunk against his skin, tightening like a membrane around his entire body, weighing him down into the deep pool. He flailed, unable to orient himself. In a matter of seconds, he would succumb to the river and inhale the Acheron deep inside him, and take his place among the remains of the thousands that lined its banks.

A pair of impossibly strong hands grabbed him by the shoulders before he could commit.

He inhaled as though he were a newborn. Andreas sputtered as Simon dragged him from the water, heels dragging along its floor, until he was laid upon the rocky shore next to the lamp light. Simon wrapped his arms around him, pinning him so he couldn't wriggle loose. All he could do was gasp. Within mere moments, the red subsided, as though the Acheron had flushed it from his body. Free from the red episode, Andreas breathed, just like Simon had urged him. After several deep, rhythmic breaths, he opened his eyes.

Gone were the writhing bodies. The bones remained, but they were inert, no longer threatening. Andreas's body relaxed, and Simon released his grip. He stayed prone on the bank of the river, moving only his eyes around the cavern. In the brightened lamp light, he began to notice more details around the chamber. It was much longer and wider than he'd first thought. Much of the area was carved and shaped in an unnatural way. The chamber hadn't eroded into its shape.

It was mined.

"This is Sheol, son."

He knew it was, even if he hadn't been forewarned. His red episodes had been showing him the underworld all his life. With a new found awareness, Andreas sat up.

"If the Ansati know of this place, and what—*who* is down here, why have they not been Reclaimed?" The Ansati never left human remains behind. It was central to their belief—that all human remains must be harvested, prepared, and placed in the Ossuary with dignity, not to rot alone, unknown, forgotten. How could they have left so many bodies in this place?

Simon sighed. "Many years ago, people were forced to work deep beneath the earth, tunneling and excavating deep pits and mines, like this one. The work was hazardous. Many lost their lives. But the masters who ordered the mining were cowardly. They could not recover the bodies of the workers killed under their mandates. So, they found the deepest caverns and piled the bodies, one by one, away from the eyes of the outside world."

As Simon recounted the tale, Andreas surveyed the chamber. Gloves. Helmets. Boots. Traces of all of these peppered the piles of bones. He began to see seized equipment and tools. If he closed his eyes and allowed the red to come back, he would surely imagine a busy industrial complex, workers like drones digging in dirt and gouging through bedrock, choking on black dust. But the red stayed away.

"Our earliest Brothers and Sisters came upon this place. They decided that this place was its own Ossuary. The people left to rest here had given of themselves for the benefit of others far more fortunate, more rich, more ambitious. They were left here to be *forgotten*. And there was nothing the Ansati could do. A thousand lifetimes wouldn't be enough for us to salvage their memories, their souls. That is the domain of the *Acheron. Of Sheol.*"

That's why he'd been told not to drink of the river. Not because it was unsafe.

It was holy water.

"We come here to witness the worst of humanity. As a testimonial to what happens when we forget. In the darkness beneath the earth, we are all forgotten."

Tuesday, 19 June AD 2590
The Ossuary, Moab
Brother Andreas

"As a boy, you taught me the definition of 'Syballine'. In the eyes of a child, I understood it to mean clairvoyant, prophet. Seer."

Andreas slumped against the Ossuary stack, drawers opened to different depths around him. Cluttered around his slovenly shape, dried bones poked through the off-white lace of a burial gown. Rings, bracelets, and a hairpiece lay strewn on the thick burgundy carpet. When he closed his eyes, Andreas could smell a sea of blood instead of the musty floor. A metallic taste along the edges of his tongue, sour and profane.

"What was never clear, Mora, is the criteria to that title. What have *you* ever done to be called *Syballine Sister?* Many women come and go from Moab. But only some are ordained. What made *you* so special?"

Reaching his flat palms to the floor, a puddle of blood oozed through his fingers, wrung from the upholstered carpet. Crimson rivulets ran down the stacks, leaking through the open drawer, dripping like a faucet on the shoulder of his crumpled robe. This wasn't the Library. There were no books morphing into undead corpses. The faces of the drawers were marbled in grey swirls and white. Forty rows from floor to ceiling, and nothing more than a row of Roman numerals to identify whose remains and belongings were contained within. Syballine Sisters kept the files that contained the matching identities to their tombs. *Surely, the role required more than basic bookkeeping skills…*

"*You knew*, Mora. You knew how Sheol would affect me. You agreed with the Catholic Forty. You knew what I would see, but more importantly, *how* I would see it. *Syballine*, indeed."

The blood was only going to grow rancid. Andreas had a choice. Either clean it up while the red kept at bay within him, or leave it and move faster. How many times had he polished the brass handles of the Ossuary drawers? Wiped away dust from the edges?

Andreas hoisted himself onto his two feet, slipping on the bloody carpet before he caught his balance. He faced the stack and pushed closed each drawer until he reached the one gaping and leaking.

"MCMLXXXV. *1985* would have been so much easier, don't you think, Mora? Leave it to the Ansati to make things harder than necessary." His feet nudged the remains of the former occupant of drawer 1985. Her gown was splotched with blood, but not her own. Andreas hadn't bothered to research her identity. There were volumes in the Library that could have told him who she had been, when she had lived, whom she had loved. But none of that was important. To him, or to anyone. This woman could have just as well been stuffed deep in an underground grotto, as anonymous as the rest of the dumped bodies from another time. Washed in the holy water of the Acheron. What made her so special that she got to rest for all time in a felt-lined marble enclosure, surrounded by possessions a complete stranger had deemed important?

At least the Library told stories. But how many of those stories were worth remembering?

Andreas leaned on the face of the 1985 drawer. There was plenty of room for him to lay Syballine Sister Mora in a formal, respectful repose. Instead, he'd heaved her body over the side, still gushing from the gaping neck wound, one arm kinked over her head and one of her legs contorted in an unnatural bend, dislocated at the knee. Even bereft of life, Mora had fought the red surge within Andreas until the last.

All he had asked her was the exact location of *one body*. Somehow, she knew his motive. Perhaps she *was* Syballine after all.

"But you weren't clairvoyant enough to know what came next. Must have been your eyes…" Andreas spat the words at Mora's dead body inside the drawer, mouth hung open, her swelled tongue hiding the bottom row of teeth. In life, she had had a warm smile. Deep, soft eyes that used to pierce his heart. In the afterlife, her face was frozen in permanent disbelief.

Except for her eyes.

In the opening salvo of his red rage, he had plucked them from their sockets with one of her writing tools before plunging it into her throat.

Reaching into his pocket, Andreas rolled the squishy bulbs from his fingers to his thumb and back. "They did you no good, anyway, Sister. You won't miss them."

The Cleansing

Viernes, 22 junio NE 267
Residence of Eminence De Léon, Motherland
Colonel Tirel Desantos

What do we do about the Council of Regents? The Magister will ask questions." Alvara stood at attention only a few steps from the open door. Tirel leaned back into the plastic-leather chair, just like Andreas had done back in the chapel. Eminence De Léon had always insisted that throne-shaped chairs were provided for him—public ceremonies or private quarters alike. In his claustrophobic office that looked more like a museum, De Léon had pretended to be hard at work, when his slouching posture indicated otherwise. Books and loose papers and folders littered the mahogany desk top. If the cleaning staff hadn't dusted them, any visitor of any frequency would notice the piles never shrank. How many times did he pick up the top-most book, an omnibus of folktales from the motherland deep to the south of the Red Line? Tirel often wondered if De Léon could even read old Spanish.

A leader needsssss… a good chair… De Léon would hiss his wisdom through drawls and stutters. Tirel had seen through it from his earliest days as a ward. Even as a child, he'd wondered if the Eminence realized that everyone knew how phony he was.

"I will deal with the Regents. Magister Solanis is a reasonable man. In effect, I've done him a favour."

Alvara shifted his weight from one foot to the other, glancing around the room. The colonel couldn't blame him for keeping a quick escape as an option. The events of the last few hours were enough to unnerve the most hardened witness. Tirel plucked the omnibus from the book pile, leafing through the yellowed pages.

"Captain Alvara, have you heard the story of our first Eminence?"

"I've heard the legend, yes." The captain swallowed.

"The first Eminence of our people wasn't an inherited title from the motherland. In fact, he was elected—can you believe that? He was elected from a small number of priests of the old faith. The faithful cast their votes to select the most wise, most pious, most high. And do you remember who they chose, Tomás?"

The captain nodded. "I do, Colonel."

Tirel flipped the pages until he reached a cluster of coloured photographs at the center of the book's binding. The first was a faded, yet still vibrant still shot of a foppish older gentleman in long red robes. A white robe encircled his waist, and a long pendant on a silver chain dangled from his neck down to his abdomen. Tirel held the book up for the captain to see.

"Eminence Santiago. The first to carry the name. He was an inspiration, Tomás. You see, they had elected him when they were at their lowest. They were exiled from the diseased southern lands, roaming the wilderness from swamps to deserts, hills to plains. Poisoned wells and burnt crops. Children were starving to death and the old were left behind. But Santiago—he knew what to do."

Tirel flipped a few more pages. "He noticed something the others did not. Instead of looking to the ground, he looked skyward—and there he saw it. *La Golondriña.*"

The photo of a swallow in flight, soaring in a pale blue sky occupied half the two-page spread. The other contained an early photograph of the early symbol of the bird, wings spread and tail forked downward, its head looking to its right. Around the office, De Léon had adorned the space with paintings, carvings, and even taxidermised specimens, some perched, others in flight. Tirel never cared for the tacky decor. He'd be more than happy to burn the lot of it.

"Perhaps the Reapers know, but in our records, Santiago's full name is lost to time. It doesn't matter. We know that Santiago was a good man, a hard-working man. He tilled the earth, planted seeds, harvested crops. But when everyone was busy looking down, he looked up—and in the sky he found the key to our survival. You see, swallows are a constant throughout the land. They travel to where the land is green and the water is clean. So, Santiago followed *La Golondriña*. And the people followed Santiago."

The eldest of the two cleaning women scurrying about the room appeared to be in her fifties, deep lines on her face accented by tufts of long, grey hair. Mariana had cleaned more than her share over the course of her adult life. She may have even cleaned up after an incident like this. Tonia, who couldn't have been more than twenty, shadowed her like an intern. Tirel admired Mariana's earthy beauty. She would have been around Karina's age. She motioned to her young helper to change the mop water frequently, so the blood wouldn't streak the varnished hardwood floors. When they had arrived, Tonia couldn't contain the horror on her cherubic face, so she had covered it with a cleaning mask worn for working with strong chemicals. But Mariana, she was unfazed. She must have been accustomed to the chemical solution.

"Santiago led us for years until we reached this place, this land we call *Motherland*. For, you see, legend has it, he christened our new home *The Colony of the Mother Land*. But soon, it was decreed that we were no longer a colony from our old home, because we no longer had any reason to return. There, the land was ruined and crops were destined to fail. The young would starve before they could walk, and the old would fall one by one until we became extinct. No, Tomás. There was no going back. Here, the new water was clean. The new air was pure. The new forests were teeming. The food at our new table was rich."

Tomás spoke up. "It's our Motherland, and it's worth fighting for."

"Worth dying for, Captain." Tirel smiled at Mariana and she returned the gesture. Karina used to smile that way, and for an instant, a pang swelled in his chest. Behind her mask, Tonia's eyes were narrow, her irises pinpoints as she flexed the wringer of the bucket, reddish-brown water cascading into the frothy soap.

The colonel rose, stretching until he stood his full height, revealing the deep crimson stains that patched his uniform beyond any recognition of its original deep green. Traces of blood smeared on his forearm sleeve as he had wiped it from his cheeks, peppered with days-old scruff. His eyes burned like the crops of the old country in the fall. The smoke swirled in his pupils. Mariana had turned her attention to the spatter radius, wiping droplets off shelves and book spines with a tattered cleaning rag. Tonia over-wrung her mop, sloshing reddish, soapy water on the floor.

"Over the generations, we *fought* for it. We kept the Reapers in the shadows. We fought to keep our city from the threshing machines. And we fought the Federation on the ground and in the air, until Allentown was in ruins and a truce was drawn. At last, we were free! New Inland encased themselves under their superstructure, but we kept the sky as our blanket. But you see, Tomás, the Federation was once and always a cancer on the land. Their soldiers seeped out of their concrete sarcophagus, and their poison leaked into the ground beneath. It was inevitable that the water table was poisoned."

Tirel peered at the river of red washing water that wound its way along the wood grain of the floor boards until it mixed with the congealing blood pool. Tonia hurried to soak up the mess, but she was fighting a losing battle. It was unlikely that the cleaning women would ever be able to remove all traces of Eminence De Léon's lifeblood from the cracks in the floor.

"The Regents," Tomás interjected. "They'll want answers."

"When I tell Magister Solanis what New Inland has concealed underground—the atrocities they've committed—I am confident the Council of Regents will elect me just like the priests of old chose Santiago."

Tirel circled in front of His Eminence's desk, knocking a stack of books to the bloodied floor. He stood over the twisted, broken body of the pathetic monarch, frozen exactly as he landed after he'd thrust the knife over and over into his gut. The hapless old man, dressed as though he were half his age and had a fraction of his charisma, never saw it coming. It was De Léon who had sent Paolo to Allentown. He'd insisted they carry out small-scale attacks on the New Inland city most known for tourism and finance. This man who had had the audacity to call himself *Santiago* never appreciated the scope of Tirel Desantos's ambition. Even the Regents were growing tired of De Léon's whimsical ideas.

Andreas was right. He had to go.

"Captain, it has been brought to my attention that Reekan has been hiding the witnesses to Paolo and Grant's planning. My source tells me that they will move their assets out of Capston to their facility in the southern mountains. Ap-Oz, they call it. Send your sleeper in DefCorps, have him compromise the tandem-rotor crafts they use to fly." *If Reekan wants to migrate, he'll learn soon enough it's the wrong time of year to head south.*

"Your source, Colonel?"

Tirel smiled. He selected a stuffed swallow from its perch on the nearest bookshelf. He stroked a puff of dust from its long feather. "Let's just say a little birdie told me."

Crossing the Line

Friday, 22 June AC 0245
North of the Magna-Rail Line
Ian Null

Factoring in the average temperatures in early summer, the lay of the land, density of the forest, and his own stamina, Null expected to cover forty kilometers before nightfall forced him to rest. There were obstacles, of course. The foothills were gradually leveling into less-cumbersome slopes, but the brush was denser than he was accustomed. Motherland was situated near sickly and dying woodlands, where the ground was drier and trees had to work that much harder to grow. This far south, the flora was far richer. That meant for slow moving, since Null chose to travel off the roads and trails. He wasn't sure how far away from either Motherland or New Inland he would have to go before he was safely anonymous.

By his calculations, Null could live off the field rations for at least a week, especially if he supplemented his food with the bounty of the land. He imagined the elite from New Inland, if dropped into the wilderness, staring in horror at their surroundings, eventually starving to death for fear of eating anything poisonous. His own men were trained in basic survival, but even they wouldn't likely notice the culinary possibilities in the bush. Wild berries were only starting to emerge, but there was so much more. As he passed around a swamp late in the morning, he noted watercress and lilies, rich in nutrients if he harvested the roots. Beneath the darker canopy of old-growth forest, shielded from the midday sun, he spotted a dozen edible mushroom varieties. And if he were really desperate, he could forage for grubs beneath the moss-draped deadfall. With a quick glance at his key, the area was uncontaminated, so there would be plenty of wildlife to boost his protein intake. Bigger game was pointless—he would have to clean and preserve it for travel without any means of refrigeration, and he didn't have any curing salts. Rabbits were easy to snare, but the meat tended to make him lethargic. As he emerged in the early evening into thinner brush, the likelihood of finding wild turkey increased.

As the sun widened into a broad, deeper orange colour in the western sky, Null thumbed open the app on his key that could source nearby water. He wouldn't stop moving for the night until he was satisfied he could fill his canteen. The last rays of light were still visible when the app blinked a logically blue cursor. An artesian well, and clean, from the looks of it. He would be camping here for the night.

The same process repeated for the next three days. Null came across evidence of other nomads—a hastily covered fire pit here, remains of slaughtered game there. Anytime he came across traces of other people, it was a signal for Null to go in the other direction. He wasn't afraid of what they could do to him. He was afraid of what he could do to *them*. No matter how he tried, Ian Null couldn't be sure that Paolo Desantos was truly extinguished. Every time he woke to a snapped twig or an owl's mournful call, his eyes flared and his hand gripped the knife hilt by his side. *Paolo's* instincts could determine in half a second if there were an imminent threat. In a way, *Paolo's* lingering presence in Null's memories kept him alive. And it would have to keep doing so until the open expanse of the Pacific greeted him and the sand sifted between his toes. His former self would have to stay rent-free in his mind until then.

As the earliest streaks of light emerged in the east on the fourth day, Null breakfasted on the remains of a roasted wild grouse and a handful of golden-gilled chanterelle mushrooms, rich in nutrients for a long day ahead. The first true obstacle of his journey lay before him, by his calculations, around 1000 hours. Null slapped a horsefly and spread open the paper maps he'd salvaged from the Junquer shop. It still smelled of sickness and decay. Once he'd passed the next hurdle, they wouldn't be needed, and he could use the stained paper to start a campfire.

Within the next few kilometers, he would reach the wide-open corridor of the magna-rail trains. Null was confident that Paolo could have made it through just about anything, but the heavily monitored and electrified rails were too much even for the legendary Motherland Lieutenant-Colonel. The only magna-rail he would have to cross on his way had only one upside—wildlife couldn't just walk across them either. There would be more opportunity to corral a young doe if he decided it was the right time to take down bigger game. Sure enough, within about half an hour of leaving, he raised his silenced sidearm and shot one between the eyes. The pitiful creature was staring right at him and still didn't recognize her death was imminent. In his life as Paolo, more often than not eyes that met his longer than a half-second understood the danger they were facing. Null wasn't sure if the knot in his stomach was hunger or something else.

In less than an hour, he had carved off the striploin and even kept the flank cuts for drying out. Null wished he had some spices to make proper venison, but the dried strips of deer meat would be tasty enough. The key told him that the entrance to the mineshaft was within a few kilometers, and once below ground, there was no guarantee any wildlife would be available. Since there would likely be other travelers passing through the maze of tunnels beneath the magna-rail lines, starting a campfire wasn't smart. He'd have to break his own rule of avoiding travel routes until he came out on the other side. Following his electronic green-lined map on the key screen, Null stepped out of the bushy greenery into a flattened, well-traveled path that led directly into a square-shaped opening in a layer of sandstone. He had set the key to recharge as soon as the sun was fully above the skyline, and the battery read full charge. The light of his handheld would have to be enough to get him through, by his estimation a full day's traveling under the murky earth. Null paused, listening for footfall from inside or outside the tunnel, framed by greyed, splintered timber beams. Once upon a time, the supports were strong and immovable. He doubted that they were as immovable today.

Navigating his way through the tunnels was much easier than he expected. The key picked up movement well before anyone moving in his direction would notice him, allowing Null to hide and extinguish the light. He couldn't see what the passers by were wearing. The swoosh of a long cape or robe indicated that Reapers used the route as much as other outsiders. Through twisting, descending and rising corridors, marred with fallen debris, leftover animal remains and discarded belongings, Null wound his way slowly but steadily until the corridors began to ascend. He was too far below ground for his key to pick up the magna-rail signal. At least he was far enough underground that surface-penetrating heat registers wouldn't pick him up.

No one is looking for you, fool. Paolo's essence scolded him from deep in his gut. Eight and a half hours, and none of the dozen or so travelers he saw from the shadows had to die today.

Emerging from the tunnel on the southern side of the magna-rail, Null strained his eyes in the late-evening waning sun. The egress was a higher elevation than the timber-framed sandstone entrance to the north. He inhaled deeply, almost forgetting to take a radiation reading. He couldn't afford to make that kind of mistake in the southern land. So far, his prescription for Radiogardasse was untouched in his rucksack pocket. Inevitably, he'd have to cross some swaths of radioactive land, and the medicine would offer him an insurance policy when navigating his way through pockets of old-world radiation that still possessed the land like the malevolent ghosts of folktales.

Null stepped onto a ridge overlooking the wilderness to the east, just like he did the day he burned the last bits of Paolo's disguises while the smoke plume of the Allentown bank explosion curled into the air. They would have found the remains of Mott Wrengel by now. If Slava Allen had done his job, whoever had identified the remains would come to the conclusion that Paolo Desantos had burned to death, not some low-ranking orphan nobody would miss.

Keep telling yourself that, "Ian".

Null squinted and gazed over the eastern horizon. Below the plateau, he noticed a fine line between the heavier old forest and the shorter, thinner woodland that stretched beyond his sight to the faint, half-spherical outline of New Inland, nestled into the foothills of the old Appalachian range. The demarcation between old and new growth indicated that he was just over a hundred kilometers from the superstructure. Paolo's essence smirked. The New Inland ancestors were so paranoid about their security, they built machines large enough to mow entire forests to act as a buffer zone. Anyone making a move against the new blight on the land would be spotted long before they could inflict any harm. Besides, the old-world rich held most of the weapons. They still kept a perimeter of about ten kilometers thin, especially when the magna-rails connected them to other like-minded monstrosities across the continent. Null imagined how naked it would feel to walk in such an exposed, denuded land. His training as Paolo had made him nervous of open, vulnerable expanses.

He was about to turn away when a glint of light caught his eye from further down the bluff. The trees were full and lush, but something from beneath the canopy was reaching out for someone to notice. Null narrowed his brow and looked deeper. Something was there that nature didn't approve. A quick scan with his key confirmed that no human-shaped heat signatures were hiding.

Maybe there's something you can use, "Ian".

Null tightened his rucksack straps and wound his way down the drop, gripping branches and trunks, feeling the sting of thin whips across the stubble on his cheek. He'd made good time crossing the magna-rail line. A few minutes scouting for useful materials wouldn't kill him.

It was about fifty meters below his vantage point when the shape of the old-world thresher came into view. Null hugged the wide trunk of a gnarled tree and gazed upon the relic, long-dormant on the outer reaches of its old cutting zone. At first glance, it looked like one of the ruined buildings of Allentown, if they had been built of steel rather than concrete. Square-framed and stained, the open cavities of long-blown out windows stared back like hollow eye sockets. Moss, underbrush, and animal droppings laced across the roof of the thresher's living quarters like an antique quilt. Layered beneath the upper-most story, a wider level perched above track wheels that would dwarf any functioning construction vehicle today. The glint of light was likely sourced from broken mirrors that came to rest facing upward as though they were eternally calling for help. Such an enormous hulk of old-world engineering, rotting in the under-canopy of the same forest it was designed to kill.

A Silent Killer

Saturday, 23 June AC 0245
South of the Magna-Rail Line
Ian Null

Null had once come across a Reclamation-era machine on one of his excursions into the sub-Lake Region, months before the Yael incident. The area had been known to be the site of an urban sprawl, only a short hike from the Great Falls. It made sense that machines would have been there. But his father had told him as a boy that the great city-eaters were long gone—rendered in the smelters, deep in the bowels of New Inland and Hyacynthe. Too many precious metals in the electronic systems to leave in the wild for brigands to steal and trade. Early-generation nuclear cell-generators that, left under the elements, would breach and wreak absolute havoc over untold hectares. Maybe the greatest fear was that someone on the outside would replicate the city eaters—maybe even improve on their designs. Many a New Inlander must have shaken under their covers at the thought of an army of city-eating behemoths bearing down on their sanctuary under the dome.

Null lowered himself through the tangled brush until his boot touched the soiled roof of the thresher. *Hundreds of machines still wouldn't breach the shell of New Inland.*

To do that required stealth, the likes they had never known.

He shifted his weight from foot to foot and determined that the roof wasn't going to cave. Remarkable, he thought to himself. The thresher had to be well over a century old. The best machines Motherland could produce might last a decade—maybe two if they were well-maintained.

Looking up, Null couldn't see the plateau where he'd spotted the glint of light. He analysed the roof and spotted a thin ladder hooked to the roof, disappearing over the edge to the main level. Leaning over the edge, he saw that halfway down, the rungs had collapsed, causing an uncomfortable fall to the climber.

And by the looks of the disturbed vegetation, that was recently. *As recently as this morning.*

Null cursed under his breath. People had been here, and were likely not far. It occurred to him that someone could still be inside the machine. His father once told him that the biggest of the giant threshers contained entire barracks. A squad of twenty could live comfortably on the backs of the metal monsters, enjoying cold drinks while entire villages were shredded by those spinning blades beneath their bellies. The death toll this thresher must have incurred in its prime was enough to make Null's head swim.

Rather than take his chances on the broken ladder or scaling the walls, Null shimmied along an overhanging tree branch, until he came to rest on the wider deck. From there, he couldn't hear any movement, but drew his sidearm just to be safe. The silencing muzzle was still secured from his hunting excursion yesterday.

I have no quarrel with anyone who might still be here. He couldn't tell if that was Ian Null convincing himself, or Paolo Desantos mocking his mercy.

At the bow of the machine, Null spotted the control cab. All windows were long gone, not even a shard of broken glass beneath his soft steps. The machine beneath the deck would have had several dual-sided blades the length of banquet halls, layered so they would oscillate at different heights. If one blade missed a grove of trees or the peak of a wooden-gabled home, the second would not. They most likely were mounted on springs the height of the great falls, to rise and fall according to the terrain or the quarry of the culling. His father told him that the blades could cut as close as two meters to the soil. Close enough for the burning of the chaff that remained. But that would require another kind of machine.

One machine to do the cutting, the other to do the cleansing. Were there

Reapers in those days? Were they slaughtered beneath the spinning blades, or did they scurry away like the vermin they are?

Clearly, three distinct sets of footprints had caused the mossy growth to slide and smear along the walkways, in and out of the main cabin door that hung lifeless on its bottom hinge. Null set his rucksack on the floor and moved on the balls of his toes, soundless apart from the rustling of the breeze in the canopy above. He gripped the key in his left hand, lightly fingering the trigger with his left index. If necessary, he could manipulate the handheld with his left thumb, but he admitted to himself he needed more practice. The Junquer might have obliged him, if he'd had enough time, of course.

If he'd had enough time, he would have been impressed at the speed his attacker came at him from his right blind spot. Instead, a flash of light from behind his right eye and the sensation of a wooden club cracking against his skull blacked him out. He wasn't conscious to feel himself hit the deck.

"Don't play with that, Jamiss. Your fool ass'll make it self-destruct!"

"Fuck you, Berg. Elms, tell Berg to fuck himself."

"Berg, fuck yourself, and get up front. We're passing through the trader lands, I need another set of eyes..."

At first, Null could only see deep grey splotches with his eyes wide open. His head was still vibrating. He'd been concussed before—he only hoped that the symptoms would subside quickly this time.

His chin rested against the sternum in his chest. Lifting it made his head bob like it was full of helium. The deep grey lightened, and the outline of a man roughly his own size came into shape, leaning against an adjacent wall. As his senses caught up to him, Null felt the vibration of the moving vehicle beneath his bare feet. His captors must have worried about the steel toes in his boots. It was then Null realized that his hands were clasped together between his back and a warm, metal machine of some sort. The smell of petrol told him the brigands were riding in a common model cargo vehicle, likely an off-roader with reinforced rubber and chain-gripped tires. It ran remarkably quiet, but the swiping of branches snapped and dragged against the outer shell, likely not much more than aluminum for a covering. Blinking a few times, the grainy blur sharpened into focus. Breathing deeply, he rested his thoughts and his head settled until he could no longer count the pulse in his forehead.

The man guarding him had to be Jamiss. He held Null's handheld key in his right palm, tinkering with the switches inside its exposed innards. Whoever Berg was, he was right. This idiot had no idea what he was holding, and what it was capable of. Null almost wished that he'd just toggle the wrong app and set off a small explosion, killing them all.

No you don't. You know you'd rather take care of him yourself.

Null grimaced. Paolo was right.

"Well, well. Had a good nap, did you?" The guard couldn't have been older than twenty, if Null was being generous in his assessment. Jamiss spoke with a soft crackle behind his voice, as though puberty had arrived years too late. "You're just in time. Tell me how to make this rig work."

Null didn't answer. Straightening his posture, he nudged his shoulder blades against whatever he was chained to by the waist and ankles. Pipes jutted, one the shape of a valve or a handle, pressing against his lower back. The cargo transport rumbled along, and the machine was getting warmer. Null's mind raced. The brigands had found something worth their time, and secure enough that they could fasten their prisoner to it. And it was clearly heating up.

Come on, "Ian". What else could they have found in the thresher?

Null gulped. "Show me the screen."

Jamiss laughed. "Now you want to talk? Fine, see for yourself." He aimed the screen at him, and the main menu tabs were visible, flickering from a likely loose connection. Jamiss tampered with the insides, but luckily he hadn't ruined anything yet.

"Press the second tab from the bottom right. Then click 'yes' three times." After the third click, his fears would either be confirmed or denied.

Jamiss fumbled, clearly missing the steps and having to start at the home menu again. "Fuckssakes," he grumbled. The guard held the screen closer as though he had lost focus. He was going to lose a lot more than that if the key told him what he suspected. Sure enough, a distinct beeping sound emitted in rapid bursts of three. Null's mouth went dry.

"Jamiss, is it? You need to listen. What do you have in this cargo hold?"

"Pfft, like I'd tell *you* anything!"

"Fine. At least tell me what you see on the screen."

"Um, okay. It says 25… *rem*? No wait, 27. 28. It keeps changing! Is this thing broken, or…"

Null barked. "It is *not* broken, fool. You are reading radiation levels in this cargo hold. And they are rising, quickly."

"Well, I don't feel anything."

"Not now, you don't. But in a couple hours, you will be vomiting blood."

Jamiss's eyes widened. "You're shitting me! I oughta throw you off the back!"

"Suits me fine. I'll be away from the nuclear cell you and your friends harvested from the thresher. You will die." Null panned around the dimly lit cargo hold. His rucksack was leaned against the front right corner. Once free from his bonds, he could have it in less than two strides. He would have to take his first doses sooner than he had expected.

First, he had to convince the kid to free him. And he had to do it quietly. Berg and Elms in the cab didn't sound as simple.

Dull Blades

Saturday, 23 June AC 0245
South of the Magna-Rail Line
Ian Null

Listen to me. The key—*handheld* needs my fingerprint and code to shut off the reaction." It was more complicated than that, but Null tried to explain the situation in simple words that even a simpleton like Jamiss could understand. The youthful brigand shook, nearly dropping the device several times as he frantically tapped and swiped the screen with his greasy fingertips. Null's heart rate was climbing. It was hard to remain calm when the radiation leak was like a runaway train. If he didn't find a way to contain it, everyone within several kilometers would die. Some sooner, most later, and very gradually.

Come on, "Ian", you didn't sacrifice everything to die this way.

Null closed his eyes and inhaled through his nostrils. The breathing technique always calmed him, seemingly freezing time for a half-second. It was all the time he needed. He exhaled through narrow lips, his trepidation evaporating along with the spent oxygen.

"Free me, and I will spare you your life. Otherwise, you die."

Null's glare pierced Jamiss's wide, bloodshot eyes. Whenever Paolo stared into someone's eyes like this, he tethered himself to the recipient's soul. Ian Null prayed the effect was still there, even from his current position of weakness.

Jamiss didn't barter for the lives of Berg and Elms. Typical of a brigand. Always looking out for himself. Null couldn't blame him. The kid nodded, drew a short, dull pocket blade and dug it between Null's wrists and the tight bonds. If the kid had shown any care for his blade, they could both be free instead of waiting for him to seesaw the knife over and over. A real knife would have been able to slice the knot like butter. If Jamiss had have been raised as a ward…

"There," Jamiss knelt and hacked the binds around Null's ankles. "Now what?"

"Give me the handheld." One brisk kick sent the frayed cords flying. His wrists itched from rope burn, but there was no time for that. "Now."

The cargo transport jostled, almost causing the kid to drop the key. Null snatched it and moved to the front of the hold. It was instinct to get as far away from the massive nuclear cell as possible, but he knew it made no difference. The kid had swiped so many tabs, he had to reboot the device and start from scratch. Ordinarily, the minute or so it took wouldn't be a problem. A minute *now* was a difference of about 10 rems, and that was a huge problem. Null eyed the rucksack a stride away from him in the corner. If everything went wrong, he needed a plan to grab and go.

The key dinged and the screen flashed the main menu. A quick tap of his left index finger and a six-digit code later, he was flying through menus and tabs. Jamiss babbled incoherently in the background, and Berg and Elms up front were arguing about something. As long as they stayed in the cab, Null could lock onto the nuclear cell. The noise was almost too much.

Push it all away. Focus.

Paolo's training slowed the moment enough for Null to fix on the mass of metal and concrete. The fool had managed to lock onto it, unknowingly accessing the electronic system that controlled the cooling chamber. Today's nuclear cells were much smaller and safer. These old ones used to be big enough to fill a living room, and were half as efficient. The reactor required an adjacent but separate cooling chamber that served as a failsafe for the radioactive elements. They were contained inside lead-infused coverings back in those days. Null wasn't surprised that they'd corroded over time, accounting for the leak. But, if the failsafe was still intact, they might have a chance.

Locked into the control system, Null pressed the screen. It was slick with Jamiss's filth. There was no way of telling if the interior works of the cell were shifting. The only way he would know is if the Geiger readings stabilized. That might take more time than either of them could afford. Null initiated his escape plan.

"What the *fuck*, Jamiss?" The voice of Elms roared from the cab as the older brigand's head popped through the opening. "Y'only had one job!"

Null reached for his rucksack, and to his surprise, Jamiss drew his unsharpened knife and lunged at the leader, too stunned to react. The kid hacked with uncoordinated thrusts and swipes, carving Elms as though he were flailing in the dark. Paolo would have made the first stroke deadly. Jamiss was inflicting torture through his seething assault. In his training, Null had been taught that a dull blade was far more dangerous than a sharpened one. He doubted his teachers had imagined what he was watching. Between the kid's primal screaming and the howl and gurgle of Elms, the cargo transport's brakes squealed as the driver—presumably Berg—ground to a jerked halt.

"Elms? What's going on back there?" The biggest of the three brigands called from the driver's seat. Jamiss was flailing his knife at the fell corpse of Elms, as though he'd just cut down a tree of the same size. Null swiped the tabs back to the main menu and keyed open the Geiger reader. 30… 31…

It's jammed on the inside. Go, now.

"The only way out is through the cab," Jamiss stuttered, blood spattered on his shocked, pale face. "Berglund is too big. I can't take him."

Null pocketed the key and slung the rucksack over his shoulder. His glare told Jamiss to move, and the kid understood instantly.

No weapon in his hands. No room. No visual of his quarry.

No matter.

He rushed through the opening. The big man named Berglund was already on his feet and facing him. What the brigand didn't know was how quick Paolo Desantos could neutralize a foe. It was probably for the best.

Berg had almost twenty kilos on him. Size didn't matter. It didn't matter with Yael. It didn't matter with Grant. It wasn't going to matter with Berglund. Null charged the big man in less than two steps, wrapping his arms around his left arm and neck before dashing his skull against the dash.

"Hurry, if you want to live." Null shouted to Jamiss behind him, and the kid emerged into the cab, still stuttering from the shock of his own savage kill.

The cargo transport had come to a halt on an uneven, tree root-gnarled road. The sun was nearly set. These "trader lands" would likely be crawling with nomads, traders, and brigands by twilight. Null's feet landed on the compacted dirt and he darted off the side of the trail under cover of the brush that was still uncontaminated. Jamiss stumbled after him.

"Is it gonna blow?" Jamiss was young, but his question sounded like something a frightened little boy would ask his mommy.

"I don't know." It was all he could say. Null retrieved the key and tapped the screen. The Geiger app was still open. 30… 30… 29… The mechanism must have loosened, because by now, the rem reading should have been well over 40. But that was no guarantee the reactor would shut down completely. Or that the containment chamber would fully shut.

"What do we do now?"

"That depends." Null dropped the rucksack and opened the outer pouch, pulling out the bottle of medicine he'd purchased from Lacraie all those weeks ago. Three pills would have been a standard daily dose when passing through the seams. Null swallowed six.

"Depends on *what*? And what is *that*?" Jamiss's eyes darted from side to side as though he were suffering withdrawal from an illicit drug.

"It depends on how well you know the traders," Null answered, pocketing the pill bottle in his rucksack and slinging it back over his shoulder. "You will need their help."

Jamiss protested. "But… I freed you… You're still going to help me… Right?"

Null turned away. He couldn't look the kid in the eyes. Jamiss was better off without the abusive company of Elms and Berglund. Distancing himself from the nuclear cell gave him a chance, however slim. The traders might even pity him and offer him new clothes, a shower to wash the surface radiation from his dirty skin, maybe even a full canteen and a buggy to get farther away. Start a new life. Both Null and Paolo understood all of that.

If you didn't have that Junquer key, none of this happens. Those three boneheads bring their cell to market, they sell it, they go on their way.

Except, they found you—not a lion, but a highwayman, an assassin.

And you've killed them.

The kid still had a chance. Null paused and thought about the bottle of Radiogardasse. A strong dose right now might buy him time.

"What are those pills?" The kid's voice was breaking, but a sliver of hope rang in his question. Null turned and looked him in the eye.

If you're going to sentence him to death, you owe him that.

"Pain medication," Null lied. "Nothing more."

Jamiss glared back. The kid knew he was lying. Null's stomach knotted.

The kid nodded, then turned for the brush and darted into the deepening twilight shadows. He was no longer Null's problem. Except Paolo would remind him when he closed his eyes, whether to sleep or to die.

Heartbeat

Saturday, 23 June AC 0245
East of Farbend Trading Post
Ian Null

Null couldn't afford to waste time. The further he traveled from the transport and its toxic payload, the lower the Geiger readings, but to pause and take a reading delayed escape and hastened exposure. Ideally, he would strip and discard his clothing, and wash himself more diligently than a young mother washing her infant. A second set of clothing was still packed tightly in his rucksack—but that would have to go as well. Radiation was a bad house guest. It arrived, settled in place, and refused to leave. The best Null could do was accept defeat, leave, and get as far away as possible.

Null wanted nothing more than to curl up under a tree and sleep, if only for an hour or two. It might have been the poison, but more likely fatigue from the lingering concussion vibrations. Whether it was muscle memory or the will to survive, he continued walking briskly along the road Jamiss and his partners were traveling. As the sky darkened, the width of the road narrowed. Gnats harangued him, but he didn't waste time opening his pack and applying the bug-repellent ointment.

Mind over matter. One step after the next. Minute after minute.

"To what?" Null barked at the voice of Paolo in his mind. "Clean water?"

If you're thirsty.

Null closed his eyes. The gnats became brigand drones, only this time there was no one there to shoot them out of the sky. Instead of leading a legion in search of Yael, he marched alone. The earth was brown and diseased.

"I am not thirsty." Null's answer was an act of defiance.

Maybe you should be…

The buzzing flooded his brain, disorienting him enough to cross his heavy boots. Stumbling, Null struck the compacted mud of the road face first, shifting the cartilage of his nose. He lay flat, draped over the protruding root that had tripped him. Fitting, he observed. If he couldn't stop this death march himself, the land would have to do it for him.

Null sat up, every vertebra in his spinal column crackling back into posture, and retrieved the key from his rucksack. He could have stood up and pressed on, but eventually, he would fall again, this time for good. The whole point of moving on was to survive. Then again, why keep moving if it was only to the grave?

"If I'm going to die, a few minutes will make no difference." Null spoke the words as he fumbled with trembling fingers to open the Geiger tab. This time, the voice of Paolo didn't answer.

The reading was well below 2 rems, reading into the thousandths. Null sighed. The medicine he'd taken immediately after leaping from the transport should offer enough protection for the night. It was too early to take more—he'd already doubled the recommended dose. Even at a slower rate of movement, Null was in a far better position than the kid Jamiss, still out there in the thickness of the forest at night, directionless, unmedicated, and doomed.

Allowing himself fifteen minutes for his heart rate to settle, his breath to catch up, and his inner thoughts to quiet, Null resumed his travel. He walked throughout the night, undeterred by the snapping and crackling of branches off the road. Maybe Jamiss was stalking him in the shadows. Null shook his head. That was Paolo whispering to him.

As dawn began to flare to life, he noticed that he had walked straight into a settlement of ramshackle cottages. The shadows along the road receded to reveal scattered junk, tufts of grass and shrubs, broken walkways of black asphalt and cobbled stone. With every step, a light blinked to life in a window. A baby cried for its first feeding of the day. Doors opened, generators hummed, dogs barked. It reminded him of Motherland, when Paolo rose before dawn to complete his first workout. The city came alive in concert, all the sights and sounds greeting the rising sun in one united offering.

Inhabitants crept out their front doors, all of them ignoring the stranger as he continued passing through their settlement. Traffic increased as one by one, more villagers crisscrossed the road, greeting one another, laughing, coughing. Someone was cooking breakfast. A circular saw carved its way through lumber, and a hammer struck an iron spike. The heartbeat of the trader settlement kept in time with his own.

The road led to an intersection wide as a courtyard. At the center, a wide and squat building drew people from all directions. The entire front of the building had only half a wall, topped with a countertop, sheltered by a tattered canopy that was once multi-coloured, now faded sickly and pale. Null didn't know what help he needed, but if anyone had the answer, it would be here.

"Not open for another hour." A woman back-to the counter muttered as she tinkered with some piece of junk among the piles inside her shop. "And before you ask, I'm not buying anything until I hear from Elms. S'posed to have something big."

The woman had no idea.

"He isn't coming."

Null expected the trader to spin around, drop her trinket and curse at him. He did not expect her to keep puttering and laugh.

"Just like the bastard to take his loot to the Carroway camp." The woman's hair hung well past her shoulders in hanks of blond and grey. "Sounded too good to be true, anyway."

She turned to him and set a twisted iron chunk upon the counter top, shedding flakes of rust. "Aynslie. And you are?"

The question was simple, but he wasn't sure how to answer. He was surprised with what he finally decided.

"Ian."

"What brings you to Farbend, *Ian*?" She stressed his name as though she wasn't buying it.

"Elms and his company did not go to Carroway." Null didn't know where that was. "They have had a terrible accident."

That's one way to put it.

Aynslie smirked, wrinkling her face like a peach pit. Null looked closer. He couldn't guess how old she was, but her eyes were deep and blue. How would she have looked five, ten, twenty years ago? Was she aging from time, or from the elements? Motherland women appeared wise in their aging. Aynslie could be dying for all he knew.

Would Crystal Sheppard have aged this way, if she lived on the outside? Something in Aynslie's appearance reminded him of the intern from Lacraie. He wasn't sure why.

"I'm guessing they were robbed, or the damn thing blew up."

"You could say both." He wasn't lying.

Aynslie picked up the chunk of metal, rust staining her cracked, veined hands. "Do you know what this piece of junk is? Proof, they said. Found a thresher, down over the plateau, they said. I told Elms that if they harvested a cell from it, it had better be cleaner than this."

"The youth ignited it." Technically, that *was* an accident. "I was able to stabilize the cooling backup, but it will not hold. Your village is not far enough away, if…"

He couldn't bring himself to say the words. Aynslie said them instead.

"If it melts down." The old woman stared into his eyes. "You aren't lying."

Null retrieved his key. Aynslie gazed at the apparatus. He opened the Geiger tab, and the rem count had remained around 2. At this distance, it should have been out of range for an accurate reading. The leak was worsening again.

"If the level reaches 5 rem, anyone exposed can expect to be sick from radiation. Unless you are able to contain it, your best bet is to flee. South and west—the drift will be north and east."

Aynslie nodded her head, either confirming that the traders had no means of containing the radiation, or that they should indeed flee immediately. "Your device. How far is its range?"

"Fifty kilometers by radio wave. Geiger range is half that."

The shopkeeper turned and reached for a small control box that dangled from a twist of black cords. One press of a button, and a howling siren wailed, echoing through the streets and cottages of the settlement. Dogs roared, children shrieked, and the peaceful bustle of the morning descended into a panicked urgency.

"We've had to move before. And we will again, *Ian*. Take whatever you need from the shop, but do us one favour?"

Panning through the open space behind Aynslie, Null spotted a rucksack hanging from a rusty hook that would be a good replacement for his contaminated one. There were clothes of various sizes, shoes, belts, tools—with a little digging, he could find anything he needed for the next leg of his journey. All he needed to bring was the medicine and the key.

"Of course."

"We're expecting a transport from the badlands today. It's not too late to warn them."

It was too late for Jamiss. Null suspected the youth lay under the forest canopy, hiding under a rotted log, or in the hollow of a stump, shivering from the cold and the sickness. It hadn't been so difficult to ease the Junquer's pain—he was old, riddled with the disease, and begging for it. Jamiss, he was only a child. He *could* make it.

Only if you'd helped him. And you didn't. But there was time to help others.

Null opened the radio tab. In the chaos of the evacuation, his heart beat to the rhythm of Farbend's determination to survive. "What is your message?"

Lepers

Sunday, 24 June AC 0245
Hyacynthe/Ozarck Magna-Rail
Crystal Sheppard

Crystal Sheppard had two changes of clothes in her travel pack, but she didn't have enough time to change out of her button-down, white-collared intern shirt and grey, straight-legged cotton work pants. She tucked the long, white lab coat under her arm as inconspicuously as she could. At least she remembered to unclip and pocket her name tag. If anyone called her by her name, she knew they were after her.

"Crystal, is it? Crystal Sheppard, I presume?"

At the time, as a fresh-faced new intern, safely behind plexiglass, she had been nervous when the outsider Ian Null called her by her name, only to point out that he was reading it off her name tag. It was when he'd called her by her family name, with his awkward, half-built handheld that caught her off guard. Still, the stranger showed her kindness and more, transferring an exorbitant sum of money to compensate for making her miss her ride home. How could an outsider have so much money that he could give *that* much away?

Between his swashbuckler looks and mysterious motives, Crystal couldn't stop thinking about him. Mireil and Druna teased her mercilessly about the "one that got away". The notion was ridiculous. She never had him in the first place. Ian Null was as anonymous as Dr. Jonathan Doherty, the fictitious doctor who had "signed off" on his purchase. This was the work of an outsider with dangerous plans. It was just as well she never see him again.

The purchase of the travel pass went without hindrance, which meant Laurent wasn't trying to find her. Yet. If the magna-rail train departing Hyacynthe Station could reach the Badlands Crossing without incident, she would be out of range from any Hyacynthien tracking towers. She'd have to move enough money out of her own account during the layover, and quietly. Once Laurent realized that she was skipping town, he had the ability to freeze her account. Without money, she wouldn't last a day in the outside world. At least that's what Druna would have said.

The usher allowed her to bring her travel pack into the coach, where she stowed it in the overhead compartment. The train was about to pull out of the terminal when a late-coming passenger, dressed head to toe in a clean-cut formal suit and with close cropped, styled hair occupied the seat next to her along the aisle. As a teen, Crystal had been in awe of the spacious and plush seats on the magna-rail train from New Inland to Hyacynthe, four years ago, before the embargo came into effect. She had gazed out the window at her three brothers, waving as the coach slid silently above its magnetic conduit line. Robbie had raised one hand while Cadlen waved his with gusto. Lorrie just stood there. Before the train accelerated, Crystal saw him turn away.

As the train lilted out of the terminal, no one was there to wave to her. And for that she was relieved.

"Oops, sorry." The gentleman nudged her in the arm as he struggled to fit his pack below the seat. His sport coat bunched and twisted, tangling him up in himself as sweat beaded on his forehead. "It never fits, but I'll be darned if I'm paying the extra stowing fee."

Crystal forced a smile and turned to the window while the traveler sorted out his space limit problem. She couldn't feel the motion of the train as it picked up speed, but the whirling of the terminal and its descent into the tunnel below the security perimeter was enough to compensate for the feeling. The window tint deepened until it was opaque black. She had no idea if the tunnels were lit or dark, and she didn't care to find out. Four hours before they pass through the old sprawls, across the great lakes and into the badlands. If the guy sharing her row could settle, she might get a few hours of sleep.

She didn't share the row for long.

"Pardon the interruption, we need to do a scan." Crystal snapped to attention as the usher in his neat, snug vest held out his datapad—wider and flatter than a standard handheld, used usually for more complex business transaction stuff. She didn't have time to ask what the scan was for.

"I spoke with my doctor. There was nothing in her scan." The traveler stuttered and his face flushed. "And the coach is so darned hot—do you folks even have climate controls?"

The usher scowled as the datapad beeped. He shook his head slightly. "Sorry, sir. The readings are high, and we can't let you ride in the front coach with so high a temperature. It's red tide season down south."

Red tide. The utterance of the malady pierced Crystal's heart. Both Julia and Robert Sheppard had died due to complications of what was determined to be red tide. The doctors had reasoned that both her mother and father contracted it years earlier, and that the silent killer laid in wait, in the sub-atomic spaces of their cells, until the time was right to strike. They'd barely had enough time to mourn her mom when her dad showed the symptoms. There was no inoculation against red tide, she knew. But there were cocktails of vaccines, developed at Lacraie, no less, that offered as best protection as one could get. Red tide was a stow-away disease, hiding alongside other more known viruses. It had free reign over the immune system until it was spotted. But at that point, all a physician could hope to do was drive it back into remission.

"You are *not* suggesting I have to ride back there with the lepers, are you?" The traveler barked at the usher, digging in to remain in the comfy seats. Crystal didn't know what the accommodations looked like for the "lepers". She didn't even know what a "leper" was, but by the way the traveler spit it through his clenched teeth, it sounded less desirable than a Reaper.

The usher didn't break a sweat. "As per the fine print at the point of purchase, Hyacynthe reserves the right to freeze all accounts of uncooperative passengers."

The irate traveler continued to protest. The usher pressed an open tab on his datapad, and two enormous bouncers emerged from behind them. Their dark sunglasses were as black as the tinted windows. Not a word was said. The men hoisted the traveler from the softness of his seat, and as they hauled him kicking and blubbering down the aisle, the usher retrieved his pack from beneath the seat with less difficulty than the man had faced putting it in.

"Hmm, pack is too large for carry-on. Looks like another surcharge…" The usher muttered as he tapped the datapad screen. "Apologies, miss. Your readings are normal. And for the trouble, I've arranged an entree to be served to you on us."

Crystal wasn't hungry. "Thank you, there's no trouble." She smiled genuinely this time, and the usher nodded before leaving for the "leper" car. With any luck, the rest of the journey would be much less eventful.

She bunched up her lab coat between her head and the darkened window. She didn't know who the traveler was, or what his business could have been in either New Inland or Ozarck. He could have been the biggest asshole this side of the Rockies, but she didn't wish the red tide sickness on him. Crystal knew all too well how that story ended.

Julia Sheppard's Little Girl

For the next five hours, Crystal couldn't shake the thought of the gentleman who was briefly her row mate, before the ushers hauled him to an isolated cabin near the rear of the train. It came as a relief that he was the only one. No more passengers with too-high temperature readings were ushered through her car, unless there was another "leper" car in the front. The thought had never occurred to her before that there would ever be a need for such accommodations. She remembered how both her mother and father were allowed—instructed to quarantine in the Sheppard Family Inn. The Public Health Authority had insisted that first Julia, then Robert remained in one dedicated room. Upstairs was best, a white-coated and goggle-masked doctor recommended, only for Robert to shout back. His wife was not going to be banished to the far corners of the Inn. To live like a ghost in her own home. He had been convincing enough that Public Health had acquiesced, provided a quarantine could be maintained between the business and the living quarters. Willits had become the de facto manager in those months Julia declined, as Robert would not leave her side. Crystal remembered standing next to her big brother Robbie, so stoic and guarded during those terrible weeks and months, looking through the temporary window that had been sawn through the adjoining door. While she was still lucid, Julia could hear when her children spoke through the improvised microphone and speaker system. Crystal remembered beneath the breathing apparatus, through sinking cheeks and deepening lines, Julia Sheppard smiled when it must have been as strenuous as running a marathon.

When it had become her father's turn to face the disease, he wasn't able to do it with the same determination. And as a result, Crystal believed, he died sooner for it.

How many travelers in the quarantined cabin at the rear of the magna-rail reacted the same? Did they put on a brave face for the ushers, or did they allow their true emotions to overtake them? Crystal wasn't sure which was better. Julia had never once admitted she was dying, vowing to stay strong for her husband and her children. Robert, on the other hand, had accepted his fate, choosing to be forthright with his children, spending his last days and weeks teaching her and Robbie everything an adult would need to know to keep going:

This is how you reach Laurent… If the embargo happens like they say it might, he'll know what to do… Robbie, pay attention, the bills come due on the 15th, and you have until the 21st of the month to transfer the funds… Crys, this is the number for the occupational therapist… We have a requisition for Cad, might be some time yet, so keep checking… Be sure you go watch Lorrie ride, it's all he has…

A bell rang and the windows in Crystal's cabin faded from opaque to translucent in a soft wave of black to daylight blue. While she daydreamed, the train had emerged from its lengthy leg of the journey beneath the great lake. She wasn't permitted by the magna-rail to see the ruined urban sprawl that crawled with hostiles. Outside, the train glided through green rushes in an early-evening golden dusk glow. The badlands would swallow the healthy vegetation in due course, and somewhere in the dust bowl of sickly beiges and yellows, the junction waited for incoming rail trains to converge and swap prisoners, exchange cargo, and go on their way to their ultimate destinations. With some exceptions, of course. There would be no legal means for Crystal to board a train for New Inland, not while her electronic identification still indicated her Hyacynthien credentials, anyway.

As the green morphed into yellow outside her window, Crystal realized that she had a real problem on her hands. Those credentials would become a real barrier once they arrived at the junction. By now, Laurent would definitely know that she had not reported to Lacraie as instructed. She had made no attempt to travel illegally, so her identification would have scanned into the system when she purchased her ticket for the Ozarck run. The badlands junction was so far away from Hyacynthe. Still, she knew that officials from her adoptive dome waited there for people just like her to arrive. It wouldn't have surprised her if Laurent himself had somehow arrived ahead of her, to retrieve her on the landing platform with that old-man, shriveled smile that she had come to distrust. How would she greet him? With timid resignation? Or a swift slap to the face, in hopes that she could outrun him and anyone else who would abduct her away from any chance of seeing her brothers again?

And what of her money? More than a hundred-thousand Hyacynthien dollars remained in her account—but likely frozen by now. Even if Laurent didn't find her, even if Hyacynthien officers didn't greet her as soon as she stepped off the train, even if everyone looked away while she walked off into the unknown, she would be penniless. Destitute, in a world where her credentials meant nothing, and likely made her a target for brigands. If she wasn't killed immediately, she'd die of starvation, of thirst, of exposure.

Maybe the leper car was the best option after all. At least she'd receive medical care and nourishment in her final days.

The magna-rail was so smooth, Crystal hadn't realized the train had come to a stop at the frontier town in the wilds of the badlands. Through the fully transparent plexiglass windows, she spied officials from Sascota, Arctica, and to her dismay, Hyacynthe, preparing to inspect documents on handhelds and to search baggage and cargo for contraband.

No sign of Laurent. But they're looking for me. I know…

In a moment of panic, Crystal rose from her seat and aimed for the rear of the train, where they'd dragged away her protesting seat mate. She couldn't do this. She'd flub her words the first time a Hyacynthien officer approached her. She'd spill her guts and melt onto the platform in an undignified mess. As they'd lift her and shackle her wrists, she'd see the New Inland contingent —so close, but a lifetime away as they ignored her pleas and went about their business.

"Miss, you're going the wrong way," said the usher that greeted her at the rear of the cabin. "You don't want to be back there!"

"I—I think I'm feverish," she sputtered, praying that her forehead was warm and clammy. It wasn't.

"Nonsense, your readings are fine! Here, let me help you." The usher smiled and motioned her to turn back toward the front of the train. Hopeless, she resigned and made her way up the aisle. Through a sliding door, into the next cabin, and repeating for several more before disembarkation, Crystal's mind raced through a thousand different outcomes before a stern voice brought her back to reality.

"Credentials, please." He wore a tan and green Sascotan official uniform. Behind him, hundreds of passengers from the magna-rail crisscrossed the platform to and from a cluster of buildings made of wood, staggered in height like uneven cut bangs. Crystal breathed, the chalky air causing her to cough.

"I'm looking for the connection to Ozarck," she squeaked as she offered her handheld to the officer. He squinted through his partially-shaded sunglasses.

"Hmm, looks like Hyacynthe needs you back."

I knew it.

"No, there's a reason I'm traveling. I have a family emergency…" That was the extent of her explanation. She knew it wasn't enough.

"Sorry, I don't know what your story is, but I have to pass you on to the Frenchies. I don't have the authority to—

The guard was interrupted by a sharp pop that split the hazy sky that hung over the Badlands Junction. The throngs of people shrieked and scrambled and the officer drew a sidearm, silver and curved in his grip. "Get down! Brigands!"

Crystal dropped like a ton of bricks to the wooden-slatted platform floor just in time to witness the officer splay his arms as a bullet struck his torso, leaving a ragged exit wound that sprayed speckles of blood onto her hair and face. The gun he hadn't even had a chance to fire clattered onto the floor beside her. Shrieks became wails, and with only instinct as her guide, Crystal tucked her head between her knees and held her hands over her head in the hope that the brigands wouldn't see her. Gunfire erupted from the guards and shouting drowned out the cries as the platform clattered and vibrated beneath her. She had been right. *The leper cabin would have been safer.*

A strong, soiled hand grasped her by the right wrist, yanking her to her feet and to exposure to the carnage that surrounded her. She kept her free hand over her eyes as her captor dragged her stumbling across the deck, slipping and either water, oil, or blood before the platform gave way to solid earth beneath her shaking legs.

"Open your eyes, you dumb bitch! You're gonna get killed!"

Her captor smacked her hand from covering her eyes and the light strained grainy. They had traveled maybe one hundred meters out of the open among the nearest buildings that made up the junction settlement. Wooden doors and window sashes slammed and voices muffled. As her vision cleared, Crystal saw for the first time that her captor wore a cloth wrapping around the dome of his head, tied and dangling down the nape of his neck and shoulders. A muffler concealed the southern half of his face from the nose beneath his neckline. Silver-lensed glasses shielded his eyes.

"Come on, I'm trying to *save* you, here!"

Save me? Something in the way he patronized her gave Crystal that one burst of energy she needed. Violently, she thrust her shoulder blade with enough resistance to break from his grasp. All she could think about was her mother, smiling in the face of death as she defied her fate to the last. Julia Sheppard's little girl did *not* need rescuing. Julia Sheppard's little girl did *not* have to lay down and die, in a quarantine cabin or in the dust of the badlands.

Crystal Sheppard brought her knee into the brigand's gut, doubling him over in a deflated groan. She didn't have time to celebrate her small victory, as two more pairs of hands grabbed her, one by the shoulder and the other beneath her breasts. That was a little too close for comfort. A black fabric hood draped over her face, disorienting her before she could discern anything her new captors were saying.

At least no one had discovered the Sascotan guard's sidearm she'd plucked from the platform and tucked up under the bottom strap of her *brassiere*. She wasn't as full-figured as Druna, or even Mireil. But if the brigands kept their filthy hands away from there, maybe she could figure out how to fire it when the time was right. Julia Sheppard's little girl exhaled.

The Third Man

Sunday, 24 June AC 0245
55 km West of Badlands Junction
Crystal Sheppard

The irony wasn't lost on her. Keeping her blind to her surroundings beneath a fabric hood clumsily sewn together was not dissimilar to the blackened window panes of the magna-rail train. Both were designed to keep Crystal unaware of her surroundings. As she sat on the muddy aluminum floor of the petrol-powered cargo vehicle, her shoulders digging into protruding rivets and slatted panels, she couldn't help smiling. Hadn't Laurent kept her as much in the dark—for nearly six weeks? The band of brigands that had kidnapped her during the skirmish at the badlands junction were at least honest about it.

She couldn't see, but the improved quality of air suggested that the rig had crossed into more hospitable territory. Her body jostled as the rig oscillated on its shock springs, the rear driver side one beneath her ass squealing with every bump. Crystal's wrists were bound with some sort of rope that dug into her if she fidgeted too much. She assumed the same bound her feet, though she was grateful that her pant legs acted as a barrier between her ankle skin and the binding agent. Two hours, maybe three had passed, but who could really tell? Sensory deprivation plays tricks on the remaining senses.

Two for certain, possibly more, kept her company in the rear hold, but no one spoke. Crystal had made an attempt to converse with someone—anyone. They weren't falling for it. I don't suppose there's any water back here, she'd asked, reminding herself of her smart-mouthed teen brother Lorrie. She sighed. Lorrie would have driven them nuts. They'd have either offered him a four-course meal to appease him or thrown him from the back. He had that effect on people.

Despite the blackness beneath the hood, she knew that the sun would be mostly set, whatever the actual time. The brigands had shrouded her under a heavy blanket that irritated her and made her sweat through her own clothes. It was a blessing as much as a curse, however. The small sidearm gun she'd managed to collect from the fallen Sascotan officer aimed upward beneath her undertop, nudged awkwardly between her breasts. The coolness of the metal faded, and she prayed that the firearm wouldn't accidentally discharge and blow her head off. Druna always bragged about what she could conceal in her top—keys, drinks, even her handheld. If she ever saw her precocious roommate again, she'd have a hell of a story to one-up her.

The rig churgled along before the road smoothed out, and when it finally came to a halt, the petrol combustion engine popped and ground into a calmness, as the exhaust fumes wafted beneath her hood.

"Can I get a little air, here?" Crystal called out on the off-chance one of her captors cared whether she suffocated or not. It turned out that one did.

Her eyes didn't take as long to adjust to the darkened sky. Her captor, like the unfortunate fellow she'd kneed in the breadbasket back at the junction, covered half his face behind a cowl-like scarf. When he spoke, his lips vibrated under the stained fabric.

"Breathe. But shut up until we're indoors." He didn't touch her. Crystal hoped she'd proven herself wily enough not to take the risk. Instead, he motioned to a short building crouched among several, shadowed behind a rocky outcropping. Her feet had been freed, but her wrists remained bound beneath the blanket, crossing just beneath her navel. With every shaky step, the gun shifted, digging into the sensitive flesh under her top.

Once inside, she counted three men huddled around a stone fireplace, the glowing embers teasing wisps of flame. Overhead, the beams were exposed, long planks intersecting them and acting as haphazard storage. In the glow of the firelight, she spied a small kitchen covered with dirty dishes and three cots, none of them made. She didn't expect one would be made for her.

"There is water, if you're still thirsty." The man who had ushered into the hut must have been in the back of the rig with her when she was still protesting. A second man, around the same age wearing a week's worth of scruff on his face and a patch over his left eye tossed a stomach-shaped waterskin that she made no effort to catch. The bulbous container bounced off her blanket covering and splatted on the broken-tiled floor. Crystal gave him a look as if to say, "Hey, how am I supposed to catch anything with my hands tied?"

"Suit yourself." The brigand sighed and sat on the nearest cot, stretching and grunting as he peeled off his socks and flexed his toes. Crystal ran her dry tongue over her teeth beneath pursed lips. She was thirsty, of course, but the likelihood she'd have to be unbound if they were to allow her to urinate was the more enticing reason to give in to the temptation. She squatted down and worked the blanket over her head, letting it fall behind her. Was her shirt baggy enough to keep them from discovering her weapon? In the dimness of the hut, likely, at least for now.

Crystal twisted the cover until it fell alongside the leather pouch, dangling by a thread. She leaned ahead and took a long gulp, beads of water dribbling down her chin.

"Have as much as you like," the man on the cot said. "Water source is clean. That's why we set up camp here."

Crystal slid down onto her buttocks and leaned into the bunched-up blanket. "The place could use a little work."

The man laughed and stretched his arms forward, then loosened the ties of his tunic shirt. He worked his head out from under it just like she had done with the blanket. "Name's Hamm—two Ms."

Hamm with two Ms swung his legs up onto the cot but he stayed upright. Tucking his feet beneath him, he picked at his toenails. "This is where you tell me *your* name."

"That's none of your business."

"I mean, we already *know* your name, Crystal Sheppard." As he spoke, the left brigand facing the fireplace thrust her handheld above his head. "Just thought you'd be a little more polite, is all."

Hamm clicked his tongue. "We saved your life, after all."

There they go, "saving me"… Crystal scowled. "Is that what you call this?"

The brigand by the fire tossed the handheld to Hamm and it fell in the nest of his folded legs. "Really, though. Who *are* you?"

"I thought you already knew my name," Crystal retorted, taking another mouthful of water. The gun was itching beneath her brassiere. Her finger was itching for the gun.

"Two words: Crystal. Sheppard. That's what we know." Hamm twiddled the device in his fingers and Crystal felt nauseous that the same hands that were picking his toes were invading her private information. "But where do you come from? I mean, you came in from the Hyacynthe line, but you don't sound like a Frenchy."

"I could swear you sound like a New Inlander, but that don't make much sense." The brigand that had tossed the handheld finally turned. It was the same voice of her original kidnapper, only this time the scarf was gone, exposing a face with scars and dimples. "What would an 'Inlander be doing traveling a Frenchy rail?"

"Why don't you look up my whole story, since you have my handheld."

Hamm cut in. "That's the trouble. The damned thing is too well encrypted. We got your name from the passenger manifest back at the junction. This thing is one big paperweight—unless you feel like giving up the password."

Crystal snorted, and Hamm smiled. "Worth a try, I guess. All I'm saying is, we can move you across borders for quite a sum, but it's easier if we knew exactly who we were… trading."

Trading. She was sure he was going to say "selling". "Free my hands, and I'll tell you whatever you want."

Hamm raised his eyebrows. She'd raised the stakes. "I bet you would. And I just bet you'd waste no time pulling that gun from under your tits, wouldn't you? If you even know how to use it!"

Crystal's heart sank, and the gun felt like it was ten times as heavy. Hamm continued. "You rich people, you're all the same. Just because we don't live in your insider world, we're dumb. Guess again. That right, Duncam?"

The brigand she'd kneed in the belly, apparently called Duncam, laughed. "You aren't the first rich bitch we've met."

Rich?

"Watch your manners, Dunc. Crystal Sheppard, it's like this: We can sell you to any number of bidders. Most of the towns in the dust bowl from here to Sascota would buy you in a heartbeat—and what they do with their property is none of our business."

Crystal nearly threw up.

"No, I think you're someone important—educated, at least. I could fetch more in a trade with the Allens, but maybe even more with Rust." That name was familiar. Rival organizations to the Allens peppered the outside world, each usually specializing in something. The Allens, they were the preeminent money and information traders. But the Rust Syndicate, they were better known for moving contraband. Medicine, weapons.

People.

"So what, you think I'll just tell you what I'm worth so you can make more money?" Crystal huffed. Duncam squinted in the flickering firelight. His scars were deep, and the pockmarks on his face didn't appear to be inflicted wounds. Her mind began to flip back through the medical text pages in her memory.

"How long ago did you have smallpox?"

Hamm let out a long whistle. "I knew it! She's a doctor—med student at least!"

The third brigand, who, until this point, had been unfazed by the small talk, spoke at last. "Do you know medicine?"

The third man twitched but kept his gaze on the embers. Hamm swung his legs back over the edge of the bed. "Don't even think about it, Hewer. She's worth more to Rust than that."

"What do you mean, *that*?" The brigands were withholding something substantial. Crystal saw a tiny crack worth chipping away.

Hewer stood, but didn't turn to her. "You know medicine."

Crystal played along. "I'm not a doctor. But I'm trained in nuclear medicine."

"So, if I gave you a *diagnosis*, you would know the best treatment?"

"Like I said, I'm not a doctor, but if you were sure of the sickness, I could point you in the right direction. Assuming you had the right medicine on hand, and this—*this place* doesn't make me think you do." The brigands may not. But the Rust Syndicate might.

Hamm stood. "Hewer, settle down. She's an asset, not—

"She's the best chance I have." Hewer seethed, and Crystal thought they might come to blows. If she had any chance of escaping her situation, it was through Hewer. He didn't appear to be motivated by a quick payday.

"What are your symptoms?"

Hewer walked over to Crystal and drew a curved pocket blade. She backed up against the wall but knew there was nowhere to run. Before she could process anything, the third man reached for her bonds and with a quick sawing motion, sliced free the cords. Crystal's first instinct was to cover as much of herself with her small hands as she could. To her relief, the man stepped back, allowing her personal space. He didn't put the blade away just yet.

"The gun."

Crystal nodded, and reaching under her top, she pulled the metal weapon into the dimness of the cabin light. It sat in her cupped palms like a dead mouse. Hewer nodded.

"It's useless to any of us. Sascotans use fingerprint activation. Strict about their firearms." She looked at the contraption. The handgrip was not rough or dimpled like the guns the Lacraie guards used. It was shiny, smoky grey where the tech would confirm the identity of the holder. Of course the weapon was useless. Why else would they have let her keep the false sense of security?

Hewer motioned to the chairs by the fireplace. "You should get some rest, Dunc." The polio survivor nodded and left his chair for Crystal to sit. The wood crackled and sparked, and the smoke breezed upwards through the flue. Hewer took his own seat and continued glaring at the fire as he had done before.

"The symptoms aren't mine. It's my son." For the first time, Crystal noticed the pain on his weathered face. His eyes were naturally wide, yet fought to stay fully open, whether from the heat of the fire or the weight of the world. His hair was receding and dusty greys wisped around his temples.

"I'm sorry for your boy. Maybe I can help." Crystal swallowed. She remembered the hopelessness in her parents' voices and eyes over Cadlen's mutism. There's no greater fear than that of a parent over their child, Robert Sheppard once told his daughter.

"Breathing trouble at first. Loss of energy, high fever. But it got worse *after* he recovered." Hewer turned to face her. "You know what that is."

All too well...

Crystal Sheppard knew a lot about red tide. She knew of some medicines that helped control the sporadic bouts that reared back into the victim's life months, even years later. The sickness manifested in a wide array of visible symptoms. She nodded acknowledgment but remained silent to let Hewer continue.

"He was young, maybe twelve. In the years since, he gets these spiked fevers, and he just... I can't explain it." Hewer's eyes glassed over. "He starts to think about things, see things that don't make sense. Gets confused, and that's when he lashes out."

"Hallucination is a symptom of red tide for some, but not all." She counted her blessings that neither Julia nor Robert descended into that disease-induced madness. It was rare in the domes. Red tide was a much more broad threat on the outside.

"A few months ago, he had it bad. Started screaming at me,

breaking our things. Even pulled a knife to his own neck before I calmed him down."

Hamm spoke up. "That was scary. Came right out of nowhere."

Hewer nodded. "He was so embarrassed, wouldn't look me in the eye. Next day, he's volunteered to do a run down south, salvaging." He smirked. "Not everything we do is dishonest, you know."

For the first time, Crystal didn't feel like she was surrounded by wild outsiders. She was in the company of people. Didn't the Sheppard family do all they could just to survive?

And with that realization, everything began to fall into place.

"I can't cure your boy, but I can buy the medicine you need to manage his symptoms from Rust. They're very expensive, though."

Hewer sighed. "I can join the salvage. I'll steal if I have to."

"I'll buy the medicine—if you can help me access my funds."

Duncam held up Crystal's handheld. "I *knew* you were rich! Hamm, Hewer—we don't need her for anything!"

Hamm cuffed Duncam in the shoulder. "Shut up! Let her talk."

"I have money in a personal Hyacynthien account, but it's blocked by now." She turned to Hewer and her eyes pleaded. "If you can help me access my funds, I'll help you get the treatment for your son."

Hewer offered Crystal a calloused, dried hand. She received it, gingerly at first, but the warmth in his grip assured her that a deal was made in good faith. Hewer's eyes widened as he blinked a tear.

Hamm laid back on his cot. "Sounds like we're hitting the trail— good three days ride to Farbend."

"That's right. Jamiss and the scavengers are supposed to sell to Aynslie, ain't they?" Duncam passed Crystal her handheld. "Elms was blabbing about some big old-world rig—be a fortune if they found one!"

Bedtime Stories

(Date Unknown) AC 0235
Sheppard Family Inn, Capston
Lorrie Sheppard

"**F**or the last time, Lorrie, get under your covers! You need to get your sleep!"

With a snap of her fingers, the light dimmed to one-quarter brightness. Julia Sheppard struck the pose, where her hands rested on her hips, elbows out, her head cocked to the left. Lorrie knew there would be no more delaying his sleep time. Except…

"Mom, tell me about the Retreats again!" Lorrie tugged the covers up to his chin in an attempt to curry favour for a story. It never failed.

"Oh, Lorrie, I've told you those stories hundreds of times!"

"Not *hundreds*, Mom. I forget…"

Julia's full-bodied caramel hair was in a hasty high ponytail, locks loose and ringed around her ears. She blinked her naturally long lashes to reveal a faint glint of reflected light in her deep brown eyes. Sighing in resignation, she sat at the side of his mattress.

"Let me see… Oh, I know. How about this…"

Lorrie closed his eyes. His mother's stories were best when he pictured them himself. She was a wonderful storyteller. One day he would like to interview her like a reporter, and write her stories in a chapter book so children all over the city—the whole dome, even—could find the same comfort in the dark. Even in a superstructure designed for safety, the night time was still terrifying to his eight-year-old imagination.

"I think it was my second summer. Our patrol was on a hike, about fifteen kilometers north of the Great River, the one that passes beneath Hyacynthe. There were four of us girls. I was fourteen, I think? Fifteen? No, fourteen…"

The older he got, Lorrie noticed that his mother struggled with the details a little more with each story. Time was separating her memory from the moment, further and further with each passing day. Maybe she just made up small stuff to fill in the cracks? It wouldn't have bothered him if she did.

"There was me, Jeanne, who was my closest friend at the time—you remember Jeanne from the cabin clean-up story? Stéphanie was there. And… Sylvie. Us four, and our guide Gisèle. I think she was in her mid-twenties. I remember she had a really thin face, her cheekbones were sharp—that much I remember, for sure. Short hair, cropped right down in back. Said she hated the tangles when she was in the brush."

In his imagination, Lorrie tramped through thick underbrush, his wavy, dirty-blond hair tamed to his scalp under a bandanna. The kind secret agents wore when they hunted fugitives in the outside world. At least, that's how they did it in the shows.

"Sylvie, as always was more worried about getting wet or dirty. I never knew why she even came to the Retreats—I mean, that's what they were all about, right? Steph found a tick on her pant leg and squealed. I told her to just squish it, she'd be fine. Gisèle just kept walking. She had a long machete blade that she used to swath her way through the shrubs. I think she liked to swing the big knife just for the heck of it!"

Lorrie's eyes widened. One day he'd have a long blade of his own. For now, he wasn't allowed to cut his own meat with a sharp knife.

"As we were supposed to be getting close to a cabin where we would stay the night, Gisèle called to Steph for the map and compass. Guess what?"

Lorrie blurted out. "She didn't have them!"

Julia laughed. "Of course she didn't! She was more worried about bringing extra clothes so she wouldn't be stinky or sweaty, and she accidentally left them back at the lodge. Well, she wasn't too worried, because Gisèle was really good at finding her way in the woods. Or so we thought."

Lorrie turned over on his left shoulder. "She didn't know?"

"Not a clue. Turns out she was all talk and no action. She could do just fine with a map and compass, but when she turned around and realized she had no idea where we were, she completely broke down! Jeanne, Steph and I just watched her as she dropped to her knees and bawled like a baby!"

"Like Cadlen!" chirped Lorrie.

"Leave your little brother alone." Julia wrinkled her brow disapprovingly. "He can't help cry like he does. It will pass one day, and you won't believe how quiet it will be."

"Sorry Mom." Lorrie feigned regret. "How did you get out?"

His mom's eyes twinkled in the faint light. "They didn't send us to the Retreats for nothing, my boy!"

Julia Sheppard went on to explain to her son how she was able to find shelter by layering boughs from spruce trees. How to detect which leaves you could eat and which ones you had to avoid. How the girls started a small fire out of dried tree moss and deadfall, even how to snare rabbits to eat for supper. They had been out in the brush for almost sixty hours before they were found, and according to his mom, living more comfortably under the stars than back at the lodge.

"And when I woke up, there were still smoldering coals in the fire pit and enough berries to feed us two full breakfasts, before the rescue squad came tramping through the bushes. Gisèle wanted to go hide in the woods and never come back, she was so ashamed! But we told her that all the training worked—it kept us alive, after all. And someone would know we were out there and come find us.

"And take a guess who was part of the rescue crew?"

Lorrie sat up straight. "Was it Mr. Laurent?"

"Well yes, he was with them and he looked right the fright until he saw we were all okay! But no, that's not who I meant."

Lorrie scrunched his face in deep thought. "Then who was it?"

Julia's eyes widened as she smiled. "Only a handsome young camper named Robert!"

Lorrie huffed. "No, Mom, you told me you met Dad in the rec hall, or playing lawn tennis or something!"

Julia belly-laughed, loud enough to stir the fragile sleep of her colicky toddler in the adjacent room. "Oh, is that how it happened?"

Sunday, 24 June AC 0245
Eastern Shore, Inland Open-Pit Lake
Lorrie Sheppard

Anything.

To have his mother or his father with them to help them build a camp, find food and water, to reassure them it was going to be okay. Lorrie had woken from a shallow sleep under the ripped-up root system of a tree long dead, crawling with termites and centipedes. His shirt snagged on a root, ripping a swatch of fabric enough that it hung below his waist. He and his brothers were much further than fifteen kilometers away from any sort of lodgings. He remembered the silly treasure maps Cadlen liked to draw as a toddler, with a starting spot and an 'X' that marked where the loot was hidden, at the end of the trail. They couldn't have been in a more different situation. They'd fallen into the center of the page and there was no 'X'. They couldn't even tell which side of the page was up.

Anything to have someone even half as qualified as their mother, who had probably padded her resume with her fantastical bedtime stories.

Cadlen had woken earlier. Scrounging the immediate perimeter, he had managed to find what looked like raspberries. Without saying a word, he reached forward, offering a handful of berries to his brother who was still rubbing the sleep from his eyes.

Lorrie raised his hand in a stop motion. "No Cadlen, don't eat those. We don't know for sure."

Cadlen shrugged his shoulders and placed his bounty in a cone-shaped fold of fern leaves. Lorrie stood up, shaking loose moss and dirt from his damp khakis. His joints were stiff.

Looking around as he stretched, he realized his older brother was not in sight.

"Where's Robbie?"

Cadlen made a motion with his right thumb and pinky finger to emulate an airplane, diving it downward. He pointed in the direction of the lake. Lorrie nodded. It was remarkable how much of Cadlen's hand motions he understood.

"He went back to the lake, did he? Think he'll find supplies washed up on shore, maybe?"

Cadlen shrugged and turned away. Lorrie kept muttering to himself.

"As if he's going to find anything. Maybe the pilot has a four-course meal all laid out for us…"

The pilot.

"The pilot!" Lorrie shrieked as Cadlen poked about in the bushes for dry tinder. "If we could survive a crash like that, a pilot with years of training must have been able to make it!"

"Maybe." Robbie's voice emerged from the direction of the lake. He stepped into view, a canvas sack slung over his shoulder. "But if he *did* survive we may never know. I mean, we're in the middle of nowhere out here. How would he find us?"

"Did you make it all the way back to the lake?"

"I didn't stay down by the water very long, in case someone was watching. But yeah, I was there. No sign of the wreck at all except some supplies that drifted. Most of the supplies didn't look too useful…"

"What's in the bag?" Lorrie grabbed the loose strap and yanked it from his older brother's shoulder.

Robbie sighed. "The bag was in a plastic tub, washed up on the bank. I saw a glint of light—it was the reflective lettering on the outside. The tub was broken but some of the stuff held up pretty well."

Cadlen dropped an armload of tinder and joined his brothers as they emptied the contents.

"First-aid kit, which is handy—Holt's doctors aren't any good to us out here!"

Lorrie picked through the trinkets and supplies, unsure if any of them were useful. His eyes widened and a huge grin appeared when he reached down for the gun.

"Don't get too excited." Robbie grabbed the wide cylindrical-barreled firearm from his over-excited brother. "It's a *flare* gun. You know? They shoot off these sticks that burn and make smoke…"

"Well that's a *good* thing, right? If we're desperate we can fire one of those off, we could be rescued!"

"You forget—we don't know who wants to help us or hurt us. And besides, no flares left. I checked…"

Lorrie grabbed the flare gun back, tucking it into the waistband of his pants. "Well, maybe we'll come across some flares. I'm keeping it."

Rolling his eyes, Robbie continued to scrutinize the loot from the knapsack. "I guess you're not interested in any of these *knives,* then?"

Gasping, Lorrie tore into the supplies with renewed vigor. "I'm getting one! Don't you tell me I can't!"

There were two long knives with curved hilts, clearly designed for survival purposes. Each had a serrated rear edge, presumably for sawing. But the real prize was a long, straight blade about the length of Lorrie's forearm. He gripped the handle and waved the machete, feeling the weight of the weapon as its sharp point dipped. Cadlen backed up several steps.

"You guys can have the hunting knives, but I want this one!"

Also in the mess of supplies were coils of twine, tightly-wrapped plastic bags and mesh netting big enough to fit at least two full-grown adults. Several packages that held food rations had appeared to have been soaked when the tub cracked open, so Robbie had discarded them. Small bottles with long, complicated medical names indicated medicine of some sort. Robbie pocketed them, though Lorrie questioned the usefulness of medicine they couldn't identify. Robbie reminded him of the useless flare gun he insisted on keeping.

A small pocket radio device that would not power on when the switch was toggled rounded out the recognizable supplies. Both brothers agreed it was worth keeping, in the event they were able to find someone friendly who could either repair it or trade it. Neither knew anything at all about radios. They were obsolete technology inside New Inland, although the necessity of cheap long-distance communication would have to be essential on the outside.

Lorrie reached down and picked up a rectangular chunk of metal that Cadlen had absentmindedly tossed over his shoulder. Looking a little closer, he could see it was rough, like sandpaper. Robbie squinted his eyes as he examined it a little closer.

"Wait a second, were there any other chunks of metal?"

Lorrie poked through the remnants of the supplies. He knew what Robbie was thinking. If the chunk of metal was a fire flint, they'd need something to strike against it. He narrowed his sight on the machete blade, then on the pile of dry tinder Cadlen had gathered. Julia Sheppard must have told the same stories to all of her children.

"Think about Mom's stories, Lorrie! From the Retreats, you know, where they were lost in the woods?"

Cadlen took a handful of small branches and tore them into smaller bunches. Lorrie pulled the hanging rag of his t-shirt and used the machete to saw it free, leaving his lower left abdomen exposed. He tied the fabric over his head like a bandanna. The Sheppard brothers wouldn't shiver under a tree root tonight.

"We're making a fire."

Unexpected Company

Sunday, 24 June AC 0245
Farbend Trading Post
Ian Null

Preferably, Ian Null would have traveled as lightly as possible. His Motherland issued rucksack, a change of clothing and a waterskin, a hunting knife, and his handheld. The Junquer had called it a "key". True to its name, it had opened many doors—only those doors operated with electronics. On the outside, metal keys would have been more practical. The handheld would occasionally need recharging, of course. Junquer had installed a long-life power cell, but even it had its limits.

As the settlers of Farbend fled, Null lingered in Aynslie's trading post. Take what you need, she'd told him. There was no telling how long before the radiation of the thresher cell started leaking once again, eventually melting down beyond means of control. They were close enough to New Inland that their scanners may detect the spike in radiation. Possibly they'd even send a task force to contain it. But none of that was guaranteed. Evacuation, far and fast—that was the only option.

Behind Aynslie's shop, Null spied a frame-bare off-road rig with just enough space for two riders and scant else. Denuded of its coverings, Null determined that it ran on petrol rather than nuke cells. No wonder they left it behind, he remarked. A full tank of petrol might get him far enough from the radiation, so long as the tank was actually full, or there were reserves on site. A quick inspection and he confirmed both. The rig was fully fueled, but appeared to have been unmoved for quite some time based on the tall grass grown around its wheels. Null rummaged through the drawers of Aynslie's counter desk and found a few dozen keys of all shapes and sizes. Scooping the lot into his hands, he climbed into the driver's seat of the rig and a family of mice scurried from beneath the cracked and rotted cushion. Even the rodents had the sense to get away.

Half a dozen attempts later, Null turned the right key and the rig coughed to life. A burst of black smoke spewed from the tailpipe. He checked his new rucksack one last time. The change of clothes included loose-fitting slacks, held up with a snug rope belt, short and long-sleeved shirts of different fabric densities for light wear by day and warmth by night. Hunting knife with a cracked wooden handgrip. Snare wire coiled tight. Clean gauze and antibiotic salve in an air-tight container. The radiation medicine he'd purchased from Lacraie, swapped into a different pillbox to be sure there was no lingering trace of radiation. He'd tossed the original container into the bushes after he'd parted ways with Jamiss. Someone could find it and trace its origins to Lacraie. Maybe even to Ian Null.

By then, he would be on the west coast, a range of mountains and a lifetime between them.

He checked his handheld one last time as the engine idled, less caustic than when he'd first turned it over. His last transmission was a warning to any oncoming transports to steer clear of Farbend. It was up to the travelers, now. He'd gone above and beyond to warn strangers of the danger.

South. Away from both New Inland and the radiation. The rig rode smoothly thanks to its robust shock springs and fat, wide tires. Polymer-infused rubber, he'd suspected. Probably lined with steel fibres. This rig existed for life in the deep wilderness.

Null piloted the machine into the brush, making tracks that could be spotted from the air. He calculated that he would have enough fuel to wind up within ten kilometers of an open pit mine that had long ago flooded into a lake. Several creeks bled into the surrounding land from it. If he could reach it by foot, there would be plenty of means to shake anyone who might have picked up his trail. That's what Paolo told him, anyway.

No one is looking for me. Null shook off the insecurity of his former self as bushes thwacked the roll bars.

The sun waned in the mid-evening and the rig sputtered the last of its fuel. He'd encountered several outsiders throughout the afternoon. All of them had ignored him, most shying away from the rumbling engine noise. Null's stomach growled almost as loud, but he didn't stop to eat from the road rations he'd pilfered from Aynslie's kitchen. There would be time to eat and sleep. But not yet.

According to the Junquer key, he was 8.6 km from the northernmost tip of an open-pit lake. Well-rested and quenched, Null was nonetheless famished, and even on a full stomach he knew he couldn't make it to the edge of the water before sundown. The land was even, grown with stands of poplar, cedar, and ash. He'd managed to squeeze just enough petrol through the fuel lines to rest the rig beneath a wide cypress canopy. After a quick scan of the key, he slung his new pack straps over his shoulders and ducked into the heavy cover of the nearest stand of hardwoods.

An hour later, the last streaks of light stained the western sky. The cabin couldn't have revealed itself even a minute sooner. On the edge of a clearing, grown waist high in rushes and shrubs, the quaint structure appeared sturdy enough. Roof was taut and even. Windows were intact and the door was shut. No tracks in or out. Overhead, a swallow peeled across the sky in a wide, swooping arc.

La Golondriña. Paolo Desantos's ancestors had followed the swallows until they'd settled permanently in their new motherland. No radiation. No exotic diseases. Clean water. The birds had delivered on their promise, to deliver them from the toxicity of the old world into the salvation of the new.

Null shook his head. No birds led him here.

In the lengthening shadows, Null approached the cabin and peered through a window. The modesty inside matched the outside. A main living area boasted a fireplace, kitchen area, and a heavy lounging chair.

Two closed doors led presumably to a restroom and a sleeping quarters.

It was perfect. At least for one night.

Before darkness had completely fallen, Null had scouted a rain barrel on the south side of the cabin. It was faded blue polymer plastic, listed to one side and topped with a layer of algae. A quick scan confirmed the water beneath wasn't radioactive; in fact, the rem levels were negligible. It was one less thing to worry about. Only a few paces beyond the barrel, Null spied game tracks. It appeared that rabbit was on the menu for the night. The knotting of his stomach and unsatisfactory freeze-dried ration packets he'd taken from Farbend convinced him that using the fireplace wouldn't do any harm. If the cabin were on a more traveled route, smoke and the scent of roasting game would be a magnet for wandering brigands.

Null wasted no time setting snares. Rabbits should still be active at dusk, he reasoned. As he waited for his traps to do their work, Null busied himself scouting the cabin and building the fire. There was enough kindling, and scrap paper in the form of old books to set the heavier softwood quarter-cut log chunks. He filled an iron kettle from the kitchen and placed it on the glowing embers once the fire had seasoned itself into a searing heat source. Around 2200 hours, he slipped outside to check the snares. To his relief, the wire had tightened around an unfortunate rabbit's neck, strangling it in seconds. Null made quick work dressing the animal, leaving the entrails and fur in the bush before retreating indoors for the night.

As the rabbit roasted in a shallow pan over the fire, Null circulated about the cabin to ensure it was secure. Any window could easily be broken, but at the cost of a racket that would alert him to a would-be intruder. Fortunately, none of the windows could be opened from the outside. The door, however, proved a little less certain. Turning the knobby bolt mechanism, it didn't lock, but kept turning without resistance. The inner mechanism had either been removed or was seized. Either way, Null would have to leave the front door unlocked or find a way to lock it, at least so no one could just breeze in on a whim. He was in no mood for unexpected company.

If only there was something that could warn him of approaching danger…

The key. Paolo's voice in the back of his mind reminded Null that he had one other option. He retrieved the handheld from his pack and thumbed open the main menu, retracing in his memory as best he could how to access the motion sensor application. The Junquer had used the technology in his hideaway to alert him to Paolo's arrival all those months ago. Surely it would be effective to alert Null if anyone encroached on his shelter.

For about half an hour, Null sat in the big armchair, digesting his roast rabbit, sipping an herbal tea from his road ration packet, and fiddling with the settings of the motion sensor. Once he'd set the range, alarm volume, vibration, and trigger size, he doused the coals in the fireplace. 16 degrees would be warm enough not to need extra heat, and the bed was made with layers of warm linens. He could have slept under the stars, but the thought of a proper mattress, linens, and a pillow was enticing enough.

He set the handheld alarm to 4am, allowing him an easy five hours of sleep. Just over a week ago he'd left the memory of Paolo Desantos beneath an Allentown explosion. Since he turned his back on the billowing smoke of the Allen city, it was as though he'd traveled a month or more. Null removed his boots and crawled under the bed covers. In the silence and darkness, he stared at the ceiling. Elms, Berglund, Aynslie. *Jamiss*. The young man was dead by now, most likely. Null's stomach was heavy. It could have been the rabbit.

It was probably regret.

Null wouldn't have needed to set an alarm to wake himself up if not for the fatigue of his tumultuous eight days in the wild. Even after the ill-fated five-day march to find water in the Lake Region, even after he'd killed Yael, he had been able to regulate his sleep pattern. Maybe he'd have been better off sleeping outdoors. Maybe the comforts of the cabin would betray him. Maybe he'd sleep right through the alarm, and the motion sensor, and an intruder would kill him before he had the chance to even acknowledge his mistake.

Null hadn't slept an hour when the handheld vibrated. His eyes snapped open. Floorboards in the common area creaked. In the darkness of his room, Null listened for any telltale patterns or movements. Rather than distinct up/down steps, the unexpected guest shuffled. Perhaps they were trying to stay quiet. Perhaps they were ill or elderly. If it were daytime, the intruder would surely have known someone was in the cabin—signs of a fresh fire in the hearth, plenty of tracks in the tall grass, algae cleared off the rain barrel. Null had made no attempt at concealment once he'd decided to stay the night. He had bet on the lengthy abandonment of the cabin to remain for one more night. As the intruder shuffled across the cabin floor, Null tried to determine if they were a threat. He curled his fingers around the grip of the hunting knife he'd tucked under his thigh. Paolo's voice whispered to him.

You've done it before. And you'll do it again. Survival, Ian. No one will ever know.

The voice of his former self retreated into his memory and Null channeled his perception in the pitch darkness. There was no natural moonlight. With every passing second, it became clearer that the intruder was less and less a threat. If they were fit, intent on making the first move, they would have crossed the common room in less than ten strides. A full minute had elapsed, and the intruder was shifting his weight from one foot to the other unevenly, until he collapsed into the big chair, expelling a gasp of either relief or agony. Null kept a tight grip on the knife.

He heard raspy breathing, the sound of someone who was not asleep, yet in a state of forced rest. Several minutes passed with no change. The intruder laboured to control his breathing, forcing his body to calm.

"I am no threat, friend." The stranger spoke, barely above a whisper, yet in the stillness of the cabin, it was as if he were sitting at the edge of his bed. "If you wish to be left alone, I can find another cabin, but I'd prefer to sleep on this chair, mind you…"

Null stayed perfectly still, awaiting his guest's next gesture. He was an older gentleman—perhaps in his sixties. There was discomfort behind his words, though he was clearly exuding bravery in the face of a serious injury or illness. Null had not survived this long trusting people he knew, let alone those he did not.

"As you were, then. I'm not ill. Just a little broken, is all… If it's all the same to you, I'll just stay here. If you decide to kill me once I've fallen asleep—and I assume you can tell—I won't hold it against you."

The man coughed, shifting in the chair to stifle his pain. "I'm unlikely to make the morning as is, so I suppose I'm no worse for it."

Null lay in perfect stillness until the man finally drifted into a deep sleep. The breathing was heavy and natural, stirring every so often from what was clearly a severe pain in his abdomen. He allowed himself to sleep for thirty-minute intervals, waking to the same pattern of breathing over the next three hours. Null shut off the alarm before 4am, and with the heavy breathing slowed considerably, he rose from the bed and left the room.

The sun had yet to rise, but the falling moonlight strained through the cloud cover, revealing exactly what he imagined: An older man, bearded with streaks of grey beneath a tangle of shoulder-length silver-grey hair matted and tangled, a canvas shirt stained with deep patches of blood, some browned over with traces of fresh flowing crimson indicating an untreated wound. His deep green pants were too short, the rope belt tied loosely to allow his breathing while he slouched. This man was clearly no threat to anyone, and Null assessed that even in full health he'd have been of no concern.

The man had no gear or equipment, unless he had left it outside. He had no weapons on his person. Clearly, he was simply passing through, possibly looking for a quiet, out of the way place to die alone. Null imagined himself one day in the same state—slumped in a big chair, in a cabin, far away, counting down his final breaths.

Alone.

Without opening his eyes, the man startled him when he spoke. "I should thank you for not killing me, sir, while you had ample opportunity."

The man smiled, his eyes remaining closed as his chest heaved. "Although I should ask, if you could spare any pain medication, the contents of my cart are yours—I won't likely need them where I'm going."

Away from the Sun

Sunday, 24 June AC 0245
Beneath Allentown
Mayor Steven Reekan

It began with a faint scraping, like a rat dragging a scavenged meal along a hollow pipe. The silence in the bomb shelter, deep beneath the streets of Allentown, had nearly driven Steven crazy. The silence, or the endless time he had to think about what could be happening back in Capston. With no contact, Ling would assume the lead. She would send the Sheppards and the Connellys to Ap-Oz, unaware that Motherland's lieutenant-colonel had sprung a trap. Paolo Desantos had possibly succeeded in his two-pronged assault—he'd nearly killed Steven and his command team, and he'd smoked out the witnesses from their protection within Holt Tower. As the scraping intensified into a grinding, squealing of metal echoing through the conduit pipes, Steven and Kenzy saved their breath. Kenzy's handheld had long depleted its power. They had since burned the few wax candles from the emergency supply kit. In the sheer darkness, Steven imagined he was comatose, yet still aware of the world continuing on without him. His weakened body, reduced to only simple movements and breathing, leaned against the steel wall, ready to use his last shred of voice to alert his rescuers that he was in fact still alive.

"They're getting closer," Kenzy wheezed, only inches away in the darkness. "They're close enough that their heat sensors should pick us up."

"Heat… Then why is it so damn cold…" Steven had lost blood when he'd torn open his hand during the initial blast. Kenzy had dressed it well. But between the lethargy in the confined space and the scant, powdered ration packs, he had to have lost ten pounds.

The scraping intensified into crushing excavation. Memories of the industrial rhythms of the Foundries flooded back. The smell of the smelters, the flashing of the white heat, the specks of minuscule sparks and shavings against his cheeks. He was back there again, back to the start of it all. Young, fit, and angry while his father lumbered towards early retirement, cancer in his lungs and resentment in his heart.

And no one waiting for him at home.

Trahearn Reekan left the workforce a shell of a man. Dianne had left him years before. Steven had taken up his father's role—that of a curmudgeon in training, the next generation of Reekan men to spend the prime of his life underground, away from the sun, destined to leave with the same conditions.

One loud crash snapped him to attention, and as though he'd been jolted with a live wire, Steven found his voice.

"We're here! Two of us!"

Over the course of the next two hours, the rescuers from Allentown pressed downward, ultimately breaching the wall where the conduit had indeed alerted them to their survival. The artificial light flooding into the bomb shelter blinded Steven and he stumbled backward by instinct. Kenzy shielded her eyes with one hand and reached with the other as an Allen glove flexed through the breach. Before leaving the shelter, Allen medics descended into the chamber and provided instant care to both Steven and Kenzy. It would take some time before a safe evacuation could be done, so Madam Allen insisted that Steven lie down as she fastened an intravenous line to his wrist. Something about dehydration and nutrient deficiency. *Nothing a decent meal couldn't fix…*

While the evacuation route was being secured, the only good news involved the survival of nearly everyone from the collapsed tunnel. Shore, Gry—all but Swift had survived the initial blast. According to Madam Allen, a remote-controlled drone had detonated in the courtyard above the tunnels, causing the collapse. It was unknown if the drone had intended to target the fleeing Capston squad, or if it was intended to strike the Grace hospital, only a block away. With the knowledge that his senior officers suffered only scrapes and bruises, Steven protested less and left Kenzy to do the talking. He smiled as she negotiated with the Allens. Capston had done nothing against their agreement. She had concrete evidence against Paolo Desantos and Motherland for a litany of offenses in and out of Allentown. Kenzy made her case, hand-gesturing with every syllable.

"Madam Allen, it is crucial that we find Desantos—for both of our sakes!"

"We're sorry, Major Wall. You're too late for Desantos."

As Madam Allen revealed the second, more devastating explosion in Allentown's north end, that leveled the stronghold of the Motherland forces, had taken the life of Lieutenant-Colonel Desantos, Steven lurched from the bed.

"You say he's dead? Have you confirmed it?"

Madam Allen nodded. "We have conducted a forensic examination of remains found beneath the debris. Dental records match Paolo Desantos, as do traces of his officer's uniform."

Paolo Desantos is dead. Steven sat back on the cot before he could pass out again. He should have been happy to hear the news. Instead, the death of his prime suspect ruined everything. There was no one to arrest. No one to throw in a cell. No one to hold accountable for the terror that had been wrought on Capston. Steven couldn't even claim the kill for himself.

"But who would have taken out Desantos? Madam Allen, with all respect, do you know who could have done this?" Kenzy pressed the Allen agent as more rescuers emerged through the breach, cables and straps in tow.

"The Allen Consortium conducts its own investigations, Major."

"They tried to *kill* us!"

"This does not concern Capston. That is all."

"Kenzy." Steven interrupted her before she could respond. "Drop it. We have all we need." Her handheld might be out of power, but when it was recharged, there was more than enough evidence that

Paolo Desantos and Motherland had been behind everything.

How to explain it to the DHC, now, that was another matter.

Obsolescence

Monday, 25 June AC 0245
25 km West of Badlands Junction
Crystal Sheppard

Whatever it takes.

Crystal had never thought about the depths she'd go to be with her family again. When she'd accepted the offer to study in Hyacynthe, there was reason to believe that the trade embargo would be temporary. Only a diplomatic squabble, nothing more, Monsieur Laurent had said. You'll be home to visit after the first term, and you'll be fighting with Lorrie and dying to come back.

All those lies played back as she tossed and turned on Duncam's crooked, slim cot as the light of the fire died and the air cooled. It took only one stern look from Hewer to convince Duncam that sleeping on the floor for one night wouldn't kill him. And if he didn't like it, he could always sleep outside. That seemed to be enough persuasion.

What exactly *would* she do?

The gun she'd hidden on her person gave her the slightest bit of confidence. The longer it stayed wedged between her cleavage the more that confidence waned. Guns were used by police officers and criminals. Soldiers and brigands. She'd never even seen one up close, let alone held one. In truth, she would have likely hurt herself before anyone else. And her captors knew it.

Still, something in her gut told her that if the time was right, if the circumstances were just so, if the urgency was high enough, that she would hold the weapon, aim its muzzle at her enemy and fire. Not all guns had the palm-print recognition sensors. Yes, she was convinced she could do it. She wasn't sure if she would do it with her eyes open or closed.

Despite the warming of relations between herself and her captors, she was still very much a prisoner. Hamm drew the short straw and waited outside the privy while she used the bathroom and splashed water on her face. What if the outsider tried something while she was at her most vulnerable? Duncam had already taken her knee to the belly. Hamm would take it the same if he pressed his luck.

As the four loaded onto the cargo truck, Crystal studied her surroundings. The rising sun in the east illuminated rocky terrain with tufts of green rushes and short, round shrubs. To the north, trees rose taller. She grimaced at the thought that they were going to travel in the opposite direction.

"We're not in a seam," Hewer explained as the truck roared to life, its engine gargling petrol like rancid mouthwash. "We'll come close, but we won't have to pass through one. No, this is just badlands. It used to be worse, but it's shrinking. My old man used to say, anyway."

Crystal knew that seams of old radiation still swathed across the land. Most in the north east were weak and relatively harmless, so long as a traveler didn't disturb too much soil or drink water without testing first. But farther south, there were pockets of land that just shouldn't be traversed.

Unless you made adequate preparations.

She wondered how Ian Null made out on his trip. With the amount of medicine he'd purchased from Lacraie, he was most likely moving through some of the most forbidding land. The thought of the mysterious outsider who had gifted her a small fortune reminded her— if we ever get to trade with the Rust Syndicate, it would be wise to buy some Radiogardasse. Just in case. She might even buy enough for her captors, but that depended on how they acted over the next few days.

They started on the right foot. Crystal wasn't forced to wear a slight-blocking hood, and she wasn't bound. Hewer did convince her to wear a long-brimmed hat, tucking her wavy hair up inside, and to cover her face with a cowl and sunglasses.

"You need to look like us," Hamm said. "Out here, if you look like a fresh cherry, you'll be the first to get plucked."

Crystal had expected to drive over rocky roads in the sun, harried by other lowlifes every fifteen minutes. Instead, over the next several hours, her captors brought her into a number of smaller encampments—some nestled in wooden stands, next to low streams of chocolate-coloured water, others concealed in rock formations. One was a surprisingly intact village of wood-framed houses with gabled roofs. Hewer instructed her every time not to speak to anyone. Her accent could set off unnecessary alarms. She wasn't convinced—nearly everyone who spoke did with either a bastardized dialect of English or a spectrum of accents from all over the continent. One thing in common, she noticed, was that everyone wore earth-toned clothing. Anything white wouldn't keep its virgin sheen out here. Fabrics were tightly woven, most tied in the front rather than buttoned, no hint of metal zippers or clasps. Who in the outside world had the facilities to loom textiles into clothing?

Hewer insisted that the three men would take turns keeping watch at night, and that Crystal remain incognito in the rear cargo hold of the truck. He had even brought a bedroll for her. As the three men settled into a nighttime rotation of watching guard and sleeping in turns, Crystal rested her head on a rolled-up blanket for a pillow and couldn't shake the thought that she was a fraud.

So what if we buy the medicine? I'm offering depressants, not a miracle cure. No one can cure red tide.

Despite her worries, the lack of sleep over the past few days allowed her to sleep far deeper than she had any right. Her captors didn't wake her. She was jolted awake by the ignition of the engine. She pulled the dirty blanket up over her face as the truck started off on the second day of their journey. Maybe she could force herself to sleep a little longer.

The truck stopped just after high noon in a more thickly wooded land. Hewer seemed to know exactly which routes to take, which would offer no resistance, no threats, only familiar faces with fresh water and food to barter or buy. Crystal shared the cargo space with crates of metal gears, tools, electronics, and scrap metals. In the evening, Duncam hooted in elation after trading the Sascotan gun for a banquet's worth of food. He and Hamm roasted a wild turkey on a slow-turning spit over the evening campfire, like the pilgrims of old. She watched through the narrow slats of the cargo bay as the pair sang songs off-key and toasted earthen mugs that frothed over the rims. She couldn't help but smile. They could have been brothers for all she knew. If she weren't their captive, she'd have been happy to join in.

A pang knotted in her stomach. *Don't forget why you're here, Crystal.*

The hatch from the cab to the cargo hold slid open and Hewer poked his head inside. "You'll be okay here. Come on out, if you want."

By now, she trusted Hewer's judgment, if only because she knew how much she was worth to him. "That wild bird smells delicious."

Hewer offered her a hand as she stepped down from the hold onto the ground. She didn't take it. "We got more than just food from that last trading post."

Hewer sat alongside his brethren on a fallen log half-covered in a green blanket of moss. Crystal sat cross-legged opposite the three as Duncam poured her a ceramic mug with an unfamiliar logo on the side facing her: A large circle with an arrow pointing downward and bisecting lines. It was no letter or number, and Crystal had never come across the symbol in anything at Lacraie or elsewhere. She'd come across unfamiliar alphabets—always in transactions that dealt with Arctica, due to the northwestern federation's business contacts in the far east. But there was no way any one person could remember all symbols from all corners of the world.

"Never seen that before, have you?" Hewer chomped on his wild game, the grease dripping into his wire-brush whiskers. "Probably a good thing."

Crystal sipped from the symboled mug and winced. The drink was sour and made her tongue ripple. "And why is that?"

Hewer swallowed and followed with a long gulp of his own ale. "Next time you see that symbol, you'll be in the company of Rust."

Duncam and Hamm refilled and emptied their mugs, and with every clink of the ceramic, their voices warbled further and further off key. Crystal sipped more of the tart alcohol and narrowed in on the circle and lines. Were they random markings? Or did they have some sort of meaning, connection to a time long passed? One of her teachers in second year had told the class that the words of today looked very different even a hundred years ago, let alone three or four hundred. Logos of corporations that were known around the globe might today be as unrecognizable as a child's sketch, their power and influence reduced to obsolescence, like cave paintings or disintegrated data. A byproduct of societal evolution, the professor had said.

"There's a town—not really a town, more like a trading post," Hewer explained as he stirred the embers beneath the spit. "Farbend. Trader by the name of Aynslie, no nonsense bitch. Fair, but nothing gets past her."

These fellows had a habit of calling women "bitches". It was such an ugly word, rarely spoken in Hyacynthe or New Inland. Clearly an example of how language didn't evolve in equal measure everywhere. Crystal dismissed the slur as she had the rest of their poor etiquette and manners. *Never let them call you names,* Cherise had told her during her orientation at Lacraie. *They might be clients, but anyone who talks that way is just an outsider.*

Maybe that's why Ian Null had surprised her.

"Aynslie, she's got an in with Rust." Duncam and Hamm stopped singing and glanced at each other, then each took another drink. Crystal tried to piece the spare bits of information together.

"Aynslie. Farbend. Your son will be there."

The embers continued to glow, but they dimmed after Hewer stopped stirring them. He tossed the stick into the dying fire and one last gasp of flame gasped into the cool evening air. "That's when you do your magic. Fix my boy, and we'll fix your money situation."

Magic. Talk about obsolete ideas. Magic is nothing, only an excuse for ignorance.

And that was her problem. A pharmaceutical intern is not a doctor. And there were no doctors that she knew of, in the far east or behind the bushes, that could perform the miracle Hewer was expecting, if his boy—Jamiss was his name—*did* in fact have red tide-induced delirium. If she couldn't convince anyone that her treatment was successful, she may as well throw away her handheld.

Seeking Death

Monday, 25 June AC 0245
9 km North of Inland Open-Pit Lake
Ian Null

The rain barrel water bubbled in the kettle. The handle was too hot to grasp with bare hands, so Null had to improvise. A moth-riddled rag folded over three times did the trick. He poured the boiled water over a square pouch of citrus-infused herbal tea.

"Man of few words, are you?" Null didn't answer. The old man dug his elbows into the arm rests and lifted himself straighter in the chair. Null noticed brownish-red splotches on his shirt, still wet from fresh leaking. A wound on his torso was deep enough not to have healed over in what must have been four days removed from the assault. Assuming, of course, it was an assault rather than an accident. It was in Paolo's nature to assume the worst.

"I'll say, a cup of hot tea is the last thing I expected to find here." The man couldn't help chuckling even though it induced more coughing, doubling him over. "I'll be sure to savour it."

Ian broke his silence. "You are certain that you are dying."

The man raised a shaking arm and clasped the handle of the cracked tea cup. "Aren't we all, friend?"

Ian poured himself a cup of tea and set the kettle on the kitchenette countertop as it continued to billow steam.

"Death comes easily out here."

"Is that what you believe?"

The man shifted, leaning forward to straighten himself before spasming in pain from his wounds.

"You see, out here, death comes easily two ways. Either you deal it, or you seek it."

Null fetched the medical kit he'd acquired from Aynslie. Opening the lid and laying it 180 degrees on the kitchen table, he selected the clean gauze. Soaking a swab with leftover tea water, he approached the old man. Up close, his eyes were webbed with thin, wiry veins. His face was dotted with age spots, and there were traces of healing scratches.

"And which are you?" Null stood over him. The old man sighed as though he were crippled and needed help moving his legs. Without directions, the man unbuttoned his stained shirt, revealing two notably wide swaths of slash marks across his chest and abdomen. Both were stuffed with fabric, saturated and beginning to crust around the frayed edges. The skin surrounding the wounds was deep red. Null swallowed. The old man might be right in his self-diagnosis.

"Until recently, I would have said neither. I suppose I'm *seeking* at this point."

Null grimaced. "I can treat you with what skills I have." He proceeded to gently wipe dried blood and dirt from the unblemished skin, avoiding the wounds until he was able to approach the makeshift bandages with some sort of plan. Paolo had learned basic first-aid. If nothing else, he'd learned how to survive.

"I have little of value to offer in payment, except my gear and my cart." The man squinted his eyes and dug his wrinkled fingers in the arm rests. "Whatever you need, please take it."

Ian retreated to the bedroom, returning with the rucksack. Flipping open the outer flaps, he retrieved a small white box with a series of markings and logos.

"Your kit, the tea rations… Traded with Rust recently? Carroway?"

Retrieving a pair of nylon gloves and tweezers, Ian dipped the tips in boiled water before turning his attention to the soiled fabric stuffed into the wounds.

"Farbend." Null started to probe the infected wound for a loose end. There was no anesthetic in his medical kit. The old man stiffened as Null gripped loose fabric strands and tested how difficult it would be to remove them. Trial and error.

"Ah, Farbend, of course. Aynslie must have charged you plenty.

Deep pockets, you must have…"

Null jerked on the fabric, loosening it instantly as the old man winced. "Riches don't concern me."

He continued cleaning excess blood and pus while extracting every last thread from the first slash wound. Given the split of the skin and depth of the wound, Null guessed the assailant had wielded a longer blade—a machete, most likely. He didn't ask.

"I suppose not. Perhaps you bought it, or maybe stole it—I'm just grateful you have it today." He tightened up in anticipation of Null reopening the second wound.

Null locked eyes with the old man. He was prodding Null just as much as Null was prodding him. He turned his attention back to the wound. Carefully grasping the free end, he peeled away the fabric. The pain would have been considerable, but the man bore it with striking fortitude.

"You're familiar with Rust."

"My brothers, my sisters—we're well-traveled. We're familiar with your country, too."

My country?

When the wound was cleaned to the best of his ability, Null applied antiseptic salve to disinfect the perimeter. It was clear the bleeding was not going to stop easily. The location of the wound ensured that whenever the old man coughed it would reopen, exposing his torso to infection. It would need to be stitched. But before that, at least part of the slash would need to cauterize. He took the old man's right hand and set it upon the gauze to keep pressure while he inserted a cast iron poker into the coals.

"From which country do you presume I hail?" Null pulled an ottoman foot rest close to the big chair and sat.

"You've done well to conceal your past. All new clothing, supplies. Not speaking—that is important. But your accent still gives you away. Your people once followed *La Golondriña*. Which makes me wonder why you've traveled this far south."

Retrieving the poker from the fireplace, Ian eased the glowing end to the edge of the wound. The old man closed his eyes tightly and gripped the arm rests. The searing took only a few seconds, but the smell of burned flesh filled the cabin instantly. To Null's astonishment, the man didn't make a sound. After returning the poker to the hearth, Null sat back on the ottoman. The old man held the gauze to the freshly burned patches.

"Brothers and sisters, you said." Leaning forward, his elbows resting on his knees, Null clasped his hands. "Who are you?"

The old man sighed and rolled his eyes to his shirt pocket bunched up over his left bicep. Null spotted the outline of a heavy medallion through the stained fabric. He didn't retrieve it. The last time he'd seen an Ansati pendant, his father was using one to carve the same logo into Andreas's forehead in the pouring Motherland rain.

"It appears you do seek death."

The old man smiled in resignation. "My name is Raël."

Windows at Five

Monday, 25 June AC 0245
Office of Phil Fox, Capston
Interim-Solicitor Karyn Kendall

Karyn Kendall's calendar application indicated that Phil Fox had been away for thirty-five days, and his expected return date of July 20th couldn't come quick enough. She shifted her weight to the left side of the cushion, as Phil's posture had worn the right side shallower. When you're chucking firewood at the Homestead, don't blame me if you slip a disc, she'd chastised him more than once. You try to sit up straight for ten hours in court, he always answered. She couldn't blame him for wanting to slouch.

And she couldn't blame him for wanting to get out of Capston for a while. The office remained open, lease paid and utilities on, in the event he opted to reuse the workspace in his role of city solicitor. Karyn worked from his old desk, on his old datapad, while his old office decor remained packed in boxes. Sixty days isn't a long time, she'd reasoned. No point paying to store them if he's just going to set them back up again. Reekan could insist he move his office to Holt Tower all he liked. If Phil didn't want to move, he simply wasn't going to move.

"Climate to four." The office temperature adjusted within moments. "Light to two." The windows to the downtown core of Capston brightened, adding a warmth to the atmosphere. Captain Ling always complained about the coolness of the 400-Block offices. Karyn hoped to make the room as welcoming as possible, ahead of some difficult conversations.

A soft alert from the datapad, and a touch of her index finger released the electronic doors in the lobby. The scanners had confirmed Ling's presence. Karyn had just enough time to shift her weight again and take a sip of water before the captain came through the door.

"Thank you, Captain Ling—though I would have been happy to meet you on the 93rd." Karyn stood as Ling approached the desk, offering a greeting hand. Ling was an imposing presence despite her size, barely a meter and a half and toned. Dressed in her casual seamless shirt and crisp-cut trousers, the captain would have been anonymous in the pedestrian throng of business folk of downtown Capston at midday.

"Not at all, Miss Kendall. I thought it best to meet you here." Her tone indicated the subject of Ling's requested meeting carried heavy. The captain looked around the empty office. "You really miss Mayor Fox's personality when all of his things are gone."

Karyn smiled. "You wouldn't miss it if you had to have all those baubles and toys cleaned. Besides, he'll make himself at home wherever he decides to set up."

"He's expected to come back—"

"July 20th." Karyn spoke the words out loud, although she'd recited them silently to herself many times. "Unless he tells me otherwise."

"You've spoken with him, then?"

"Not since he almost missed his shuttle." She could still imagine the drip of toothpaste on his collar. "I don't expect to hear from him ahead of the next DHC meeting. I swear, he planned it that way, to miss it by five days."

Ling laughed uneasily. "Can't say I blame him. Those can get touchy."

"Speaking of touchy, I'm surprised we're meeting, and your boss isn't with us."

The mention of Reekan caused Ling's expression to darken. "I asked to meet with you, Karyn, because there has been... a development."

First, she dropped the formality. Second, a "development".

Karyn leaned forward. "Go on."

Ling straightened her posture in the guest chair. "Yesterday, 0200 hours, we received word that Steven and Major Wall were rescued from the catacombs beneath Allentown.”

Karyn lowered her face into her palms. She knew Reekan was determined to scout the Allen city for leads, even if it meant disobeying DHC laws. She had been in the office when Phil explained up and down exactly how many laws he’d be breaking. The two of them barked back and forth at each other like chained fighting dogs. Somehow, she had known that he was going to do it anyway.

“Rescued. From what? And why the hell was he in Allentown in the first place?”

“We found evidence in the Sheppard Inn debris that lead us there.” Ling looked around, as though she were expecting someone was spying on them. “And in Allentown, Major Wall came across even more—”

“Ender.” It was Karyn’s turn to drop the formality. “It doesn’t matter what you found, it’s *how* you found it. Marribel and the rest of the Council are not going to let this slide. You know!”

“And you know that he wouldn’t have done it if he didn’t think it was worth the risk.” Ling pounded a half-closed hand into her palm. “You know Steven Reekan. He’s pigheaded—but he’s a *good* man.”

Karyn couldn’t help but laugh. “In my experience, Steven Reekan is boorish, arrogant, and reckless. Maybe you know him better than me. But this… this is bad for Capston.”

“People blowing up is bad for Capston. Damn, we nearly lost our senior command in one in Allentown! How he and Wall survived all that time—”

“All that time? How long?” Karyn hadn’t spoken directly with the mayor in almost two weeks. She had enjoyed the silence.

“They wouldn’t have survived a week if they hadn’t found a bomb shelter. Steven’s healing some serious cuts to his right hand. They’re both malnourished and dehydrated.”

A week? The mayor of Capston was missing and presumed dead for seven days?

“You thought he was dead and you never thought to fill me in? Windows at five.” Karyn stood and faced the open panes as they darkened. Anyone below looking up would only see a silvery reflection.

They wouldn't see Karyn looking back. They weren't the only ones looking at the wrong side of one-way plexiglass.

"His vitals read he was still alive, but there was so much debris from the blast. The Allens couldn't even figure out where to begin digging."

"Okay, so you found him. And Wall. How many did you lose?"

"Only one."

Only one. Only one more casualty from terrorism, only *this* one could have been avoided if they'd stayed the hell out of Allentown. Karyn watched the people of Capston on the streets below. They rushed up and down, interweaving and crossing streets at corners. They said hello to some and ignored others. They bought street food. They gawked up at the artificial sky. They looked over their shoulders and hugged their loved ones a little tighter before leaving for work every morning.

And Reekan almost got himself *and* his executive killed. He got at least one officer killed. He might have made things worse.

"I have to tell Marribel, Ender. You know that."

Captain Ling stepped beside her, following her gaze on the busy downtown. "Do what you have to, Karyn. We only have one favour."

Karyn sighed. She knew she'd have to make the call. Just not under the present circumstances. "Just say it."

"We need our solicitor when we go to the DHC. We need Phil Fox."

Pixelate

The floor to ceiling projection in the gallery looked so real, Steven had to remind himself not to walk right into the artificial foliage. The climate controls even wafted the sweetness of dew-fall, the rich pungency of forest floor decay, and the sense-cleansing scent of pine and tamarack. All that was missing was the dripping from the forest canopy after a brisk rain.

Steven could live without all of it. The natural scents didn't help his nausea, still plaguing his stomach after a week of stale powdered rations. Sufficiently re-hydrated, he'd removed the intravenous tube against Holt's doctor's warning. There was too much to do to have a pole on swiveling wheels and a sloshing bag of water dragging behind him. He could have sworn the fluid was making him thirstier, anyway.

He stood alone in the gallery of the 93rd level, squinting at the whiteness of the decor. It was too white. Steven always felt safer in darkened rooms. Spaces where the colours were deeper, redder. Harder.

Holt Tower was soft. He had never realized how much until his return from Allentown. No wonder Phil Fox chose to keep his offices elsewhere. Steven cursed himself for allowing himself to become complacent.

"Ling told me I'd find you here." Steven didn't turn toward Jason Holt. The proprietor walked softly, as though he were afraid to poke a sleeping bear.

"You know, I used to be amazed how lifelike this is. I've been out there. I've seen it, smelled it, tasted it. But you know something, Jason?" Steven closed his eyes and cradled his bandaged right hand close to his chest. The infection had set deeply, despite Kenzy's best efforts to keep the wound clean. There was no telling the bacteria lurking beneath Allentown. "This doesn't look *anything* like the real world outside."

Jason Holt didn't dare stand too close. He leaned on the backrest of one of his white, lazy chairs. "You did your best, my friend."

You did your best. What a load of shit.

"Tell that to the Sheppard boys." A sharp pain shot through Steven's temples. There was nothing left in his gut to throw up. As soon as he and Kenzy had realized that the saboteurs had been trying to smoke the Sheppards and Connellys out of the sanctuary of Holt Tower—and that there was nothing he could do to stop it—Steven had realized that Paolo Desantos had won. Maybe not the war. But a key battle. And that pained him more than the dehydration, the undernourishment, the injuries, and the fatigue combined.

"It's terrible, just terrible." Holt sighed and twiddled his thumbs. "Keeping the news from the Connelly family, that's been hard."

"About that, Jason." Steven turned away from the screen and glared at him. He was so put together. Hair combed perfectly straight. Suit and jacket pressed and trim. And behind the outward luxury, Steven detected uncharacteristic worry in the proprietor's comportment. "How is it that the Connelly family weren't on that Tan-Ro copter?"

"And thank goodness. Losing the Sheppards, after they lost so much already…"

"Ling tells me you forced her hand."

"It wasn't like that."

"Then tell me *how* it was."

Holt reached out in a gesture for Steven to sit. "I admit, I lost my temper. You know how that Lorrie kid is—"

"You got into an argument *with a sixteen-year-old!*" Steven glowered. He didn't need a mirror to know his face was reddening. "We had a deal. Seventy-two hours."

"Ling had no idea you were missing in action! And you'd be proud to know the captain held onto your orders—she's no pushover. But if we knew what was going on in Allentown—"

Steven swung his good hand at a porcelain vase perched on a glass-topped end-table, sending it crashing to the floor. "And if you weren't trying to impress your new girlfriend, maybe a kid wouldn't have got you so worked up!"

Jason held his breath as the fragments scattered on the floor. The vase could have been a priceless heirloom, and it could have been a cheap knock-off. As long as it didn't damage the projection. He might have tested negative, but Steven could have sworn the red tide was fomenting inside of him.

"Let's just be thankful the Connelly family didn't take that flight." Holt spoke as though he were ready to duck and hide.

"Of course, they're lucky to be alive. Did you explain to Charles and Warren that it was your hard-on for Clara that saved their lives?"

"That's enough, Steven! You can be pissed at me all you want, but that doesn't change anything."

As much as it hurt to admit, Jason was right. Blame couldn't change anything. The Sheppard brothers were gone. The Connellys had survived, even if by dubious decision-making. Paolo Desantos was dead. The colonel of Motherland would surely retaliate—even if Steven had nothing to do with his assassination. The whole damned operation in Allentown might have yielded undeniable proof that the Motherlanders were the terrorists. But in reality, it had only lit a long fuse.

The implications made him dizzy. Steven lowered himself onto the same sofa Cadlen Sheppard had sat on that first day they'd met, cross-legged, drawing in silence. So young. So talented.

"It would be best if we moved the Connellys to a new location. There's no guarantee the danger has passed."

"I would agree with you, but Clara—*Mrs. Connelly*, she won't agree to that. And I can't imagine her husband and her son will go without her."

"They'll go if I say they're going." Steven ground his teeth. "I've got no time for Clara and her attitude."

"So you'd send them to Ap-Oz? And what do you tell them when they show up and the Sheppards aren't there?"

As soon as he'd said it, Jason winced. If the man was trying not to provoke him, he was doing a poor job of it. Steven measured his response.

"I'm sorry, for all of this, Jason. You've been nothing but gracious. And I know how Lorrie Sheppard can… could be. He was just an angry kid. Lost his parents way too young." Julia Sheppard died of complications from long-term red tide. Dianna Langley had just walked out on the Reekan family. Steven's chest tightened.

"Whoever took down your copter, they would assume all six were on board, wouldn't they? The Connellys are as good as dead to your attackers. Capston—all of New Inland already thinks they're dead. Let me keep them here, Steven. They can stay on the 93rd. No one will know."

Jason was right. There was no more danger in keeping them in the tower than trying to move them. Until the debris from the Tan-Ro was found, the cause of the crash was unknown. Maybe it was sabotage. Maybe it was targeted by a smart missile. Maybe that long fuse ended at a stick of dynamite hidden in the cargo hold. Steven's temples throbbed at the thought of the brothers disintegrating in a burst of energy.

"Fine. Keep your girlfriend and her family here. But they don't leave the 93rd. So, if you want to screw her, you better find an unoccupied janitor closet, because your office is off limits. Clear?"

"You think the worst of me, after all I've done." Jason Holt stood. "I know this is tearing you apart, Steven. But you're not in it alone." The words rang hollow.

The elevator chimed and its doors swooshed open. Captain Ling emerged, uncharacteristically dressed down in casual dress.

"If this is a bad time…" Ender glanced between Steven and Jason.

"I was just leaving." Jason glided behind her into the elevator.

Steven turned away as the doors shut.

"It's fine." Steven motioned for the captain to sit in the white chair opposite his sofa. Ender sat, leaning forward onto her thighs.

"I spoke with Miss Kendall."

Steven sighed. "Out with it."

"She's sorry to hear about Allentown, and the loss of Swift. She's also upset that we kept her out of the loop."

"I'm sure she is. Last time I checked, Karyn Kendall is an interim solicitor, not a member of my executive."

Ender tilted her head slightly. "Technically, no. But you *did* agree to her appointment in Phil Fox's two-month absence." He had no choice, really. Kendall had the qualifications, if not her full certification. She was a proxy. But the right proxy.

"Will she summon Fox?"

"She said she would try. Hasn't spoken to him since he left. But Fox isn't the only one she's calling."

"She wouldn't." Steven seethed. "Not until Fox is back. Marribel will listen to him."

The look in Ender's eyes told him she'd already made the call. Steven's stomach heaved but nothing spewed from his mouth but vitriol.

"Marribel. Easton. Pierre. All of them—they're hypocrites. They *all* have people in Allentown!"

A surge of energy coursed through Steven's body. Springing to his feet, he seized the glass end-table with both hands, pain searing through his bandage. Ender hollered, but he couldn't discern the words. With a twist and a lunge, Steven hurled the table straight into the projection screen. Instead of sailing through the greenery, it shattered against the panel, showering glass in all directions. The lush forest crackled and fragmented into a kaleidoscopic array of ever-decreasing squares and lines, until all of the green and brown dots flashed sickly white. All the trees, the dead leaves and fallen needles, the flitting insects and scurrying rodents—gone in one giant burst of light. The natural smells gave way to burning metal and polymers, fraying and frying electronics sizzling before the sprinklers activated. Showers rained from the ceiling. Steven closed his eyes and aimed his face upward and the water ran in rivulets down his unshaven cheeks, tracing the Foundry spark scars.

"Steven, what have you done?" The pleading voice sounded as much like Ender Ling as Dianna Langley. Steven opened his eyes. The gallery lights pixelated in intermittent red pulses, turning the furniture, floors, and decor crimson.

Pixels. It's all we are. The trees. The animals. The Sheppards. Jason Holt and Clara Connelly. Dianna Langley...

Mercy

Monday, 25 June AC 0245
9 km North of Inland Open-Pit Mine
Ian Null

Null couldn't believe the old man fell asleep while being stitched. Once the hot poker had cauterized the deepest open wounds, everything else must have been fairly pedestrian by measure of pain. Unaccustomed to needing any sort of bedside manner, Null was relieved the man fell unconscious. Upon learning his patient was a Reaper, it became easier to dismiss the pain his stitch work would cause.

While the old man slept, Null's curiosity won and he retrieved the medallion from Raël's pocket. A Reaper totem, shiny and silver, save for the smudges of blood and pocket lint. The old man had been wise to conceal his membership in the cult. They were silent, hooded creatures that spoke in tongues and carried open flames in the palms of their hands. At least that was the way he imagined them as a small boy. As he neared adulthood, those images became haggard, ugly, diseased golems that skulked in shadows and looted graveyards. As a young officer in the Motherland militia, he'd seen the graves dug up and empty, tombs looted of not only valuables, but the bodies themselves. Someone once suggested that the Reapers ground up the bones they harvested and sold the powder overseas. Fertilizer, magick ingredients, aphrodisiacs. Even the Kayewati avoided them.

Null cleaned his operating tools and returned them to his kit. He sat on the ottoman and leaned forward once again, holding the totem in his hands, its chain dangling freely between his knees. The pendant was cross-shaped, the top-most appendage a loop, while the short cross-arms and the main shaft flared out at the ends. An *ankh*, it was once called. A classic symbol co-opted by this modern cult of death. Null had never understood its power or significance until the day

Andreas thrust it in the air in the rotunda. From his position on the stage, he had remained stoic, eyes fixed on the talisman. As the clouds broke, radiant light reflected, piercing his aviator glasses lenses. Captain Alvara's guards had swarmed the fanatic, but not before Null had seen unhinged lunacy in Andreas's eyes.

Andreas. This man knows him…

"You have seen one of these before."

Raël's voice startled Null to attention, nearly causing him to drop the pendant. He tossed it into the old man's lap.

"The injuries are severe." He turned to the kitchenette. "As you say, you won't likely survive."

Raël didn't open his eyes. "And still, you wasted your supplies and your time to close my wounds. I would expect nothing less of you, *Lieutenant-Colonel.*"

"My name is Ian Null." He spat the words through clenched teeth.

"Of course it is," Raël answered, his eyes remaining shut. "Mind you, *Ian Null* looks an awful lot like *Paolo Desantos…*"

Null stormed over to the man who had begun to smile as he shifted in the easy chair. He grasped the man by the shirt he had since refastened over the bandaged wounds, hauling him within centimeters of his own face. Raël kept his eyes closed.

"Now there's that legendary Desantos anger," he mumbled, wincing from the pain of his upheaval. The words slashed across Null's chest with the pain of a cauterizing poker. Raël open his slitted eyes. They were reddening and the corners pooled with tears. He set the man back into the cushions and sat back on the ottoman.

"You do *not* know who I am, old man."

The man sighed. "No, son, I most certainly don't. But I do indeed *recognize* you."

"And how is that? You don't even look at me as we speak."

With that, the man opened his eyes revealing veined whites around his deep blue irises.

"It was only when I closed my eyes, that I knew who you were."

Ian Null. Paolo Desantos. Who am I… His own eyes began to burn. "Soon enough, they will be closed forever."

As if on cue, the old man closed his eyes again and smiled. "Then I will know you forever, *Paolo.*"

The Reaper drifted into another uneasy sleep and Null paced the common room's rickety floor. The sun would soon be rising. He packed his rucksack, keeping a sideways view of the sleeping old man in the chair. His chest still rose and fell. At any moment, he expected it to stop.

Null swallowed the next dose of his radiation medicine and washed it down with the last mouthful of cold green tea. One last look around the room, and he turned for the door. His boot struck the Reaper pendant, clattering it across the floor and startling Raël awake.

"Remember. My belongings are yours now. My horse isn't fast, but she's sturdy enough to get you to Moab."

"Moab?"

"The Ansati city. Well, it used to be a city. Today, it's a ghost town."

Null cursed himself under his breath. If he hadn't been so clumsy, he could have slipped out and left the old man to die.

"You know Andreas."

Raël coughed, hard enough for Null to check his bandages for fear they'd split. Dropping the rucksack to the floor, he steadied the old man by the shoulders as the spasms calmed. He sat back on the ottoman.

"Andreas—that is how you know who I am."

Raël opened his eyes and tears leaked onto his spotted and scarred cheeks. "I know Andreas. I *knew* Andreas…"

"My father banished him to Kayewat."

Raël nodded softly. "Kayewat couldn't contain him, Paolo."

"He has returned?"

The old man sniffled. Null watched the old man shudder. He grabbed the water-skin from his rucksack and forced a mouthful of water to Raël's lips.

"Andreas is very sick."

That was an understatement. Still, for a fellow Ansati to admit as much—it must have been even worse than Null could imagine. A faint line of red seeped through Raël's shirt. The wound must have opened in the last wave of spasms.

The wounds.

"He did this to you." Null's eyes widened. *If he could do this to one of his own…*

"The red is in him. It makes people do awful things."

Red tide. Andreas had apparently survived the sickness, but not without a terrible cost. Null knew full well what the red tide could do. He had been too late to stop Commander Yael from committing awful crimes to a community of innocent people. The girl in the barn. The terrified glare in her eyes flashed behind his eyes as though it were imprinted on his irises.

"I have maps in my cart that will guide you to Moab. If you choose."

"I am not going to Moab. I have left Andreas in my past, and I intend to keep it so."

"Can I ask you, Paolo?"

Null shifted on the ottoman. He knew what the old man was about to ask.

"Why have you left?"

This time, Null closed his eyes. The scourge scars on his back itched. The scars in his memory stung all the time.

"I am leaving my name. You call me *Paolo*. Paolo is dead. I am *Null*—no one of consequence."

Raël leaned forward, straining his bandages, but composing himself as though he were twenty years younger and in full health. His hair fell in gentle waves around his face.

"You are running from your father. But you don't know your *family.*"

"I know my mother died before I could remember her. She had no family left. And I know that after my grandfather passed away, my grandmother left my father for De Léon to raise as a ward."

Raël groaned, but stayed upright, resting his wrinkled hand on Null's knee. "You know what Tirel Desantos told you. But you don't know the whole story."

"Who says I want to know more than that?" Null shook Raël's hand from his knee.

"*You* do, Paolo. If only you listened."

Both men sat in silence for a long minute.

"I thank you… *Brother Raël.* Your horse and cart will help me reach the mountains much faster."

Raël slumped back against the chair cushions, for likely the last time. Null picked up his rucksack and slung it over one shoulder. Before turning for the door, he tucked the medical kit under the old man's arm.

"Moab is empty now. You'll be able to replenish your supplies. But if you change your mind, find the Ossuary. Search your family name. *Then*, decide if you still have to make for the mountains."

Null looked one last time upon the Ansati. He remembered how pitiful the Junquer looked the day he'd purchased his handheld. The key. It had set him free from his old life. Just as Paolo Desantos had set the Junquer free from his own. He couldn't bear to see the shriveled up, leprous tinkerer suffer.

Like Jamiss after contamination, Brother Raël wasn't long for this world. Ian Null nodded farewell and slipped out the door.

Thirty Aught-Six

Wednesday, 26 June AC 0245
Gasperro
Phil Fox

Traveling before sunrise had its benefits. Under cover of darkness, Phil and Le_Renard could slip out from Gasperro into the Bay of Green relatively unnoticed. According to the old man, any local brigands were too lazy to get up before dawn. Out on the open water of the strait, it might be a different story. But at least they had time to round the cape and plot their course before any pirates caught wind of their movement. More than just the stealth, though, it meant Phil wouldn't be able to see the cemetery on Burnside-on-the-hill. As the sloop cut silently through the rippled water, Phil pretended it wasn't even there. And as if he could read his mind, Le_Renard said nothing, only focused on the navigation screen, and guided the sloop along its tangential course. Knowledge of the general routes—and how to avoid them—that's how you moved around on a lawless sea in a lawless time.

Phil had convinced Le_Renard to sleep at Albert's house in Gasperro so they could slip away quickly. It took some convincing. The Homestead was well guarded with security sensors. The village was as well, to some degree. But even the diligence of the harbour master couldn't guarantee that no one from the outside would be able to drop in. Even in Albert's flat, the old man wore a wig and false beard. Something had him spooked good.

Once aboard, Le_Renard ducked below deck and inspected the cargo. Phil stayed topside. It was just as well he not know what goods the "Sly Fox" had smuggled out of the frozen north. Whatever it was, it was small enough to conceal in the hold. No cargo crates of food or textiles. And the Rust bonds, of course, he kept on his person in a breast pocket, every so often patting them to be sure they were still there.

Phil wrapped his shoulders with a microfiber poncho to keep the sea breeze from chilling him. A tumbler of warm tea helped. The forecast called for clear skies and a slight breeze, not enough to affect their fuel consumption. A nine-hour voyage would take closer to eleven, accounting for their deviation from the standard course. Le_Renard knew who would be out on the water, where, and when. Just to be safe, he gave Phil a quick rundown of the firearms available if the need arose. The last time he fired one he had been in Le_Renard's company, only both were about ten years younger. He wondered how often the old man had had to use them in the years since.

Around the cape and north-north east, Le_Renard guided the sloop out into the middle of the strait where the water was deepest, veering close to the Jackson pier without getting too close. The broken fragments of another pier lay dangerously beneath the surface, providing an unseen barrier to interlopers. The scanners swept for miles. Every time a dot appeared on the concentric circles on the screen, Le_Renard casually identified them, although he had no way of confirming any of them. "Capers, there. Oh, wait, they have company—ho-ho, look! Dunesmen, they don't want Capers in their shoals. Funny, though, they're *both* out of season…"

Phil half-listened to Le_Renard ramble on about the drama between the different families out on the strait, as though it were a serial program. Advertising spots and "tune in next week", and it would be like watching Ranger Man. The classic western drama based around a Sascotan outlaw working the badlands used to bother him when he was young. His father, Lucas Fox, hated how it stereotyped Sascota as the wild west, and Sascotans as little more than vagabonds and rogues. His biological father, Emmanuel Jackson, scoffed at the notion. He knew *real* wilderness. It had forced him to become Le_Renard_Subtil.

It was mid-afternoon when the first real sign of trouble emerged. The blips came and went, usually fishing trawlers, with the odd pleasure craft darting in and out of the travel lanes. One kept creeping closer, as though it were tracking the sloop from a safe distance before making its mind to intercept. Le_Renard set the autopilot and ducked below deck, reemerging with a long-barreled rifle.

"Modified M1, thirty-aught-six," he explained. "These were good enough to snipe up to a kilometer away. Plenty enough for us! Huh!"

Le_Renard had weapons hidden everywhere, it seemed. Some were state-of-the-art, with sensors in the grips so only he could fire them. But back in Gasperro and Spruce Grove, the old man relied on the classics. Models that were either passed down over decades, even centuries, or facsimiles rebuilt from what remaining parts could be found. Like the FTE buggy, only deadly.

"I'll give him a friendly warning." The old man crouched over the console and keyed open the comm.

`Nothing for you here. Move along. Only warning.`

Phil's brow wrinkled as he leaned closer to the radar screen. The blip circled upon reception of Le_Renard's warning. After some consideration, it continued to encroach on their position. The Sly Fox chuckled.

"Enter the aught-six." Phil crouched below the rail, peering in the direction of the mainland shore. The unwanted visitor had emerged from Massiemi Bay, where the river wove deep into the heavily forested settlements known to harbour brigands. Le_Renard perched the forearm of the rifle upon the railing, bringing his right eye to the scope. Phil could have sworn the old man was humming a tune under his breath. The sloop lilted in the late afternoon breeze. Even the shore birds that squealed and wheeled in the sky over the strait had gone silent, as though they knew what was coming. Phil knew his father would see the power boat before they saw him.

A crack split the sky. The approaching craft was too far off to hear if anyone was crying out in pain or despair. There was no smoke, no flare of light, no panic. Instead, the blip that represented the brigands halted. Le_Renard muttered a challenge for them to come closer as he reloaded, sliding the bolt action with a click. When the dot retreated back toward the bay, he sighed in disappointment. Patting the pocket where he kept the bonds, he huffed and set the rifle on the deck beside him. It would remain within arm's reach for the rest of the trip.

179

The Lighthouse Keeper

Wednesday, 26 June AC 0245
Bas-Étang Island
Phil Fox

With no further incidents, Phil and Le_Renard guided the Jackson sloop away from the visible coast into the gulf, putting distance between themselves and anyone tracking their movements. The scuffle between a crew of coastal brigands and Le_Renard's thirty-aught-six would have been witnessed—word of mouth moved quickly despite the limited means. The old man might live an incognito life in the maritime coast, but Emmanuel Jackson's name carried a certain gravitas, whether on the open water or deep under the forest canopy. If they only knew about the fox in their henhouse…

"That's it… Huh! Looks like they closed off the dunes. Bring'er northeast, 'bout thirty degrees should do it." Clouds had moved in, and the old man had gone below deck, emerging with his yellow, rubber jacket and rain hat. For someone who wanted to draw as little attention to himself as possible, he had no trouble dressing up like an old-time seaman in an outfit any pair of sturdy binoculars could spot from shore.

Phil spun the spindled wheel and guided the sloop away from the approaching sandbars of *Bas-Etang*. The marshy island offered few points of entry from the sea, and less by land. The old bridge was long sunk into the gulf, and the few who remained on the mossed and mucked island preferred to keep disconnected. The sloop was shallow-hulled enough to be able to skirt the northern shore, but they'd have to wade a few hundred yards. Phil sighed. He'd wear the rubber chest waders, but he was not going to put on that stupid hat.

The sun was waning but they had a few hours of natural light yet. Phil dropped anchor and opened the cabin door, resigned to having to wear the rubber suit for their amphibious assault. Le_Renard raised a hand.

"Hold on. If the dunes are closed, Fisher will expect us." The old man sat at the comm and switched on the screen. Two blips appeared, but they were small, and their movement indicated they weren't interested in the Jacksons.

```
Calling F. Supplies for textiles. EJ
```

After a few minutes, Phil caught the glint of a light in a tall structure just up the coast. The comm read back a response.

```
Confirm EJ.
```

"Confirm? Fisher's tightening up," grumbled Le_Renard. "Okay, I'll confirm."

```
FTE2075.
```

It wasn't a very clever code. "Front Toward Enemy", followed by the incorporation year of Jackson Auto. Le_Renard wasn't concerned. "Confirmation code, my ass. Fisher's already scanned us. That's all for show."

"So, this fisherman is going to just let us come ashore?" Phil reached for the door again.

"*Fisherman?* Huh! This old fart has the sea legs of a Capston lawyer. No offense…" Ten years ago, the jibe would have hurt. Today, it was a term of endearment. "No, he's no fisherman. *Fisher*, that's his name. Pretty common one where he comes from."

Before he could ask again, Phil heard the buzz drifting over the rippling early evening surf. Within seconds, the rubber-hulled dinghy bobbed up against the sloop. A figure even more cartoonish than Old-Man-of-the-Sea Jackson waved his hand and tossed a guy-rope over the rail. He cackled as Le_Renard secured the line to the mooring.

"Well, if the code wasn't enough, that outfit sure'n hell is! Still have that getup, do ya?"

Le_Renard reached for Fisher's hand and coughed through a belly laugh. "Think I can just go to the store and buy a new one? Seen good and plenty of rough seas with this'n. Huh!"

As the two bantered, their accents thickened almost to the point Phil could barely keep up. He'd heard it before. Traders that came to port in Gasperro from a certain northerly origin spoke the same. It made sense, now.

Fisher. The most common Kayewati name, Le_Renard once told him.

"Supplies, y'say? Prol'ly need a tow skiff. You fellas come ashore— you're not sailing back tonight, are yas?" Fisher squinted. His smile looked like a dull saw blade, every other tooth missing, the rest black and rusty.

"Sounds like an invite! Whaddaya say, my boy?"

Fisher's eyes widened, his deep brown pupils floating in sickly yellow. "Your boy, here? So y'wasn't shittin' me!"

"All grown up, ready to take over the shop." Le_Renard rapped Phil's shoulder almost enough to knock him into the dinghy. "Trust the sloop'll be safe here?"

Fisher nodded. "You c'd fire off a flare and spell 'take me' in the sky, and y'd be safe. C'mon, soups on!"

The three boarded the raft and made for shore. The structure that had flashed the light emerged as a white-painted lighthouse, vertical in the evening air of *Bas-Étang*. The low marsh that gave the island its name was cropped with few trees, splotched with wide bogs and swampy lakes. You can't walk across the island without a walking stick, Le_Renard had told him. There were spots where the moss was a carpet over bottomless marsh muck. Use the stick to see if there's solid ground before you take a step. As they stepped ashore, Phil regretted not wearing the rubber waders.

"I'll have the rouses load yer supplies. We'll lug your *textiles* first light."

Phil looked out on the water. Another watercraft was approaching the sloop, a small crew of three or four "rouseabout" workers shuffling and coordinating their task. Fisher went on to explain that he kept a small but loyal retinue of labourers on the island. The threat of being sent to Kayewat and submitting to the stamp process was enough to buy their loyalty. Phil accepted Fisher at his word. If Le_Renard trusted him…

A short hike to the lighthouse, and Phil breathed easy for the first time since they'd shipped out from Gasperro. The inside was deceivingly spacious. Comfortable chairs and a roaring fireplace reminded him of the Jackson Homestead, except for the concentric spiral staircase that coiled up to the higher levels. The aroma of fresh-baked bread and rich stew wafted throughout the tower. If they had to stay the night, Phil could imagine worse scenarios.

The Lighthouse Keeper, as he was known on the mainland, was a gracious host. "Make y'rselves home," he slurred after guiding Phil and Le_Renard up the spiral stair to the bunks. There was plenty of food in the galley, as he called the kitchenette. Extra blankets in the armoir. And total security, as if they were hidden in the Spruce Grove, nestled into the Homestead with state-of-the-art security measures armed to the teeth. Those were Fisher's words. *Should I take his word on anything to do with teeth…*

Despite the Kayewati trader's assurances, Phil couldn't fully rest. The bunk was soft and warm. His belly was full. There was no one from Bas-Étang to Bermude who would know who he was and why he was even there. It wasn't enough to allow him to drift into a proper sleep. Movement from the uppermost level stirred him enough to open his eyes in the salty-aired darkness. Making himself at home, Phil swung his feet to the floor and climbed the spiral stairs.

The topmost level of the lighthouse was laid out just as he'd imagined. Glassed-in with one-way tinted panels allowed for the beacon beam to flash its warning to approaching watercraft. The message was two-fold. The coast is shallow. And company is not wanted.

"If y'r hungry, you went the wrong way, feller." Fisher slouched in a woven wicker chair looking out onto the ink-black sea.

"Couldn't sleep. Just used to my own bunk, that's all." It was a partial truth.

Fisher raised his arm and pointed off to the coast. "Look close. You can see y'r boat. Anything gets close, we'll know."

He'd explained that sensors would alert the tower to any intruders. Phil gazed into the darkness half hoping something would swim up alongside the sloop to prove it.

"I'm sure it's fine." Phil squeezed his eyes, blinking away sleep sand. "How come you're up so late?"

Fisher chuckled through closed lips. "Y'could say I couldn't sleep neither. We din't sleep so good in Kay'wat. Y'r old man, he'd tell y'as much."

If only.

"He doesn't say much about Kayewat—at least not since we've been home." Phil wasn't sure what to expect from the lighthouse keeper. Everyone from Kayewat had their secrets.

"Can't say I blame the ol' fart." Fisher continued watching the darkness outside the glass panels. It was as unsettling as it was serene. "Not my story to tell, feller. 'Magine he'll spill when he's good'n ready. But I know he got spooked good up there."

Le_Renard was obviously hiding from something or someone. Fisher's confirmation only made Phil more curious. Le_Renard_Subtil had crossed a lot of people over his lifetime. Phil Fox had first heard his name when he was still a young man in Sascota. The reputation of the outsider frontiersman preceded him—criminal mastermind, smuggler, trafficker.

Killer.

The infamy surrounding the old man had him on even ground with the Reapers.

"My father gets agitated whenever I try to bring up Kayewat. I've never known him to be… afraid."

"Ah, I r'member one time he was *really* 'fraid." Fisher finally turned to face Phil, his squinty eyes and jagged smile wide. "When he was tinkerin' in that g'rage of his, that same damned buggy he's itchin' to finish. Bay door was open, and in walks this lass—but she's carryin' a babe wrapped up like a bedroll. She leaves the lil' bundle-a-joy right on the hood and walks away. Er, that's how he tells it!"

Phil swallowed. Le_Renard had told him that his birth mother was from the coast, but had more than a few bad habits she couldn't escape.

Fisher sighed. "He was scared witless, feller. Man could go toe to toe with the meanest sumbitches y'ever met. But a lil' *baby*…"

"I doubt he's running from another baby."

"Ndeed." Fisher leaned his elbows on his knees. "But if he's this scared, it's for *you*, feller."

Phil already knew it. There was something about how the old man never let eye contact hang more than a second. How his jokes and his nervous tics landed a little less hapless. How determined he was to fix the roof. The buggy.

Everything.

It was as if he was on borrowed time.

"We'll have yer nuke-cell loaded to yer boat before sunrise. I know yer old man has the bonds." Fisher stood and, true to his name, fished out a small device about a quarter the size of a handheld. He twiddled it in his dirty fingers.

"This is for yer old man," Fisher whispered. "Came t'me a while back, but I wouldn't risk sending it. Comes from Kayewat—urgent message, I'm told. But promise me, don't let on till yer back at the house, kay?"

The lighthouse keeper offered the device to Phil just as the light beam flashed out to the sloop. Phil spun in the direction of the laser light and Fisher shrunk away into the shadow, retracting his hand and the correspondence in its grip.

"Watch, pod a-dolphins! See?" Fisher gestured to the window as though Phil would actually see anything.

"How do you know?" Phil strained to make out any shapes in the stillness of the shallows.

"Cause there's no gunshots." The rouseabout workers must have been on watch. Phil's eyes were just starting to adjust to the brightness when the beam extinguished. It must have been dolphins, after all. He closed his eyes to stifle the residual light. Before he could open them, he felt Fisher's clammy hand tucking the device into his own.

"Not till yer home," Fisher whispered. "And you can tell 'im it's from Walpurgis."

Rules of the Road

Wednesday, 27 June AC 0245
45 km WNW of Farbend Trading Post
Crystal Sheppard

For three days rumbling through dense bushes, over dried patches of dying earth and back into oases lush with leafy canopies and mossy floors, Crystal and her captors pressed on. She had seen a drastic change in their temperament, particularly Hewer, once they had realized she was of greater value than simply a tradable commodity. Hamm and Duncam avoided interacting with her as much as possible since Hewer had made the decision to hold onto her. She was negotiating from a position of weakness. At any time, the brigands could change their minds. They could take her handheld to the Rust contact in Farbend and sell her, like they had originally planned. They owed her nothing. Integrity was fleeting on the outside.

And still, for three days, the brigands stuck to the plan. Wake, cover tracks, travel, stop, eat, travel, eat, travel, sleep, repeat. Conversation lacked what life on the road delivered in plenty—stories, sights, insights. Every passing stranger, every roadside stall selling vegetables and raw meats, every abandoned house or wrecked car—everything had a story of its own. Sometimes they blurted it all out, like the nomad that wouldn't give Hewer a full canteen of potable water until he'd told his life's story. The guy was down on his luck, but not stupid, Hewer told her later in the cargo hold while Hamm drove. The guy was tedious, but trustworthy. And that was more valuable than the ten minutes spent listening. The water trader dribbled words through broken and half-rotten teeth, but he'd traded an invaluable resource for only a few Rust credits. Not everyone in this region even accepted Rust credit. If Hewer was indeed good on his word, Crystal would need to convert Hyacynthien money into Rust credit if she was going to make it on her own to Ozarck.

Assuming, of course, they were good on their word.

It was mid-morning, and Hewer was at the wheel. Crystal sat in the passenger seat, her backside chafing from dirty pants scuffing on cracked and torn vinyl-covered cushions. The air was cool—not quite Hyacynthe, but closer to New Inland's climate-controlled breeze in the Hanging Gardens. Hewer gazed at the road, both hands on the steering wheel. He had moments when he would go silent for long stretches. Hamm had advised her to just leave him be. He was probably thinking about Jamiss, his wayward son who was prone to irrational outbursts amidst his long-term red tide symptoms. The boy hated scavenging, and hated his bosses even more. Hewer knew they would push him. He'd only hoped that they wouldn't send the boy home in a zipped-up body-sized sack.

Hewer's handheld vibrated and a wailing alert siren jarred the driver awake from his daydream.

"I'd answer that, but I don't know how yours works." She really meant that she didn't know how to respond to an incoming transmission.

Hewer smiled, and released one hand from the wheel to press the answer toggle tab. A different alarm sounded, and Hewer slammed the brake pedal to the floor, grinding the big cargo truck to a halt and causing Hamm and Duncam in back to tumble and curse.

"What is it?"

Hewer didn't answer. He gripped the device in both hands and wove his index fingers and thumbs faster than Crystal could process. His thick brow wrinkled and his eyes widened.

"That is a Geiger counter application," Hewer breathed. "We can't go any further."

Radiation. Unless the brigands were keeping it from her, the party had no medical defense against it. Surely Rust would be able to sell them some Radiogardasse, like the prescription she'd filled for Ian Null all those weeks ago. Five days on the outside, not counting her time on the magna-rail, and this was the first time she'd encountered a dangerous radiation situation. They weren't supposed to be traveling close to any seams. Something unexpected had happened. She could see it on Hewer's dirty face.

Duncam poked his head through the partition and cussed. "Fuckin' hell, Hewer! What's going on up here?" As soon as he finished speaking, he recognized the Geiger alert, regret falling over his expression. "Shit, how high is it?"

"Not high. We got a transmission from Aynslie."

"What did she say?" Duncam reached a hand back through the partition to hush Hamm who was still grumbling.

"*She* says there's been a radiation leak, from a harvested thresher reactor. Keep the Geiger app on, go wide around, meet in Carroway."

"You don't look like you believe her, boss."

Hewer had enunciated "she" with obvious doubt. "Because the transmission didn't come from Aynslie's account. And, we're still too far out of tower range for her to send."

Hamm emerged from the rear, a quizzical dirty face alongside Duncam. "Then who sent it?"

Hewer tossed the wailing device onto the dash. "No one. At least that's what the account name says." Crystal narrowed her eyes. Anonymity was no stranger to her work, but even the doctors who filled prescriptions outside of the rules used the pseudonym Jonathan Doherty. A client could use any name as long as it was registered somewhere. No one could buy from Lacraie without a name at all. Rules really were different on the outside.

"Did she say anything about your son?" The pair of henchmen, heads bobbing through the partition like hand-puppets knew enough not to ask. Crystal suspected she already knew the answer as soon as she asked.

Hewer only shook his head and shifted the big truck into drive. The petrol engine gargled and revved as he swung wide the wheel. No one said anything else for the rest of the morning, and for about half the afternoon.

Deny

After backtracking a few kilometers, Hewer steered the truck off-road through high grass and rooted terrain without slowing down. The Geiger alert had fallen silent on the dashboard. Crystal gripped the armrests as Hewer plowed on through abandoned roadways and trails before emerging onto a smoother, more-traveled path. Her stomach rumbled, only a murmur drowned by the engine's roar. Hewer hit the brakes again, only this time the brigands in the cargo hold didn't shout or complain. He keyed off the ignition and grabbed his device from the dash, thrusting wide the driver-side door. Crystal unfastened her safety straps and leaned forward, her eyes squinting in the glint of sun off the untarnished chrome spots on the hood. Waves of heat rippled, and the form of a fallen body laying across the road wriggled some twenty meters ahead.

Hewer's big boots hit the ground and he strode in the direction of the body just as the rear cargo doors clanked open. Crystal grimaced as the now-familiar Geiger alert wailed to life again. Whoever was laying in the road was emitting enough of a radiation signature to set off the app on Hewer's device.

"Stop!" Crystal cupped her hands around her mouth and yelled out of instinct before she opened her own door. "Stay back!"

Hamm and Duncam stopped at her side. "Is it him?" Duncam called to Hewer who had not stopped, only increasing his haste. The Geiger app screamed as the big man knelt alongside the lifeless body. Without looking up, he hollered, his voice straining.

"Bring her here! *Now!*"

Hamm pushed Crystal between her shoulder blades causing her

head to jerk. "You heard him, you're up, doc!"

Crystal spun and slapped his arm. "Don't push me! And I told you, I'm not a doctor!"

Hamm stepped into her personal space, nearly nose to nose. "I told you, get moving!"

"Make me!"

"*NOW!*" Hewer's voice crackled like radio static. It was clear they didn't have to make it to Carroway to find Jamiss. He had found them.

Crystal stood, defying Hamm as Duncam protested. They weren't stupid. They knew what the radiation meant, and they weren't going a step closer. And they thought they could make her do it.

"*PLEASE! IT'S MY BOY…*" Hewer's bark melted in a caterwaul, discordant with the screaming Geiger alert. Crystal turned away from Hamm. Hewer was on both knees, cradling the body in his shaking arms, ignoring the poison leeching from his son. She was still too far away to notice any welts or burns on his exposed face, neck, or hands.

Duncam grabbed her arm. "Listen, we gotta get out of here! If Jamiss has radiation, that means he has that *and* red tide! Hewer ain't gonna leave him, but *we* don't have to catch any of that shit!"

Crystal shook his hand from her forearm. She looked from the terrified eyes of Hamm and Duncam back to Hewer and Jamiss. The sun above burned down on all of them.

What if it was Robbie? Or Lorrie, or Cadlen? Or Ian Null? Or anyone…

It didn't matter who it was. Hewer, or his boy, or Aynslie, or the toothless water trader, or whoever sent the warning. Integrity was lacking in the outside world.

But it didn't have to lack in her.

She didn't offer an answer or an explanation to Hamm or Duncam. Crystal ran toward the father and son, dropping to her knees alongside Hewer. The boy in his arms was really a young man, though she understood that he must have still looked like a boy in his father's eyes. Like how Cadlen still looked like an eight-year-old in her memories.

Jamiss's face was mud-stained, but she could already see blotches of red rash—telltale signs of radiation burn. His torn shirt was still damp with blood, as though he had slaughtered livestock hours before. Without hesitation, Crystal pressed her fingers into the veins of his neck. She was amazed that there was still a pulse. Hewer read her body language and sat back, allowing her to assess his condition. She tilted her head and leaned her ear over his gaping mouth. Jamiss wheezed slowly, as though his lungs were half-full of mucus.

He's alive. But he's dying.

"Get the water jugs," Crystal ordered. "He's parched. And if you have any medicine at all, bring it to me!"

Hewer bolted for the cargo truck and Hamm and Duncam backed far away as he approached. Crystal wanted to judge the fair-weather associates as cowards. Still, they were following the ways of the outside world. It was a lawless land, and the only rule that mattered was that you did whatever you had to do to survive. If Hamm were the father and Hewer the gawker, he wouldn't have acted any differently. That was the rule.

But it isn't my rule.

A minute that felt like ten later and Hewer returned with two canteen jugs, a first-aid kit with a broken hinge, and the cleanest linen he could find. Crystal used every ounce of strength she had to lift the young man under his shoulders, dragging his feet as she hauled him off the roadway beneath wide-canopied trees. The spongy moss made for an adequate surface to lay him flat. She forced water to his lips, holding his head slightly to the left so he wouldn't choke. Half the water leaked over his cracked, bleeding lips. Crystal took some coiled gauze wrap and dabbed them. Jamiss's eyelids flickered.

"Jamiss? Stay quiet, I'm here to help." Crystal exhaled. With every passing second, the young man aged by years, yet somehow, retrogressed with every laboured breath. From his throat, a murmur emanated painfully, a futile attempt to communicate. His eyelids parted; the sclera that should have been white was a blood pool keeping his blue irises afloat. Jamiss moved his eyeballs until they found Crystal's.

"Get… away…"

Even in agony, in the final moments of his life, the boy was trying to save her from contamination. Crystal cupped her hand on his oozing, infected cheek. It didn't matter. If Hewer could get them to his Rust contact, they might be able to purchase some medicine—with any luck, iodine pills—clean clothes, and lots of fresh water. A thorough scrubbing with basic soap in a moving stream. The exposure was minimal, she reminded herself, so long as they didn't linger around the doomed boy.

Jamiss flexed and relaxed his fingers, tightening fists and releasing them as though he were breathing through his hands. Tears leaked out of his eyes, deep crimson droplets. His fever was so high Crystal could feel it pulsating from his forehead. Her mind raced through all the years of instructions on how to comfort a patient. She'd written in her quarterlies about what not to say to a patient in shock, in the final throes of death, comatose. All of it jumbled together as though every character in every data file somehow shook out of order and lay in a digital haystack, without a needle to be found. Every patient she'd practiced on were actual patients, but none had appeared as though they had already died and come back to life. None of them had posed any risk to her or anyone around her. None of them had gasped their last breath in her care.

"I… I… k-k…" Blood and saliva boiled from his mouth. "K-killed…" His eyes had shifted to the silhouette of his father, who knelt next to Crystal, shaking and exhausting his energy on keeping himself strong. "D-d-dad…"

Jamiss didn't finish what he was trying to say. His last breath seeped like a slow-leaking balloon, and his fists relaxed one last time. Crystal wiped the beaded sweat on his forehead as though he were still alive. So many things she wanted to say.

It came as a whisper. She wondered if Hewer heard the regret. She hoped Jamiss could.

"I'm not a doctor…"

The Human Factor

Monday, 2 July AC 0245
DHC Rotunda, New Inland
Mayor Steven Reekan

The DHC rotunda echoed every tiny sound when it was empty. Steven scratched his boot across the floor of the Capston mayoral desk and it could just as well have been a grinding wheel in the Foundries. The tap of his finger snapped like Chair Marribel's gavel. Even the wheezing of his breath whooshed like a Tan-Ro copter's twin blades.

He felt the weight of a glass plate pressing him flat, arms and legs splayed, unable to move. The DHC was the microscope. Marribel would appreciate the analogy. After decades of work in laboratories, she approached politics the same way—analysis, data, scientific method as ideology. No room for the human factor.

The Mayor of Heartsburg lacked heart. Irony of ironies.

New Inland's artificial daybreak had yet to rise and the chamber's lights were still dim after the overnight cleaners had punched out. Steven stared at the blue light of his datapad, propped at an angle that he could reread his prepared statement while leaning back against the cushions of his chair. The first dozen pages read with defiance, his eyes moving diligently across the text, his internal voice speaking with conviction. By the time he'd reached the twenty-page mark, he had come to realize he wasn't fooling himself. How in the hell would he convince Marribel? Anyone?

The chamber doors clicked and opened, echoing as though they were thrust open with two pounding fists. The tap of feet approaching the Capston pod were hammers on Foundry anvils. By the time the interim solicitor sat in the Second seat to his right, Steven's ears rang from his own imagination.

"It isn't like you to be here before the java is ready." Karyn Kendall's voice somehow dampened the acoustics around them. Or, she'd only cut through the echo inside his own head.

"Already had two back at the office." Steven waved a finger across the datapad screen, bringing his notes back to the opening comments. "The swill they serve here tastes like shit anyway."

Kendall chuckled. "Phil always said the same—in so many words, anyway. I thought I'd find you here. Figure we ought to go over your remarks."

"You like him, don't you?"

"Mayor Fox? He's a great boss, if that's what you're asking."

That was only half of it. "I mean, you like *him*, as a person. A friend." It was best to clarify that. He needed Karyn Kendall today.

"He is a friend, yes. A valued friend. Why?"

Steven reached for the datapad and pulled it face down. "What is it about him that you like? That Jennings Marribel likes?"

Kendall shifted in her seat. Her hair was pulled back in a business-like ponytail. As the artificial sunrise increased, her eyes brightened. "For starters, he's polite."

"Point taken. What else?"

"He's very smart, obviously. But he doesn't make others feel less smart."

She made a great point. Steven remembered all the times Phil spoke as Mayor, as Capston First Representative, even during their candidacy debates. His way with words was exceptional—he could express so much with such clarity, uncommon among lawyers. At least the ones he'd known. As a young man, he remembered the stiff-suited, heartless advocates his father had hired when he filed grievances with the Foundry. For so many years Hearn Reekan had been passed over for promotion. And when he paid steep fees for someone with all the right words to say in his defense, all they'd spoken was jargon and legalspeak. The whole ordeal had resulted in the advocates getting richer, and his father crawling into retirement with an underwhelming severance proposal.

Worse, the advocates Dianna Langley had hired were sharper than any machine in the Foundry. Not once did Steven's mother ever appear in court. Everything was delivered in prepared statements, which may not have even been her words. Young Steven heard the advocate read them, but they sounded nothing like his mother. Then again, he'd done all he could to forget Dianna Langley's voice.

Steven shook his head to clear the memory. None of that mattered today.

"That must be it. He knows how *not* to sound like a lawyer."

Kendall crossed her legs. "I met him in my second year at the Arcadian Bar Academy. I could have gone anywhere—I fielded offers from abroad, Arctica, even Hyacynthe when it was an option. But where I really wanted to go was Sascota. The Bar Association there is tops. Ask anyone."

"So, why didn't you?"

"Because they turned me down," Kendall huffed, bobbing her ponytail. "Quite a shot to the ego, that was. Worked my ass off, had all my ducks in a row. When I sent the application, I figured I'd be accepted as soon as I hit the send tab."

"Arcadia is great, I hear."

"Oh, it's excellent. In the end, I made out just fine. But when I found out I was articling with a Sascotan lawyer, it was all I could think about. So, I was introduced to Phil Fox. And he was as friendly as you would imagine. Firm, but fair. He expected you to put in the work."

Steven tried to imagine a younger Phil Fox, interns clamouring to work under him. He couldn't picture it. "And the rest is history, I suppose?"

"Not quite. I worked in his office for months before I finally had the courage to ask him. Where did I go wrong in my application to Sascota? What was I missing?" Kendall sighed. "He looked at me and said Karyn, you have all the tools—always have. But there's one thing Sascota looks for. They want to know *who* you are. Not who you *think* you are."

What the hell does that mean?

Kendall continued as if she'd heard him ask. "I spent so much time trying to convince the recruitment committee that I could say all the right words, that I knew what they were looking for. And in so doing, I didn't tell them *who I am.* That I enjoy reading and listening to the classics. That I used to take my little sister to the shows. That we kept a garden. That I played racquet sports."

"But what does any of that have to do with being a lawyer?"

"It means everything, Mayor Reekan."

Steven turned his eyes to the Chair's pod. In a few hours, Jennings Marribel would be behind her desk, gavel in hand, eyes of steel ready to cast judgment over him. It started to make sense. He wondered if Phil Fox were in the seat if he would offer more humanity, rather than dictate statutes from decades-old documents. If he would see the big picture—that everything he had done was for the security of the federation, not just Capston. His thoughts returned to his father, pleading with the advocates to listen to him. The whole damned thing was predetermined. And so was this hearing.

Under Blackout

Monday, 2 July AC 0245
DHC Rotunda, New Inland
Mayor Steven Reekan

Karyn explained how the hearing would take place. The procedure would follow DHC protocols, adhering strictly to the order of questioning, and the time limit for each representative. Steven squinted at the shared document on his datapad as the rotunda buzzed with the arriving pages, surveillance sweepers, and cleaning staff. Pages from all five cities traveled to and from their respective city offices, bringing java in carafes, loading datapads, fluffing cushions. An overly cheerful page from Capston tried to hand Steven a hot cup of black java, only to slosh it over the rim and drip onto his desktop. The young girl, no more than eighteen years old, apologized over and over, and backed away when he glared at her. "Thank you, dear," Karyn said in an effort to diffuse the tension. "She's nervous, that's all. Nice kid, Melinna. She'll be with me, don't worry."

"The kid's the least of my worries." Steven dabbed the java spill with a disposable napkin. "Okay, I see the order here." Double tapping the data screen, the list expanded.

"The Chair opens the proceedings with brief opening remarks. Greetings, charges, basic housekeeping stuff." Karyn leaned in and highlighted the order list. "As you know, each city's Mayor and 2nd Representative are granted time for questions. The order is generated in DHC city priority order, such that the final speaker is the sitting Chair."

Steven rolled his eyes. "Of course, Marribel gets the last word."

"No, you do. The final allotment of time is your rebuttal. So, your biggest challenge is to keep it together for your final remarks after she's had the floor for questioning."

Steven zeroed in on the order list. At least she'd prepared an organized table:

	DHC Representative	Title	Portfolio	City	Minutes
1	Shal Adem	2nd Rep.	Aquaculture	New Mills	5
2	Wynn David	2nd Rep.	Energy	Arcadia	5
3	Blythe Easton	2nd Rep.	Foreign Affairs	Preston	5
4	**Pax Brien**	2nd Rep.	Agriculture	**Capston**	**5**
5	Cooper Fellows	2nd Rep.	Treasury	Heartsburg	5
6	Jeffres Marsh	Mayor	Solicitor	New Mills	8
7	Harus Salter	Mayor	Public Health	Arcadia	8
8	Sylla Pierre	Mayor	Defense Corps	Preston	8
9	**Karyn Kendall**	1st Rep	Solicitor	**Capston**	**8**
10	Jennings Marribel	Chair/ Mayor	Public Health/ Medical Research	Heartsburg	8
11	Steven Reekan	Mayor	Defense Corps	Capston	10

The order of representatives had a few bright spots. Heavily-industrial Arcadia held down the second and seventh spots, and historically, Wynn David and Harus Salter gave him little trouble. Shal Adem from New Mills was younger, and rarely raised any hackles during DHC meetings. Those three, plus the Capston representatives, made for half of the scrutineers potentially being friendly.

The remainder, however, could be hostile. Blythe Easton third and Cooper Fellows fifth had potential to be hard-nosed. Sylla Pierre from Preston could go either way. She'd been both supportive and critical of Capston's crises. Steven had once questioned her qualifications to sit as a DefCorps rep. That might come back to haunt him, Karyn pointed out.

As Steven narrowed in on the Chair and Heartsburg Mayor's name at ten, Jennings Marribel and her delegation entered the rotunda, early as always, and made their way to the Heartsburg pod. Melinna, the page, fretted in the empty pod to their right. If only the impetuous teen were asking the questions instead of the grizzled, hawk-nosed veteran.

"You'll be in the center of the chamber. The witness pod is oriented to the questioner, so you'll be speaking directly to them. At least you won't be staring at a row of people all staring at you."

"Except they will be, and I won't be able to see the whites of their eyes." Steven had no fear of speaking in public. The notion that his peers were judging him without looking him in the eye—that was unnerving.

"The best you can do is answer the questions as clearly and concisely as possible."

Clear. Concise.

Honest…

"The Special Hearing will come to order. I am Jennings Marribel, Mayor of the city of Heartsburg, Chief Officer of Public Health and Medical Research of Heartsburg and sitting Chair of the Domestic High Council of the Federation of New Inland. Let the record show we have convened on this day, the 2nd of July, 0245. Our mandate is to determine whether Steven Reekan, Mayor of the city of Capston, has violated the New Inland charter. This hearing is under blackout. The viewing gallery is closed, and DefCorps has swept the chambers for any recording devices."

From his central pod, Steven suppressed a smirk. Jason Holt wasn't able to keep Paolo Desantos from infiltrating the closed circuit inside Holt Tower. If someone wanted in on the proceedings badly enough, they'd find a way.

"Steven Reekan has been accused of the following charter violations: Failure to disclose technological innovation to the Federation; entering into agreement with a foreign entity; conducting business with an unsanctioned entity; violating a legal treaty with foreign entities; entering and conducting military operations in the territory of a foreign entity; and defiance of DHC decrees."

Karyn had explained the use of 'foreign entity' in a legal sense. Anything outside of a friendly federation beneath a dome fit the designation of 'foreign entity'. Kayewat? Foreign entity. Hyacynthe? As long as the embargo remained, foreign entity. Motherland? Steven would have preferred to call it what it was—a terrorist state.

"I reserve the right to address the accused during my allotted time. In the interest of expediency, I yield to the first representative from New Mills. 2nd Representative Shal Adem, you have the floor."

Steven's pod rotated to Marribel's left, stopping in front of the New Mills pod. Representative Adem nodded.

"Thank you, Mayor Reekan, for your time today. I understand this must be difficult for you, given your city's troubles these past several months."

"To put it lightly." Steven wanted to retort that he had no choice in attending the hearing. But Adem was a potentially friendly to his cause, and he needed all the help he could get. Besides, he was clearly nervous himself—the second button of his dress shirt was undone, and he was visibly perspiring.

"The attack on the Sheppard Family Inn was the fifth in as many months in your city. Is that correct?"

"It is."

"Could you tell—could you *reveal* to the council the number of victims?" Adem corrected his words to sound more official.

"Victims? A family of four lost their home and their livelihood."

"I'll clarify—how many lives were lost in the attack, Your Worship?"

It was worth a shot. Victims and dead bodies weren't necessarily one and same. But in this case…

"One."

"Thank you. One deceased, yet the official report indicated seven. Can you explain this to us?"

"I would except the details you're suggesting could be detrimental to our ongoing investigation—"

Chair Marribel turned on her microphone. "I understand that you wish to protect witness identities, but you're reminded that the hearing is under blackout, and sensitive details will be redacted. Please answer the question, Mayor Reekan."

Steven turned to Karyn Kendall's pod. She nodded.

"Very well. We moved six individuals into witness protection custody in light of retrieved evidence. Those six individuals were either witnesses or immediate family, and we felt it was necessary to let the public believe they had died in the explosion."

"Understood. And the seventh?"

"The seventh is the one actual death from the explosion. He was found in the debris, and was confirmed as one of the perpetrators. His was the lone body found in the rubble." The other one would be found under his own pile of rubble.

"Your forensics team was able to identify him?"

"We confirmed that his name was Ennis Grant." Steven straightened his shoulders, bracing for more probing into Grant's identity.

"Thank you, Your Worship. Madam Chair, I wish to yield my remaining time to Mayor Marsh."

That wasn't a good sign. Marsh was far more seasoned in committees and hearings. Adem had been instructed to open the proceedings with soft, fact-based questions. Steven took a sip of java.

"Arcadia 2nd Representative Wynn David, you have the floor." Marribel tapped her microphone, and Steven's pod rotated until it came to a stop in front of Arcadia's delegation. Wynn smiled, wrinkling the dimples of her round cheeks. Steven's nerves relaxed slightly. He had worked with Wynn David before. She came from a long line of Foundry workers.

"Good morning, Mayor Reekan. It has been discussed in Council that Capston has failed to meet the requested 2.5% GDP spending on New Inland Defense Corps. Could you confirm Capston's current percentage of defense spending?"

"We currently budget 2.2% to DefCorps."

"It's my understanding that this is an increase from your predecessor?"

"Under Phil Fox, we were spending 2.0%. I pressed to increase that to 2.4, but I was met with opposition to that." He didn't dare look at Karyn Kendall.

"I see. I know from working with you on various portfolios how passionate you are about security."

"It's my job, Wynn. I'd add that our budgetary expenses in the industrial sector are second only to Arcadia, and nearly double one other city."

Marribel's microphone crackled. "Mayor Reekan, you are to address the representative by title, please."

Steven smiled. Marribel's interjection might have been over protocol, but she knew he was referring to Heartsburg's meager contribution to the Foundry. And he hoped Wynn David caught the jab.

"Thank you, Mayor Reekan. I have nothing further, and I yield."

"Very well, Representative David."

Steven turned his eyes down to his datapad, not to examine any notes, but to avoid making unnecessary eye contact with Blythe Easton. The pod rotated clockwise before coming to rest in alignment with the Preston 2nd Representative. Marribel introduced her, but Steven kept his gaze downward. Everything in this hearing was out of his control. He would look up only when he was ready.

"Do you need a moment, Mayor Reekan?"

Steven casually raised his eyes. Blythe glowered at his sleight.

"Ready when you are."

"Good." Blythe launched into her line of questioning without hesitation. Steven avoided her steel-grey eyes as much as possible. The 2nd from Preston sat in perfect posture, suit jacket trim and long hair tied back, silver streaks gleaning tight against her scalp in the chamber light.

"Does the City of Capston have an agreement with the Allen Consortium?"

Karyn had gone over this. Answer honestly, because perjury will result in immediate expulsion.

"Yes."

"And you are aware that this contravenes the Federation of New Inland statute—"

"I am. And so is Preston, I assume?"

Marribel buzzed. "The 2nd from Preston has the floor for questions, Your Worship."

Blythe continued, unfazed. "Does that agreement allow for Capston to enter into and move about freely inside of Allentown?"

"I wouldn't say freely. We're restricted as to which parts of the city we can access. No different than any other city's agreements." His phrasing meant Marribel had to allow it. He imagined her scowl.

"Was the agreement in place before you took office?"

"If you're asking if Phil Fox had an agreement with the Allens, then, no. I made the agreement, as a result of intelligence we'd gathered in our investigation—"

"Thank you. Mayor Reekan, have you traveled to Allentown?"

Steven raised his still-bandaged right hand. "I didn't get this from taking a roast out of the oven. Yes, Representative Easton, I was in Allentown."

"And as you have already testified, you are aware that by doing so you've contravened New Inland statutes."

"Is that a question or a statement?"

Blythe breezed past the sarcasm. "Several officers in your executive accompanied you. Is that correct?"

"That is."

"How did you incur your injury?"

Steven inhaled deeply. "We had evidence that not only was Motherland behind the attacks on my city, but that they were operating from inside of Allentown. As you are aware, Representative Easton, Motherland has also signed on to the peace treaty that pledges they too will remain outside of Allentown. We learned that a significant military presence was established in the north end of the city. Our intention was to gather conclusive intelligence as to their plans, in conjunction with what we already knew."

"Your injury—"

"I'm getting to that. An unidentified informant revealed to us that our position was compromised and that we were in imminent danger. As we left, via underground routes authorized to us from the Allens, an ordinance detonated on the surface. In the collapse of the tunnels, my hand was cut open pretty deeply. My major and I were fortunate to have found our way into a bomb shelter. We were nearly buried alive in a tin can stocked with decades-old dried rations, stale water, and human remains, for over a week."

"The Council is grateful that you were found alive. The same can't be said for your lost officer, however."

"Swift was a major loss for us. Don't pretend you feel sorry for him."

"I feel sorry for the Sheppard and Connelly families, Mayor."

Steven hammered his bandaged fist, narrowly missing his datapad. "If you did, maybe the Council wouldn't have hampered our investigation from the beginning!"

Marribel interjected. "Be careful, Mayor Reekan."

Blythe focused her cold eyes on Steven's widening irises. "One last question. Did you carry out the assassination of Lieutenant-Colonel Paolo Desantos of Motherland?"

"I did *not*. It's pretty hard to do that when you're buried alive and laying in mouse shit. And I promise you—I would rather have had Desantos answer for his crimes. I'm not out for revenge. I'm out for justice."

"Time." Marribel tapped her gavel and Blythe Easton smiled. Steven rubbed the bandage as pain surfaced in his still-healing wound. The loss of the Sheppard brothers throbbed far worse, and never healed.

Bloomer

Tuesday, 16 April KW 2590
Spleen Cavern (Third District),
Free Association of Kayewat
Le_Renard_Subtil

Tuesday nights were popular at the Spleen Cavern. Half price dialysis was a significant deal, especially for the low-level traders and their lower-life associates. Le_Renard_Subtil was known to offer robust health benefits the likes of no other Kayewati bosses. But nothing is really a good deal. To receive full retirement, accommodations in the Narrows Black, and all health services, an associate had to commit to some of the most dangerous work on the continent. Le_Renard slouched over the dirty bar, alone on the row of stools while the denizens of the spleen fought for positioning in the dialysis lines. Five terminals, no less than three slummers in each queue. He couldn't tell if the stench came from the sick or the sticky floor. Either way, his nose had never really adjusted to it. The stamp on his forearm couldn't keep the stink out of his nostrils.

"Last call, Le_Ren." The barkeep didn't even turn to face him. For someone who was always washing dishes, Le_Renard couldn't recall ever being served a clean one. He didn't frequent the Spleen for the medical services. He didn't need to—a prescription drug smuggler with reach into the Far East and south past Ozarck had plenty of access to affordable drugs. And he certainly didn't choose the Spleen for its ambiance.

The patrons provided a free shield from more respectable

criminals. Few risked the hepatitis that was rumoured to be in the air at the Spleen Cavern.

"Half-glass of Aquavit," Le_Renard sighed, pushing his dirty glass across the surface until it stuck in a half-dried spill. "Gotta know your limits. Huh."

Two bums started punching each other, one still wired up to the second terminal. He missed, swinging so hard he tangled himself in the crimson plastic tubing. Le_Renard winced and turned away. If that tube came undone, it would make one hell of a diseased mess.

In the commotion, the doors swung open and a wide-framed silhouette nearly filled the frame. *Thought you were never going to show up…*

"You missed last call, CF." Le_Renard swirled the green liquid in his glass and the barkeeper grunted.

"Got my own anyway." Claw_Finger ambled up to the stool next to his boss, nearly sliding off as clumsily as he slid on. "Least I know whose lips been on the bottle!"

He made a good point.

"Good day at the races?"

"Pfft. Mutt didn't even finish. Took a shit on the final turn, for chris'sakes." The fat-faced informant swilled back a long gulp of green liquor. "But I did have an interesting evening."

Le_Renard shifted on his stool. "How much'll this cost me?"

To his surprise, the big man shook his head. "This one's on me, boss. Too important."

Nothing was free. "Out with it, then."

Claw_Finger wiped droplets from his uneven beard with the back of his sleeve. "I'm up in the second decks—close enough to see but far enough from the splatter, you know? And down below, this feller is stumbling around, talkin' up spectators. Not one of 'em listened more than a few seconds. But he wandered close enough I could hear what he was askin'."

The agent took another swig. After two gulps, Le_Renard snatched the goblet out of his grasp. "And he was asking what?" The two sick men had fallen to the floor, presumably slipping on the spurting blood.

Claw_Finger was clearly annoyed, but when Le_Renard returned the bottle to his bear-paw hands, his eyes brightened. The big oaf might not need dialysis, but his bloodstream was probably half green.

"He tells this guy watching the races that he's looking for someone. Feller's mutt was in the lead, he had no time to listen to this jerk. But the guy keeps talking, says the name loud enough for me to hear."

"Cryin' out loud, CF—you waiting to read the credits or what? Out with it!"

CF looked him in the eye and took another swig. He sighed the name while the alcohol coursed down his throat.

"Emmanuel Jackson."

Le_Renard had grown accustomed to hiding any reaction to his "real" name. Le_Renard_Subtil was the name on the Kayewati forward database. It was the name that would scan from his stamp. It was the name that elicited respect and fear, far and wide.

But in the *rear* database, and in a small coastal village, and a spruce grove up river, Emmanuel Jackson was last in the line of a centuries-old family business that was in its twilight hour. *Almost last. No guarantee the boy's cut out for it. But still…*

Beyond that, the name should have zero consequence.

Yet, it was uttered in public within Kayewat. And that was a problem.

"And no one knew what he was talking about?"

CF shook his head. "Not that I could see. But this feller, he said it loud enough I could hear him a good fifteen-twenty feet. Not too stealthy if yer trying be 'fficient." Le_Renard suppressed laughter. It was amusing when CF tried to sound smarter than he was.

But he'd made an astute observation. Whoever this interloper was, he wasn't shy about speaking out loud in the Abattoir. Anyone accustomed to Kayewati norms would have been more discreet. It's likely he *wanted* eavesdroppers.

"You get a name of this feller, CF?"

He shook his head. "Guy was a tough customer. Good shape, strong features. Wild lookin' eyes. Kept rubbing his forehead, twitched a lot."

CF went on to describe an outfit usually given to fresh Flowers—newcomers to Kayewat: Plain tan trousers, insulated shirt, standard wool-liner boots, and mitts. In a crowd of thousands of bloomers, this guy could have been half of them.

"That wasn't all, though. He mumbled something about going way back. And then, the spectator asked him where he's from."

Le_Renard carried an encyclopedic memory of village and settlement names from decades of trade and exploitation. He grabbed the bottle of Aquavit back from CF's mitts.

"Feller says he's from Haven."

Haven. The man known to the long-dead village as Le_Renard_Subtil, but to this unwanted suitor as Emmanuel Jackson, took his own long swill from Claw_Finger's bottle of Aquavit.

"Walpurgis is in New Inland. Get the Allens to call him, CF. Now."

Wednesday, 27 June AC 0245
Ebbequit Strait
Le_Renard_Subtil (Emmanuel Jackson)

Emmanuel Jackson didn't have to conceal his identity on the deck of the sloop, on the open waters of the strait, under the navy-grey pre-dawn sky. Woken by the muffled conversation between Phil and Fisher in the light chamber above, he found himself unable to fall back asleep. Three hours was more than he could hope for on some trips. After Haven, he hadn't been able to sleep at all that night. In the same bluish sky hue, he couldn't keep the streaks of orange and red out of his mind, while the children huddled below deck. In the same quarters, Phil caught forty winks before the sun crawled up from the eastern horizon.

The sloop drawled over early morning ripples leaving a faint, fading white outline in its wake. On the port side, the rusty-banked island stretched wide, north to south. Beyond the coastline, it harboured its own cohort of settlements—some modest, others sprawling from tip to tip.

On the open Atlantic, there was no land in any direction for most of the journey from Haven to Gasperro. He was passing Sable, well wide of its southern shallows, when the cabin door crept open. A curly-haired boy with bright eyes and wide smile peeked into the early morning salty air. Emmanuel sighed and motioned with cupped fingers for him to come out. The youth hopped over on the balls of his bare toes, legs like twigs. The other children maintained degrees of fear from the moment they'd left the emptied village behind and boarded the sloop, docked in the Hudson shallows before hauling anchor.

But this little fellow… He was different. It was like he was embarking on the adventure of a lifetime, and he couldn't wait to see it all. He would have to introduce him to Bernard. A youngster with that kind of spirit would be welcome in the sleepy harbour of Gasperro.

The curly-haired boy pushed up on his toes and gazed towards the thin crest of land on the horizon. He pointed his matchstick index finger. "What's that place called?"

"Sable," Emmanuel answered. Little more than a sandbar with tall grass, seals, and horses. Any closer and the sloop might run aground, so they had to navigate wide. The boy answered with an *ahh*, as if he were mimicking a grandparent. Yes, Bernard had to meet this kid.

Meet him, he did. And as Emmanuel predicted, they got on just fine. Albert never left—Bernard Schiff raised him to be a fine young man. It had always made the cynical, jaded trader drop his façade to see Bernard teaching him how to fish, how to swim, how to repair leaky roof shingles.

How to live an honest life.

Emmanuel looked at the closed hatch to the cabin. It was a life he could never have offered his own son. He was eternally grateful that Bernard's sister Elsa and her husband, a Sascotan magna-rail driver, could offer Phil a good life.

Or at least a life without constantly looking over his shoulder.

The sloop crawled around the cape and set its sights for the Bay-of-Green estuary. Emmanuel Jackson had a lot of work to do. Everybody knows Flowers bloom after the rain. Gasperro couldn't afford a leaky roof, knowing the heavy weather that could descend at any time.

Shadows

Thursday, 28 June AC 0245
Gasperro
Phil Fox

The last streaks of daylight dimmed enough for the lamppost lights to switch on, bathing the wharf in a yellowish glow. Albert secured the mooring ropes while Le_Renard and Phil lowered the jib, securing the chains to the nuke-cell in its polymer-framed shipping container. The plastic box radiated a sickly purple-grey as though its contents had leaked, soaking the shell in radiation. Phil's Geiger counter indicated otherwise, however. The unit was tight, and if Fisher had been honest, the fusion technology was far safer than the cells of old. Thrasher cells in the later years were much more compact than the temperamental and bulky type known to still be found in the wilderness from time to time. Phil remembered the DHC meeting in which the council had resolved to dispatch a cleanup crew to contain a leaking cell from an abandoned mulcher. There had been concern that it was close enough to affect the water table. Phil had contributed little to the discussion, but he had gone on the record stating that a hundred years earlier, the New Inland DHC would have ignored the ecological disaster, preferring to stay shut inside the dome and let the outsiders deal with it.

An hour later, the cargo was stored in Albert's garage in the hidden cellar, and all three huddled around Albert's kitchen table. A creamy asparagus soup warmed Phil's belly. Le_Renard complained again that the Rex was closed, mumbling about too much soup and not enough red meat. Albert asked if his cooking was that bad.

"Rex, he used to run the eatery, my parents always said. Terrible cook, huh! Yeah, Rex was his name. Had this Mustang, one of the remake models—perfect shape, you could tell it was well-maintained. Three-sixty horsepower, eight cylinder. Gas-guzzler, but Rex loved that thing. Huh! It was this copper colour—I think he went custom. Used to rumble up and down the main strip all the time. Near the end, he wouldn't risk the suspension to bring it up to Jackson Auto. Dad always said he missed working on that old girl. See, it was around then people started piecing together bastardized cars. Cobble 'em together with what you can find." Greenish broth leaked from the corners of his mouth.

"Anyway, he held onto this old boat of a car until the end. But it was getting too expensive to keep shipping in petrol, and most of the old parts were too costly to keep fixing. So, most people went back to old ways—carts, bikes. Easier to fix and no gasoline to buy. Hyacynthe was tightening up on trade up the north shore. You couldn't get anything up the St-Lawrence without being boarded and picked apart— think the strait's bad enough now? Huh. So, I started talkin' to the Kayewati more and more. I still get the petrol I need from them today."

Just mentioning petrol conjured the smell in Phil's nostrils. Neither Sascota nor New Inland relied on the outdated fuel source. The pale-yellow liquid was pungent and toxic. Le_Renard continued his story.

"I think people were as tired of his car as they were of his food. Tailpipe always coughin' black smoke, fluids leakin' and stainin' the asphalt. Look close enough, you can still see some coolant drip stains in the carport. Anyway, I never met him, or anyone related to him in my lifetime. Don't know whatever happened to that Mustang, but I imagine some of its parts are in buggies from the Baie to the Avalon. Huh! Maybe even in the FTE!"

"So, you're saying my cooking *isn't* that bad? Albert fetched the whistling teapot and poured himself a steaming cup.

"You'll do, I guess!" Le_Renard pointed to his empty cup and Albert filled it.

"Maybe you already tore out all the hand-me-down parts." Phil nodded and Albert poured him a cup before taking his seat. "Might be able to sell the old engine. We'll have traders from the Avalon next week."

"Tell you what—sell the engine and buy some decent beef cuts!"

All three laughed, wiping their lips and sipping tea. Phil dipped a dry roll in his broth.

"Now that you have your replacement, you've got no excuses." The old man couldn't complain about finally finishing the buggy anymore. As soon as they moved the nuke-cell to the Spruce Grove, he could stay all day and night in Jackson Auto if he wanted.

Albert slurped a spoonful of broth. "Fisher sent along instructions, I hope."

"Yeah, pretty straight forward, though." Le_Renard dripped soup down his chin stubble. "Already got all the old combustion engine parts out. Biggest thing is to be sure there's enough airflow. Don't need it overheating in the dry woods in August."

Phil poured a cup of tea and scraped the last mouthful of soup. "Fisher told me a story. When you were still sleeping."

Le_Renard peered over the rim of his teacup mid-sip. "Oh?"

"He told me how scared you were when my birth mother left me on the hood of the buggy, right in the Jackson Auto bay."

"Huh. Like that old coot was even there!"

Phil smirked. Le_Renard's dismissive tone wasn't fooling anyone.

"But he's right. I've seen plenty of scary shit, my boy. Nothing scared me as much as you. Huh. Wrapped up in a blanket and drooling, never seen anything so fright'ning!"

It was probably the only time in his life Phil ever wielded that much power.

"How'd that come up, anyway?"

"I was telling Fisher that you seem preoccupied. Like something's weighing on you, and every time I bring up Kayewat, you want to shut it down."

Le_Renard snorted. "You would too, my boy. You would too."

Albert piped in. "Must be something serious—you never shut up about Kayewat otherwise!"

"Smart-ass. I'll tell you this much if yer so horny to know—I had to leave quick. Didn't even give Pretty Boy enough of a heads up. I had a shadow, wanted to find me pretty bad. Now I'm used to running into… unsatisfied clients, let's say. But this one…"

"It isn't like you to tuck tail like that," Albert said. "Any idea what his problem is?"

Le_Renard lifted the soup bowl to his lips and slurped. "Not a whit. Guy wasn't fuckin' around though. I lost a good man for it."

Phil's heart sank. His biological father was by no means a saint. He wasn't even a good man. Still, despite Emmanuel Jackson's best efforts to shed Le_Renard's skin, it always followed. Shadows never leave if you're standing in the light. People still got hurt. Sometimes they died.

"You know for sure?" Phil reached into his pocket and pinched the data clip between his finger and thumb.

"I'll save the details for back at the Homestead. When's the last time you did a sweep of your cottage, Albert?"

"As soon as you arrived. We found nothing—no surprise there. Even swept since to be sure."

"Huh. Still, I won't take any chances. Can't be too sure. Walpurgis learned that the hard way."

Walpurgis. Phil almost choked on his last swig of cooling tea. "We need to get back to Jackson Auto. I have something from Fisher. It's from Walpurgis."

Bombshell

Monday, 2 July AC 0245
DHC Rotunda, New Inland
Mayor Steven Reekan

The pod halted in front of the Capston delegation. Steven expected respite from his home city, yet his heart still pounded in double time. Behind Representative Pax Brien, Karyn focused on her datapad, tapping her narrow fingers on the screen. The Chief of Agriculture smiled, opening tabs on his own device and taking a sip of java the page Melinna had managed not to spill.

"Thank you for your honest testimony today, Your Worship. I have a few questions for you."

"Of course, Representative Brien." Steven's tone naturally softened in anticipation of a friendlier line of questioning.

"Can you explain to the Council the purpose of your agreement with Allentown, and why you entered the city?"

Steven straightened his shoulders and planted his feet firmly on the floor of his pod. "Yes, I can. After we discovered the body of one of the attackers in the Sheppard Inn debris, we found a handheld device that was not completely ruined. Our technicians were able to power it on, and inside there were financial transaction trails that led to Allentown. Specifically, a location in the north end where it was confirmed Motherland had been based."

"I see. So, to confirm, this intelligence was gained in Capston, and within legal parameters?"

"That's right, Pax—sorry, Representative Brien."

Pax smiled. "Thank you. If your police hadn't found this evidence, can we assume that you would have had no reason otherwise to enter Allentown?"

"That's right." At least for the time being. One way or another, the evidence was always going to lead to Motherland.

"Aside from the already-disclosed agreement, does Capston conduct any further business with the Allen Consortium?"

"We do not."

"That's all. I yield my remaining time to Solicitor Karyn Kendall."

Marribel didn't even answer. She tapped her gavel without looking at him. As he began to rotate towards her Heartsburg pod, Steven made brief eye contact with Karyn. She nodded in approval before sliding out of view. The 2nd from Heartsburg, Cooper Fellows, replaced Marribel in the lead seat for his round of questioning. It was going to be a long five minutes.

"Mayor Reekan, you have testified that Capston has budgeted 2.2% GDP to DefCorps, far below the ratified agreement of 2.5%. Can you tell us how much is allotted to the operation of the Appalachian-Ozarck facility?"

"Representative Fellows, I'm sure you're aware that Capston's business arrangement with the Federation of Ozarck was approved by my predecessor with DHC permission—"

"What percent, Mister Mayor?"

"*Your Worship.*" Steven eyed Marribel, holding her gavel. If he'd made a slip in formality, she would have lowered it. "4.6%."

"More than double your expenditure to New Inland's defense. Would you care to explain why?"

"Ap-Oz is a legal business investment with a recognized federation. We employ dozens of Capstonian citizens, and we contribute to research and innovation that Heartsburg in particular has benefited from."

"So you say. According to your budget, your 4.6% accounts for higher than your expenses. Any explanation for the inconsistencies?"

Steven was no accountant, but he knew why Cooper was fishing. "A significant portion of our budget is allotted to rental fees with Ozarck. We also pay our share of intellectual property licenses, travel and insurance—"

"We have access to the particulars, but there are lines that are labeled broadly. One that caught my attention is listed as 'innovation'. Now, you have submitted to the DHC a budget of innovation in science and technology, but the numbers we have seen are far lower than what is indicated here."

"I would have to speak with our accounting." Steven knew where this was leading.

"Mayor Reekan, is it true Capston has underreported its innovation budget?"

"No, it is not."

"I remind you that you are sworn to transparency."

"You heard me."

Cooper Fellows bristled at Steven's retort. "Dr. Kyle Jarren is the lead researcher at Ap-Oz. Capston has granted him fast-tracked citizenship, correct?"

"Yes. Mayor Fox signed off on that."

"I was on the committee, Mayor Reekan. I was opposed to it. Nonetheless, Dr. Jarren and his team are citizens of Capston, and therefore hold credentials for free association within New Inland, is that correct?"

"Yes."

"Therefore, any business Dr. Jarren conducts, in Ap-Oz or otherwise, is subject to the statutes of the Federation of New Inland, again, correct?"

"What's your point?"

Cooper ignored the question. "Mayor Reekan, who was the perpetrator whose remains you found in the Sheppard Inn?"

"He was identified as Ennis Grant."

"Capstonian, I assume?"

"The records showed he's from New Mills."

"Except he wasn't from New Mills. Ennis Grant is Kayewati, is that correct?"

The air in the room thickened and Steven swallowed hard. "We determined that he was not in fact from New Inland."

"I will take that as a yes. Mayor Reekan, as you're aware, anyone of Kayewati origin is detectable by all point of entry scanners because of their stamp. How is it, then, that your forensics were able to determine that Grant was *concealing* his stamp with a biosynthetic covering?"

That was the bombshell. "Dr. Jarren and his team had been developing the biosynth technology for years before we entered into our lease with Ap-Oz. It's in our opinion that the advancements by his team predated their citizenship—"

"But once that process had been completed, they now fall under your jurisdiction, isn't that right? Or are they still Ozarckian? You can't have it both ways."

"We were prepared to disclose with the DHC when we felt it was appropriate to do so! Look, the work Jarren and his team have done— we *all* stand to benefit from it! Thanks to this innovation, we've been able to confirm that Kayewati *can* gain access to New Inland."

"I don't think you understand the implications, here. If the Kayewati already have the ability to masque their stamps, how did they acquire the biosynth technology?"

Cooper was right. It sounded fishy. Ozarck was no friend of Kayewat. Still, Jarren had told him that the bio-signature was different from Ap-Oz science. Someone else was working on it. Maybe a disgruntled Ozarck technician.

"Dr. Jarren confirmed that the biosynth masquing Grant's stamp was different."

"And why should the Council trust your Dr. Jarren, when we can't even trust you?"

Steven should have had access to Karyn during the fifteen minute recess before the mayors began their questioning. She was his lead solicitor, after all. Interim, maybe, but the closest he had to an ally in the Rotunda. He laughed at his own faint hope that Phil Fox would show up, thrusting open the chamber doors at the last second before convincing the hearing that Capston had done everything for the best reasons. All he got was a new cup of java from Melinna before she slunk away, still embarrassed for sloshing the first one.

As the hearing rotated back to New Mills, Mayor Jeffres Marsh had taken the seat in his city's pod. Whereas Representative Adem was still green, Jeffres was a veteran on the DHC, and its longest serving Mayor. He'd served as Chair three times, and had no intention of not seeing the rotation come back to him for a fourth. The man looked half his sixty years, despite his double portfolio as both mayor and solicitor for his city. Steven regretted having once remarked within earshot that anyone who actually knew hard work couldn't look so good.

"Your Worship, all of New Mills grieves the loss of life in your city. I would like to focus on the Sheppard family for a moment. Is it true that the Sheppards are orphans?"

Steven sighed. "Yes."

"From red tide, I believe. I remember the press release. It's unfair for the children to grow up without them. There are four, correct?"

"Three brothers and one sister, yes."

"The sister—Crystal Sheppard—lives abroad?"

"In Hyacynthe, four years now."

Jeffres nodded. "I'd like to say on the record that this hearing does not have the mandate to investigate the Sheppard family's communication with the Federation of Hyacynthe, which is under full trade embargo."

"That's kind of you." The brothers were gone, but Crystal didn't need anything more dropped on her. As far as Steven knew, she hadn't even been told of her brothers yet.

"Your Worship, has there been any communication between Capston and Hyacynthe?"

"No. We've held true to the embargo. If anything, it's kept her safe."

"No doubt. To clarify, the three Sheppard brothers, Robbie, Laurent, and Cadlen are under witness protection?"

"Yes." It was a white lie.

"Where are they currently?"

"Due to the ongoing investigation, I'm not able to say."

"You are sworn to transparency, Your Worship."

"I do not want to compromise their safety, Mayor Marsh. I'm sure you can agree—"

"This hearing is under blackout, and you are compelled to answer." Jeffres spoke with the eloquence of a seasoned solicitor. His words were heavier than the chamber atmosphere. Steven felt claustrophobic.

"They're *dead*."

Jeffres paused, even if the clock on his allotted time was ticking. "I'm sorry. How did they die, Mayor Reekan?"

"We were moving them to Ap-Oz. They were being transported by Tan-Ro. Somewhere over the outside wilderness, the craft fell out of the sky. We're still searching for debris."

"That's awful. What caused the craft to crash?"

"We're still not sure. We suspect sabotage."

"I'm wondering, why did you need to move them from your safe house inside Capston?"

Steven gritted his teeth. He remembered the words the informant had uttered to Kenzie Wall back in Allentown. *Your house is not safe...*

"Holt Tower was compromised. The enemy hacked into the closed circuit video and made it known that the Sheppards and Connellys were there. Naturally, we were concerned—"

"Concerned enough that the Connelly family was left behind?"

"That was their choice. At the time, I was underneath Allentown. My captain, Ender Ling, made the call and I stand by her decision."

"So let me get this straight: Captain Ling decides to send the Sheppards to Ap-Oz in order to keep them safe. Instead, they're in a copter wreck and presumed dead. Meanwhile, the Connellys are still in Holt Tower, which wasn't deemed safe enough? I'm confused by your captain's logic."

"We moved the Sheppards because the middle one pissed off Jason

Holt to the point where he wouldn't keep them any longer! And on top of that, Clara Connelly has a thing for Jason Holt, and she refused to leave. Believe me, if I was there, I would have sedated her and sent them all to Ap-Oz!"

"Right. And then there would be six dead instead of three."

Before he blew his top, Karyn Kendall buzzed in. "Chair Marribel, this is badgering."

Marribel clicked her controller. "Stick to questions, Mayor Marsh."

"Indeed, Chair. Mayor Reekan, you have claimed throughout your tenure on the Council, and in this hearing, that everything you have done is for the safety of all. And in so doing, you've violated several statutes along the way, which have resulted in even more casualties. Wouldn't you agree that your efforts have only made things worse?"

Steven leaped from his chair. Marribel made to tell him to sit down, but he drowned her out. "*Made things worse?* If anything, Jeffres, I've *proved* just how much danger we're all in! It was a Kayewati that blew up the Sheppard Inn. For all you know, there could be a dozen or more Kayewati in every city under the dome! And you'd be none the wiser if not for the developments from Ap-Oz! Grant was hired by Colonel Desantos, that is for certain. If anything, the Sheppards' deaths only proves my point. *We are in serious danger here!*"

"Mayor Reekan, that is enough!" Marribel smashed her anvil and it echoed throughout the chamber, piercing Steven's eardrums.

"With all due respect, Chair Marribel," Karyn interjected. "Mayor Marsh has leveled serious allegations at Mayor Reekan, and it is permissible for him to speak in his defense. I would remind the Council that this is a hearing and not a criminal trial."

"And I would remind you, Solicitor Kendall, that you are not Mayor Reekan's legal counsel. However, your point is taken. Mayor Marsh, do you have anything further?"

"Nothing further." Jeffres folded his hands on his desk, a faint smile emerging on his smug face. Steven glowered, lowering himself back into his seat.

Why They Hate Us

Monday, 2 July AC 0245
DHC Rotunda, New Inland
Mayor Steven Reekan

There was no recess permitted after Jeffres Marsh eviscerated Steven in his eight minutes of intense scrutiny. The best he could do was wave to the page to bring him more java. Melinna scurried over to his pod with a tall carafe. As she went to pour, Steven snatched the insulated jug from her shaky hands and poured himself a refill to the brim before slamming it to the table. The page was barely back to the Capston pod when Marribel introduced Mayor Harus Salter of Arcadia. His 2nd, Blythe Easton, had already had her turn to tear him down. Harus, however, was more measured and softer-spoken. Unlike the ageless wonder Jeffres, he looked every bit his near-seventy years, wisps of white hair receded and reduced to the fringes of his head.

"I would like to bring the tone down a little, if I may. Mayor Reekan, I have questions concerning the developments that have come of your partnership with Ap-Oz."

"Sure, why not?" Clearly still heightened from the previous exchange, Steven breathed deeply.

"Yes, well, it's my understanding that Ap-Oz has innovated much in the field of agriculture, as I'm sure Representative Brien can attest. Can you elaborate on the work Dr. Jarren and his team are doing?"

"Kyle Jarren is an exceptional researcher. One of the first things that impressed us when we first consulted Ap-Oz was their desire to enhance safe agriculture. Ozarck is so close to the Red Line, and tropical diseases affect crops as much as people. So, to see them building more resilient crops was impressive. Their work in biotechnology is nothing less than incredible."

"Indeed. I'm told your mother was passionate about AgriCorps and the Hanging Gardens. I'm sure she'd be proud."

"*You're told*, are you? Well, *I'm* sure she doesn't give a shit."

For the first time in the proceedings, members from all pods raised their voices in disbelief. Marribel hammered her gavel.

"Order, please! And Mayor Reekan, watch your language!"

"And if you please, Madam Chair, I would ask that my mother be kept out of the questioning."

"Your Worship, I meant no offense by it. I apologize." Harus raised a hand in a gesture of surrender. Steven didn't bite.

"Apologize for what? For a woman that walked out on her husband and child almost forty years ago? Not necessary. You see, she didn't appreciate all that my father and I gave to the Foundry, to the industry that quite literally forms the foundation of New Inland. But I know enough to know that AgriCorps is crucial to all those workers giving the best years of their lives to keep the engines running. We all have to eat, right? So, to your last comment, if she knew what Ap-Oz has done, I'm sure she'd be thrilled. If you want to send one of your pages out to find her, she's in the Gardens somewhere."

"Again, I apologize. My point was that Ap-Oz has been beneficial to everyone in New Inland. My hope is that your developments in biosynth can further help in the domain of security for all, as it has in public health."

"Only if the Council wants it to." Out of the corner of his eye, he saw Karyn cupping her hands over her face. Steven cursed himself under his breath. She'd told him that Harus Salter could be sympathetic, given his tenure in public health. But why did he bring up Dianna Langley?

Marribel. Of course. She'd held the public health and medical research portfolio for years. She had to have told Harus to bring up his mother. They were clearly colluding.

"I have nothing further." Mayor Salter bowed his head and sat back in his chair.

"Let's get this over with. Who's next?"

Marribel ignored him. "Mayor Sylla Pierre, Preston." The pod rotated to the Preston delegation and Steven topped off his java.

"I have questions concerning your ongoing investigation into the terror campaign within your city, particularly in regards to why it has been thus far limited to Capston."

"Have at it."

"Have you been able to determine why it's only your city?"

"It's pretty hard to ask *why* now that Paolo Desantos is dead. And your 2nd has pointed out that venturing outside of New Inland is illegal. So, how do you suppose I could find out?"

"You've reported that Major Wall received intelligence from an unknown informant. Can I assume they didn't provide any motive?"

"You can assume whatever you want. The informant transferred hundreds of files and photos. None of them offered any explanation. But I have my hunches."

Sylla blinked her long lashes. "I'm sure you do—so do I. Your perpetrators have a clearly defined target. It's obvious to me that the motive is to direct some sort of revenge against your city, or someone in it. Would that make sense?"

"That would make sense to a fourth grade student, but yes."

"So, it would stand to reason, Mayor Reekan, that you've investigated business dealings, external affairs, and connections that may have come in contact with Motherland, perhaps through the Allens?"

Steven sloshed his cup after a long gulp. "You're the foreign affairs expert, Sylla. Maybe you could give me a lesson. *Yes,* we've followed up on correspondences, illegal transfers, and business ventures outside of Capston and New Inland—hell, Phil Fox advocated for that! And all it got us was dead end after dead end, and more attacks."

"And still, you—"

"Let me tell you a little story, Sylla. Long, long ago, I sat at the dinner table with my mother and my father. He'd come home from work with a new bandage over a new burn—nothing new when you work in the Foundry. I have my share of scars. Anyhow, as he's picking all the green vegetables out of his supper, he goes on to tell us all about how he got his latest burn. Was it the smelter? Not this time. No, he was volunteered by the asshole foreman to move tailings. For those of you who don't know, those are the leftover chemicals used in rendering reclaimed rare earth metals."

Marribel clicked her microphone control, but Steven shouted her down. "I'm making my point, Madam Chair. Turn that off and let me finish." To his surprise, she acquiesced.

"Why did they have to move tailings? Surely they have a safe disposal site for chemicals so dangerous—I mean, if that got into New Inland's aquifer, thousands might get sick or die. And yes, there was a disposal site… Except that it wasn't so safe anymore. Turns out that it had cracked somewhere near the bottom, and for some reason, it went undetected—by us, anyway."

"Steven, you're filibustering to use up Mayor Pierre's time." Marribel's hand trembled making her gavel wobble.

"We didn't notice it right away. But a small settlement not too far away did. Ever heard of a town called Jude?"

"Steven! Your time is up!"

"It just so happens that a young boy from Jude was adopted by Santiago De Léon—he's known as His Eminence in Motherland. And that boy grew up to be his puppet master. Imagine that!"

"*Mayor Reekan!*" Marribel hammered her gavel until it cracked and the head fell to the chamber floor.

"New Inland poisoned the well of Desantos's hometown! *That's why they hate us!* And now, he has a chance to get revenge! Do you want to know who's responsible?"

Marribel's nostrils flared. "Your time is up! One more word, and you will be—"

"*It's me!*"

The chamber fell silent.

Rust to Rust

Crystal Sheppard, the pharmaceutical student, was a fraud.

All the high grades, all the nights she chose to stay home and study, all the praise Laurent heaped upon her, all the lies she told herself. All of it meant nothing in the hour she needed it most. Hewer had reached to his son's face, wiped his hair into a neat part, and closed his eyelids. She was sure the deep crimson had begun to fade back to white. As she lay him back onto the moss bed beneath some trees on some road, she saw Jamiss, son of Hewer, in a different light. His skin was patches of pink and red, as though he were a newborn fresh from the womb.

Hewer retreated to the truck and climbed into the cargo hold. After rifling through supplies, he returned with a round-mouthed spade. Crystal had retreated several arm's lengths from Jamiss. She knew she should have been as far as possible, but she couldn't leave him. Not yet. Hewer tramped into the brush and drove the spade into the dirt, shoveling load after load like a human excavator for nearly half an hour. They never spoke. Crystal let him lift his own son one final time. He carried him as gently as a crate of hand grenades. Crystal watched from the side of the road into the thicket at the shadow of a father leaning to kiss his dead child one last time on the forehead, before lowering him into the open grave. He didn't cry; the anguish had been spent back on the road. After a vigil of several minutes, Hewer began to return the turned earth into the grave, sprinkling it evenly until it was filled. He leaned on the handle of the spade. The sun began to wane in the west.

If we have to stay here overnight…

The Geiger alert back in the cab had fallen silent sometime while

Hewer was filling his son's grave. Hamm and Duncam were gone. Neither waited around for radiation poisoning. She was relieved that she didn't have to see either of their traitorous faces again. The sun had finally set when Hewer came out of the brush and back to the truck. He sat on the lip of the open cargo hold. Crystal sat beside him.

"I dug the hole double wide." The big man rubbed his fingers, blistered and cracked, leaking fluid. "I dug a hole wide enough so I could lay there with him. In the same grave, so we'd never be apart again."

Crystal's eyes watered. "He wouldn't want you to." She didn't know that for sure. *What's one more lie…*

"We're driving through the night. You can sleep back here if you want. We'll get to Carroway by morning."

Crystal shook her head and joined him in the cab. The engine coughed to life, and Hewer gazed one last time toward Jamiss's last resting place. As they lurched away, Hewer found his voice, as though his grief stayed behind with his son.

"There was nothing you could do. I know."

No! There was plenty I could have done!

"I wish I could—"

"I'll stop you right there. Weren't no one could save my boy." Hewer held the wheel loosely, weaving around jutted rocks and tree roots spotted by the yellow-white beams of headlights. "But you *held* him. You didn't run away."

Maybe it was guilt. Maybe it was something programmed into her training that came out by instinct. No matter how much white noise buzzed in her memory, she remained present. Offer comfort when there was none. Solace. Humility. She wasn't a doctor, but she didn't have to be a doctor to offer these things.

"There's a high-wattage tower in Carroway. We'll need that if I'm going to convert your insider credit."

Something in his plan didn't make sense. "You mean Aynslie?"

Hewer shook his head. "Aynslie don't know shit unless it's a hunk of rusty junk."

Crystal remembered when Hamm and Duncam looked at each other back at the campfire, like they were keeping playground secrets. The mug. The symbol.

"*You're* with Rust."

Hewer nodded. "Carroway has an apothecary, pills and potions from all across the badlands. Natural stuff, synthetic stuff like you sell. You'll find what you need."

Crystal couldn't let her guard down. *This is the outside.* "I don't know what to say."

"Don't have to say anything. Jamiss might've killed someone." The boy had uttered the words, but provided no context or details. "But I'm damn sure he didn't *want* to kill anyone. You know why I didn't lay down beside him?"

Outside the cab, the night was deep, the headlights stabbing the darkness.

"Because he'd want me to be sure he didn't kill you too."

The Weapon and the Wound

Monday, 2 July AC 0245
DHC Rotunda, New Inland
Mayor Steven Reekan

The central pod rotated to align with Capston's, and as it came to a soft halt, Steven made eye contact with Karyn Kendall. Marribel kept her microphone off. Karyn waited a few awkward seconds before speaking.

"Take your time, Your Worship. Representative Brien has loaned his remaining time."

Steven rubbed his eyes and attempted to compose himself. "Ask away, Miss Kendall. I'm ready."

"Can you clarify your last statement? You said that *you're* responsible."

Steven closed his eyes. For a moment, he was back in Jason Holt's gallery. The holographic window that once bloomed with nature was hollow, fragmented shards of polymer-infused glass like teeth on a gaping, angry maw, a portal into the blackness in that white room. Electrical components crackled and hissed, wires twitched and smoke curled from tiny bursts of sparks. The lush forest had morphed into a foundry, all the sounds of hammers on anvils, of gears and grinding wheels, of pistons and presses. It was a world he knew better than anything.

"It was *me*. It was my *father*. It was *everyone* who worked the Foundry. It was *all of us*."

Steven shuddered until his legs began to buckle. Everything surrounding the Motherland attacks on Capston came into a perfectly logical focus. Tirel Desantos had lost everything as a child—his parents, his home, his childhood, his future. Until Motherland took him in. Until De Léon gave him shelter, sustenance, education, and guidance. Until a whole nation gave him belonging, direction, devotion, and respect.

This wasn't Tirel Desantos against New Inland. It was Motherland against the world.

And despite all the means at his disposal, Tirel Desantos had wielded the most reliable weapon in his arsenal. He'd been crafting it for years, pounding his hammer on molten metal, side over side, sparks flying as the blade sharpened.

Some days you're the hammer. Other days, you're the anvil.

But what is produced between the two… now that's what it's all about…

The weapon was his own son, Paolo. It made perfect sense. Weapons are only as reliable as their craftsmanship.

"Why Capston? That's obvious—we're the easiest! We're unprepared! We're the fat, soft underbelly of the Federation! Fox tried so hard to do it the right way, to follow the rules. And you know what? I never blamed him for it. But what happens when you play by the rules? You lose."

Trahearn Reekan had played by the rules, and all it got him was forced retirement and cancer. Steven clenched and relaxed the wound beneath his bandage. Tirel Desantos's weapon had struck a blow that cost Swift their life, left an open sore on the surface of Allentown, and a deep division inside the DHC chamber of New Inland.

Through the echoes of steel on steel in his mind, Karyn's voice pierced like an intravenous line.

"I'd like to turn our attention to the evidence that was transfered to Major Wall's handheld device. It's clear that the evidence your forensics collected from the Sheppard attack led you to Allentown and ultimately Motherland. Can you explain to us why Motherland as state-sponsor of this terrorism is significant?"

"As the Council should be aware, the Free City of Motherland fought a lengthy war against the coalition of five cities that now comprise New Inland. Much of the theatre of war took place over and inside Allentown, which had chosen neutrality. Motherland accepted defeat, on the condition that Allentown would be left as a buffer zone, and that New Inland would not encroach on Motherland's right to exist."

"Of course, the conflict was more complicated, but otherwise that's a clear explanation. Thank you. Given this conflict took place generations ago, why do you feel Motherland has decided to risk hostility with New Inland now?"

Memories of his mother and father arguing about the transferring of waste chemicals played in his mind. From his darkened bedroom, Trahearn shouted over Dianna. *I didn't sign up for this... You don't understand...* Dianna pleading with him to say no... *I'll look like a coward... You already think I'm coward...* His father was no coward.

"Among the files we found on Major Wall's device, there were environmental reports—specifically about the quality of potable water in and around Motherland. Colonel Desantos has been sending expeditions further and further from the city to find clean sources. It turns out, the water table pollution has been happening for decades. The colonel himself was an orphan from an outlying community called Jude. The whole town was razed to the ground after the soil had become too contaminated."

"So, Colonel Desantos has a personal stake in all of this?"

"Wouldn't you?"

An expression of frustration came over Karyn's face. Steven's heart was still beating too fast from the last round of questions.

"I suppose I would. But I wouldn't choose to murder civilians for revenge. And neither would you."

"And that's why this situation is so dangerous—we're not dealing with a rational thinker. Desantos is feeding distorted facts to Eminence De Léon. He's a figurehead monarch with deep pockets."

"Paolo Desantos was assassinated in a massive explosion in Allentown, shortly after the one that nearly killed you and your team. Do you have any leads on who would have done that?"

"No. It wasn't us. Hell, the Allens could confirm that if you asked them. They confirmed to us that Paolo's body was found in the rubble of the Allentown National Bank—our money trail originally led us there."

"We have only a minute. Would you agree, Mayor Reekan, that with the death of Lieutenant-Colonel Paolo Desantos, an already unstable Colonel Tirel Desantos could become even more desperate?"

"Without a doubt. We have documentation in the cache of files that suggests that the Motherland Council of Regents is concerned that Eminence De Léon is compromised by Tirel's fanaticism. Popular opinion is firmly behind the Colonel. Hyper-nationalism is at an all-time high. The informant told Kenzy, 'you are not safe in your bunker'. *We* are not safe. The dome over New Inland will not protect us. They can get Kayewati mercenaries inside—"

"Time." Marribel's microphone crackled and the pod began to rotate.

"I have twenty seconds, Madam Chair." Karyn protested but the pod continued moving toward the Heartsburg pod.

"Mayor Reekan overextended his time with his outburst at Mayor Pierre. It's my time, now."

The Road from Hell

The next eight minutes were going to be the worst of his life. Worse than when his mother left. Worse than when his father died. Worse than being trapped for a week underground. Worse than when Shore told him that the Tan-Ro carrying the Sheppard brothers had disappeared.

Jennings Marribel, Mayor of Heartsburg and Chair of the New Inland DHC, had him dead in her sights for eight minutes. The pod came to an abrupt halt, sloshing his java cup. The woman sat behind her datapad like a statue, her facial features carved from granite, age spot-speckled and grim. Steven glared straight into her blue-grey eyes, stone cold and stark. Nearly a minute ticked off her time, neither blinking.

"Mayor Reekan, there is little more for me to ask. As Miss Kendall said, this is not a criminal court, and you are not on trial. But in one sense, you are."

"Be honest, Madam Chair. The verdict was already decided."

"That's your greatest flaw, Steven."

So much for formality. "And what is that?"

"Everyone is *against* you. You're *always* the victim. It's the world versus Steven Reekan!"

Steven swiveled his chair a full 360 degrees, making eye contact with every councilor, in the same order he had been questioned. The radius of the council circle was twenty meters. He could leap from his pod and in five strides or less be within arm's reach of any one of them. Sitting directly in the center of his judges, he had no cover, nowhere to hide, no escape route. He'd been trained how to fight, even against impossible odds. His training, of course, assumed his adversaries were wielding firearms.

His adversaries today were armed with much more dangerous weapons.

"From the moment I was confirmed Mayor, I knew I was up against the Council. I remember how it felt when you shook my hand that night. I remember how cold it was. How cold you are."

"I never liked you. But still, I offered you my hand."

"You offered me hypocrisy! At no time did I ever feel welcome in this chamber."

"And there you have it! You barged into this chamber as if it were Jason Holt's tavern. You ignored the rules. You violated our laws. And every time, you did it in the name of 'the greater good'. Forget that our laws have stood for generations—they've kept our federation safe and prosperous. But the minute you think you're being slighted, to hell with the rules!"

Steven's blood boiled. "Hypocrisy, ladies and gentlemen! Because you all know that laws are broken by every single one of you every day. You think no one knows every city in the federation has boots on the ground in Allentown and elsewhere? The Allens told us as much. And let's not forget about your garden, Jennings."

"I'm not the subject of this hearing. Nor are the rest of the council—only you."

"Are there any questions coming, or do you plan to use up your time insulting me?"

"Steven, the Council has heard you admit that you are indeed guilty of all accusations against you. You are in violation of the full disclosure statute to declare all scientific and technical innovation. You conducted official city business with the Allens. You set foot on Allentown soil in full disregard of a truce made long ago to keep the peace. And when given the chance to explain yourself, you chose to argue, blame, deflect."

She neglected to mention how several councilors poked and

prodded him, knowing full well he would strike back. It was a coordinated attack. Clandestine meetings had taken place. Deals had been struck. This was the best chance the DHC had to remove him before the Chair shifted to Capston. Mayor Reekan was only months away from becoming Chair Reekan. And Jennings Marribel was not going to have it.

"Steven, I have only one question. After all that has been revealed today, why *shouldn't* the council censure you?"

Steven looked over to Karyn. She remained expressionless, eyes narrow and lips tight. It was at that exact moment he knew he'd lost her. They'd discussed how the votes might play out, and all they needed was fifty-fifty. A tie meant he would be reprimanded and placed on a probationary period, but he would keep his seat in the Council. A clear victory seemed improbable. A clear loss, however…

"The Council is bound to its laws, of course. I know that! Believe me, I don't stay up at night planning to break more rules in the morning. The only reason I'm sitting here is because our city is under siege! You wish you still had Phil Fox here because he was a good guy—he's cut from the same cloth as everyone else in this room. Everyone but me, of course."

He took a long gulp of room-temperature java, a thin streak of the deep brown liquid running down his chin. "But that's the problem with the DHC. None of you are cut from the same fabric as the rest of us." Steven pointed at the floor. "All those people, scurrying around way below us, they have no idea how things work up here. To them, on any given day, we're just ghosts. Our forebears used to look up at the sky and imagine angels living in the clouds. The DHC—we're about as real. They don't know if we wear white robes and have wings, or if we carry forks and have tails. And you know what the real kicker is? I'm sitting here myself, and I can't tell the difference!"

"Then why do you even want to be here, Steven? Who's all this for?"

"I swear, Jennings, if you mention my parents—"

"Why are you doing this, Mayor Reekan?"

"Because I have to!"

And that was it. He could rhyme off half a dozen reasons. Safety. Security. Political ambition. Pride. Altruism. Only, he wasn't going to convince anyone. The road from the Foundry to the DHC had indeed been paved with the best of intentions. But no one was interested in intentions. Steven looked around him. The DHC Rotunda wasn't so different from the Foundry. Machinations clicked and whirred in impossibly intricate patterns. But everything connected into one big machine, and if anything slipped a cog or clogged a line, the whole thing would grind to a halt. The Foundry was devoid of emotion. The molten metal didn't care if it burned the flesh. The sparks never suffered the souls. And here, in the most intricate and finely-tuned instrument of law and order, the code didn't suffer the heart.

Steven Reekan was guilty. He was guilty of believing otherwise.

"You have your time for rebuttal, Mayor."

What was left to say? For the next five minutes, Steven Reekan sat as still as the twenty councilors. There was nothing left. Every second ticking off the timer brought him one second closer to the end of the line. And with every one, kilograms of weight lifted from his shoulders, until he expected to float from his seat into the air like a balloon from a small child's feeble grip. He looked one last time toward Karyn. The look in her eyes had shifted from incredulity to pity. No words were spoken, but he could hear her voice saying, *I'm sorry.*

Steven sat alone in the center pod as the last of the cleaners and pages filed out of the chamber. Above, the gallery seats came back into view as the blackout tint receded. From the skylight, artificial sunset darkened the chamber. The vote went exactly as he'd expected. 6-4. Karyn voted against him—against her 2nd, no less. Pax Brien would hold the mayoral seat until it was determined who would succeed Steven as Mayor. He *could* fight it. He could refuse to resign, and force the DHC to go down an unbeaten trail to determine who holds the first seat in the absence of a city mayor. Most likely, Phil Fox would return as solicitor, and as such ascend to Capston's mayoral seat on the council. *If* he came back.

Steven wouldn't blame him if he didn't.

His handheld buzzed.

`Take a week to think about it. I'm sorry. K`

Steven closed his eyes. Shore and Ling were more than capable of holding down the fort. Ap-Oz was looking like the best option for him. *Maybe this is how Phil Fox felt...*

Terms

Lunes, 16 abril NE 267
Eastern Lake Region
Lieutenant-Colonel Paolo Desantos

A man of your… skillsssss… should have n-n-no trouble learning." The Junquer slurred and stumbled on his words as though he were tripping down a flight of stairs. Paolo cradled the handheld device carefully in his palm. So many functions, so many applications—all crammed into a mess of capillary wires and silicon chips. Parts were tucked beneath polymer panels to keep the innards from spilling out. Most of the key was exposed. Paolo expected the machine to be warm in his hand. It was as cold as a poker.

"I am impressed, Junquer." Paolo slid his calloused thumb across the screen. It was smoother than polished marble. The engineer had quipped that the blade of his knife wouldn't scratch it. Paolo wanted to try, if only out of curiosity.

"C-c-calibrated to all known c-c-communication towers on the… continent—though you have to ch-ch-check it every so often. Might go miles without re… re…"

Junquer doubled over and hacked so hard Paolo thought his chest would collapse. All around them, the man had parts for any device, tool, or machine imaginable. None of them could help with the litany of health problems that beleaguered him. The man was a genius. That genius must have come at a high cost.

"…re-CEP-tion." When the spasms stopped, he stood upright. Blood had trickled from the corners of his mouth, over the crusted remnants of a prior coughing fit.

"I am sure it will suit my needs."

"No refunds… But I'm sure…" Paolo couldn't even assume he was an old man despite his appearance. He'd come across pitiful denizens of the outside world in as bad shape, and not all were elderly. Red tide was primarily a respiratory ailment. But there were other diseases that chose other more gruesome means of killing their hosts. Whatever had befallen the Junquer had ravaged his skin, to the point it appeared to be melting off him in places. *What a cruel end.*

"If that is all…" *…we should settle accounts and part ways.* Staying in the Junquer's underground lair for even a minute more than necessary wouldn't do. Paolo wasn't accustomed to escaping unseen enemies. He backed a step away, scanning for the nearest exit.

"Your advance is enough, young lion." Junquer hobbled from his work bench to the nearest of several metal cabinets. He knelt on a shaking knee, keeping his balance while he cleared away piles of supplies and wires. "Keep your father's money…"

The Allens had facilitated 60% of the agreed sum; the remainder was to be paid upon completion of the task. Paolo keyed his financial account onto the key screen. The remainder was staggering, even for a Motherland elite. How much of those funds were skimmed from Eminence De Léon? From the subjugation of smaller communities within striking distance of the walled city?

Forgiveness of the final 40%, that was too good to be true. There had to be a catch.

"I have one final request, young lion."

Here it comes. Paolo lowered his hands. The man wobbled, then pried open the door of a cabinet that may not have been opened in years. His head disappeared out of view, as he rustled through its contents.

"It would be… wrong of me to charge you full p-price. Not when I've… been building this k-key for many years." His voice was muffled in a tinny echo. "I was going to see… the world... You see, this was a key to my own freedom…"

He spat on something that pinged. Paolo didn't have time for any of this. No side quests. No deliveries. No Allens. No Rust. No Kayewati. Just finish the damn transaction and part ways.

The man crouched back on his ankles, clutching another handheld, similarly unfinished like the key Paolo had purchased. Junquer held it up to his cracked lips and wheezed a feeble breath. Dust whirled and a trembling, thin finger touched the screen. A faint blue light reflected onto the old man's face. Paolo's forehead wrinkled.

"I am not long for this world. When the Ansati collect my body, they will surely empty this place of its secrets… of which there are… many…" Junquer lost his balance and toppled to the floor. He wriggled on his back like a turtle helpless on his shell. Paolo grimaced. The whole scene was pathetic. Here wallowed a man of such incalculable intelligence, someone who could have changed the world… Wallowing in his own filth. The pungent stench of urine wafted through the already dank workspace. *Great. He pissed himself.*

"I've transferred the control to your key. When you have left the lair, and you are far enough… Activate the red tab." All around the room, lights blinked to life from corners on both the ceiling and floor. Every one was located at a load-bearing juncture.

He is mad. This whole facility is rigged and armed.

"The Reapers… they spread disease… they did this… to me…" The Junquer managed to orient himself, leaning on his elbow. "I wish to be interred in this place, surrounded by my life's work…"

"The Reapers brought this condition upon you?"

Junquer nodded.

"You sought no treatment?"

"Nothing… can treat… what afflicts me, young lion."

Paolo looked at the key screen. A scrolling blur of data rushed across the bottom of the window. A significant amount of information was uploading.

"I spent yearsss…"

Paolo's eyes widened. The Junquer had been a busy man. Ansati secrets were rarely sought, and never unearthed. As the old man's voice faltered, Paolo imagined the contents of the uploading files. Strongholds. Treasuries. Perhaps even the route to the Ansati city of Moab…

There were few places on the face of the earth Paolo dreaded more.

"I have seen Moab. The journey took years off my life." It made sense. Many of Junquer's wounds were reminiscent of radiation burning. In all likelihood, his immune system had been long ago compromised. Simple ailments might be life-threatening to him. "They are thieves, young lion. Thieves of culture. Thieves of humanity… They will not steal me…"

"You expect me to do it? Why not do it yourself?"

Junquer cackled. "If I died in my sleep…"

If he died unexpectedly, anyone could scavenge his lair. The old man wanted his life's work to die with him. But not just a peaceful death. He desired all of it to erupt in one glorious, final burst of light. Paolo couldn't help believe he was a hostage. 'Finish it on my terms, or face your maker alongside me.'

"You are a far superior heir to Motherland than your father, young lion. You are the sum of your nation's prosperity. I will not see the fruit of my labours. But *you*… You can rid the land of Ansati filth. You are no lamb, Paolo Desantos. *You are a lion—*"

Paolo drew his sidearm and shot the Junquer directly between his sick, streaked eyes. What remained of his carcass crumpled, his legs contorting as his head struck the floor like a ripe melon.

The key alerted him when Paolo had crossed the twenty-kilometer invisible boundary. From his position on a plateau, gazing toward the ruins of the city of lions, the mighty lake a line of grayish blue just beyond, he watched as the eruption of flame, debris, smoke, and soil blossomed into the evening sky. Paolo spat the last taste of the lair. Junquer was a disgusting coward. In his delusion, he had built this image of a saviour, sent to wash away the sins of grave-robbing druids. So convinced he was, he built a device strong enough to allow him to do it.

But he had made one critical miscalculation. He had never asked Paolo if he shared the vision.

Highwayman

AC 0240
Sheppard Family Inn, Capston
Cadlen Sheppard

You know, your brother Lorrie used to try the same tricks to stay up later."

Julia Sheppard tilted her head and smiled. Cadlen sat upright, his pillow tucked beneath his tailbone. Ever since his mom and dad gave in and let him draw until he was tired, he found himself calmer, less afraid of the shadows. Those fears took the form of marks on a sketch pad, as though drawing them was a way of imprisoning the nasty monsters. Those shifting shapes in the dark used to make him cry out, so much he grew to hate the sound of his own voice. Drawing gave him control.

Cadlen smiled. He knew his mom couldn't resist.

"I remember a story Monsieur Laurent told us girls. In the wilderness around Hyacynthe, we were safe from highwaymen."

Highwaymen? That was an unfamiliar word. Cadlen narrowed his eyes.

"Laurent called them *voyageurs, courreurs des bois*. Highwaymen are brigands that move along the travel routes looking for travelers to rob."

Oh, brigands.

"They're like pirates without ships, on the land and not the sea. Laurent told us girls that we had to be sure we were safe from highwaymen before we started a fire. Because the fire might keep us warm, might cook our catch—but it could alert unwelcome guests."

Cadlen wondered what was worse—shivering and hungry, or an encounter with land pirates.

"I asked him, how do you know someone is a highwayman? Laurent said it wasn't how they looked, but what they said. The highwaymen of the old times, they would say 'your money, or your life!'"

Cadlen flipped page after page of his sketch pad until he found a drawing he'd made while watching the shows. In his eight-year-old hands, he held it up so Julia could see.

"Oh yes, Ranger Man! He tracks down highwaymen, doesn't he?" Cadlen watched the classic program faithfully. The titular hero always got his man or woman. The enemies could be either, but they always *looked* a certain way, *spoke* a certain way. They talked like half their mouth was paralyzed. They always wanted something. Ranger Man could always tell.

"It's time to get some sleep, Cadlen." Julia leaned forward and kissed his cheek, brushing his hair to the side. Soon she would tell him it was time for a haircut. He dreaded it.

"You know—one more drawing, then it's lights out."

Cadlen smiled and flipped to an open page. When his mother closed the door, he started scrawling lines in crisscross and swirling shapes, forming a fire pit with flames dancing above a tent-shaped arrangement of sticks. He'd left his colours out in the lobby, so he had to imagine the orange and red. When he closed his eyes, the fire would be a beacon of safety. Ranger Man was hiding in the bushes, watching for highwaymen.

Wednesday, 27 June AC 0245
SSE of Inland Open-Pit Lake
Cadlen Sheppard

Cadlen worked away at a small circular pit made of rocks he had found around the campsite. Inside, he piled up some dried branches and green clumps of tree moss. He'd drawn this exact formation many times. His brothers looked at each other in bewilderment.

"Cadlen, you know how to build a fire?"

He wandered into the brush to find more fuel. His mother had told him that some kinds of tree bark was good fire-starting material. His brothers talked to each other as though he couldn't hear, or as if he wasn't there. He was used to it.

"Do you suppose Mom told him the same story?"

"Wouldn't he have been too young to remember a story like that, with all the details and everything?"

Lorrie knelt by the pit, machete in hand, raising it impossibly high before striking the flint. "Maybe? I don't know. He's always been a good listener, though."

Cadlen used the hunter's knife to saw boughs off saplings. As his brothers argued about how they were going to find food, he set about preparing a shelter the only way he knew how. Double the thickness underneath you, she once told him. Cold comes up from below. Insulate.

Rather than peel the white/silver bark for fire starting, Cadlen realized that if he was careful, and he dug the knife edge deep enough, he could peel wide strips off the trees and use them for waterproofing the bough lean-to he'd built. Weaving the strips together, he figured that if it rained, the water would run off the back of the meager shelter rather than soak his only layer of clothes. Once Robbie caught wind of what he was doing, he and Lorrie set about to make their own shelters, triangulating around the perimeter of the fire. Talk of hunting subsided. The fire had taken hold once the dried moss and twigs caught the spark from Lorrie's machete. Once he was finished with his shelter, Cadlen would have to add some heavier wood.

As the Sheppard brothers crouched inside their shelters, the fire crackled.

"Now if only we had some chops and some vegetables." Robbie smiled at his brothers. "Don't suppose you have any, do you?"

"There you go, talk about food why don't you?" Lorrie grimaced. "I wasn't hungry until you brought it up."

Cadlen wasn't hungry. In the morning, he'd look for berries that his mom once described in an adventure she'd taken with their father, where Robert almost ate the wrong kind before Julia showed him that he'd have a terrible reaction. He settled into the boughs, a gentle heat enveloping him as the three brothers quieted in the darkening twilight. He hoped the fire didn't attract any highwaymen.

The Sheppard brothers woke to the chill of morning, their fire long dead while they slept. The pangs in Cadlen's stomach woke him. He had been so worried about making shelter and staying warm that any hunger he'd felt was manageable. On day three, they would have to find food. By the look on Lorrie's face, he wasn't the only one starving. Robbie wasn't joking about chops and veggies this morning.

Cadlen reached for his leaf full of berries. It had been almost two days without food. Everything was starting to look edible—even tasty. The berries might upset his stomach, but anything would be better than the rolling pangs contracting in his belly.

Robbie crawled out of his shelter and stretched his hands above his head. Lorrie grumbled as he awoke from his slumber, scratching at the exposed side of his abdomen where the shirt had ripped. Robbie's eyes narrowed on the leafy cup of green beads in Cadlen's shaking hand.

"Where did you pick those, Cad?"

Cadlen pointed behind him to a shrub tall enough to be a small tree, with small white flowers beginning to bloom on its willowy branches. There were dozens of small clusters of the newly emerged berries. Robbie narrowed his eyes.

"We don't know what we can or can't eat out here. You could eat one of those and keel over in seconds!"

"Maybe they aren't exactly nutritious, but they wouldn't kill us, right?" Lorrie squinted and scratched his messed hair. "I mean, people live off the land everyday out here."

Robbie waved his hand. "If *you're* such a survivalist, then why don't you try one? But, if you get so much as a fever in the next day or two, you'll know why."

Lorrie grimaced at his brother's sarcasm. Cadlen gazed at the berries, the cupped leaf preventing them from directly touching him. He glanced back and forth at his older brothers. Robbie was wise for his age. He did his best for the family, but he wasn't always right. It was Robert and Julia that went on the Retreats all those years before he was born. They would have known what to do.

And then there was Lorrie. Even if he was a jerk, he was a fighter. Cadlen remembered all the times he came home with a new bruise, or a fresh cut, or ripped clothes. There were days he came home looking worse than he did after surviving a helicopter crash. But he had heard all the Retreat stories, too. He had managed to build the campfire. Lorrie was a jerk. But that didn't make him wrong.

Cadlen reached into the makeshift cup and selected a berry. It was firm, but tender.

"No Cadlen, don't you eat one." Lorrie walked over to the nearest clump of flowering shrubs and plucked one of his own. "I'd rather get sick myself than let you try it." Cadlen pursed his lips. He couldn't remember the last time Lorrie had acted so selfless toward him.

"You're an idiot," jeered Robbie. "But whatever, don't listen to me. What do I know?"

Lorrie held the berry close to his lips. Cadlen could tell by the way he rolled it in his fingers, how he smelled it, that he was just as hungry. They were all hungry. And unless a solution came charging out of the brush into their campsite, their stomachs would contort and heave until they broke down and started to chew on anything green or red. Cadlen sat very still and watched Lorrie wrestle with the choice.

The moment was only a few seconds, but it felt like an hour had passed. The two brothers snapped to attention as Robbie smacked Lorrie's hand, sending the berry flying into the tall grass beyond the range of the campfire's heat and light. Lorrie slapped his shoulder.

"What's wrong with you? I can make my own decisions!"

"And what if it's poisonous, Lor? You go act the hero, eat the berries, and then what? You start puking in the bushes and before you know it you're unconscious! *Then* what?"

Lorrie postured his shoulders wide, spreading his arms. "What do you want *me* to do, Robbie? You don't know any more about this place! You're no hunter, no great family provider! Gonna charge into the forest and come back with a rabbit or a deer, all skinned and ready to throw on the fire?"

Robbie's eyes were watering in the creases, but he glowered back at Lorrie, like so many times before. Cadlen closed his eyes and imagined how Lorrie would have reacted if it was his father and not his brother arguing with him over a couple wild berries. Of course, none of this was about berries. It was much more than that.

"What do *we* do? *We* sleep on it. Gather our things and start walking. There are people out here, and maybe we'll find someone who can help us. Who actually knows what they're doing! Someone who can give us food that won't give us the shits, or dehydrate us, or—I don't know—*kill* us!"

Lorrie huffed and waved his arms in exasperation.

"Oh yes, we'll just saunter on through the bushes—find some tiny cabin with an elderly couple who'll take us in, and feed us a stew and garden vegetables!"

The brothers argued back and forth for several minutes. Every retort was a volley from two stubborn combatants. Every comment landed sharper and harder. The pain in his chest from watching his brothers fight was almost as acute as his hunger.

"Why are you doing this, Lorrie? Why do you feel you have to go sacrifice yourself?" Robbie sighed, cupping his face in his hands.

"Don't you think Dad would have done it for us? *He* would have taken the risk so we wouldn't have to."

Robbie pounded his fist into his open palm. *"But I'm not Dad!"*

"Damn right, you're not."

And with that shot, Lorrie had struck the winning blow. Robbie's face faded into a sickly pallor; the whites of his eyes reddened.

Cadlen didn't expect Lorrie's reaction, however. The look on his face equaled that of Robbie, as though he was the one who'd suffered the low blow.

"I mean, Dad had the experience, right? From the Retreats, I meant. They taught him how to identify edible plants."

Cadlen couldn't remember Lorrie ever backtracking in an argument. The words that escaped his lips were sharper than he was letting on. And Robbie couldn't deny their truth.

It was in that awkward ceasefire that Cadlen noticed the movement from behind the berry bushes. Not a bird, or a squirrel—something that moved all at once, as though it had been there the whole time, waiting to reveal itself. And when it did, it was as though it had crawled right out of the television screen. Or from the pages of his sketch books. Cadlen startled himself with the sound of his own voice.

"Ranger Man."

In an instant, the argument was forgotten. The two elder brothers snapped to attention. Turning to their younger brother, the boys saw Cadlen glaring beyond the perimeter of the campfire. Following his gaze, Robbie and Lorrie spied the form of a man, emerged silently from the shadows of the tree line. The sun had risen. The intruder wore a stained, sleeveless shirt, his hair hanging in tangles around and over his cheeks. He spoke softly, but his words carried heavy in the morning air. Between his dirty fingers, he held up a sprig of the shrub, plump with green berries.

"I advise you not to eat those."

Interlude: The Homily

Chapel of St. Jude
Syballine Sister Ave Maria

☥

Welcome one and all who have traveled from afar. We hope you all find comfort in this place, as it has offered as much to so many over generations. The Chapel of St. Jude has changed. Once erased from history, it has been brought back to life in the image of our late designer." Sister Estelle paused and looked down at my mother and Dr. Sheppard. "Cadlen Sheppard lives forever in his work. We thank you."

Mother nodded, her lace veil rippling. Dr. Sheppard held her close, tears welled in her eyes. It was all I could do to hold myself together.

For him.

For all of them.

"We would observe a moment of silence in remembrance of that day so many years ago. When so many lives changed forever. Some ended. Others lived on with scars and sorrow." Sister Estelle looked up to the balcony. The hooded man shuddered, and the Ansati Brothers steadied him. No one else looked his way. But I couldn't look away from him yet. He needed to be present, but that did not make it any more comfortable. The moment passed, as our people would say, in the width of an ocean and the breadth of an eye.

The guests waited quietly. Among them, many faces were

familiar to me. Chair Karyn Kendall. Representative Laurent with his family. People from all walks of life and every corner of the land. Clearly, my father touched the lives of many.

Sister Estelle, only a young girl all those years ago, read another passage from the *Chronicles*:

"We came upon a room one day with a great hearth, the brick mortared together by a skilled mason. The carved wood was deep and wise. The photographs in their frames were images that made us smile, for they were our past lives. Mirrors, each and every one. Below, the embers feasted upon the logs. They engulfed the open space with the warmth of gratitude.

We could not leave them behind. We gathered the mirrors and offered our thanks, and we remembered as they slowly faded away. Cold crept back into the room, and satisfied with our stay, we moved on.

We sat around a grand table, dressed with the finest meal. Fresh greens, roasted fowls in rich sauces, pastries sweet and rich. Enough wine to redden our cheeks flowed from earthen vessels spun by the skilled hands of potters. We joined hands around the table and again we gave thanks for the bounty that lay before us. Only the sounds of consumption could be heard as we licked the platter to a shine. Yet, languishing in gluttony, we felt the first flickers of returning hunger. A voice inside said, 'you hunger still, because you can never fully be nourished'. We rose from our chairs, offered our gratitude, and moved on.

We found a great archive. Shelves lined the walls from floor to ceiling. They contained books, small boxes, jars, and artifacts of innumerable origin and design. We fed our minds with the memories of souls glaring back through their mirrors. We filled our ears with folklore and fancy as the melody unfurled from the machines of divine song. We satiated our ever-present hunger as we sought and found. But we were never satisfied, for satisfaction is impossible. Desire can only end with sleep.

Drowsy from our journey, we yearned for slumber. Behind our eyelids, a voice sounded. "Why would you surrender now, while you still thirst for more?"

We had found all we could find. We would lie down, weary as we were from the world.

The voice said, "In your wisdom, you have yet to find the door. Are you afraid of the egress, or only afraid?"

The question perplexed us. We dashed to and from each room, finding windows were waiting all along. And sure enough, we found a door. Forty pairs of hands heaved in unison.

What awaited us outside was frightening."

Chronicles of the Ansati 7-13

II: The Fox

Accession

Sábado, 23 junio NE 267
Concilio de Regentes, Motherland
Captain Tomás Alvara

You will know when it is time…

Tomás Alvara lived his entire life within the walls of Motherland. There was hardly a square inch of the free city he had never seen. The *Concilio de Regentes* was one he never expected to visit, given the sanctity of the Council of Regents and their privacy. Tomás never fully understood the duties of the Council, apart from their appearance as a senate to the sovereign. The eleven councilors always appeared at public functions, adorned in their garish robes and medallions. They never spoke. They never issued any statements. In fact, they rarely interacted with the public. Only Magister Solanis he knew by name, and nothing more.

The acrid smell of burned candles mixed with mold permeated the *Concilio*. The floors creaked from warping. Streaks from water leakage trickled like blood down the walls and tapestries hung like rags, faded despite the distinct lack of sunlight. Tomás had expected better. The instant he stepped through the wooden doors, he was overcome with the oppressive aura of a chamber that had at one time been vital. The Council of Regents had become as stale as their inner sanctum.

At the head of the room, the Regents flanked Magister Solanis's throne, five per side. Each wore their traditional cap, conical and inscribed with the image of *La Golondriña*. Magister Solanis wore no headpiece on his balding scalp. Tomás assumed he was old enough to have been De Léon's father. In the petitioner's bench, Colonel Desantos waited for Solanis to bring the emergency meeting to order. Tomás sat in the gallery nearest the exit, deliberately assigned to prevent entry or exit.

"As we come to order, Colonel, the Council would remind you that firearms are prohibited in the *Concilio*." The Magister glared at Tomás. The old man wielded more gravitas than Eminence De Léon. Tomás didn't know if he should reply.

"Magister—Councilors, you can forgive me for such a brutish display. Lieutenant-Colonel Alvara serves to protect all of us, in light of such recent tragedy."

Lieutenant-Colonel. There had been no formal promotion. No grand parade, no ceremony in *L'Estadio Real*. Not even a casual mention. Tomás had finally received his promotion, but at the cost Paolo Desantos's life, and his father's last thread of sanity. None felt it more than Eminence De Léon in his dying breath.

"The Council shares your sorrow, Colonel. Your son was a formidable man."

"My son *is* indeed formidable." Tirel's voice cracked. "Forgive me once more, Magister Solanis, as I am indeed still grieving his murder." Paolo's assassination had shaken the city. Tomás witnessed the recovery of body fragments in the ruins of the Nat Bank in Allentown. No direct proof of Steven Reekan's involvement had officially been produced. But Capston's presence in the city had been confirmed, and the Allen silence in the wake of the attack was deafening. They'd brought the fight to Motherland, just as Capston's firebrand mayor had promised.

Magister Solanis didn't react to Tirel's emotional plea. "Colonel, several weeks have passed. His Eminence De Léon has also succumbed in this time. Be assured the Council is also in mourning." Tomás shifted in his seat, the firearm stock pressed against his ribs. He didn't think Tirel could pull it off. After brutally murdering the sovereign in his own chambers, he'd somehow managed to clean it up perfectly. He'd even found a doctor to "confirm" that he had succumbed to his long-standing red tide symptoms, most pronounced being his wheezing, pained speech patterns. Once the body was burned at a pyre of his *spiritus arbor,* there would be no evidence. Tomás didn't ask what had become of Mariana the cleaner or the doctor who'd performed the autopsy.

"His passing doubled my grief. His Eminence, as you all know, was a father to me."

"And he was indeed fond of you, Colonel. You have petitioned for accession, despite no blood relation."

Tirel cleared his throat. "I am to understand that there is no precedent in our storied history. His Eminence bore no heirs. But I am also to understand that the adoption of wards provides the possibility of accession. Am I correct?"

Solanis nodded. "It has long been a concern of the Council that His Eminence would have to choose a line of accession, given his age. As it has been established, the petitioner requires unanimous consent."

Tomás swallowed. His rifle weighed heavy in his grip.

"His Eminence has long held me in favour. I was adopted as a boy, and served him as a ward through my compulsory military service. Under my leadership, the armed forces of Motherland have expanded our influence far and wide. And in the wake of continued environmental terrorism, I followed His Eminence's wishes to strike back at New Inland."

"Indeed, your successes are noted." Magister Solanis shuffled papers in his veined hands. "And you are aware, Colonel, that the Council is not unanimous in agreement with your policy towards our southern neighbours."

"With respect, Magister, I know all about our neighbours. More than the Council. Did you know, Councilors, that the Chair of their Domestic High Council, has been complicit in the environmental terrorism?"

The councilors murmured to each other. Solanis's eyes narrowed. "Be that as it may, you continued to wage a campaign of terror not on Jennings Marribel's city of Heartsburg, but on Capston. It has never been satisfactorily explained."

"As the hub of New Inland's financial sector and tourism, His

Eminence chose Capston as a means of striking them in their treasury. As you know, the federated domes live and die by their bank accounts."

"Yet, your subterfuge has yielded what? Mayor Reekan's unwavering resolve to seek revenge. And it appears that the cost was particularly high."

Tomás restrained himself from standing, taking aim, and silencing the Magister himself. Paolo Desantos had been his rival. His death allowed for his long-deserved promotion. But rhetorically alluding to his murder crossed a line.

"I petition the Council of Regents for ascension to Eminent Sovereign of Motherland."

"Colonel Desantos, for the past several weeks, you have been largely absent of the city. There has been no clarity as to our official response to the assault on our citizens abroad. There has been no evidence that your actions—even at the direction of His Eminence—have done any favour to our city. As of this hour, you do not have the unanimous vote to accede."

Colonel Desantos remained unexpectedly calm. Tomás found this more unsettling than if he'd leaped to his feet and raged against the robed councilors.

"I see." Tirel trembled. "And you have no further petitioners?"

"None." Solanis glared down at the colonel. "Until we are in agreement about the next course of action, the Council of Regents will maintain the order of the city."

"We'll see."

"Beg your pardon, Colonel?"

Tirel stood, slowly and deliberately. Tomás took his cue and stood, his rifle relaxed and ready.

"Tomás."

Before they'd entered the *Concilio de Regentes*, Tirel had outlined how this would proceed. *You will know when it is time. Start from the left. Spare the Magister.* Lieutenant-Colonel Alvara raised his weapon and fired, felling one councilor after the next. The final five had begun to flee, but none escaped Tomás's high-powered assault rifle. As the slaughter continued, Tirel didn't flinch. Magister Solanis, spared as instructed, hid behind his throne, pleading for the carnage to stop.

"I believe I have unanimous consent, Magister." Tirel turned, his face wild and speckled with blood. He strode towards the door and his new second in command. Tomás kept the barrel of the rifle raised, his fingers blistering in the vice-like grip. He breathed as he'd been taught so many years ago, when he was a junior officer, still afraid for his first kill. It gets easier, Tirel had once told him. As he gazed at the crumpled, twisted bodies, he told himself it wasn't so difficult.

Tirel placed a hand on the barrel of the rifle, gently lowering it. "Gather your agents. It is time."

A rush of adrenaline coursed through his body. The culling of the council was necessary. Tomás Alvara would at long last prove himself for generations to come.

"As you wish, Your Eminence."

Deus ex Umbra

Wednesday, 27 June AC 0245
SSE of Inland Open-Pit Lake
Robbie Sheppard

Once he'd stepped ashore, sopping from the lake shallows, Robbie had imagined a squad of Capston police rushing from the woods to their rescue. Lieutenant Shore smiling as he motioned for his team to rescue him and his brothers, assuring them they could go home. As soon as the idea of *home* arrived, the fantasy came crashing down faster than the Tan-Ro helicopter, faster than the Sheppard Inn. For three days, Robbie had scolded himself every time an ounce of hope crept into his brain. And still, it kept creeping back.

It was for that reason that he rubbed his eyes to the point they ached when the stranger emerged from the shadows of the brush surrounding their meager camp fire. Cadlen's voice made the whole episode feel more like a dream sequence, except the tone of his baby brother's voice had deepened since he'd last heard it. Maybe during those months, years since he'd last spoken aloud, Cadlen had bypassed the awkwardness of the change. He'd laughed way too hard at Lorrie's crackling and squeaking.

He's too young to sound so old. Maybe life has forced him to grow up too fast.

"Those berries will make you very sick. They could kill you."

The man glided through the tall grass without making a sound. As the flickering light from the fire revealed his physical appearance, Robbie noted that he wore tan-coloured cargo pants, stained in splotches of deep brown mud, and stringy, grass-green streaks from his thighs to his high-rising boots. He wore a deep green canvas shirt, buttons fastened except for the top two. His collar flared open, revealing some half-healed surface cuts on his neck and upper chest. A knapsack hung from his right shoulder. Wavy hair hung just below his chin, parted almost evenly to either side of his rugged face. Dark pupils peered without blinking from a face that showed several days' worth of stubble over a strong jawline. Red lines across his left cheek hinted at whiplash from rushing through heavy brush.

Whoever this guy is, he's been through hell before he found us. He certainly looked like someone not to be trifled with.

"Who the hell are you?"

Robbie grimaced at Lorrie's rude introduction. "Don't mind him. He tends to speak out like that when he's tired."

The man raised an eyebrow. "Is that so?" He dropped the knapsack into the grass and reached into one of the outer pockets.

"Whoa, there—what're you doing?" Lorrie crouched and grabbed a chunk of deadfall, pointing it like a spear.

The man retrieved a small, sealed package and tossed it to Robbie. "Soup. Mix it with clean water, boil it on your fire."

Robbie caught the packet as it flitted in the air. His dirty fingers stained the white envelope, obscuring the cooking instructions. "Are these field rations? Are you DefCorps?"

The man shook his head. "Defense Corps, no. But this is a travel ration, yes. I have more, enough for your brothers."

"How do you know we're brothers?" Lorrie hadn't let down his guard yet.

"Cadlen is the silent one. Robbie, the elder. And you, Lorrie, are the loud one."

"That's not fair! A mannequin would be louder than Cad. And just how long *have* you been watching us, anyway?"

The man reached back into the sack and retrieved two more pouches. "Long enough."

"Lorrie, don't you suppose if mister… I'm sorry, I didn't catch your name?"

"I did not offer it."

"Right. Anyway, our guest would have hurt us already if he wanted to." Robbie nodded to the stranger, hoping he would reciprocate.

He did. "I could have reached out and grabbed any one of you many times over the last hour. But as you said, Robbie Sheppard, I do not mean to hurt you."

Lorrie squinted, looked between his brothers and the stranger one last time, and eased the stick onto the fire without taking his eyes off him. "My brothers might believe you, but I'm not convinced."

The stranger brushed a lock of his hair off his cheek. "I don't blame you, Lorrie Sheppard. You are wise to keep your guard."

To Robbie's surprise, the man turned to leave the campsite. "Where are you going?"

The man stopped without turning back. "Keep your fire burning. I will be back with fresh meat to roast."

Without another word, he slipped into the shadows as quickly as he'd arrived. Robbie looked at Cadlen. He'd never taken his eyes off the stranger, the one he'd referred to as Ranger Man, from the picture shows they'd watched dozens of times. He pursed his lips like he did whenever he was deep in thought.

"I don't know, Cad. Ranger Man should be a little more… *lively*, don't you think?"

Robbie had hoped his youngest brother would answer, as if his exclamation had burst a verbal dam, and that a torrent of words would come rushing. It didn't. Cadlen shrugged his shoulders and turned to the fire, poking the embers with a wiry branch. The berries he was about to eat fell to the forest floor, scuttled beneath leaves and dried moss.

Lorrie huffed. "What's that guy about? Stalks us for hours, tosses us some freeze-dried lunch, talks like a robot—then *leaves?*"

"When you say it like that, it sounds like you're setting up for a joke." Robbie couldn't help but laugh.

"No joke, Robbie. We should get out of here before he comes back."

"What, leave this fire you've worked so hard to make?" Robbie turned to Cadlen, knelt and fed the flames with bigger pieces of wood and strips of bark. "What do you think, Cad? Should we trust him?"

Cadlen didn't answer, but he didn't wrinkle his forehead as he typically did when he wanted to say no. Maybe he believed that Ranger Man had actually come to save them. Robbie sighed. It was more than he could offer.

"Maybe he doesn't come back. Maybe you offended him and he's left us behind. More meat for himself." Robbie's stomach grumbled at the thought of roasted meat. At this rate, he'd eat it medium rare.

"Yeah, maybe the jerk left us with powdered stew. If that's the last I've seen of him, fine by me." Lorrie strode into the bushes.

"Where are you going? Think you can hunt, now?"

"We need more firewood, smart-ass! Besides, we don't have a cup to cook the rations in, anyway." Lorrie tramped around the bushes, muttering unintelligibly. He was right. Without anything to cook them in, the rations weren't very useful. As if on cue, Cadlen glared at the ground where the stranger had dropped his knapsack. Robbie followed his gaze and saw a grey tin cup lying on its side.

"Cad, think you remember where we saw that little stream?" He nodded. Robbie smiled. "I think soup's on!"

Snared Rabbits

Wednesday, 27 June AC 0245
SSE of Inland Open-Pit Lake
Ian Null

Over thousands of square miles, through all manner of terrain and climate. Above ground and beneath. Ian Null had encountered countless others in the vast wilderness. Most were wild, unsophisticated, impossible to trust for more than a transaction and a curt acknowledgment. Some were hostile. Some dangerous. All unknown.

Of all people he could have possibly encountered, it had to be the Sheppards.

There was no way Brother Raël could have known. He'd insisted Null take the extra supplies—just in case. In case of what? The wounded old man had only smiled and said with a faint twinkle in his half-open eyes *you just never know.*

He'd heard the brothers, two of them, anyway, many yards before he'd seen them. The underbrush floor was spongy with moss, very few twigs or dry leaves to give his position away. Crouched and balanced on the balls of his toes, Null peered through the foliage, and the outline of three young males came into focus. The oldest appeared to be in his early twenties. His hair was short but messy, a perpetual fear in his facial expression. He was constantly bickering with the next-oldest, a petulant teen with lighter hair and a chip on his shoulder. They argued about everything from their current situation to childhood grudges. "Lor", the teen, still wasn't over not getting his choice of bedroom, which had instead been given, apparently, to the youngest brother.

Through the incessant bickering, the youth called Cadlen, more often shortened to Cad, never spoke a word. Null narrowed his eyes on the youngest of the brothers. While the other two fought over such pointless issues, Cadlen busied himself gathering dry sticks, moss, and anything a boy would consider flammable. The boy couldn't have been more than twelve or thirteen years old. His hair was thick and straight, covering all of his forehead. He carried on as if his brothers weren't even there, as if he were alone with his own thoughts. While his brothers argued about meaningless games from their younger years, Cadlen sought out fuel for their fire. He gathered berries in folded leaves, but never once tasted his harvest. He moved the pile of kindling under the cover of hanging boughs—he had the foresight to realize that if rain came, they'd be cold and wet. And when he was tired, he used a pointed stick to doodle in the dirt.

The instant Lorrie uttered the name Sheppard, a switch flipped inside Null's memory.

He was standing in the Sheppard Inn lobby, holding a framed drawing of a young family, presumably the owners of the facility. At first, he'd assumed the drawing was a photograph. Or at least a rendering from a professional artist.

Null gazed at Cadlen through the filter of branches and leaves. *He couldn't have drawn that, could he?*

It would have been so easy. Slip away undetected, as he had countless times already. Dozens of travelers, traders, and miscreants had no idea how close Ian Null had passed. How when they weren't looking, he would help himself to untended food. How that one time he'd secured a poorly set snare for starving marauders that looked like they needed the protein. How he'd lifted a clean shirt from traders he'd witnessed ripping off others in need. Back in Motherland, or in New Inland—even in Kayewat, theft came with penalty. Under Eminence De Léon, theft was a serious crime, resulting in a day in the pillory, or possibly the removal of the offending hand. The federated cities usually levied fines or public service as reparation.

But on the outside, everything was different. The only law was that of nature.

Survive. By any means necessary. It was cruel. But it was everything.

What Ian Null had learned, however, was that Paolo Desantos could never have survived on the outside, despite his skill and experience. The "young lion" the Junquer had labeled had it all wrong. As sure as in Kayewat, thieves always became bigger targets of theft from bigger thieves and killers on the outside were the first to be themselves killed. Creeping through the forest, Ian Null had fared better using the cunning of a fox rather than the might of a lion. There was no need to draw attention to himself. Take only what you need and move on.

And in those moments when time stood still, and the opportunity presented itself to spare a stranger undue harm, Ian Null did what Paolo Desantos never could. He extended an unseen hand, as some meager payment for whatever he took. While a small group of brigands slept around a dying fire, he'd helped himself to their supply of medicated salve to treat the scrapes on his cheek. In return, he added a log to the fire.

Maybe he was reckless. Maybe he'd been inspired by Raël's selflessness.

Somehow, Ian Null felt more complete for it.

He never believed in the Ansati nonsense about magic, spirits, the hereafter. There was only one here and now. There was what you could see, what you could reason, and everything else was speculation at best. And still, the old monk who'd stumbled into his shelter, facing mortality at the hands of a vicious assault, was so… peaceful. He'd spoken in riddles and verses. He'd given away the last of his possessions, freely. And with his parting words, he'd implored Ian Null to give Paolo Desantos one last, long look before fading away.

Go to Moab, he'd told him. *Find the Ossuary. Learn about your family. Then, make up your mind…*

Null had retreated from the Sheppards back into the cover of the wilderness. Not half a mile back he'd spotted evidence of rabbit trails through the tall grass. By the accumulation of droppings, it wouldn't take long to snare a few. Null hooped the wire, coiling it taut to a sturdy branch as he hung the open trap over a frequently-traveled lane. The sun was setting, which meant they'd be on the move soon. He had enough time to gather root vegetables, edible berries, and even prepare a cup of pine-needle tea. He'd bring the rabbits back to the Sheppard campsite to show them how to skin the animals and use as much of the carcass as possible. *Out here, nothing should ever go to waste.*

Twilight had fully descended, and sure enough, the snares had strangled a pair of mature rabbits, their fur mottled beige and grey as their coats had begun to camouflage against the natural surroundings. Null preferred a quicker kill, but snares were useful when stealth was paramount. He carried a firearm and enough rounds of ammunition to hunt bigger game almost daily for the duration of his planned journey. Aynslie had left him with more than enough before the trading post had emptied. In the days since, he'd yet to load it.

"Hello there!"

Null crouched, tucking his kill beneath him and reached into his waistband for the gun. He cursed himself for being detected. There couldn't have been more than a couple of them, unless they were experienced outdoorsmen. As he quieted himself, Null heard two sets of feet moving in his direction with caution. A pair of headlamps flashed to life.

"Dim your lights," Null directed his company.

"We don't mean you any harm, traveler. We're only passing through ourselves." The leader spoke deliberately, as though he'd spoken the same line many times. As if he were a policeman.

"I am unarmed. Dim your lights." It was a lie. The weapon was empty, but it was better left unseen.

"If you come out with your hands in front of you, we'll call it even. How about that?"

The headlamps prevented Null from determining if they were themselves armed. For a moment, he imagined how Paolo Desantos would have reacted. They would have been the quarry. They would have received no quarter. They would have been dead to rights.

Null swallowed and stood from his defensive position. All of the goodwill he'd offered had to pay off one last time. Raising his hands, he gripped his rabbits by their back legs. Blood began to seep from their lifeless mouths.

"I see you've already caught supper!" The leader dimmed his headlamp. He wore a military-style uniform, clean and neatly pressed, a beret perched atop his head. The colours and style looked familiar.

"You are New Inland Defense Corps."

The leader nodded. "We are. Scouting expedition—one of our craft went down not far from here. We think it crashed into the open pit lake." The second officer switched off his headlamp completely. Both were in their mid- to late-thirties, neither had any facial hair, but both faces showed several days' growth of stubble.

Null dropped his arms, clutching both rabbits in his left hand, keeping the right free for quick action. "I have not passed by the lake. I hope your people survived."

He knew the answer to that, of course. While he'd observed the Sheppard brothers, he'd learned that the pilot of the Tandem-Rotor craft presumably died in the crash, and that there were no other crew. The fact the officers didn't know he knew this was an advantage.

"We're missing four crew and a full load of supplies—mostly food and medicine." The leader lied effortlessly. The other one nodded, but he looked nervous. Null spied sidearms holstered at their waists. In a pinch, he could subdue the pair of them before they even realized they were in danger. For now, Null determined that it was best to play it out.

"I have not come across any Defense Corps survivors." It wasn't a lie.

"We're afraid there weren't any. Still, we had to be sure. And if there's any chance we could find any supplies…"

Null narrowed his eyes. *Supplies, or Sheppards?* The pair of officers smiled and glanced at each other. Something wasn't right.

"We're only a few kilometers—miles, to you—from the lake. You're sure you haven't been there?"

"That is what I said."

"Two rabbits, there. That's a lot of meat for one fellow, isn't it?"

Null felt the conversation shifting into an inquisition. If these two were in fact Defense Corps, they were well outside of their jurisdiction. There was no sign of any vehicles. And the fact that there were only two made no sense. Reekan always sent his troops in numbers—especially outside the dome.

"If you are hungry, I can spare you a rabbit." It was better to offer kindness than apprehension.

"No thanks, friend. Our bellies are full. It's just odd you're by yourself, but you have enough meat to last for days. You know how to preserve them?"

"If you have nothing further, I will be on my way."

"Hold on, friend. That shirt you're wearing. You didn't happen to find that at a trading post? Farbend?"

That was their final mistake. New Inland forces would not trade at the outposts that far from their boundaries. These weren't New Inlanders. Null blinked, and for a second, Paolo Desantos awoke.

"Where is your transport?"

"Back a ways, about half a kilometer." The secondary officer motioned with his right arm. Sure enough, the sleeve rode up, revealing the bottom of a tattooed pattern. Kayewati, stamped but not covered with the same biosynthetic skin Grant had boasted.

Kayewati mercenaries, in disguise as New Inland Defense Corps officers. Moving quietly through the brush, and fully aware of the downed aircraft and potential survivors. This was the work of Tirel Desantos. They weren't here to rescue anyone.

They were here to finish the job.

There was a time for stealth. There was a time for passivity. Paolo Desantos inhaled and sprung forward.

When it was over, the Kayewati lay naked save for their undergarments. Null confirmed the stamped ink in the form of the stone totems that identified the pair to any sensors that recognized the toxic cocktail of elements in the ink. Without biosynth coverings these two had never set foot inside of the New Inland dome. Null cleaned up the scene quicker than he preferred. He took the uniforms under his arm and sprinted in the direction the second officer had motioned. Sure enough, an off-road vehicle powered by a newer nuke-cell power source waited for its occupants to return. The key to the machine was in the inside breast pocket of the leader's jacket. If Tirel Desantos had indeed orchestrated the crashing of the Tan-Ro with the Sheppards on board, he was determined to see that the job was finished. When his mercenaries didn't come home, he'd send more.

The decision had been made for him.

The Sheppard brothers were stuck with him if they wanted to survive.

Least-Worst

Wednesday, 27 June AC 0245
SSE of Inland Open-Pit Lake
Robbie Sheppard

Good thing we boiled water for these ration packets. I haven't tasted anything this bad since Warren and I cooked those old preserves." It was a lifetime ago, now. Lorrie and Warren had breezed into the kitchen, and of course, Robbie was out. In the back of the pantry, Warren snatched an aluminum can with a half-peeled label. He'd remarked about how it was three or four logos old. Still, there were no better options, so Lorrie cranked the lid off and heated the clumpy stew. Neither finished the first bite.

Robbie laughed, taking the metal cup and swigging back a mouthful of thin broth. "Leave it to you dopes to cook the one can leftover from before mom died."

"If you bought better easy-preps, maybe we wouldn't have to settle for pantry surprises!"

"The last time you made a shopping list, I spent half the budget on easy-preps that you didn't eat!"

"Because you bought the wrong brand, when I specifically—"

Lorrie and Robbie both quieted as Cadlen stood and peered in the direction the stranger had come and gone. The last of the light had melted away, and only the glowing embers of their fire offered any view of their surroundings. Within seconds, a whirring mixed with crackling branches intensified. Lorrie grabbed a rock from the outside perimeter of the pit. The stick he'd used to threaten the stranger had long since burned in the fire. Robbie tugged on Cadlen's sleeve.

"Come on, Cad. Let's move out of the light."

Cadlen nodded, and all three brothers backed away from the fire, kneeling behind thin bush cover, hoping that whatever was approaching didn't have a floodlight.

The crunching and whirring stopped, and a pair of boots loping through the brush intensified until the stranger burst into view of the campfire. Instead of his knapsack, this time he carried a jug with a dangling strap. He unscrewed a round cap.

"I know you are near. We need to leave. Now." The stranger tipped the container over the fire and a stream of water poured onto the coals, steam erupting in the twilight air.

Lorrie exploded. "Are you crazy? That fire took me hours to get started!"

Robbie groaned. Lorrie was going to be the death of them.

"There is no time to explain. You are in danger, and we need to leave this place." The stranger looked grim. He motioned behind him. "I have transport, food." He motioned to Lorrie's torn shirt. "And a change of clothing."

"Where did you get all that? Is there a grocery store back there or what?"

Robbie put an arm over Cadlen's shoulder. Lorrie wasn't wrong to ask. This fellow arrived in silence, watching and learning about them before revealing himself. Then he left as quickly, only to rush back with more supplies and the urgency to flee the area immediately. With them. Robbie wondered if they were being kidnapped.

The stranger emptied the canteen, dousing what remained of the ember bed. "I know you have questions. I found people not far from here. They were searching for you."

"Wait a minute." Robbie spoke up. "How do you know they were looking for us?"

"They were dressed as Defense Corps, but they lied to me."

Lorrie snorted. "How do we know *you* aren't lying? And where are these *people*, anyway?"

Cadlen tugged on Robbie's sleeve. "Highwaymen." His little brother had spoken for the second time in as many hours.

The stranger nodded to Cadlen. "You could call them that."

Lorrie's neck swung back and forth. "Wait a minute. All this stuff…" The wheels were turning in his mind, and Robbie expected he was reasoning the same. He had a feeling the people in question didn't need their belongings anymore. And if that were the case, who exactly was coaxing them to leave with him?

"You know our names. I won't let you take my brothers and I anywhere until I know your name." Robbie trembled as he spoke, hoping his defiance carried some sort of confidence.

"Ian. Ian Null."

"You could be anyone for all we know." Lorrie raised his arms in protest. "Come on, Robbie, you're not buying any of this, are you?"

"Do as you wish, Lorrie Sheppard. I have fresh meat that will spoil if we do not dress and cook it soon."

"You could have cooked it on my fire, smart guy!"

Ian Null ignored Lorrie's sarcasm. "Robbie Sheppard, I can bring you and your brothers to safety. But we must leave. Now."

For Now

Wednesday, 27 June AC 0245
SSE of Inland Open-Pit Lake
Lorrie Sheppard

Why won't anyone *listen to me?*" Lorrie protested the entire hike through the brush to the abandoned all-terrain vehicle Ian Null had managed to secure. It did him no good. Despite his sound logic concerning the stranger's unbelievable story, Robbie and Cadlen stopped arguing and followed the stranger, blindly and without reservation. What if they were being led into a trap? Maybe they'd be killed too, bodies left to rot on the forest floor with those DefCorps grunts.

"You need to lower your voice," Null barked from the front of the line without turning his head. The man sliced through the bushes, swishing a long blade when he needed to clear the path. Lorrie had asked where he'd suddenly found a machete, but Ian never answered. Just another secret.

"Lorrie, shut up!" Robbie implored in a croaking half whisper. It was just like him to give in, go along with what he was told. He'd never been a risk-taker, but since their father passed, he was less adventurous. He'd all but given up riding his bike. A bad fall and an embarrassing loss was Robbie's chosen excuse. But Lorrie suspected it was more than that. Losing his parents was like losing his armour.

When the brownish-green vehicle came into view, Lorrie saw no sign of its prior occupants. Not even a trace of a struggle. Null turned to the brothers and motioned for them to get inside. Lorrie opened his mouth to protest, but the stranger's eyes bore into his own, blue and cold. He'd keep quiet. For now.

Inside the rig, Null flicked a small key and the machine came to life. Like the Capston security shuttles, they whirred with hardly a sound.

The power source didn't depend on a combustion engine, so it didn't gargle and sputter like they did in the Ranger Man shows. If anything, it would make moving in the wild quieter. As the doors shut, the air grew dry and stale within seconds.

"Can I speak now, Your Majesty?"

The machine lurched and through the semi-opaque front window, bushes and branches swished against the outer shell. Null guided the rig carefully around larger trees and rocks. From the inside, it was impossible to know how much noise they made. But for a second, Lorrie accepted they were likely safer inside the military rig. At least for the time being.

"Twenty minutes."

Huh? "What do you mean, twenty minutes?"

Null shifted and the rig accelerated. The branches thwacked the outer shell with quicker swipes. "In twenty minutes, we will be far enough. Then you can ask me questions."

Everything was far enough already.

"Let the man drive, Lor. We're going to be okay." Robbie raised his hand as though he meant to put it on Lorrie's shoulder, but he stopped himself.

Lorrie sighed and sat back in his seat. The rig cut through the woods without incident. It made sense—vehicles like this would have to be designed to withstand off-road travel. Were there roads at all? In his brief time outside, Lorrie had yet to see a walking trail let alone a highway.

It was nearly twenty minutes, and the rig emerged from the brush onto the bank of a river. It didn't look deep from Lorrie's seat. Null hunched his shoulders and leaned forward as though his body weight shifted the whole rig. Decelerating, he guided the rig into the shallows, turning right and following the course of the water flow.

"We're not crossing?" Lorrie didn't understand.

"If our trail is picked up, the river will wash it away."

That actually made sense. There might be a track leading into the water. But if they followed it long enough, maybe they could come out of it in a place where tracks would be hard to trace. Sure enough, ten minutes later, Null spotted a rocky plateau on the far bank of the widened and shallow water. Lorrie dipped backward as the rig emerged at a steep angle. When the rig came to rest, they were nestled in the shadow of a rocky outcropping. Null turned off the ignition and turned to face the brothers.

"We are not out of danger yet. Follow in my exact steps, and say nothing." He looked directly at Lorrie as he emphasized that last point.

"My lips are sealed." Lorrie rolled his eyes and hoped Null understood the sarcasm.

Once outside, Null walked in even steps, accounting for Cadlen's shorter strides. He shoved a rucksack into the arms of each of the Sheppard brothers. Lorrie slung his over his shoulder, the weight of the contents wobbling. About twenty meters into the brush, the stranger used the jutting rocks as steps and ascended the bluff. It wasn't a difficult climb. Lorrie still kept to the rear. He wasn't going to let Cad stray behind them. If they were to be separated, would he even answer if they called his name?

"Stay close." Null nodded to Robbie, who nodded back without answering. "We will make camp for the night soon."

The party of four pressed deeper under cover of the forest canopy that thickened farther from the river. Null came to a halt on a plateau with huge stone walls that seemed to run parallel—completely unnatural.

Dropping his rucksack, Null pulled out a small shovel, not more than half a meter long with a curved blade. Kneeling, he brushed aside leaves and peeled back clumps of sod. Beneath, he dug the tip of the spade into the dirt. Heaving with his shoulders, he thrust downward, and the mouth of the spade disappeared beneath the surface. Null looked satisfied as he dug a hole carefully, leaving the removed soil in a neat pile. Cadlen crept closer and showed him some dried sticks he'd collected along the way.

"Yes. But we will need more than dead wood. Find dry moss and grass." Null motioned up the alleyway between the two rock walls. "Any sticks this big, bring them." He cupped his fingers and thumbs to form half circles with each hand, joining them to make a diameter as a visual reference. Cad nodded and went to work searching for fire materials.

Null set the spade on the grass and reached into his rucksack. He retrieved an ugly handheld device. The innards were half visible, and it was a little bigger than any Lorrie had seen. It could have been an older model, or maybe it had come apart from the struggle with the DefCorps officers he'd stolen it from. With a touch of his thumb, though, the screen blinked to life. Through a series of swipes and tabs, Null opened a screen with green swirls or patterns—in the fading light, Lorrie couldn't tell.

"Robbie." Null motioned for him to look at the screen. "These leaves are edible, and they can be found in this area. Can you find some?"

Robbie squinted in concentration. "I'll see what I can find." He stood from his crouch and moved in Cadlen's direction. Lorrie expected to be scolded, for not being polite to their guide. It didn't happen. Lorrie stood within spitting distance of him, watching him dig a second hole next to the first. Null ignored him, as if he wasn't even there.

"No job for me, I guess?"

Null kept digging. "Watch." The second hole was narrower but equally as deep. He bent forward, and with his hands began to scoop more dirt from the second hole, only this time horizontally. When he was finished, he sat back on his heels and motioned for Lorrie to come closer.

"Without experience, you managed to build a fire. You have skills." He plucked the dead sticks Cadlen had collected and placed them into the larger hole, over top of some moss and grass. From the right cargo pocket of his pants, Null took the two-part firestarter and aimed the end at the base of the kindling. Two strokes later and a wisp of smoke curled from the hole. Lorrie leaned closer.

"Wait a second, the second hole—that's for air flow!"

Null nodded. "They call this a Dakota hole. Once built, your fire will be unseen beneath the ground, and will give off less smoke."

Lorrie was impressed. They may have been well sheltered from passersby, but fire still burned bright, and any light source would be a magnet for all manner of highwaymen in the wild. Credit where due, this Ian Null guy knew how to survive in the outside world. Maybe it would be best if they stayed with him for a while.

"You said you have meat that'll spoil?"

Null motioned to Lorrie's pack. Peeling back the outer flap, a rich scent wafted from the inside. Lorrie reached in and found the limp, furry legs of some animal. Instinctively, he winced and pulled back his hand, a streak of blood from his finger to his palm.

"What the hell? You made *me* carry the dead animals?"

Null snatched the sack and pulled out a rabbit by its legs, mottled brown and grey with a streak of blood. "You need to learn how to dress wild game. I am not sure your brothers could handle it."

In the distance, Robbie and Cadlen had come together, each with arms and hands full of their respective assigned findings. Lorrie looked at Null. His gaze was still intense, like it was always that way, even at rest. This time, however, there was a calmness, a sense of trust.

"Cad won't like the sight of blood. And you're right—Robbie isn't much better. Cried like a baby when he cut his knee open on the velo track." He wasn't sure if Null knew what a velo was.

Within half an hour, the fire was cooking thin strips of rabbit meat, hanging on branches Null taught Robbie to trim and tie as a roasting hanger. His leaves were boiling in a small collapsible metal pot, likely found in the DefCorps rig along with the tarp shelters and sleeping mats. The scent of rabbit roasting made Lorrie's stomach rumble.

Null had proved useful. At least for now.

The Silent Highway

Thursday, 28 June AC 0245
SSE of Inland Open-Pit Lake
Ian Null

Leading a cadre of highly trained army corps officers for days through unknown lands—that was second nature to Paolo Desantos. A thousand troops marched through the badlands, and four-fifths of them made it home over a total of nine days. Paolo's only adversary had been an unseen one, the emergence of red tide that had corrupted Yael and had led to the summary execution of the rest of the sappers before it spread through the rank and file. Paolo Desantos hadn't flinched as each shot popped from the muzzle and the heads jolted before hitting the floor of the barn. The job had to be done. There had been no time for second guessing. Still, he'd led hundreds of men over hellish terrain under a cruel sun. And every pair of boots marched in step to his every motion and command.

Ian Null didn't think Paolo Desantos could have handled the Sheppard brothers.

They spent their first night under an outcropping of shale, insulated for the evening with heaps of dried grass and shorn boughs. Lorrie complained that they were sleeping too far from the Dakota hole where they'd roasted two rabbits, some for supper, and some for jerky. They'd prepared enough for three days—four at most. The thin strips of meat hung on a crude spit, drying over the glowing coals of the slowly dying fire. Robbie took an interest in the curing process, carefully turning the strips and adding wood shavings to make the smoke richer. Lorrie had been correct—Cadlen looked away while they flayed the carcasses and removed the innards. Ever the dutiful guardian, Robbie had faced the task like any other, but Null saw him quiver at the smell of the gut pile, the sight of the coagulating blood, and the emptiness of the skinned hide.

Null explained to Lorrie that the fire would die over night, but with adequate insulation and some heated stones, they wouldn't be too cold. Robbie and Cadlen fell asleep within about fifteen minutes. Lorrie continued to mutter for half an hour, and Null expected he'd complain in his sleep. Null perched at the front of the outcropping as night fell, the key in his palm switched to its dimmest backlight. Junquer had programmed more old-world routes than he'd expected. The Sheppard brothers weren't sleeping in a natural outcropping. Sometime long before the Age of Reclamation, dynamite had blasted trenches through the rolling hills to clear way for highways, once black-topped in asphalt long since disintegrated or harvested for re-purposing. The highway once streamed sleek cars, petrol-fueled before they evolved into electric, then into the earliest models of nuclear-celled propulsion. In a different time, Null would have been sitting in the middle of traffic, in a world that moved so much faster, so aimless. The scarred hills lay silent, only smoldering coals and the last curls of its existence the only signs of survival for miles.

He followed the old-world maps Junquer had uploaded into his key. Tracing the old highway along a digital thread across the map, Null estimated that they could travel more than a hundred miles with relative ease in their stolen rig. The only complication, as was always the case in the wilderness of the mid-south, was the chance of encountering brigands. They were fortunate to have traveled anonymously thus far. That wouldn't last.

While the Sheppards slept, Null scrolled through pages of data, everything from historic weather patterns and known trading routes, to settlements and trading posts. As the night's chill caused him to shiver, and the cool air of the altitude and shelter of the blasted corridor made his breath visible, Null cross-referenced Junquer's maps with the information Raël had relayed. Moab, home of the Ansati. To reach the fabled city, they would have to navigate through land with significant radiation poisoning. The Reapers knew how to travel in the least-contaminated swaths, but it was nonetheless dangerous to anyone traveling without a Geiger counter or any medicine to combat the toxins. Null reached into the outer pocket of his sack. The Radiogardasse he'd purchased from Lacraie was a strong grade—enough to keep him relatively safe as he passed through the region.

Lorrie snorted and muttered as he almost woke himself up, before settling back into slumber. Robbie and Cadlen didn't stir.

The Sheppard brothers had no protection from the radiation.

Null opened the tiny bottle and let a tablet tumble into his palm. In his hand, the ovoid and blue tiny capsule weighed as if it were made of cast iron. Without water, it would taste metallic if he rolled it around his dry mouth. The roasted rabbit meat had his stomach rolling until he'd finally excused himself, retching the half-digested protein in the bushes safely out of sight of the brothers. It took a dose of antiemetic to settle the nausea enough to eat a few mouthfuls of wild mushrooms. He was lucky to have found some in Raël's provisions.

Two adults, two adolescent boys. Not more than fifty miles before the earliest traces of seam radiation, and another fifty at best before Moab. Null shone the light of the key screen into the open mouth of the pill jar. His heart sank. If they moved briskly, took all precautions not to eat any game, drink from any springs, rustle any vegetation…

He tipped his palm and let the pill fall back inside.

Opening a new tab, Null searched the database for trading settlements. They would be passing through the southern-most reaches of the Rust traders—mostly money and commodity peddlers. To the south, La Cumbre held more sway. They were known to deal in a wider range of goods and services, with a deep reach below the red line into the wilder deep south Motherland's ancestors had once fled. It was against his nature to even consider traveling that way. Paolo Desantos would have relished in the challenge, to barrel into hostile territory, carving a path of death in his wake. Only Paolo Desantos wasn't poisoned from a leaked nuke-cell, weakening by the day, and now responsible for three other lives.

Ian Null had choices to make. And in the pre-dawn hours on a silent highway, he had no answers.

The old highway wound in wide arcs down the far side of the hill into a valley, itself winding between the foothills. Null piloted the DefCorps rig using his key as his guide. Every so often, the rig dipped into a deep fissure in the trail or had to detour around unexpected obstacles, usually fallen rocks or trees. They slept the first night sealed inside the rig, but after a sleepless night in cramped quarters, Null had decided it would the last. For the first time, all four agreed. On the second night, Lorrie dug his first Dakota hole while Null sourced clean water. Deep in a valley, there was a good chance of finding a natural spring. Sure enough, following the Junquer maps, Null spotted an oval-shaped stone basin surrounded by high grasses. The lush vegetation was a clear sign of fresh water. He'd seen these before—old troughs for horses along trade routes built at artesian wells. Null filled his own canteen and the water reservoir from the rig. With rationing, they had enough water for the next couple days.

Making the hike back to camp with the heavy four-gallon jug took more energy than Null had been accustomed. Maybe too many meals of wild game and not enough balanced nutrition. Not enough sleep since he'd found the Sheppards.

The poison. That's what it is.

"Clean water! Guess we won't have to drink our piss yet?" Lorrie sat next to his fire, constructed in the shade of a fallen tree's roots. There was a ring of rocks, evidence of a simpler campfire some time ago. No tracks through the brush, however.

"You drink what you want, Lor. I'll go with the fresh water," Robbie said. He and Cadlen emerged from the nylon emergency shelter they'd found in the DefCorps provisions. The domed tent wouldn't shelter all of them. Null had insisted the two younger Sheppards would sleep inside.

Null dropped the water jug next to Lorrie. "Save the rabbit cuts.

We'll use ration kits tonight." They were designed to provide all essential vitamins. The boys needed a balanced diet now in case it became more challenging later.

A weak spell washed over him. He'd straightened his posture too quickly and blood rushed to his head. He could have used a nutritious meal himself.

Lorrie's fire proved to be efficient. With stomachs full on whole-grain crackers, oatmeal, dried fruits, and lentils, Null and the Sheppard brothers went to work securing the campsite for the evening as the sun waned. They had already established norms. Cadlen had become skilled at finding edible plants. Robbie gathered wood, grass, and moss for building both shelter and fire. Lorrie had become the keeper of the flame, in his own words. In his previous life, Paolo Desantos knew how to deal with cocky young officers. Give them something to call their own, to be proud of. With any luck, Lorrie's cockiness would fade sooner than later.

Robbie insisted on sleeping outdoors, and Null obliged. He knew the eldest Sheppard felt he had something to prove—to his brothers, and to himself. Robbie set up two bedrolls from the DefCorps rig, one each for himself and for Null. He climbed inside of his own, covering himself with the weighted blankets from his toes to his waist as he sat upright, back against the fallen tree roots.

"Aren't you going to use your blankets?"

Null shook his head. "I prefer sleeping with less warmth." It was much easier to oversleep when too comfortable.

"I suppose you're used to sleeping under the stars." Robbie lowered the blankets to just above his knees. "I don't think I could ever get used to nights outside."

"Your parents. They were outdoor folk?"

"When they were young. Before they settled and had me." Robbie took a sip of tea. "Hyacynthe Retreats. That's where they met."

Null had heard of the Hyacynthe program. It was controversial among the federated cities—teaching insiders about life on the outside.

If life was so good under the domes, why would anyone want to venture outside of them?

"They would be proud of their sons." Null remembered the faces of Julia and Robert Sheppard from the drawing he'd held in his hands while Grant rigged the inn with the explosives that would bring it down. Hopefully, Reekan and his people would find where he'd hidden it.

"I hope so." Robbie sighed. His eyes sparkled the reflection of the coals, watery either from smoke, allergens, or memories. Null admired him. He knew all too well the weight of expectation. But the drawing of Julia and Robert was so lifelike, it was as though they were still alive on the page, *immortal.* And their eyes. Null expected that if he stared too long, he'd see them blink.

"You have a sister." Null didn't have to remember how Crystal Sheppard appeared in the family picture. He'd met her. In his pocket, he carried a prescription bottle she had released to him at Lacraie. She had unknowingly handed medicine to the man who had destroyed her family home. Who had set in motion their exile from New Inland, their near-death in the Tandem-Rotor copter crash.

Who had a moral duty to see them to safety. He'd already given Crystal enough money to rebuild their lives however the Sheppards saw fit.

Null studied Robbie's face at profile. He didn't resemble his sister as much as Lorrie. They had the same eye and hair colour and same facial structure, reminiscent of Julia Sheppard more than Robert. But Crystal and Robbie shared the same reservation, that same awkward charm. She was nervous, on the verge of panic when he'd walked into the dispensary. Her eyes were wide, deep, open. As though she saw through him. And then she fussed and dropped her keys…

"Crystal. She's two years younger than me. She lives in Hyacynthe—Mom and Dad's old mentor from those Retreats, he promised that when she was ready, he would sponsor her for school."

"Even with the trade embargo?" Null didn't know how their benefactor pulled it off, but he'd managed to arrange for Crystal

Sheppard to move from New Inland to Hyacynthe despite the strict travel and trade ban. *He must be powerful.*

Robbie nodded and the fire crackled as a coal burst. "Laurent explained that it was all legal because he'd arranged it all before the laws were passed. But she still had to travel in secret because New Inland wouldn't allow it."

"I am not aware of how the city states conduct their affairs." It was a half-truth.

"Well, if it makes you feel any better, I don't know much more than you."

Lost and Found

Thursday, 28 June AC 0245
Jackson Homestead, Spruce Grove
Phil Fox

The Grove slept under the midnight sky, peppered with stars and humid, farm machines idle and silent. Albert piloted the shuttle up the old road, bypassing Jackson Auto entirely. Phil scrunched up in the rear seat, designed for someone no older than ten. At least he'd lost some kilograms since he'd been home. Mayor Fox wouldn't have fit.

Le_Renard rested an arm on the shuttle's door, his greyed hair waving as he stared outside at the woods. He didn't say a word the entire trip—a first, at least in Phil's time with him. Maybe the memory of baby Phil falling in his lap had terrified him. Whatever had happened with Walpurgis must have been far worse.

Once they were parked next to the Homestead, Albert opened his handheld and ran a precautionary scan. "Settings are unchanged. No visitors. No unrecognized ears. All good." Albert exited the shuttle and unlocked the front door. Inside, Le_Renard made for the kitchen and boiled water for tea. There was no need for a fire this evening.

Settled in their usual seats, Phil poured a capful of Aquavit into his tea. Le_Renard took out his handheld and Phil passed him the small device Fisher had given him in secret. It contained no buttons, only a retractable plug the size of nothing he'd ever seen before.

"Ah, yes. We called these tiles in Kayewat. Not compatible with most handhelds, and bloody hard to hack. Junquer keys won't even scan 'em."

"What's a junker key?" Technology outside of the federated domes often surprised him.

"Junquer is a *who*. Makes really smart devices, but they'n't cheap. Huh! Here we go." Le_Renard slid a thumb alongside Walpurgis's tile, and the plug extended about a knuckle's length. Inserting into the corresponding jack on his own device, the screen flashed to life. Le_Renard leaned closer so both Phil and Albert could watch. A red tab appeared on the screen, indicating an e-folder labeled, predictably, <WALPURGIS>.

Le_Renard swallowed, his thumb hovering over the tab. "These tiles are set for a specific purpose. All of my agents were required to keep accurate notes of their jobs. Encrypted, filed in the Kayewati secured database. The fact that he sent this…" He never finished the thought.

Tapping the tab, a cursor blinked, and a title page emerged in green script.

"Yup, this is his journal. Says here the timestamps, location—and how many *copies?*"

"Is that unusual?" Albert leaned closer, stroking his chin.

"Very. Let's see." Le_Renard tapped the bottom of the screen. "Two copies. One to the Allens—we have an ID number, too. That might be handy. And looky here…" He held the screen up. Phil's eyes widened.

"Mayor Fox of Capston. You sure you never seen this before?"

"No, not before I left. Miss Kendall would have—"

She would have sent it to your handheld, except you turned the damned thing off on the magna-rail. Then it came back to him. He had checked it, briefly, and the name *Walpurgis* hadn't been familiar at the time. So much on his mind, he'd dismissed what he'd considered junk mail, and never thought of it again.

"I need to power up my handheld," Phil said. "I think I might have received it—but I didn't recognize the name. Could I have even been able to open it?"

"Oh yeah, but you'd have had to jump through Allen hoops to get the double encryption codes. No matter, my boy. We have it now."

But if he'd opened it then, maybe he could have prevented the Sheppard Inn attack. Phil's heart sank into his stomach.

To his relief, Albert broke the silence. "So, tell us about Walpurgis. Who is he?"

Le_Renard grimaced. "Who was he, you mean. One of my most trusted agents. Worked for me nearly twenty years. He had an in with everyone—Allens, Rust, La Cumbre, even the western townships. Hard worker. Knew how to blend in."

Phil understood the importance of reliable staff. Karyn Kendall was the best. Even if she was pushy at times, he always appreciated her efficiency.

"Not long before I left Kayewat for here, I got an emergency call from another one of my agents. CF, we call him. He don't stray far from Kayewat, but he's nosy—if it's happening in the third district, he probably has a bet on it. Anyway, he tells me there's some guy asking around about me."

Phil took a sip of his tea, the added Aquavit adding a necessary punch. "I'm sure you have lots of people looking for Le_Renard_Subtil, though."

The old man nodded. "Sure do. But no one comes lookin' for *Emmanuel Jackson.* Huh." He reached for the Aquavit and sloshed some into his own tea.

"So, if he knows your name, what does that mean?" Albert raised a hand to refuse the green alcohol.

"It means he's learned about my business before I took the stamp. Before I registered in Kayewat as Le_Renard."

Phil asked even if he didn't prefer to know. "And what business, exactly, did that entail?"

Le_Renard swallowed a long drink. "A little of this 'n that. You remember the human trafficking stories?"

Phil nodded.

"You'll be happy to know that most of those were misunderstood. Y'see, out *there*, outside of your comfy, domed cities, things you take for granted are hard. Imagine you have small children, you're working, living your dreams. And one day, people in your neighbourhood start getting sick. One by one, they drop like flies. And you know you need to get your kids as far as fuck from this place before they get sick too. What do you do?"

Phil wrinkled his brows. "I'd move them to another city. When breakouts happen in New Inland, we quarantine cities from each other until it's finished." Heartsburg medicine was strong, and protocols had proved successful. But Phil knew what he was getting at.

"No quarantine out here, son. No magna-rails. No planes. Lucky if you have a horse and a carriage in some of the settlements." Le_Renard pointed a finger to his own chest. "That's where *I* came in. I knew the *right* people to *move* people."

Albert sighed and leaned back into his chair. He and Le_Renard glanced at each other, and the old man continued. "CF told me that the fella looking for me, under my old name, was from a village called Haven."

"It must be small, I've never heard of it," Phil said. He watched Albert's expression change from serious to sombre.

"It doesn't exist anymore. Ansati burned it in that cleansing ritual of theirs." Le_Renard turned again to Albert. "Not before I moved out the last surviving kids."

A tear welled in Albert's eye. It made sense, now. Albert Schiff never resembled Uncle Bernard Schiff. Phil's cousin was a survivor of Haven, and Le_Renard had profited from trafficking him.

"I don't have many clear memories of Haven," Albert said in a low tone, wiping his eye. "I was six years old, almost seven. My birth parents were gone. Our mayor, Mr. Harp, he took me to meet Emmanuel. He explained as best he could that he had a home for me, safe from the red tide."

The rest made sense without any need for elaboration. Emmanuel Jackson—in his life before becoming the infamous crime boss Le_Renard_Subtil—brought young Albert back to Gasperro, and Bernard Schiff adopted him.

"If I didn't bring Pretty Boy home with me, he'd be living in the western townships."

"Or I'd be dead." Albert sipped his tea, his voice cracking.

Le_Renard coughed and took another drink. "Anyway, it's history now. Point is, CF tells me about this. I need to get the high hell out of town until I sort this shit out. CF contacts Walpurgis, he's in New Inland at the time. I never did get to see him again."

Phil remembered standing over the memorial marker for his father, Lucas Fox. How Le_Renard had paid his respects incognito, and how his mother had pretended she didn't know who he was. And how she kept the secret to the grave. "So, whoever is looking for you knows you're both Emmanuel *and* Le_Renard. He knows you did a job in Haven."

The old man turned back to his handheld and pressed his thumb to the chapter tabs on the right side of the window. "Anything else we need to know is here. No time like the present, boys."

I'm just about finished, I think. These small jobs pay but there's so much work for the reward. Moving contraband is fairly safe, I admit, but I'd make more selling this junk out of a lost and found most days. The Allens have me delivering personal junk between New Inland and Hyacynthe, mostly. Just think, if I can deliver a few more care packages of baked goods and kids' finger-paintings, I can finally pay off Junquer. Pardon the sarcasm.

Mind, without his rig, there'd be no profit. That's what I get for taking on the less-risky jobs, I guess. Access to places other agents can't. I found a low-risk spot in Capston, in the 300-block where rent got too high and Jason Holt put them out of business. Junquer's key allowed me to come and go, and no one was paying any attention anyway. Perfect set-up. Until I found someone else hiding out here too. Lucky for me, I had the scanner app open. They had no idea I was only two doors away.

I thought it was funny that they got inside. Turns out they'd managed to get in through the back service door. I waited until they were settled in their room, and I set the key to record on the highest frequency I could. Through my headset, they sounded like they were talking right into my ear.

I'm including the audiofile separately, so the file size doesn't trip any alarms. But here's what I learned:

- Two men—Kjell Sundland and Baylor Zayne. The first has an Arctican name, the second could have been a Heartsburg pseudonym. I've met several Baylors. Third was a woman, Jeremie Beth—again, I've heard Jeremie as a surname, so likely it was chosen to fit a profile. All three of them spoke with a Motherland accent. It's odd to hear that in New Inland. It was a first for me.

- They're making a lot of small talk, but they're clearly planning something big. They keep talking about the "next one". Jeremie lets slip that their job is being called "Jewel Heist".

- Baylor says the Jewel Heist will make the first four look like nothing. He's referring to the bombings. These guys are the saboteurs Fox and Reekan are looking for.

- Sundland argues with Baylor about where Florian is going to stay. Baylor questions whether or not Florian ever gets the chance to lead. No idea who Florian is.

- Jeremie says he has to pair up with one of them, since The Lion gets his own room. Baylor teases that Jeremie can bunk with him, and she loses it— says you don't joke about shit like that.

- Sundland mentions a Kayewati, Baylor shoots that down, since they can't get past the New Inland scanners with their stamps. I admit, that last one made me chuckle.

The room got quiet. I didn't make a sound, but I started to wonder if they could scan like me. I waited around until the small talk continued, then I slipped out of the room and down to the service door. I didn't wait around to see if the door secured. A few blocks

away, I hailed a shuttle and made for New Mills, hoping
I didn't raise any hairs traveling so late at night
alone.

I didn't get a date or a time, but it sounded like
it was taking a long time to secure the materials. I
know the Motherlanders are planning to hit Holt Tower.

And I know The Lion is going to lead it. You know
who I mean.

All three leaned away from the screen, and all three finished their tea. Phil's heart raced. As he read Walpurgis's journal entry, visions of the exploding four-story office complex flooded his memory. It was the fourth of four attacks, and it was the final straw for his leadership. It was the reason he was sitting in front of an extinguished fireplace in the Homestead opposite his criminal father and adopted cousin.

"Of course, Holt Tower wasn't the fifth target." Le_Renard broke the silence. "Instead, they hit some floundering hotel, and didn't even manage to kill anyone in the process, except their own."

Which one of the names in Walpurgis's account did Reekan's forensics find? Was it the Kayewati?

One question came to Phil's mind ahead of all the others. "Walpurgis said you know who *The Lion* is. Do you?"

Le_Renard stood and stretched, likely for dramatic effect. He took the Aquavit bottle and poured a half glass. "Ever met a Desantos, my boy?" He tipped the cup and downed its contents. "*The Lion* is a fella by the name of Paolo Desantos. And lemme tell you, huh. If he's half of what they say he is…"

Modus Operandi

Friday, 29 June AC 0245
Jackson Homestead, Spruce Grove
Phil Fox

Once his handheld had fully charged, Phil scrolled through more than a hundred messages. Three quarters of them were junk mail. The first was a reminder from Ms. Kendall to confirm his docking fees at the Hudson, which he'd forgotten. The second, a flagged and encrypted message sent from Walpurgis, which he now remembered dismissing on the magna-rail before turning off his data reception. It didn't matter at this point. Fisher had relayed the same message, albeit through a more arduous journey. Of the most recent messages, however, another flagged message, this time from Kendall, caught his eye.

```
                                   25 June AC 0245


    I hope your travel to Azore was smooth. I know I told
you to take your full sixty days, but there have been
developments that need your attention. Reekan moved into
Allentown on leads found in the Sheppard Inn debris. As
you might expect, it was a disaster. Reekan and his
senior leadership were targeted by an assassin, all
survived except one of his junior officers. In a
separate attack, Paolo Desantos of Motherland was killed
in a mass-casualty event in Allentown. Marribel caught
wind of it, and the council came down hard on Reekan. I
tried my best, but there's only so much you can do to
help that man. DHC voted to censure him. He's on leave,
gone to Ap-Oz. Pax Brien is interim Mayor and Capston's
1st. I'm 2nd as Interim Solicitor.
    Captain Ling is running security while Reekan's out.
She's more than capable, but she's in a tough spot as
```

well. She came to me asking if you could be reached. I can handle the solicitor portfolio—you taught me well. But Ling is right. We need you back on the council. You're going to love reading this, but you bring poise, and a sense of reason to the DHC. The council is divided. We need you to restore that balance.

If that doesn't convince you to come back, maybe this will: Motherland has planted agents inside New Inland. Two DefCorps infiltrators sabotaged a Tan-Ro that was moving the Sheppards to Ap-Oz. The copter went down and all on board are presumed dead. The Sheppard family were honest, hard-working Capstonians, and because they accidentally got caught up in all of this, they've lost everything. It's only a matter of time before Motherland strikes again, and the next time could be massive.

Please respond as soon as you receive this. If I don't hear from you, I know you at least did what you were told—to relax and recharge. By the way, I re-upped your docking account at the Hudson. You're welcome. K

Phil lingered over the Sheppard family developments. He had never met them. Julia and Robert Sheppard had died of red tide-related symptoms—he remembered that from the press releases. The fact that they'd spent time in the Hyacynthe youth retreats added to the case for keeping the embargo. Hyacynthe was too loose with their outside ventures. Indeed, during his time as mayor, he'd supported the embargo.

But now…

Le_Renard chomped on his breakfast. The sun had yet to rise, but the trio talked into the wee hours about Walpurgis's information. Albert curled up in the crook of the sofa and pulled the decorative throw over himself. Phil started a fire and put on a kettle for java. By 0430, Le_Renard had eggs frying in the kitchen. All three needed to digest all of the information in play.

"So, what are you gonna do?" Bits of egg flaked from Le_Renard's mouth onto the plate in his hands.

"It'll take me a week to sail back. If I'd checked my messages—"

"If you'd checked your messages, my boy, you'd have turned the rig and headed straight for the Hudson and paid your docking fees. Then you'd have taken the first magna-rail home. And guess what? *Nothing* would have changed."

Albert stirred and turned his face toward the back rest. Phil poured himself a cup of black, ungarnished java. It tasted as bitter as his father's comment.

"You, of all people, should appreciate responsibility. But then again, it's your MO to run at the first sign of trouble."

"Well, sue me for staying alive! Huh!" Le_Renard looked genuinely hurt.

"And what about the Sheppards, *huh*? They didn't even do anything, and look what that cost'em!"

"Don't mock me, boy." Le_Renard scowled and tossed his plate onto the empty seat next to him. "We all have our reasons we do what we do."

"Right. Like living with a fake name and always looking over your shoulder?"

Le_Renard stood, towering over him. "And isn't it about time you got over that?"

"Got over *what?* Growing up not knowing who my biological father is? And then having to wait *for weeks* only to find out he's an emotionally detached crime boss?" Emmanuel Jackson had avoided him when Uncle Schiff first brought him to Spruce Grove. When they finally met, it was anti-climactic at best.

"Keep your voice down! And listen—your parents gave you a life I knew I couldn't, right? Better to grow up bored in Sascota than dead on the outside!"

"At least they were there for me! They raised me to be who I am today."

Albert shifted again, and interrupted without opening his eyes. "Then how come you haven't gone to see them yet?"

For once, Le_Renard didn't offer any kind of retort. Phil swallowed the last half cup of java, nearly coughing it onto the living room rug. His eyes welled. Without answering, he threw the porcelain mug at the dead fireplace, shattering it over the coals. Snatching his jacket off the hook, he stormed out the front door as the sun peeked through the trees.

His cousin was right. Before he made any decisions, Phil had to visit Burnside-on-the-hill to see Elsa and Lucas Fox.

Roll Call

Domingo, 24 junio NE 267
Garcia Pub, Motherland
Tomás Alvara

Gentlemen, welcome. I'm grateful we could all meet at this late hour, so far out of your way. Rest assured your anonymity is safe here." Tomás signaled for the barkeep to fetch him another ale. He had to be mindful not to drink too much to cloud his critical thinking. Besides, the ale didn't block the memory of his actions in the *Concilio de Regentes.*

Elbie Garcia's dive bar was in a poor, ramshackle end of the city, within the walls yet rarely patrolled by the night watch. A street culture of bribery and racketeering kept honest men nervous and risk-takers wealthy. It made perfect sense to meet there. Garcia went about his business polishing silverware and standing by to serve drinks, well past last call.

Six other men sat around two tables pushed together. Tomás looked at each in turn.

"Gentlemen, we move in four weeks. Therefore, it is crucial we know each other—that we know *ourselves.* I'll begin."

Instead of his standard fatigues, Tomás wore ragged, unseemly clothing. His tunic was stained from too many sloppy meals and beverages, and the left seam along his torso was unraveling. He hadn't shaved since the shooting, and his hair was tangled and greasy. He was the best dressed and groomed of the company.

"My name is Florian Willis. I am thirty-seven years old, and I live in the tenth ward of New Mills with my wife, Lene. We have no children. I have lived in New Mills all my life— my father was a smelter in the foundries, and I apprenticed in his footsteps before a back injury forced me to retire from heavy labour. After my recovery, I enrolled in post-secondary at New Mills Academy, completing the two-year criminology program. I was hired by DefCorps, and I work to this day in the Arterial Corridor Security Detail."

The seven spectators nodded, impressed by his backstory. Tomás took a drink. "In my leisure, I enjoy cinema, classic literature and watching local athletics. My wife and I are doting parents to our schnauzer Rufus!"

Tomás smiled, his teeth smudged with remnants of food. The other men chuckled, sipping their ales and eating nuts from the wooden platter dish at the center of the tables.

He turned to his right and nodded, the cue for the next agent to introduce himself.

"Very good, Mr. Willis. Where do I begin…"

"Perhaps with your name…"

"Ah yes. Of course. Hastings Benjamin, thirty-five, I live in Heartsburg. My parents were medics. They always pushed me to follow along in their field, but I never wanted that. Couldn't stand the sight of blood, you know?"

Tomás pressed his fingers together, like Colonel Desantos at his most patient. Hastings had a nice, natural flow. Clearly, he'd been practicing.

"One time, my father brought me up to the Hanging Gardens— most of my friends would have killed for the chance to see them first hand, but it pays to have parents well-connected! When I saw the Gardens, I knew I wanted to work with plants. So I studied biology, majored in vascular plants, and now I work in the AgriCorps—"

"Your family, Mr. Hastings?" Tomás cut him off, giving the man a nervous moment. His eyes narrowed on the "agriculturalist".

"Family… My wife, of course. Her name is Sareyna. We have a daughter, Macie, she turned… nine in February."

Willis took a long drink from his tall glass, emptying a third of the ale.

"Hastings Benjamin, you're uncertain of key details in your life. You wouldn't be *lying* to us?"

Hastings grabbed his glass and tipped it back, leaving a ring of white froth around his stubbled moustache and beard.

"No, Mr. Willis, of course not. I was only nervous. First time, you see."

"Precisely why it is so important that we work out the details now. If I don't *know* you, how can I *trust* you?"

Hastings nodded. "I understand, sir. Should I start over?"

Tomás shook his head. "It does no good now that you've already had a false start. I suggest you practice. And I'll be disappointed if improvement hasn't been made."

He raised his hand, and Garcia poured another tall ale. Tomás motioned to Hastings, and the barkeeper delivered a refill to the visibly shaking recruit. Some operations required a heavy hand. Others, a softer touch. Hastings was no good in the field if he lacked confidence.

For the next hour, the remaining agents introduced themselves, to varying degrees of accuracy and concision. His calm yet unsettling rebuke of Hastings was sufficient motivation for the remaining five men to step up their game.

Halston Rivers, a twenty-eight-year-old security guard from Capston, employed by Defense Corps in the Arterial for almost two-years. His girlfriend, his high-school sweetheart Anna, also twenty-eight, a shopkeeper in Capston, where the couple rented in the downtown district, fifth block. No kids, no pets.

Abrams Livingston, forty-two. Divorced, father of two sons: Shal, eighteen, and Monte, fourteen. Both attend Central Station Academy. Rents in the low-end district, double-shifts at a local convenience store. Sees his children every other weekend.

Creighton Anthony. Forty-one, administrator at First Heartsburg National Bank, branch twenty-six. Never married, no children. Serves on the board of directors for Hearts Alive wish foundation. Owns a condominium in the West End. Avid musician, plays several instruments, but has an affinity for strings.

Russ Cedric. Thirty-two, married to Arvit for four years. Both are textile workers in Arcadia. Russ is a weaver, while Arvit works in advertising. No children. The pair enjoy traveling and have invested in property in Sascota. They have a poodle named Mitzi. Tomás admired Cedric's confidence. He suspected the man could continue sharing the minute details of his life for hours.

Finally, Gerardi Phelps. Originally from Ozarck, moved to Preston with his parents at age four. Today, at age fifty-three, Phelps was night-shift foreman at Steelco, an intercity giant in hardware and construction. Widower, his wife Madileen died of red tide. Though he was cleared by doctors, Phelps always felt that his Ozarckian heritage somehow carried the virus that took his wife. His eyes teared up when he shared this most powerful memory.

Tomás smiled. *Now that's experience…*

After an hour discussing personal lives, hobbies, spouses, education and training, Tomás signaled to Garcia for one final round. As the six agents finished their drinks, the leader gave each man a slip of paper with the address of the next clandestine meeting. Changing location was crucial. They would meet the following morning, six sharp. With only a matter of hours to return to their homes and rest, the six left quickly. Tomás remained at his seat, raising his hand for one more tall ale. He didn't have to focus on details until morning, after he'd slept off his latest hangover.

"One for yourself, Mr. Garcia," he said as the bartender tilted the glass diagonally to stem the foam. "I'll settle the tab this evening."

Garcia sat in Hastings's seat. "I know you're good for it, Captain Alvara. I don't know about *Florian*, but I know I can trust you!"

Tomás grated his teeth. He didn't want to hurt the barkeeper. Besides, he'd been a trusted confidante. It hadn't been his fault the Reaper Andreas had manipulated him all those months ago. Still, Tomás wouldn't hesitate to neutralize any threat. The colonel was right. It *was* easier…

"*Lieutenant-Colonel* Alvara." Tomás planted his glass onto the table with enough force to nearly crack it. Garcia's expression changed to fear. "And you will never say the name Florian Willis again."

Heart in Hand

Friday, 29 June AC 0245
SSE of Inland Open-Pit Lake
Robbie Sheppard

Robbie slept deeply knowing Ian Null was alert and well-adjusted to the nature of the outside world. He knew every snap of a twig, every coo or hoot of an unseen bird, every footprint and disturbed pebble along their path. His pupils narrowed and his brow tightened upon the detection of any of these things. Usually, he dismissed them, but now and then he would pause. A few times it led to a change of course. Robbie never asked why. He didn't really want to know.

The Sheppard brothers slept peacefully in the open air, save for Lorrie mumbling incoherently through his dreams. Cadlen hardly stirred. Even unconscious, Robbie's baby brother was alarmingly quiet. It hadn't always been that way. He never forgot all those sleepless months when Cadlen suffered severe colic, how he'd whispered to Crystal in the twin bed on the other side of their shared room that he couldn't wait until Cadlen was finally quiet. He still regretted it.

They'd covered a lot of ground yesterday—by Null's calculation more than forty kilometers. Traveling through long-forgotten roads, overgrown with maturing pioneer trees and warped lanes long stripped of their blacktop, the journey was slow and cumbersome. They'd move barely a kilometer before Null brought the shuttle to a halt and slipped outside to remove debris from the sensors and the radiator grill. Tramping through heavy brush, they left a clear trail. Null had explained that if anyone was pursuing them, they would have a hard time determining which of the thousands of beaten paths was theirs. Despite minimal contact with other travelers, there was evidence everywhere of countless folks living and moving in the region. It was both comforting and disconcerting.

Robbie woke as though emerging from anesthetic to Null gently jostling his shoulder. He didn't say a word. The aroma of herbal tea was enough. The fire in the Dakota hole smoldered. Lorrie had become deft at the skill. It gave him something to call his own, since the Sheppards now owned nothing. The early morning sun had yet to rise. With any luck, their pursuers hadn't either.

Robbie took a sip of tea. Before he could speak, Null raised his index finger to his lips, eying the slumbering youths. Even Lorrie was in a deeper sleep, his lips still as he breathed through his nostrils with a faint whistle. Robbie nodded. They had another long day ahead. They had many long days ahead. *Null thought of everything. Let them sleep while they can.*

Null sat arms-length from the pit, propping himself against a fallen tree that had uprooted a bank of clumped mud. Crossing his arms gently over his scrunched torso, he closed his eyes and seemed to fall asleep immediately. This had become their routine—Null stayed awake for the earliest hours, when it was hardest to stay alert, no matter how cold or hungry or afraid. When the first Sheppard woke, Null settled into his own needed rest, never more than a couple hours. Robbie observed their guide as he breathed in time like a metronome, as if he'd somehow trained his breathing reflex. His left foot crossed his right slightly. His chest gently raised and receded. Robbie began to hear the natural soundtrack of the woods around him once more, as though Null was only a mute hologram.

Two hours crawled while Null and his brothers slept. Robbie tried his best to emulate his calmness. Crackling and snapping came from all directions. Occasionally the flapping or whooshing of birds. Nothing came close to the fire pit, as though the light projected a force field in which the small party was impervious to whatever lurked in the shadows.

The first rays of the emerging daylight streaked the cloudless sky. As soon as Robbie began to wonder if he should wake him, Null's eyes snapped open. He listened for a few seconds before rising, curling forward, and flexing his legs in one motion until he was on his feet. He began to stretch, performing a full regimen of motion exercises to wake his muscle system and coax blood circulation to his extremities. The routine never changed, and Robbie figured he could set a clock to Ian Null.

"Good… morning?"

Robbie wasn't sure what else to say. Null peeled off his shirt, revealing a mess of scars, both fresh and healed, on his chiseled torso. Stooping over his rucksack, he retrieved a small kit and a new shirt, folded neatly but visibly stained from prior ownership. He'd shared similar clothes with Robbie and his brothers. It would help them blend in, and blending in was crucial.

"Did you rest well?" Null sat and stretched his legs wide, his fingers reaching the tips of his bare toes.

"Better than the night before, that's for sure. You?"

Null didn't answer. "Your brothers slept deeply. Especially Lorrie." He finished his stretches and put on his boots, tying the laces in bows that looked like they were machine-woven. Back to his feet, Null turned to leave the campsite.

"Going for a shower?"

Ian paused. "There is a water hole not a hundred meters from here. It may be the last for a while. When I return you should clean up."

Robbie nodded and Ian disappeared into the brush beyond the tall grass, leaving a glossy trail through the dew. Lorrie began to stir and Cadlen's eyes opened, although he stayed still as if he were home in his own bed. In the first days of the Sheppard adventure in the wild, Cadlen woke and rose quickly. The last few mornings, he greeted the day like a teenager. He'd be thirteen in less than a month. Robbie looked at his mute brother, his thick, sandy hair growing faster than weeds.

"Gone already, is he?"

Robbie turned to see Lorrie sitting up, wide awake, legs crossed as though he were at a retreat campfire.

"He went to clean up. Water hole's not far. He says we should do the same before we leave."

Lorrie stood. "Yeah, good idea. Only whenever we find water, he tells us to stay away from it until he waves his magic hunk of metal. Any idea what a *microsievert* is?"

It had something to do with radiation, though Robbie had to admit that he didn't understand how it worked. Crystal would know about it, if she got to spend any time at all in Lacraie, like she always wanted. Nuclear medicine, it was all the rage, according to his sister.

"He wouldn't warn us if he didn't have a reason. And besides, it's been a week. If he was going to hurt us, don't you think he would have by now? I thought you were finally starting to trust him."

"*Trust* him? No chance. I mean—yeah, he seems decent. But how much do we *really* know him?"

"You can ask." Null's voice interrupted their conversation like a machete. The guide reemerged, hair damp but untangled, hanging loosely around his scarred and tanned face.

"Stop doing that!" Lorrie's yelp crackled from the surprise. "We get it, you're like the wind…"

Several days' worth of stubble patched the southern half of his face, tawny-brown like his mane. The morning light gave it a lighter shade.

"Your turn." Null nodded toward the waterhole trail, ignoring Lorrie's sarcasm.

Robbie motioned to Cadlen. "You can come too, Cad. Lorrie?"

"I think I'll stay back, keep an eye on the camp," Lorrie looked over at Null packing his supplies. "Just in case."

"In case of what—I steal your things?" Null didn't even look up. Robbie tried his best not to smirk at his sarcasm. "If you're staying with me, I suggest you help pack. The sooner we leave, the better."

"Oh right, where do I begin," groaned Lorrie. "*So* much stuff…"

"Either help the man or come with us! He's done nothing but help us, for crying out loud!"

Null filled in the Dakota hole with mud and rocks, smothering the life from it until the last curls of smoke had exhausted. From his pack, he retrieved the handheld device he'd relied upon over the last week for directions. Robbie's device had long since died. But Null's gadget, half-exposing circuits and wires, ran as efficiently as if it had just been unplugged from a full charge. It was a curious machine. Robbie had watched him carry it lightly in his palm, wiping prints off the screen, and blowing dirt and dust away from its open core. As if he was carrying his own heart in his hand.

"I can show you how to use it." Null held the device up for Lorrie to see. "If I were to be injured. Or if you steal my things while I sleep…"

Robbie laughed. Null always parried Lorrie's insults, and it drove the teenager crazy. He'd have paid a small ransom for half of his comebacks any of the times Lorrie had outwitted him in an argument over the years. Robbie motioned to Cadlen to start up the trail.

"Real funny. Whatever you say." Lorrie pointed to the handheld. Robbie watched his brother and their guide as they each held their ground. It was an emotional tug of war. For an instant, he wasn't sure if he should leave them alone together. Then again, Null had offered an olive branch. Offering the secrets of his device to the sometimes-hostile teenager—that was unexpected. Robbie was certain he wouldn't have been so trusting.

Knives Out

Friday, 29 June AC 0245
SSE of Inland Open-Pit Lake
Lorrie Sheppard

There was no way Lorrie was going to leave Ian Null alone with the sum total of their meager survival provisions—even if Null was the reason they had it. Null spread out the tools on a small rectangular swatch of fabric that could have been either a small tablecloth or a large handkerchief. The knives were familiar, of course. A knife is a knife. Until Null explained that one of them was designed for whittling, one for filleting, another for stripping flesh from bone, and another again for skinning. The long-bladed machete was the flashiest, and the one Null had yet to allow him to carry. Lorrie had already sharpened the field-dressing knives as Null had taught him: How to slide the blades across the sharpening tool, at what angle, and how often. How to wipe them clean after use. How to apply oil and wrap them in the fabric so they would be ready for use in an instant. Lorrie watched Null care for his tools with the care of a parent, ensuring that each of his children were flawless and sharp.

If Null were to abandon them, there was no way he'd leave his tools behind. And Lorrie was going to be damn sure he wouldn't leave them with no means of survival.

"The machete." Null carefully wrapped the filleting knife and nodded to the long blade. "It needs oil."

Lorrie's heart raced. It was harder to dislike Null when he kept offering him responsibilities he knew weren't extended to his brothers. "On it." Lorrie dug into the backpack and retrieved the small bottle of oil. Removing the cork, he dabbed a few drops on the cleaning rag and ran it in slow, deliberate strokes the length of the blade.

"Careful." Null still hadn't looked up. "It is very sharp. Keep your fingers back and always wipe outward."

"I know, it's like the others. Just longer." The machete was heavier than he expected. With every stroke, Lorrie felt stronger with the weapon in his hands. "Does everyone out here have one like this?"

Null wrapped the knives individually, coiled the fabric in one big roll and tucked it into the backpack. "Some do. But I don't worry about them."

"Why not? One swing and you could take someone's arm off!" Lorrie gripped the handle, his fingers settling into the grooves like he was slipping on a glove. Swiveling his wrist, he maneuvered the blade in awkward swooshes.

"Keep that up, and you will remove your own arm."

"I'm not going to—"

He didn't finish the sentence before the blade dipped low, dragging his freshly oiled blade in the dirt. Null had already moved onto the non-lethal devices in his kit. He didn't have to say it. Lorrie set the blade in his lap and reached again for the oil and rag.

"So if you're not scared of maniacs with machetes, what are you afraid of?" Lorrie wiped the dirt from the tip and started oiling again.

Null stopped arranging the tools, from familiar cooking utensils to foreign gadgets in different shapes and sizes. He pulled a slender, symmetrical bladed knife no more than thirty centimeters from hilt to tip. Null fingered the handle, making an imaginary circle with the blade. "Anyone who knows how to handle a knife should be feared." He looked through the range of the blade, eyes locking with Lorrie's. Suddenly the machete offered little comfort to him.

"I'm not afraid of you." Lorrie blurted the words he wished he'd kept to himself. "I mean—I know you won't hurt us. Right?"

Null didn't blink, but he returned the knife to his inner shirt pocket. "I do not mean to harm anyone."

"No? What about the owners of the shuttle? Did they just give you all their belongings? 'Here, Mr. Null, we don't need the car—we'll just walk!'" In the days since he returned to camp with a vehicle and all its contents, Robbie hadn't asked. Cadlen sure wasn't going to say anything. Lorrie's little brother followed Null's lead to the letter, as though he were the real Ranger Man coming right out of the shows. But that didn't mean the question wasn't warranted.

Null didn't answer. He returned his attention to his tools, reaching for a small handheld device that looked far more sleek than his general-purpose device. The casing was yellow and its front was almost entirely a viewing screen. Null turned a dial on the right side, and the small device came to life. A faint beeping sound began to emit while the display screen flashed digital numbers that meant nothing to Lorrie. Null looked directly at Lorrie with narrow eyes.

"This is a Geiger counter. It detects radiation."

Lorrie focused on the small machine. "What does it say here?"

Null tilted the reader so Lorrie could see the screen. At an angle, the sun made the numbers hard to determine.

"0.20 microsieverts." *There's that word again.* "This is about what I would expect around this area. We're still some distance from the red zone."

"So, at what point do we start to worry? Does it go up gradually or is there all of a sudden a big spike in those pinging sounds?"

Null knelt on his left knee. "There is no telling how high the levels will go, but I am certain that with precautions, we can pass through without serious risk."

Lorrie raised his right eyebrow. "Precautions?"

Null set the Geiger counter on the ground. "The radiation is not measured simply in numbers. It is important to track the exposure time." He pointed to the screen. "These numbers, they will accumulate."

Lorrie's eyes widened. "Oh, so we can't stay long then."

"Ideally, no."

To Lorrie's surprise, Null offered him the reader. It was light in his palm, like the smallest knives in their set, or the one Null kept concealed on his person. The number on the screen flitted in the hundredths, but averaged around 0.30 as Ian had told him. He resisted the urge to press any buttons. He knew how knives worked. But the Geiger counter, that was something completely different.

"Okay, so we have to cross a radiation zone?"

Null nodded. "The seam is not a clearly defined area. There are different levels of radiation, depending on many factors." Lorrie could tell he didn't want to explain it in detail. "We have to pass through if we are going to reach Moab."

Moab. "And you say we *have* to go there? Why?"

Null reached for his Geiger counter, taking it into his dried and cracked fingertips. "You and your brothers are free to go where you please." With a tap of one of the buttons, the device beeped to life.

"So, if we hightailed it back to New Inland, you'd be fine with that?"

"I would advise against it."

"And why is that, pray tell?"

Null returned all of his tools into his backpack and closed the flaps, buckling them tight. "You asked what became of the owners of the shuttle."

Lorrie gulped and reached for the machete. This time he didn't wave it around. He gripped it tight in his hand, waiting for Null's explanation.

"They were dressed as New Inland Defense Corps officers. But they were not." Null turned his eyes away as though he were reliving their encounter. "There are forces that saw fit to target your flight and blow it from the sky. Those forces would not be overjoyed to learn you survived."

"What did you do to them?"

"They are no longer a threat."

"That's not what I asked." *They're dead, aren't they?*

Null slung the pack over his shoulder. His hair had begun to dry, the waves tumbling along the sides of his strong jaws. "They are no longer a threat."

"Okay, fine. But why not another dome? We have family in Hyacynthe."

"Oh, you remembered you had family there!" Robbie had emerged from up the trail with Cadlen, almost as quietly as Null. Cadlen's thick hair looked darker, neatly combed with a part in the middle.

"Look, I'm not happy with her, but it beats wading around in radiation," Lorrie countered. "Hey, maybe we'd surprise her—does she even know we're *dead* yet?"

Cadlen's face dropped and Robbie grimaced. "Watch what you say! Maybe you don't miss your sister, but we do."

"Your sister in Hyacynthe."

"Yeah, we haven't seen Crys in years." Lorrie tried to imagine her. In his memory she looked more and more like a stock photo, less real with every passing day. "Why, are you single? She's not your type."

"LORRIE!" Robbie smacked him on the shoulder. Null's eyes widened.

"No. Hyacynthe is not an option." The mention of Hyacynthe seemed to snap him to attention, and like clockwork he was back in machine mode, as though one of the Geiger counter buttons changed his function.

"What?" Lorrie raised his arms as Null brushed past him. "I was only kidding…"

"You've said enough," said Robbie. Cadlen took his cue from Null and gathered his bedroll. "You've always said enough."

The Choices We Make

Friday, 29 June AC 0245
Burnside-on-the-hill, Gasperro
Phil Fox

From the hillside, the grey, stone grave markers watched over the Baie of Green like sentinels. Veterans of forgotten wars, still answering the call in death as they did in life. Phil left a path of footprints in the dew-tipped grass of the cemetery as he wandered through the markers in rows. The names on the stone slabs read clearly thanks to diligent maintenance. The Fox plot hid among the others, inconspicuous to anyone seeking them out. Phil knew to look for three distinct stones. One each for his parents, and a third for the most recent burial he'd missed.

As the Fox plot came into view, Phil approached with careful steps as if he would wake them if he were too loud. Kneeling in front of Elsa Schiff Fox's stone, he released the torrent of tears he'd been holding back.

"I'm sorry, Mom. I didn't know what to say." Looking around him, Phil saw flower arrangements placed with care in front of the markers. He reached into his pockets, as if he would magically find something he could offer as a token of affection.

He pulled out the small wheel-shaped barometer. The atmospheric pressure had dropped according to the small needle. He placed the obsolete device on the trim grass at the foot of his mother's marker.

The breeze of the bay prevented him from hearing the sound of approaching feet. Crouching next to him, in front of the third marker, Albert reached for the wilted flower arrangement on his father's grave, replacing it with a fresh wreath.

"I had to change the flowers anyway," he said, sitting back on his heels.

"I wish I'd been here." Phil couldn't look his cousin in the eye. "I'm no better than Le_Renard_Subtil."

"He understood, you know." Albert sighed. "He knew you'd come when you could. He spent a lot of years with Emmanuel. Believe me, he got it."

"And he was a great man for it, Albert. I wish I'd gotten to know him better. At least he was there for me when I first came to the Grove."

"I know. Your father and I bicker. A lot. But when you get to know him, you know he's just doing his best."

Phil didn't agree with that assessment. "The choices he's made have hurt a lot of people."

"Every choice we make risks hurting someone else. Best we can do is keep the damage to a minimum." Albert's wisdom sounded like it once came out of Le_Renard's mouth. Phil inhaled the salty air as gulls wheeled overhead. He knew it was true. As a solicitor, his decisions led to either guilty or not guilty. As mayor, they led to either prosperity or squalor. He'd taken a measured approach to the spate of terrorist attacks, and it only led to more of them. It even cost him his job.

The easiest thing to do was the third alternative—to choose neither and walk away. What did that accomplish? The Sheppards were killed, the administration of Capston was in shambles, and Phil didn't feel any better. *Turns out the third option is the worst.*

The roar of a petrol engine interrupted his self-pity. Cresting the hill, Le_Renard roared into view in an old rig, puffing black smoke that looked like it hadn't been started in years. The old man turned off the engine and wandered through the rows to the Fox and Schiff family plots. He stayed upright.

"It hurts when you're right. Huh." Le_Renard crossed his arms. "Running is all I know. It's easier than facing stuff head on."

"I remember when we met. It wasn't in the garage. It was outside Sascota, Dad's memorial service. You had these wide sunglasses on, and you had an inch of dust on you. Mom said she didn't know who you were, but I knew she did. And I remember after you paid your respects, you walked off into the badlands, like you were walking off the face of the earth. Every now and then I remember…"

Le_Renard knelt to Phil's left, in front of Lucas Fox's marker. "She asked me to bury him here, even though he'd never seen the place. She knew that one day, she'd come home. Elsa Schiff—Bernard's little sister. Y'know, if he was here, he'd tell you that she always wanted to get away from here. Always said it was like a living cemetery, the whole damn town."

Albert laughed. "Guess he told you that story, too!"

"Lucas, he'd go anywhere Elsa wanted to go. I meant it, son. He was a good man." Le_Renard placed a white flower on Lucas Fox's grave. "When the Kayewati stamper told me to pick a name, first thing I thought was *The Sly Fox*. Bravest man I ever met."

Reaching into his other coat pocket, the old man tossed a handheld in front of Phil's knees. The silhouette logo of a man wielding a sword covered the back panel. Phil shook his head.

"I can't take it. It's not even road-ready!" The FTR buggy sat in Jackson Auto's service bay, waiting for the nuke-cell to give it a new life.

"It'll take a couple days to refit the block, but then only a couple more to go by land. Yer lookin' at a week by sea at best—and that's if the weather cooperates with ya."

The land route from Gasperro to Allentown led through seams, trading posts and other communities that may or may not be friendly. But if anyone could plot a secure route…

"You once told me that the family motto was a joke. Front Toward Enemy—brave words for someone who always ran. It's only fitting you use the buggy, my boy."

The FTE buggy, fitted with a nuke-cell block, could cut his trip by half. Maybe he was already too late. *Maybe it's never too late.*

Phil stood. "Well, come on, then. It isn't installing itself!"

You First

Saturday, 30 June AC 0245
SSE of Inland Open-Pit Lake
Ian Null

Be careful with that," Null called ahead to Cadlen. He was swishing the machete blade in wide, exaggerated strokes. Despite Lorrie's care, the sharp edge didn't cut through everything. Occasionally, the silent Sheppard struck a wiry branch that whipped back behind his stride. Most of the time, it caught Lorrie in the face.

"Dammit, Cad—watch it!" Lorrie rubbed his eye. "If *I* was in the lead—"

"If *you* were in the lead, Lor, you'd do no better." Robbie took up the rear, the next-longest hunter's blade tight in his grip. Null didn't want to be too far from the lead this close to the earliest reaches of the seam. Robbie carried more gear than the younger siblings, and needed a well-cleared path. Lorrie had learned how to monitor the Geiger counter and took the job seriously; Null had to remind himself that despite his deeper voice and broader shoulders that Lorrie was still a child. The teen held the device out as though it were radioactive, adjusting the knobs when he didn't need to. If the ticking increased even a quarter of a beat, he froze on the spot and declared that the readings had changed. Null had to reassure him that the slight changes were mostly natural, and had little to do with the approaching radiation-contaminated zone.

"Cadlen. Eleven o'clock. Aim for that white pine." Null had to teach the Sheppard brothers what the directions of an analog clock meant. Eleven was almost straight ahead, only slightly left. There wasn't enough time to teach them how to navigate with his key, but the Sheppards had proved hardy and adaptable. Cadlen obeyed his directions to the letter. As a result, Null awarded him a chance to wield the machete after early morning practice around the smoldering Dakota hole. Lorrie wasn't impressed, but his charge over the Geiger counter pacified his sulking, at least for this leg of the journey.

Cadlen swathed in a beeline to the tall pine tree Null had given for reference. The Sheppards were lucky they hadn't traveled far before Null had found them. Even after their brief sojourn into the woods from the pit mine lake, they had begun to arc when they thought they were moving straight. The forest is a lot like the ocean. If you didn't know how to mark your location, there was no chance you could find your destination. Keeping an eye on a landmark to keep moving straight was one of his first lessons. The youngster picked up on it right away.

Null stared at the screen of his key. The terrain was too difficult to maneuver the shuttle without following the worn roads. Null didn't know the land. They steered clear of most other travelers thanks entirely to his heat-signature application. It had alerted him to Raël's presence before the cabin door even opened. It had allowed them to hide from several traveling bands that could have been brigands. The power cell of the shuttle had dipped to less than twenty percent, and there was no known means to recharge the nuke cell generator without risking overheating, or worse, another Jamiss situation.

As his mind wandered, Null stumbled, dropping the key for a second before snatching it from midair. His head swirled. He'd missed a step a few times before, but fortunately the younger Sheppards were ahead of him and hadn't noticed.

But Robbie did. "Ian, are you okay? We can stop." He was a decent fellow. He showed compassion, even if it was to his detriment. Null straightened himself out.

"Only a tree root." He'd used the same excuse before. He expected Robbie knew it was a fib by now. He didn't need Robbie to know that he was feeling worse, despite taking the Radiogardasse pills. It was getting harder and harder to keep his food down—especially greasier wild game. His thoughts returned to Jamiss. The boy was only a few years younger than Robbie, but he must have suffered greatly from the exposure without any medication to help stave off the symptoms. Surely he'd died by now.

And Ian Null had done nothing to help him.

"Ian! The counter is picking up now. Do I adjust the—"

"No, leave the knobs." Cadlen halted just a few strides before the white pine. Null and Robbie caught up and the three huddled close to the Geiger counter in Lorrie's outstretched hands. Null looked at the screen. This time, the readings had indeed spiked. Reaching with his free left hand, he plucked the yellow-cased device from him.

"Give me a moment." Null's eyes darted back and forth between the counter and the maps on his key. They were still several days from the outskirts of Moab, but were closer than he'd expected to the seam. Once inside, the ticking would increase to a much more concerning pace. It was time.

"It is 1700 hours, 16 minutes. Remember this time." Null passed the Geiger counter back to Lorrie and reached into his knapsack for the pill bottle. The instructions on the side had faded slightly, but the name Dr. Jonathan Doherty was still legible. Any purchase secured through the Allens used the fictional doctor's name—it was a guarantee of anonymity. For a second, Null was relieved that there was no trace of Crystal Sheppard on the label. She had only been an intern, probably unaware that there was no such doctor as Doherty, at least at that point.

Lorrie's eyes widened. "Hold on there. What are those?"

"These pills will help your body process radiation poisoning." Null unfastened the cap and passed the oldest two Sheppards each a pill. Robbie and Lorrie both held it between finger and thumb, examining it as if they were holding a fly by the wings.

"These are safe?" Robbie held his up at eye level. "Where did you get them?"

"It should say on the bottle, right? It looks like something you get back in Capston." Lorrie snatched the prescription bottle from Null. His eyes widened. "Hey, this says Lacraie! Isn't Crystal supposed to work there if she gets good grades?"

She got the grades. And she was working there. Null snatched it back and scowled. "These are not easy to find out here." He fished out a third pill and motioned to Cadlen. The boy joined the huddle and tucked his machete blade into his waistband, letting the metal hang by his leg. Cadlen set the pill in his palm.

"I don't know where you come from, Ian. But in Capston, we're taught not to take unfamiliar drugs from strangers. No chance I'm taking that."

Null couldn't blame Lorrie for this one. They'd known each other for less than two weeks. Up to this point, he'd been taking his pills in secret, and planned to keep it that way. They were, by his estimate, half a mile from a known settlement that should have had Rust ties. This close to the seam, they would likely have more Radiogardasse—even if it was so expensive they had to steal it. There was simply no other way he was going to get the Sheppards anywhere near Ozarck, let alone Moab, without at least three times his current pill count.

And that wasn't accounting for the extra dosage he'd begun to swallow earlier in the week. The sickness had settled inside of him, and it wasn't going to get better without better treatment. Raël had told him that Moab had stockpiles of it. But he had to get there first.

"Ian wouldn't give us anything that would hurt us, Lor." Robbie held up his pill and made to take it, but stopped. "But you're *sure* it's safe, right?"

"Easy solution: Ian, *you* first." Lorrie smirked matter-of-factly. "If you take one, I'll think about it."

And therein lay the problem. He'd already double-dosed before daybreak. Too much of the medicine would cause more harm than good to his organs.

"I am on a schedule different from yours. I had to begin before we met." The statement was one hundred percent accurate, but even to himself it sounded like a feeble lie.

"Oh, that's handy. So what, were you exposed?"

"Lorrie! That's not our business." Robbie scolded his brother, but brought his own pill no closer to his lips. If the elder brother would just take it, the younger two would believe him.

"Since I began my dosage time at 0500 hours, I must follow it. To the minute."

"Yeah, well, I'm not buying it." Lorrie thrust the pill back to him. "Take it here and now, if you want me to believe you."

Null was about to take it just to prove his point when Cadlen plucked his pill from his palm and without hesitation popped it into his mouth. Null watched as the youngster grimaced at the tart taste of the pill's coating, swishing it around what saliva he could conjure, and gulped it down dry.

"Cad! You don't know if that's safe!"

Cadlen shrugged, and turned back to the white pine, drawing the machete from his waist. The boy had shown fortitude from the beginning. But even now, he continued to surprise Null. One extra dose to prove it to the others was a small price to keep the peace among their party. He snapped a pill into his mouth and forced it down without water. As the ovoid capsule sank down his esophagus, his eyes watered. Lorrie was blurry, but Null could tell he was satisfied, at least for now.

"Come on, Lor." Robbie swallowed his pill and washed it down with a swig from his canteen. Lorrie looked at each of his brothers, then down at his pill. He only opened his lips wide enough to shove in the pill, and he turned away Robbie's offer for a drink. All the while he kept eye contact with Null.

"1700 hours and… *20* minutes." Lorrie glanced at the Geiger counter to confirm the exact minute. He turned toward Cadlen who had reached the white pine, awaiting further instruction. "But if you hurt either of my brothers, you're a dead man."

Null nodded. There was little chance Lorrie Sheppard could actually harm him. But then again, with the right motivation, anyone could do anything.

Villains

Tuesday, 3 March AD 2544
Village of Jude
Tirel Desantos

Your hands are so cold, Tirel. Are you sure they're keeping you warm enough?"

Hazel's hands felt cold. Their home was too warm, too stifling, adding to his shortened breath and making it that much harder for him to calm down. Cold was his friend.

The room was walled in white gypsum board, stained from leaking, rusting around the nail heads. The floor was a square linoleum tile pattern laid in a diagonal, the edges jagged from a combination of natural wear and Tirel picking and peeling at the edges. Opaque, plexiglass-covered windows prevented him from either escape or self-harm. Still, there were two plush chairs, one each for himself and his mother when she visited, which was daily, and more frequent than he would have preferred. Still, she brought him clean clothes, soups, and company when he needed all three, even if he didn't want them.

"I'm fine, Mother. I like it cooler anyway, remember?"

Hazel's face had grown a web of age lines since the murder. She cupped Tirel's hands gently in her own, shaking ever so slightly yet enough for Tirel to feel her anxiety.

"I have been speaking with your doctors. I think they understand what happened." Her voice trembled. "They know how he treated you."

"*Us.* How he treated *us.*" Tirel pulled his hands away. "I couldn't…"

The blue of Hazel's eyes deepened as she began to tear. "Let's talk about something else. They are keeping you warm enough?"

Tirel gritted his teeth. *You still don't hear me, Mother. You still don't hear.*

A commotion outside provided a welcome distraction from the mundane conversation. For days, Tirel begged his orderlies to tell him what was going on. The best he could discern was that the village was being visited by an armed unit from somewhere. It could have been an expeditionary force, maybe a brigand militia, maybe even invaders from the bigger, more established walled cities in the northeast. There was no mistaking the sound of heavy vehicles rolling through the streets, troops marching in military precision, an air of urgency.

"I'm thirsty." He reached for the hard plastic tumbler, covered except for the small spout. He was delivered a new tumbler twice a day, but lately he found himself taking bigger sips, emptying the cup sooner and leaving him parched longer.

After a few more minutes of awkward silence and Hazel asking if he was well fed and warm enough, an orderly rapped on the door twice, signaling their time was finished for the day. She stood, straightening her arched torso as best she could, even though she had developed a permanent hunch. She wrapped the scarf over her hair, wisps of grey locks dangling down her cheeks. "It's raining," she said. Hazel always worried what others thought about her hair. Tirel despised her vanity almost as much as her weakness.

It was the last time Hazel visited him.

Days passed, and the welcoming absence turned to alarm when the orderlies refused to speak of his mother, fake smiling when they delivered his meals and his refilled water tumbler. Hazel's absence was not the only change to his routine. The tumbler had been replaced with a new, stainless-steel model, and it was filled with bitter tea. On the first day, he refused to drink it, spitting the pale beige liquid at the walls, providing a contrasting colour staining the pale, rust-streaked gypsum. When he asked for water, Tirel was told that the water was being tested by the visitors, and they insisted that patients be served from a different source than the town water table. The tea was meant to take away the taste of the purification process. The tea was probably poisoning him.

On the fourth day, no orderlies came. Tirel begrudgingly drank the tea. The tumbler was dry, and when the starchy paste in his mouth began to cake around his lips, he pounded at the door, shouting as loud as he could handle the echo. In the distance, he heard a deep rumble that he could feel in his chest. Shortly after, another louder and closer boom shook the room, only this time the pop of gunshots peppered the village streets. Men and women shouted in alarm as vehicles hummed, and boots began to tramp around in a chaotic, undisciplined discord.

"Hello! Anyone? *What's happening?*"

Tirel's pulse raced as he pounded his small fists until they hurt. Voices barked nearby, and as the gunshots began to fade and more explosions sounded further away, he turned his attention to his new tumbler. Grasping it in his right hand, he pummeled the door, splintering it as he screamed. His voice shorted out like a broken radio signal. Tirel slumped against the door, every ounce of his energy drained.

He woke to the door jarring his limp body, pushing him further into the room with each thrust. The hallway outside was abuzz with commotion; boots were clopping up and down the corridor as voices hollered over top of one another. The shape of what looked like a laboratory technician came into view. The man wore a white coat and pants, but no helmet, and carried no weapon.

Tirel's hearing was as distorted as his sight. The person looking down at him was trying to speak, but his words were indiscernible. The man turned out to be a woman with short-cropped hair, blue eyes, and a husky voice. He'd never seen a short-haired woman before.

"Are you okay? Can you tell me your name?"

Tirel couldn't answer. His mouth was like chalk and to speak would have taken the last bit of energy he had. All he could do was stare at his rescuer.

"Get him over to the cot. I need to look him over…"

Two medics wearing breathing apparatus lifted the boy by the arms and legs and moved him back into the room to his bare bones cot, laying him gently on his back. Two masked medics entered the room with portable monitors and began to attach colourful wires to his head, his chest, and his abdomen. A pinch in the soft flesh at his elbow and the needle began to extract his blood. Tirel tried to cry out, but his voice was gone, his words absorbed in the dryness of his mouth.

"Run the sample," the woman ordered.

The needle withdrew, replaced by a swab of cotton and adhesive tape. The medics continued to study their devices until a loud beep emanated. They huddled together, conferring over the results of the blood test.

"They were giving him water directly from the table..."

"His numbers are way too high..."

"Do we bring him in?"

"He needs the treatment..."

"What if this gets to the press?"

"The water table is ruined. We can't just leave him here when all the others are leaving…"

"Do we know if he has any family…"

Tirel couldn't tell who was saying what, but it was the woman who'd posed the last question. He shook his head, but the medics didn't acknowledge. No, he had no family left. Hazel had left him in this secure room for the doctors and town leaders to poke and prod him like a science experiment. He was the boy who took a steak knife and slashed his father's throat. Cold blood. No provocation.

No remorse.

Mother had only stayed out of some false sense of duty. Not once did she tell him she still loved him. *No, there's no family left.* He was ashamed that he still longed to hear the words.

Domingo, 1 julio AC NE 267
Chapel of St. Jude
Colonel Tirel Desantos

Tirel knelt over the back of the pew. "While they locked me in a white room and forced me to drink the water disguised as tea, the whole of Jude was under siege. I didn't know who the villains were—my captors or my liberators."

From atop the officiant's throne, Andreas listened, hands folded. "It's never easy to tell, Colonel. Everyone is the villain eventually."

The Reaper stood, looming over the altar and the front rows of pews. Tirel watched his face shift from that of the fallen Ansati to his fallen son, Paolo. A red hue bathed him in an equally mystifying and terrifying aura. In one instant, Tirel could embrace him. In the next, he could squeeze the life from him.

"Who decides, Colonel? Who has the moral authority to say what is right and what is wrong?" The Reaper circled to the front of the altar, crunching glass under his steps. "When that authority is given to those who seek to *restrain* you…"

Village elders. Doctors. Parents…

"*They* are the villains, Colonel Desantos. Councilors, too cowardly to speak for themselves. Too busy shrugging their shoulders to swing the hammer." The Reaper's words flowed like a river into the sea. "Those who would call themselves family… They are in fact our oppressors."

Tirel's lips trembled. The chalky dryness in his mouth caused his throat to spasm.

"You are thirsty, Colonel. Why not drink from your bottle?"

With shaking hands, Tirel grasped the water canteen. Tilting it back, the fluid poured over his lips. It tasted like bitter tea. Without swallowing, he spit the contents, hurling the container across the sanctuary.

Andreas smiled. "Why settle for tea when wine is the better choice?"

Crucible

Tuesday, 15 March AC 0219
New Inland Foundry
Steven Reekan

Steven's muscles screamed but like the gnashing and pounding of the Foundry machinery, he kept moving. His father was right. The foreman was an asshole. Four hours before break, not a second less. A new assembly of casting molds had arrived, and according to the foreman, they weren't going to unload themselves. A team of four, of which Steven was the youngest and least experienced, were tasked with unloading the skid and lugging them across the floor. On the other end, a more experienced crew waited to assemble the series of rectangular hulks so the crucibles dangling from their pulleys and cables could pour the molten metals.

The oldest of the crucible crewmen urged his son onward while the others jeered. Steven scowled at his father, tuning out the other men. He stumbled, straining his ligaments as he straightened his posture. His heavy gloves were loose enough to allow airflow, but the Foundry heat still made his palms sweat. Drifting a little too close to a hammer press, a stray spark caught him high in his cheek, just beneath his round goggles. The right lens always fogged a little, so he tended to squint that eye, making the left his compass. Ten more strides and he could drop the almost 40 kg weight onto the treadmill. Then it was back to the skid, and repeat the process all over again. One hundred molds. Steven had lost count at twenty, but he could have sworn they'd unloaded the lot and the foreman had doubled their labour, expecting it done in half the time.

The mold dropped from Steven's gloves and the treadmill grinded under the impact. "Watch it, Reekan!" The foreman barked as the hammer press pounded, showering more sparks. "Break one of those rollers and it's out of your pay!"

"Ah, leave him alone," Trahearn Reekan croaked. He was much older than the rest of his team, and a full step behind. The rest teamed to maneuver the molds into place, according to the order they'd been unloaded and that which they'd need for efficient casting. This whole place was built on efficiency. There were two kinds of machines—the metal ones, and the breathing ones.

"Was I talkin' to you?" The foreman looked up from his datapad. He held it in gloved hands, only his were skin tight and thin, themselves molded of a metal and polymer hybrid material designed to keep molten metal from burning his dainty fingers. His hardhat perched on his scalp like a bad toupee. Steven squinted both eyes. Through the right lens, he was a foggy shape of a thin man, too long out of the manual labour pool. By break time, Steven couldn't tell anyone apart.

Trahearn Reekan opened his mouth to answer back, but instead of a sarcastic retort, a loud coughing spell erupted. The pair of workers nearest him laughed. Steven wanted to punch them both. His father was right. The Foundry was a brutal workplace populated with jerks not smart enough to land the easier jobs, and not clever enough to find their way out. Deep beneath New Inland, the infernal presses kept their workforce in invisible shackles, even if they had the means to forge them of metal.

"It's a means to an end, son," his father told him when he punched the clock for his first shift nearly three months prior. "You can do better than this, Steven." The words rang in his ears like hammered anvils. The zeal his father had shown him when he was a boy, after he came home from a long workday and Dianna Reekan fluttered in the kitchen, was long gone. Dianna had long left them. Recovery from those long shifts took longer, and required more medicine. Some nights, he couldn't reach down to remove his own boots.

When his cough didn't subside, Steven crossed the floor and wove behind the treadmill. He pulled off the goggles and let them fall to the floor. With newfound energy, he reached an arm around his father, doubled over and spewing blood.

"Reekan! Back to the skid!"

Steven glowered at the foreman. "He needs the medic!"

"He needs a medic, all right. And I need a vacation. Now, move!"

Trahearn wove a hand. "Go… I'm fine." The words wheezed through spittle and blood droplets. Steven refused.

"No, you need the medic. I'm not going until they get you help."

"*Hearn* Reekan, take your break. You're holding up the production anyway. And *Steven* Reekan—"

"*Get the medic!*" Steven hollered, tightening a grip around his father as the spasms jerked his frail body. Trahearn kept his eyes turned down. Steven knew he was embarrassed.

"All right, all right. Don't piss yourself over it." The foreman waved to his counterpart across the floor. "And you can skip break—you owe me time."

The medic arrived ten minutes later. Steven refused to return to the skid. He already owed overtime, so the extra ten minutes wasn't going to matter. The medic in a stained reddish-brown jumpsuit beckoned for assistance. Two more medics arrived with a spinal board, and it took the three of them plus Steven to secure him to it. Between spasms and stubbornness, Trahearn wasn't going easily or quietly. By this time, the rest of his team had stopped joking, grinding the production to a halt to the chagrin of the complaining foreman.

They carried Trahearn Reekan out of the Foundry for the last time. His treatment required a lengthy stay in the hospital and half of Heartsburg's supply of drugs. It turned out that after Steven filed his report, the foreman had ignored several medical incidents, not only from his father, but from others on the Foundry floor. After almost a year to the day, Trahearn won a substantial settlement for both his early retirement, as well as compensation for his lung cancer—neglected long enough to pay out a six-figure sum that could have seen him live a life of comfort for years to come.

Only there weren't any years left. Trahearn Reekan died before the ink on the settlement dried.

But Steven Reekan remembered his father's last words to him on that final shift. *You can do better than this.* For almost thirty years, his father poured all of himself into a thankless job that ultimately cost him his life. The day after his father left the Foundry in a medical shuttle, Steven stepped to the foreman. He punched him square in the jaw. He didn't wear the goggles, because he wanted to see every detail, not just from his left eye.

He walked out the front door, just like Dianna Reekan had so many years earlier. For an instant, he understood why.

Tuesday, 3 July AC 0245
Ap-Oz Research Facility
Steven Reekan

Steven held fast his grip and peered down at the gaping maw that was the entryway to the Appalachian-Ozarck mountaintop facility. The Tan-Ro copter descended toward the open hangar jutting from the grey-green metal roofed structure. Commander Gry's gruff voice had greeted him over the radio as the craft made its final approach, listing back as it angled downward. To anyone watching from the foothills, the craft would have vanished into a maelstrom of blasted rock.

John Gry emerged from behind the security barrier, his hair buffeting from the thrumming blades as the craft came to rest on the heliport. The blades were still winding down as Steven leaped to the stone floor, briskly making his way under the overhang.

"Hope your flight was smooth." Gry extended his right hand.

"Like silk," he muttered, brushing past the big man who fell into step with him. "Report from the scanners?"

Gry shook his head. "Lots of life out there. Camps everywhere, people in little pockets, mostly nomads. None matching the descriptions of our kids."

Our kids. Steven winced at the thought of the Sheppard brothers, but he couldn't shake his conversations with them from his mind. At least, from Robbie, the only adult of the three. Anything with Lorrie was sarcastic or rude. And the youngest one didn't talk at all. If their lives hadn't depended on him, he wouldn't have considered them his *kids.* Still, their loss left a pit in his stomach worse than his own mother leaving him. Than his father coughing up blood on his last shift, and again the last day he saw him still alive.

Steven continued marching, the doors to the complex sliding open as he approached. He would have collided with the heavy iron had it remained shut.

"Transponder?"

"Nothing. No debris. We're sure the Tan-Ro went under. And that lake was an open mine; it could be a long way down."

Steven slowed his pace. Ap-Oz personnel skittered about as though it were a routine day. It could have been the 93rd at Holt Tower if not for the humidity and the dank smell. The pair approached the offices.

"We need to get out there again." Steven had dispatched three Capston DefCorps officers. He hadn't heard back from them before leaving New Inland. Pax Brien had frozen Steven's access to Capston funds. He figured Kendall was responsible. He couldn't blame her. They both knew he would drain the coffers trying to find out what had become of the missing Sheppards. "We can't be sure they're gone until we find some *evidence*—a panel, a doorknob, a dirty sock—*anything.*"

The two entered the offices. Steven took his seat behind his desk. Gry remained standing, not quite at ease.

"Steven, we need to be careful," Gry began. "Our nuke-cells are good for the short term, but only if we pace ourselves."

"Get Enstrom on the line." The Ozarck Chair ran a tight ship, but surely there was something he could do. Steven always found him fair.

"They've already bought biosynth. Besides, you summoned Jarren to New Inland." Gry hunched his shoulders. "Since the DHC cut us off, we don't have anything to offer."

Steven raised a hand. "I don't want to hear it, John."

The big man sighed. "You have to hear it anyway. The lien on the fleet—bank's calling us on it. Without Capston support we can't maintain it."

"Then Ling can talk to Kendall. We need time."

"Ender's already met with her. She runs a hard bargain, but so far, no go."

Steven leaned back in his office chair, as rigid as the surrounding walls. Ap-Oz had a lot in common with the Foundry. Only the crucibles were empty and dry. Heaving a sigh, Steven stood and inhaled a lung full of mountain air.

"Where are you going?"

Nowhere, John. Nowhere.

"I need a nap."

No_Underscores

Wednesday, 4 July AC 0245
Allentown
Slava Allen

S hall we obscure his sight?"

The receptionist's voice crackled through the speaker. Slava glanced at his reflection in the datapad screen. Not a hair out of place, though he noticed a few were greyer.

"Ask our guest politely if he will consent to a hood. Remind him that his request for personal interaction without standard privacy barriers is highly unusual. He is a reasonable man. I expect he will comply."

"Sir," the receptionist replied and the speaker switched off. Slava brushed the fabric of his suit coat downward to clear away any unseen loose fibres. Such an unexpected visit demanded attention to detail.

It took about twenty minutes for the DNA examination to be completed. Slava circled his sterile desk and moved the guest chair back a metre. After careful examination of the office area, he returned to his office chair, squaring his posture. The secretary informed him that the examination was complete, and by all accounts in their database, the guest was indeed who he claimed.

The Allen agent sighed in relief. "Send him." A flicker of static from the intercom, and the door of his office opened.

The guest emerged into the cold light of Slava's office. He wore the black fabric hood which hung to his shoulders, resting upon the neatly pressed sport jacket fastened by only a single button over his blue and white plaid shirt. His pants were deep navy blue and spotless, unusual for his chosen mode of transportation.

"Welcome. Please keep your hood drawn over your face. Advance seven steps to your seat." The words were abrupt. He wondered if his guest sensed his apprehension.

The guest nodded and moved seven steps forward to the backrest of the chair. Without reaching to confirm it was there, he circled in front and sat directly on the seat. Slava noted the implicit trust he displayed. The first test was passed by both parties.

A green light blinked on Slava's console. As though the guest could see it, he spoke for the first time. "Your secretary has my data uploaded to your system. You should see it any moment."

"Indeed, I have received the access," Slava replied. The hooded man before him understood the process. *Such poise. My, how you would make an exceptional agent.* "Now, Mister—"

"I would prefer to conduct our business eye to eye," the man interrupted. "You've waived your protocol this far. I'm sure you could indulge me."

"I have a few questions before we cross that threshold." Slava tapped the datapad screen and a menu with New Inland business tabs appeared. "What is the nature of your call?"

"You know why I'm here."

The guest held his ground. Slava respected him for it.

"I wish to open a client account with the Allen Consortium."

Fair enough. "And you submitted my personal identification. Sir, very few individuals have access to that."

"It's all who you know, right?" The hooded guest chuckled.

"That is what puzzles me. How are you connected to Le_Renard_Subtil?" The identification number the guest had submitted was unique to Slava's dealings with the infamous kingpin. The Allens had access to more information than any other organization in the outside world. Yet, this hadn't been anticipated.

"Your organization trades in information. My answers are currency, *Slava.*"

Slava sighed in resignation. "You may remove your hood, sir."

The man reached up with his left hand and pulled the fabric over his head, dropping it to the floor. His face wore a weeks-old beard. All data Slava had reviewed showed a clean-shaved face, rather than the auburn-reddish facial hair that revealed itself from beneath the hood.

"You received my proposal three days ago." His eyes narrowed. "I'm sure you've had enough time to consider it?"

"Indeed I have," Slava replied. "Your offer is very unorthodox. I'm understandably concerned that you will not be able to carry out your end of the bargain."

The man nodded. "Naturalized relations with a city in New Inland is worthy of your doubt. I think my offer protects your interests, both within Allentown and abroad."

Full sovereignty of the Consortium within the boundary of Allentown. Recognition by New Inland of Allen identification. Status quo trade relations with Hyacynthe, even Kayewat. It sounded too good to be true. "You mean to tell me, sir, that you can guarantee all of this with the DHC?"

The guest nodded again. "Guaranteed."

"And if you fail?"

"I'm prepared to offer compensation to you, Mr. Allen."

The men glared directly at each other in a silent tug of war. Slava relished in the game the two played, but the carrot his guest dangled before him was way too tempting. He'd read the insurance proposal. He'd read it twice just to be sure he'd understood it correctly.

"If I were to agree with you, sir, I would have conditions of my own. I trust you understand?"

"Don't waste our time, Slava."

"Very well. Your full name, for the documents."

The man leaned forward, smug in his victory. "Phileas Jackson Fox. No underscores."

Slava had expected a less assertive man in the former mayor of Capston. He'd expected a desperate man seeking information on Paolo Desantos. He'd predicted the price for that information to be prohibitive. When he saw just how much Phileas Jackson Fox was prepared to pay for the Null/Desantos files, he had to hear it in person to be sure he wasn't bluffing.

Either Jennings Marribel's DHC agreed to naturalize relations with the Allens, or Phil Fox forfeited his family estate. Worst case scenario, Slava could retire immediately to the comforts of the Jackson Homestead. He could taste the salty air already.

Cold Tea

Saturday, 1 February AC 0239
Holt Tower Lounge, Capston
Steven Reekan

"Cripes, Jason, jazz night again?" The discordance of brass instruments and tinkling piano keys drove Steven nuts. "Is it that hard to find a decent bass and guitar combo in this city?"

Jason Holt belly-laughed and sloshed Steven's refill of whiskey onto his bar top. "Come on, Reekan! Don't you feel it in your bones?" Jason snapped his fingers intentionally off the beat.

"No, that's early onset arthritis. And this shit you call music is about as painful!" He grabbed the whiskey and took a swig. Drops beaded in his mustache. Keys and brass made sounds as foreign to him as a nursery of crying babies. Guitar, drums, bass—distortion from electricity. Steven liked his music as punctual and disciplined as the machinery of the Foundry. Even if that place was a cesspool, and his father got cancer by the lung along with his severance and pension from it. Fat lot of good the money did him.

"Here." Jason tossed him a bar towel. "Wipe your hands—you want to give the mayor a good impression, don't you?"

"I'm charming enough as it is." Steven wiped the sloshed whiskey off his hands and tossed the towel back. "Besides, if he's half as mild as he looks on the news—"

"Mild? That's a new one." Steven cursed under his breath as the mayor's familiar voice cut through the jazz behind him. Swiveling his stool, he greeted Phil Fox with a puffed-chest and firm handshake. The mayor didn't squeeze back. He was dressed less formally than he'd expected—usually he was in full suit and tie on the television screen. His voice was louder, too. Maybe the music bothered him just as much.

"How about this band?"

Great. He likes this shit. "They're something else. Steven Reekan. Pleasure."

Fox nodded. "Phil Fox. The pleasure is mine, sir." He took the bar stool next to him and motioned to Jason. "If you have it on hand…"

Holt was one step ahead of him. He'd already pulled a green bottle from beneath the counter. Its contents poured equally green. Steven wondered if it was alcohol or cough syrup.

"Thanks, Mr. Holt. And put Mr. Reekan's tab on mine."

"That's not necessary, Your Worship."

"Phil—I don't like *Your Worship*. It sounds way too important." The mayor took a mouthful of the green liquid. The smell of it overpowered Steve's own drink. He couldn't figure out what combinations of herbs and additives made it so pungent.

"There's no more important job, don't you think?"

"I'd think the service your company can provide is far more important." Phil leaned an elbow on the counter. Jason puttered around behind the bar, clearly eavesdropping on the meeting. Phil didn't seem concerned. "My administrative assistant briefed me on your proposal, and I have to say, I have a few concerns."

Miss Kendall, as she'd introduced herself, was more intimidating than Phil. "By all means, I'm happy to explain—*elaborate* our services." Hopefully the mayor wasn't judging him by his choice of words.

"Reekan Security Services has been successful, I see. You have positive feedback from your previous clients. You had the Foundry account—that's no walk in the Gardens!"

Steven smiled. There was no greater retribution for his and his father's treatment in New Inland's basement level. Half of his original hires were disgruntled Foundry-men. His security team had managed to do the unthinkable. Theft, aggression, everything tightened up down there under Steven's watch.

"I'm thorough. I treat my staff with respect, but I take no shit." Maybe he shouldn't have sworn.

"Our current police force has been adequate, but tourism has grown, and that brings more opportunity for trouble. My concern, though, is your current payroll. We need at least five times the bodies if you're going to be able to police the entire city."

This was the tricky part. By now, he'd already read Steven's proposal, or Kendall had read it to him. "I'm sure you've read about our business with Ozarck?"

Phil took another drink of the cough syrup liquor. "Ap-Oz, you call it. Yes, I did read it. To my understanding, you have a lease agreement with the Ozarck Federation."

"That's right. Ozarck has this facility up in the southern Appalachians. Old-world military bunker, fully stocked and well-maintained—but expensive. So, when we applied for an in-house training facility—"

"I remember, it came up in Council. We were concerned about the scope of your plans."

Those plans were for research and development akin to what Hyacynthe was doing up in their Lacraie nuclear medicine fortress. Mayor Marribel, Heartsburg's Chief of Medical Research and Procurement, had been heavily against a similar set-up under New Inland's dome. Steven had never met the woman, but he already didn't like her.

"As it turns out, we came across Ap-Oz during our expansion in research and development. Can't live off security alone. You have to diversify if you want to get a leg up on the competition."

Phil blinked. "No doubt. I'm no businessman, but Jason tells me constantly."

"I heard that!" Jason was back to them, wiping dry glassware and listening too intently. The band had shifted gears into more mid-tempo drawling.

"I'm sure you did! Now maybe give us a few minutes?"

Jason sighed. "Fine. My bar, and all. But you two take the time you need." He moved an arms-length further down the bar. Steven knew he could still hear, but the point was made.

"Ap-Oz employs almost a hundred scientists, and that's on top of the hundred or more guards that Ozarck laid off. I met with Mayor Enstrom. Ozarck Fed is willing to lease the facility if I take on the contracts of the employees."

"And how can you afford that, Mr. Reekan? You don't have the Capston contract yet."

Maybe not yet… "My father died from working in the Foundry. You might have heard about him? Trahearn Reekan?"

Phil wrinkled his brow. "Can't say I recognize the name. Sorry for your loss."

"Before he passed, he won a large settlement on top of his pension. As his only heir, I inherited the lot of it. So, I invested back into my business ventures. I know it's what he wanted." *You can do better than this, he said. I will. I did.*

"I'm sure he'd be proud. Now, just to be sure: You threw all of your inheritance and earnings into a lease agreement with Ozarck that gives you a military compound, laboratory, and a full staff to pay—all on the assumption you could land the Capston account?"

"My father always said to go big or go home." He'd never heard him say that in his life, but it sounded impressive. "So I'm going big."

Phil nodded and took another drink. The mayor sat up and shifted his legs. Steven tried to read his body language, but Phil Fox didn't give up his position so easily.

"If we were to make this deal, there are a few obstacles. Your Ap-Oz employees aren't New Inland citizens. The DHC will have a problem with that."

"The condition of hire for the Ap-Oz crew was to seek New Inland citizenship, as I expected the Council might be concerned. I have vetted and referenced all of them. Enstrom can vouch for me."

"I know Enstrom. Reasonable fellow. Pays his solicitors terribly, though." Phil laughed. Steven thought all lawyers were rich. Evidently, not in Ozarck.

"Ozarck's having a rough go. Rust is undercutting them on everything. Anyway, I let go anyone without a spotless resume. I won't request for even one of them to enter New Inland unless you and the Council are completely satisfied."

"Makes sense to me. You'll have to sponsor the citizenship applications."

"As long as you can convince the Council to expedite the process?"

Phil curled his lip. "I'll do my best. Now, you're aware of the covenant on research and development, I assume?"

"Full disclosure and five-way equal sharing of all development." New Inland was no different than any of the treaty-bound domes on the continent. "As it stands, my head of research has completed all contract work with Ozarck, so if we close this deal, we'll start the clock from then on any future work."

"Fair. What's the nature of your work in Ap-Oz?"

"Biotech, mostly in medical research since we're closer to red-zone resources." Kyle Jarren once tried to explain that exotic ingredients made better medicines, and were difficult to cultivate in artificial climes. "We don't have functional nuclear research though, so Heartsburg loses nothing." Steven took a long drink. *That should please Marribel…*

Phil flexed his fingers. "I think we can make this work. I'll need to report to the Council, so that may take a few weeks. But we can discuss it further in my office."

"Yeah, *your* office." Jason Holt had inched his way closer until he was practically the third man in the conversation. "Now, I have a whole floor up on the 93rd if you need a headquarters at a reasonable rate."

"While you're up, Jason, how about a drink for my new chief of security?"

Jason brought out the green bottle and poured a half glass, sliding it along the counter until Steven trapped it with an open hand. "I can drink to that!" He took a mouthful and his eyes immediately watered.

The strange elixir tasted like dill brine mixed with lemons, and it was lighter in colour up close. The aftertaste wasn't nearly as bad as he'd expected.

And neither was Phil Fox.

Wednesday, 4 July AC 0245
Ap-Oz Research Facility
Steven Reekan

From the vantage point of the crow's nest, Steven was certain that on a clear day, the shape of New Inland, some hundreds of kilometers away on the northern horizon, was staring back at him, mocking him while he waited in his time-out corner. In the best of times, the thrumming of the engines of aircrafts approaching the hangar provided white noise that reminded him of the transience of Capston. The 93rd level of Holt Tower was so quiet it felt sterile. He was most comfortable when the gears of industry were grinding, showering him with sparks and steel dust. If nothing else, it kept him alert.

Outdoor life was difficult to reconcile. Though quieter in the forest, there was still a rawness to the air, the sounds, and the feel. He understood the funk of seasonal rot. Rain on his face jabbed sharper than smelting sparks. He'd sooner take his chances with a brown bear than a Foundry overseer.

It was most unsettling to be exposed, all the time and in all ways.

Ap-Oz was in remarkable repair when he assumed the lease. Toxicity levels were much lower than he had expected, given its position within range of the red zone. Several notable communities peppered hundreds of hectares of abandoned land. They were nearest La Cumbre territory, though it was known that the Allens and Rust both operated in the region. Steven had a connection with the Allens, but events in Allentown did no favours to either party. Neither La

Cumbre nor Rust were in any hurry to talk. Word travels just as fast on the outside as it does in New Inland, apparently.

This tea is the worst. Almost worth going back to have a proper cup of java… Steven grimaced at the bitterness. If only they could broker more trade with Ozarck, Ap-Oz could stock its pantry with better than field ration packets and cheap green tea. If only they had a Hanging Gardens of their own. The upper levels could be easily converted…

And who's going to work the gardens? Dianna Langley? Jennings Marribel? He couldn't decide which he dreaded more.

The crow's nest was really an old observation tower. In a bygone time, Ap-Oz was once a highly fortified army base, built inside a mountain for maximum protection—not unlike the bomb shelters beneath Allentown. Ozarck held several properties in the outside world, most of which weren't profitable.

When Steven's security business made the shift into a fully armed militia, upon securing a contract with Capston's fresh-faced new mayor, he scrambled to claim the hideout before anyone else could. Steven even assumed payroll over the research scientists and other employees of the facility. Reekan Security Services blossomed from about thirty to three hundred faster than a hammer press.

Steven's handheld buzzed. He took another sip of tea, curling his lip. He didn't want to talk to anyone. At least Cal Merrick didn't video call.

```
-You're a hard man to reach. C
-Only so many places around here I could be. S
-Crow's nest? C
👍 S
-Gry said if you weren't up there you'd be sulking
in your cot. I didn't believe him of course. C
-What can I do for you on this lovely morning? S
-Lovely? Thought it was twelve degrees and frigid. C
-Get to the point, Merrick. S
```

The small talk was no less annoying via text than in person. At least he could turn off the handheld.

    -Unsecure channel. But news from DefCorps. C
    -Go on. S
    -We sent a team of three to search out the assets. C

Steven winced at the thought of the Sheppard brothers as 'assets'.

    -Team has gone silent. C
    -Where are they? S
    -Unknown. We followed up with their family contacts.
Two don't have any. C
    -Unfortunate. S
    -They should have. Turns out their listed families
were false. C

Oh, shit. Grant and Desantos weren't the only outsiders in New Inland. Two managed to infiltrate his security force. Where had they come from? Ozarck by way of Ap-Oz? Kayewat by way of Motherland?

    -Still no black box signal from the Tan-Ro? S
    -No. C

Maybe the same interloping terrorists had sabotaged the flight in the first place. Maybe they'd learned about Ling's clandestine move to smuggle them out. And maybe they went to confirm they'd got the job done.

    -DHC? S
    -Not yet. But Brien needs to know. C

Pax Brien wouldn't take any chances with the rest of the Council. Steven couldn't blame Merrick for that.

    -Tell him. Make sure Kendall is there. Keep me posted.
S

```
-Go take your nap. C
👍  S
```

All Steven could do these days is nap, pace the cage, and drink piss poor tea. He pocketed his handheld and threw the cup over the edge. He didn't stick around to hear it shatter.

Don't Touch Dead Things

Wednesday, 4 July AC 0245
WSW of Inland Open-Pit Mine
Robbie Sheppard

Outdoor life, though exhausting, exhilarated Robbie. Early mornings, short bursts of sleep, swift setups and takedowns—these were the rhythms that fueled him. The harder the task, the more rewarding the spoils—be they fresh-cooked meals for supper or soft boughs for sleep. His back wasn't as sore as the first few nights. His stomach had acclimatized to strict meal timing and modest portioning. Robbie smelled more—wisps of smoke from other camps, richness of wetlands, soft decay of nature's life cycle. He noticed his abdominals tightening, his legs toned and firm, his arms and shoulders more defined. And he saw the changes in Lorrie too. Longboarding helped him keep a strong core, and his hours of riding every day had built stamina ideal for life on the outside. But most of all, Lorrie appeared calmer. The sarcasm remained, of course. Jibes toward his brothers, and pointed jabs at Null continued, but fewer and farther between.

Robbie adjusted the straps of the large rucksack, packed with bedrolls and provisions. The weight of the cargo made the straps dig into his shoulders if he didn't adjust them every so often. It was all a part of the routines at this point. No sense in complaining. Robbie and his brothers weren't only alive, they were thriving.

It was in no small part due to Ian Null. And as the days passed, Null was visibly deteriorating.

It made no sense. The man was a specimen—absolutely cut from head to toe. When he changed his shirts, beneath the scars across his back and the blemishes on his torso, the man had a physique the likes Robbie had only ever seen in films. Rather than exercise with improvised weights, Null held fast to slow stretch and pose routines.

Lorrie had asked him how he became so fit. Good food, calisthenics, meditation… and stillness, he'd answered.

"Stillness?" Lorrie poured swamp water from his hiking boot. The bog was deceivingly lush, and he hadn't noticed the spongy moss bed along the outskirts. After his foot sank into the unseen marsh mud, Null used the twisted dead branch he'd been using as a walking stick to measure the depth. He jabbed it into the moss and proceeded to push it down until his knuckles touched the moss. And that wasn't the bottom.

"Stillness of body and mind, yes." Null knelt and ate a strip of smoked meat.

"You have to *move* to exercise, though."

Null finished half the strip. Robbie watched him chew softly, his lips and cheeks barely moving before he swallowed. Over the last several days, Null had eaten less each meal. At 1720 hours every day, the Sheppards took their pills while Null supervised the dosage. Not once had Robbie seen him take his own. It appeared as though he needed more and more stillness.

"Movement must be deliberate. Purposeful." Null wiped his forehead with the back of his hand. "Otherwise energy is wasted."

"I get that, but too much stillness—don't you find it…" Lorrie wrinkled his brow searching for the right words. "*Too* quiet?" That was the best he could conjure.

"Quiet does not equal silence." Null took a small sip from his canteen.

"What do you mean?"

Null closed his eyes. "Listen. If you are still, you will *hear*." Robbie closed his own eyes. Sure enough, between words, there was a lot to hear—trickling water, wind through shrubs, animal noises, insects buzzing. The quieter he became, the fuller, richer the symphony of nature played.

When Lorrie spoke, the music slipped into the background. "So, you mean *I* have to be quiet is what you're saying?"

Null sniffed. "If there is nothing to say."

The shuttle had finally drained of power, and with no means to recharge, Null informed the Sheppards that travel on foot was their only option unless something presented itself. They'd investigated two separate settlements that appeared on Null's handheld device maps. Neither yielded anything more than collapsed dwellings and barns, long ransacked and left to wallow in dereliction. One structure contained an abandoned vehicle of some sort, easily decades old and pockmarked with rust holes. Null scanned the machine with his device. Shaking his head, he peered inside before turning away.

The next day, however, Null scanned the brush that lay ahead and narrowed his eyes. "There has been movement recently." He scrutinized a broken branch that still clung to its parent tree. "This was not game. Someone passed this way and did not return."

Cadlen handed his machete to Null and Robbie tugged Lorrie's sleeve. His brother nodded, crouching in the tall grass. Null crept forward, using the blade to move branches aside rather than hack them away. Twenty paces on, he motioned for the brothers to follow.

In a clearing just beyond the tree line a cabin with a sagging roof peak waited next to a small shed that had begun to list to one side, its door revealing a black open space in one corner. Grass matted in a trail leading to the door. Robbie swallowed, peering through the shrub cover.

Null stared at his device for a solid five minutes. Turning to the Sheppards, he raised an open hand instructing them to stay put. Robbie watched him glide through the foliage over the exact trail that had already led to the cabin door. He looked to his device again, and slowly opened the front door.

"Is it clear?" Lorrie shouted. Null turned to him and nodded. Cadlen stood and followed Null's trail.

"Cadlen, wait," Robbie breathed. It was no use. Lorrie joined his younger brother, leaving him with the supply rucksack back in the brush. Setting the pack beneath a fallen root, he followed until he came alongside the other three just inside the front door of the cabin.

The first thing to greet him was the stench. The drone of flies emanated from across the room. Null placed a hand on Cadlen's shoulder.

"No closer." Null kept a pointed gaze inside the living space at the body of a man slouched in the cleft between the armrest and back. *Clear*, yes. *Empty*, no. Robbie's skin shifted and crawled at the rolling and shifting of insects on his torso, neck, face.

"What happened to him?" Lorrie listed back toward the open door.

Null tapped his device screen. "Red tide, most likely."

Lorrie turned away and heaved, wretching in short gasps. *Red tide*. The illness that had taken their mother and father in the prime of their lives and orphaned four kids. It had passed this way. Robbie wrapped his arms around Lorrie but maintained his stare at the decomposing corpse. Julia and Robert Sheppard didn't look like this in the end. They had been nurtured in their last days. This person had no such fortune. He died where he sat, and no one came to clean him up, to treat the body for burial.

Cadlen took a step closer to the body. Thus far on their journey, he had shied away from any field dressing of game. But something about the body piqued his curiosity. Null reached and snagged the back of his shirt.

"No, Cadlen." Null stepped in front of him and crouched. "Never touch the dead."

Cadlen looked him in the eye and nodded. The four stood side by side near the exit. Lorrie recovered from his nausea and straightened his posture, gently cupping his hands together at his waist. No one said a word for more than a minute.

"It's quiet," Lorrie murmured. "Too quiet." Robbie closed his eyes. The sounds of nature were muffled inside the cabin. In his darkness, he could only envision his father laying on the couch in place of this stranger, crawling with insect larvae. If that's what Lorrie saw when his eyes were closed, he understood why he threw up.

"So, what do we do about… him?" Robbie struggled to find the right words. "We just leave him there, like that?"

Null motioned for the three brothers to step outside. "We leave him." Cadlen narrowed his eyes for one long last look before turning for the door. Null was the last to leave.

Lorrie broke the uncomfortable silence. "That's how it is out here? People just leave the dead to rot?"

Null moved toward the tilted shed. "No. He would not have been left to rot." Creaking the door open, he peered inside and retrieved a plastic jerry can similar to others they'd found empty in the previous abandoned settlements. This one, however, sloshed in Null's grip. Turning to Robbie, he made a nod to the heavy brush.

Back under cover, the rucksack slung over his shoulders again, Robbie watched intently as Null circled the small cabin, splashing the fluid from the container all over the outside walls, dripping off the staggered clapboard shingling. He slipped inside one last time, and reemerged moments later without the container, a grim shadow descended over his face. As he approached the Sheppards, Robbie spotted the billows of smoke wafting from inside the cabin. By the time Ian had reached the others, flames licked and curled from the rafters. Within a matter of minutes, the entire building was engulfed.

"So much for the Dakota hole to keep the smoke down," muttered Lorrie as windows shattered from the internal heat. The party of four stood side by side, transfixed by the inferno that consumed the building, timbers creaking and splitting while embers floated with the exhaust into the evening sky.

"It is not ours to collect the dead."

Robbie turned to Null, whose stern face glowed in the firelight. His eyes were embers, glowing with a fire of their own.

"Then who?" Lorrie gazed into the fire.

"The people who roam these lands… It is their province to *Reclaim* them." Null turned to face Robbie. His eyes burned. "The Ansati."

"Reapers? Then, if it's their job to clean up the mess, how come you burned it down?" Lorrie's question was valid.

Robbie closed his eyes. The heat from the burning cabin surged, causing beads of sweat to roll down his forehead into his eyes, stinging him. In the stillness, the quiet of early evening melting into dusk rang with crackling and snapping of fire consuming wood and flesh in a terrible, discordant symphony.

Null stood at attention out of respect for the stranger in the cabin, who had found not stillness, not quiet, only silence. "Because they are gone."

Real World Credit

Thursday, 5 July AC 0245
Carroway Trading Community
Crystal Sheppard

*L*orrie, *don't let your little brother watch those crazy shows! He's too young!* Crystal had heard her mother's pleas from the kitchen. Those damned frontier serials where the swashbuckling antihero ran from the law, fired guns, and rescued the helpless. Lorrie had watched them with rapt attention, making the popping sounds of the gun muzzles and aiming his index fingers as though he were living in the Wild West. The stories were as old as moving pictures themselves, told and retold generation after generation. And the bad guys were always the same—unkempt, uneducated, unsavoury.

And Ranger Man always saved the day.

Crystal arrived in the trading town of Carroway, and immediately likened it to one of Ranger Man's old haunts. The buildings were in rows along a main thoroughfare, gaunt and malnourished. All manner of transportation from wagons drawn by horses to petrol-fueled vehicles crawled along the avenue, wobbling over uneven road surfaces. Most people on foot covered their hair with shawls or drooping hats. Either no one had ever used laundry detergent, or the sheen of pure white fabric didn't exist to them. Most wore pale yellow tunics, stained like piss and smelling as much. As if to match, most wore trousers that were sickly greens or browns. Rope belts and hanging drawstring pouches hung from their waists like decorative bulbs, presumably to carry loose coins, or handheld devices that allowed for digital transactions. Some traders preferred tangible currency. Most dealt in Rust credit, though she had begun to notice more traders exerting influence the further south she moved. Fortunately, La Cumbre accepted Rust exchange. Otherwise, she wouldn't have had any fresh water the past three days.

La Cumbre, Rust… As long as Hyacynthe couldn't track her movements through her financial transactions, Crystal could keep moving to Ozarck—to Robbie, and Lorrie, and Cadlen. As she glided along the main street of Carroway, she smiled at the idea of watching Ranger Man with her littlest brother. He wasn't too young anymore. Lorrie likely grew out of watching those silly adventures. Besides, Cadlen was more likely to curl up beside her anyway.

Crystal flinched as a street vendor hollered her way. Fresh greens, natural-grown, not under lamps. She turned to the old woman hunched under a full-body robe, faded blue head scarf tailing over her shoulder.

"No, no, no 'lectronics." The vendor shook her head and her cheeks flapped. "Coin."

"I'm sorry, I don't have any coin." Crystal's stomach rumbled. A basket overflowing with crisp green beans, ends snipped and washed, called to her. Road food was full of preservatives and salts. The idea of nutritious greens made her mouth water.

"Here." It was a familiar voice, graveled and broken, behind her as a coin tumbled over her shoulder, bouncing on the vendor's tabletop. It took her a second, but when she remembered, she gritted her teeth.

"I don't want your money, Hamm." Crystal tightened her fists. The traitor had fled from Hewer at the first instance of danger. The man was laying in the middle of a road, his dying son in his arms, and his closest friends had left him. She'd vowed that if she ever laid eyes on either of them again, she would punch him in his fat face.

"Buy the damn beans. And get some radishes while you're at it." Hamm staggered into her peripheral vision. If the traderfolk of Carroway looked dirty, Hamm looked like he'd crawled out of a sewage tip.

"Yes, yes, yes—radishes are good! And I throw in snap peas. Good morning, love!" The vendor lady smiled, revealing zero teeth. Crystal couldn't help smiling back. She plucked a handful of beans and a half-dozen radishes by their greens. Inside of her own tunic, she tucked her produce inside a concealed pocket lined with clean nylon. It was probably the cleanest location for kilometers around.

"Did you abandon Duncam too?"

Hamm closed his eyes and folded his hands. "You could say he abandoned me. Got what I had comin', I suppose." The brigand looked pitiful.

"If you were wondering, Jamiss died—you wouldn't have made it a kilometer by then. Hewer buried him. You know, if you cared."

A commotion from an adjacent town block whooped. People shuffled along quicker and vendors drew the covers down over their lots. When it appeared as though whatever was happening had abated, the traders opened their kiosks carefully, one by one. Back to business.

"I cared about Hewer. Even cared about his kid. But you don't get it, *Doc*. Out here, you gotta look out for yourself. I seen that kind of sickness before. You don't come back from it."

Crystal chewed on his comment. It was bitter and dry, but not entirely wrong.

"So Duncam left you."

Hamm nodded. "Started acting all funny, woke up one night in a panic and pulled a knife on me. Took everything—food, clothes, handhelds. He took off straight away, never even put on his shoes. But he didn't know…" Hamm reached into one of his belt pouches and scooped out a handful of greyish coins. "Like I said, out here, you gotta be prepared."

Indeed. Hamm's coins bought Crystal some essential nutrients. Duncam might have the Rust credit, but any highwayman who crossed his path could slit his throat for them. Hamm looked like shit. But he was alive.

The brigand turned to walk away. "Thank you." It still hurt to say the words, but Crystal had been taught to show gratitude. More than once, Julia Sheppard had called out from the kitchen to remind her.

Hamm teetered from foot to foot. "Still going to Ozarck?"

"I am."

Hamm didn't look her in the eyes. "Hyacynthe has people out on the main travel lanes. You oughta stick to the backroads."

Another commotion, only this time, a rush of frightened townsfolk scurried from the same direction as before. Like clockwork, the vendors shut their kiosks in rapid synchronism. Hamm pulled his cloak up over his rat's nest hair.

"Move off the street." His bloodshot eyes made contact with hers, and the pair ducked in behind the old woman who was covering her produce and muttering. The nearest shop pulled down its window shutters and the front doors latched. Hamm motioned to Crystal to follow him in between two buildings.

Crystal peeked around the corner. A lone figure strode, robes waving in the cross breeze from the main street. A heavy hood covered his face. The figure didn't accost anyone, but he did stop briefly at the old woman's vegetable kiosk. The vendor trembled, rocking in the fetal position on the dirt while the hooded man reached into his robe. With trembling hands, he placed a small pile of coins on the table and helped himself to the beans and radishes before nodding and turning away. Within a minute, the figure had vanished up the street, gone like a puff of gun smoke.

"Who the hell was that?" Crystal gazed at the old woman. She stood, straightened her clothes, and stumbled away, leaving her produce and the pile of coins behind her. Out here, who would leave their livelihood behind, unless they were terrified…

"Ansati. They're on the move." Hamm stepped out into the street as the vendors reopened once again. He walked over to the old woman's kiosk. Passers-by arced around them in a wide berth.

Ansati. Reapers, Crystal always heard them called. She'd never seen one before. He wasn't half as spooky as she'd dreamed all those years as a girl, listening to ghost stories about the morbid monks.

"In the daytime? I thought they only moved around at night."

Hamm looked down at the pile of coins. He scooped them into an open palm, pocketing the lifesaving currency for himself. "Word has it they're looking for someone. If they're traveling by day, they must want him bad."

Crystal tried to imagine how desperate someone had to be to risk being caught in public, to be exposed under the spotlight of public scrutiny. Even in this lawless land. It wasn't hard to imagine, after all. Laurent was sparing no cost to find her and bring her home. What had this fugitive done to draw the Ansati out of the shadows?

"You shouldn't take her money."

"She won't take money from them. People around here think it's cursed." Hamm pinched a few coins between his fingers and offered them to her. "How about you, believe in any of that stuff, Doc?"

It was the second time he'd called her that. Crystal was no doctor. But lately, nothing was as it seemed anyway. In Hamm's eyes, she was a healer. Maybe that was enough.

Crystal took the coins and dropped them into her pouch. Hamm wasn't trustworthy. He was filthy. He was a thief. But he might just be useful in navigating her past Hyacynthe's sentries. She grabbed a second handful of beans.

Mareel

After the Ansati monk breezed through Carroway, everyone went about their business, indifferent to the colours of tunic shirts or the nature of their trade. A group of children used sticks to direct balls toward a goal. A pair of hefty men heaved their backs into a sunken wagon wheel in soft mud. Vendors tended to their wares with a gentleness Crystal had never associated with the outside world. When she breathed, she noticed all of these examples of life, however difficult or improbable.

After the Ansati disappeared, the air of the trading town changed. The children were hastened indoors by worried parents. The stuck wagon remained in its rut. The vendors slowly reintroduced their product, but with caution. The old lady that had sold Crystal the vegetables never came back. Indeed, she and Hamm could have taken all of her produce and no one would have stopped them. The Ansati had stopped at her kiosk. He had left coins and taken food into his ghoulish hands and he'd whisked away on the breeze. It was as if the Ansati were indeed Death itself paying her that inevitable visit. For all Crystal knew, she might be lying on her back, eyes shut and breath expired. It was moments like this that had fueled the legend of the Reapers.

Crystal and Hamm agreed to travel the next leg of their journey together, despite their misgivings. Hamm confessed that he didn't completely trust her, which came as a relief to Crystal, as she completely distrusted him. Still, the brigand had offered an olive branch in the form of stolen money, and she'd accepted. She'd even stolen food herself. She remembered Robert Sheppard used to say something to the effect of "when in Rome"… She had no idea where Rome was, but it sounded like a terrible place.

Relieved to be able to use her Rust credit with La Cumbre traders, Crystal negotiated transport on a horse-drawn covered wagon for herself and Hamm. They shared the coach with three other travelers, all of whom looked as poor as anyone in Carroway. One was a teenaged boy who could have been anywhere between Lorrie and Jamiss's ages. He sat in a corner, sniffling constantly. The man and woman with them could have been old enough to be his parents, but she suspected they weren't related. The pair muttered to each other in a slang she couldn't clearly interpret. The coach lurched along a backroad trail, rickety and creaking as the hoop-spoked wheels negotiated the trail. Crystal offered a handful of beans to their fellow travelers. All three declined.

"Nothing is free." Hamm talked while he chewed. "If they take your offer, they think they'll owe you something."

All Crystal wanted in return was to be left alone. It wasn't going to cost her anything to get that, apparently. She ate a couple beans before putting the rest back in her concealed pouch. It didn't seem right to eat in front of them.

She had dozed off when the rear drape of the coach drew open and a cadre of uniformed officers peered inside. The three travelers didn't flinch. The boy had fallen asleep, and the man and woman looked up long enough to notice, then turned their attention back to each other. Hamm clenched his fists but remained silent.

"Good afternoon, could we have a word, Miss?" The front officer spoke directly to Crystal. "We're looking for a young lady that matches your description. We have urgent news."

Urgent news. Nice try. Crystal recognized the Hyacynthe officer uniform immediately.

"Just making our way, Mister." Crystal gave the local accent her best shot.

"Do you mind telling us your name?"

Over the course of her journey from Hyacynthe Station through the wilderness, Crystal had decided on dozens of fake names. In the moment, she'd forgotten all of them.

"*Mareel.* My name is Mareel." The first name that came to her was the mispronunciation of her flatmate Mireil's name. The only time she'd heard her big brother utter the name, was when Crystal had read it from the letter Laurent sent before she left for Hyacynthe. The day she'd finally met her, Mir had offered her tiny hand and pronounced it in the thick French accent it was meant to sound. "Mee-hray." It was a beautiful name for a beautiful soul. Leave it to her brother to butcher it so.

The officer smirked. "Nice try. We know who you are, Miss Sheppard. The scan had you confirmed before we opened the curtain."

Hamm leaned forward and the officer raised a sidearm. "Don't even bother, fella."

"Listen, I don't know how much Laurent paid you. But I can't go back. I just can't." Crystal chose her plea carefully. These men didn't need to know any more about her brothers than they may already.

The officer kneeled on the edge of the coach and waved off his back-up. The curtain fell back over the opening.

"Miss Sheppard—can I call you Crystal?"

"No."

"Fine. Mareel. Listen, I've been all over out here. I know how it works, and if you've survived this long, you do too. Follow me?"

A knot twisted in her belly. The officer had dark eyes that were darkening by the second. The officer motioned to the man and woman to leave. Without a word, they crawled from their corner of the coach and slipped through the curtain. The officer paid no mind to the youth, still comatose. Hamm glowered at the officer.

"She has red tide," Hamm blurted. It was an attempt at spoiling the prize, of course, but the officer wasn't having it.

"Well that's handy. She has red tide, and I've got the blues." The officer knelt directly in front of Crystal who had lurched as far back in the coach as she could. Her eyes stung with tears and sweat while the officer unfastened the buckle of his trousers with his left hand, keeping the sidearm trained on Hamm with the other. "Time for you to take a hike, fella."

Crystal remembered the night Druna had come home after a patron at the *Marais* had gotten too hands-on in a darkened booth. She'd cried and cried, describing how dirty she felt, and that a shower wasn't going to make it go away. After a sleepless night with her flatmates, it was Mireil who contacted Monsieur Laurent. The creep was tracked down, and Crystal never saw him at the club again. Or anywhere.

And here was this new creep, sent at Laurent's behest. Even if she was still angry with him, she couldn't believe that he knew he had a rapist on his payroll. Despite his clear intentions, Crystal's thoughts remained with Druna.

"Touch her and die." Hamm gritted his teeth, vibrating his whole body over as if he were about to detonate.

"I told you to—"

Before she could process what was happening, the teenaged boy lunged from his corner, slamming into the officer and sending his sidearm clattering on the coach floor. Hamm acted immediately, thrusting his right hand into the shocked officer's crotch. Crystal's eyes widened as Hamm squeezed his fist over that most sensitive region, causing the officer to pass out from agony before he could even breathe. Squeezing his balls so hard had to have literally taken his breath away.

Outside, the other officers rushed to the curtain. The two men gasped at the sight of Hamm still gripping the leader's package in his tightened fist, like a rabid dog unable to unclench its jaws.

"You wanna shoot me, you better not miss, 'cause I'll rip your cocks off if you do."

"Let him go, and you folks can go on your way! We didn't see anything!" By this time, the youth had retrieved the limp officer's sidearm and was pointing it back at them. Crystal tapped Hamm on the shoulder.

"Let him go."

Hamm nodded. "Sure thing, *Mareel.*"

The officers glanced at each other and nodded. "Sorry for the confusion, Miss. Looks like we made a mistake. We'll take our friend off your, um, hands…"

Hamm released his grip and the junior officers dragged him back to the edge of the coach and through the curtain. The man and woman never re-entered. Crystal didn't have enough emotional energy to worry about what had become of them.

Within minutes, the coach lurched forward again. The youth kept the sidearm in his waistband but curled back into the corner. Crystal offered him a handful of beans, and this time the boy accepted. He nibbled on a few before nodding off to sleep again, as if everything that had just transpired was a dream.

Crystal turned to Hamm, still tense from the confrontation. "And thank *you.*"

The brigand nodded. His tension began to ease after she'd spoken her gratitude. "That guy won't think with his dick next time."

It shouldn't have been funny. It wasn't funny. Crystal couldn't help but laugh.

"If Lorrie was here, he'd say that took a lot of balls!"

Hamm laughed and lay on his side. "Safe to say, you have the biggest balls in this coach, *Mareel.*"

Norm

In her hospital bed, Cadlen's mother was frail, clinging to life despite tubes and wires, humming machines and respirators. He was very young, but he was old enough to understand what was happening. It was his first experience with death. Life was suddenly more fragile, more precious. He hadn't cried when the machine whined a long, unending scree and the doctor nodded in solemnity to the attending nurses. Cadlen and his three siblings watched from behind plexiglass. Crystal sobbed in Robbie's shoulder. Lorrie gazed down at his shoes. But Cadlen couldn't feel anything—at least that he could identify as feeling.

When the vital signs machine was switched off, Cadlen thought he saw the last gasp of life leave his mother's body. Her eyes had glowed only a second ago. Now they were glass, like marbles inserted into dolls' heads. Her chest fell, no longer drawing breath to keep it inflated. Despite all the sudden changes, the body on the bed still *looked* like Julia Sheppard. Just… *different.*

As he led the group away from the burned cabin, Cadlen couldn't block out the image of the dead body they had found. There was no hospital bed. No machines. No doctors or nurses. No loved ones mourning from just out of reach—only four strangers who had never met him, never known his name.

There were maggots and flies. There was a stench unlike anything he ever wanted to experience again. There was a shell of a person, disintegrating from the inside, life long exhaled. When Ian Null burned the cabin down with the body still inside, it felt right. It was an act of mercy. If the mysterious Ansati people weren't able to give him a dignified funeral, or whatever they did, this was the next best thing.

He had never been more grateful that his mother and father each received proper funerary rites. Both had been cremated, because New Inland had strict laws about how to take care of the dead. Monsieur Laurent—an old friend of his parents and someone Cadlen had never met—had paid for their ashes to be kept in the Capston Memorial Mausoleum in perpetuity. It was the first thing that had crossed his mind when he found out the Sheppard Inn had been blown up. At least his parents weren't lost among the ashes.

That night, Cadlen couldn't sleep. He kept seeing the dead body, only his mother's face covered with filth and seething larvae. Or his father's, who'd died not long after her. He huddled in his bedroll, the Dakota hole simmering but giving off just enough heat that he didn't need the second blanket. He tried to breathe in a way that sounded like he was sleeping. He was certain he could fool his brothers.

Ian Null sat down next to him. He knew it was Ian because he was on watch. A few minutes passed and Cadlen gave up the pretense, stopped forcing a false sleeping rhythm.

"I am sorry you saw the body." Ian's voice was soft despite the darkness and the sounds of the woods. "It is never pleasant."

It couldn't be more unpleasant. Cadlen rolled over. Ian was sitting back against a tree, only a soft glow from the remaining embers lighting his face. He held the Geiger reader, muted for the night so he and his brothers could sleep without incessant beeping. In a way, he wished the counter was beeping, like his mother's and father's life monitors. There was a certain silence that came with death.

Cadlen lifted his weight onto his elbow. Ian read the counter. "We will reach the outer part of Moab tomorrow evening. We cannot stop moving until then."

Cadlen nodded. He had grown accustomed to the walking. He'd learned how to wield the machete less with strength and more with purpose. He'd trained himself to drink small amounts to preserve their water for the most contaminated part of the journey. He'd gathered and dried enough fruit and mushrooms to last a trip twice as long. The promise of Moab, a safe city smack in the middle of a radiation seam, and all that could be discovered there was enough motivation. Maybe the city wasn't abandoned like Ian believed. Maybe there were friendly Ansati—the kind who cared for the sick and the dead—just as willing to help the living. There was so much cruelty in the outside world. Surely there was some kindness to be found.

In the glow of the fire, Cadlen studied Ian's face. There was something similar in the lines below his eyes, in the unevenness of his scruffy stubble, in the way he breathed when everything was still. He had seen it before.

Twice.

Cadlen swallowed. "You're sick."

Ian didn't look at him, but for the first time a smile crept across his lips. "You see everything, Cadlen Sheppard." He poked at the Geiger reader, fidgeting with the knobs. "I will be fine."

Cadlen pursed his lips like he did every time he concentrated. He used to do it when he drew, or so his parents used to tell him. Crystal said it too. Lorrie often poked fun at him for it. "Red tide?"

Ian shook his head. "If that were so, I would have stayed far from you and your brothers."

Minutes passed in silence. Embers snapped in the hole and some bird cooed in the distance.

"I am told you are an artist."

Cadlen nodded.

"Perhaps one day you will show me your work."

Maybe. Cadlen smiled and turned back over, pulling the second blanket on top of himself. "Maybe" was a promise too easy to break.

The next morning, Cadlen was the last to wake up. Lorrie complained, Robbie scurried to gather their belongings into the big rucksack, and Ian plotted the day's course. He didn't mention to his brothers that they had spoken with each other. It wasn't mentioned as they left the campsite, nor through the afternoon under a punishing sun, and it was all but forgotten when the forest gave way to fields and the Geiger reader dipped until it fell silent.

"We are in safe land, but we will still be cautious." Ian turned to Robbie and Lorrie, wiping sweat from his forehead and pulling his hair from his eyes. "Keep to our rations for now."

"But we're almost *there*, right?" Lorrie sipped his canteen. "The land of plenty you keep telling us about?"

Ian didn't answer. He took the lead, striding through the tall grass like he'd found a second wind. Like he wasn't struggling. Robbie kept pace while Lorrie grumbled that they should have arrived hours ago. His stomach had just begun to rumble when the faint outline of a cluster of buildings stretched out before them, the early evening sky bathing them in a gentle spotlight as it lowered in the western sky. Before he could realize it, they were on a cleared mud-topped road with baked wagon wheel grooves. Houses guarded the road, all in better repair than any they'd seen in over a week. Some met the road with stone-covered walkways. None showed any signs of life. None of the chimneys emitted any smoke. The silence of the seam followed them.

Up the road, Cadlen squinted at an unusually-shaped structure. Lorrie saw it at the same time.

"What's that one? Never seen a house that tall and thin before."

Ian didn't answer. As the four approached it, the building looked even more peculiar. There was a tall tower-like part that reached up to the sky. On its top was the familiar Ansati symbol. Calden watched the sun lower just as its light fed through the hoop at the top like it was threading a needle. On the outside, all of what Cadlen presumed were windows were boarded over. The double doors were tall, perched atop a wide staircase that a dozen people could climb side by side.

"You have never seen one before?" Ian turned to Lorrie, a quizzical look on his tired face.

"I think I know what it is." Robbie shifted the weight of his pack from one shoulder to the other. "A church?"

Ian nodded. "Wait here." He strode over to the stairs and climbed them, each step slower until he was nearly wobbling for the last one. A quick scan with his handheld and a peek inside the door, and he motioned for the Sheppards to follow. "We can stay the night here."

Cadlen wrinkled his eyebrows. *As long as there aren't any dead people inside.*

How could anyone sit in benches so rigid and narrow? Cadlen tried to cross his legs but his ankles pressed into the stained wooden seat. He tried to lean against the inner-most armrest but his elbow kept slipping. If there was a complete opposite to the lobby couch back at the Sheppard Inn, he was sitting on it. The cavernous open space inside the church was stale. Four-armed fans hung from the ceiling like bats, asleep in the darkness. The only source of light, apart from the lantern Robbie had rescued from the dead shuttle, threaded in around the imperfect boarding over the windows. As the sun crept into the western sky, the light changed colour, yellow to blue, to a faint violet. It sparkled on shards of broken glass and ceramic, on the carpeted aisle, on the blocky wooden table up front.

"You see that light, Cad?" Lorrie was stubbornly shifting the bedroll in different angles in an attempt at making a comfortable bed on the bench ahead of him. "It keeps changing."

Cadlen nodded, though Lorrie was facing away from him and wouldn't have seen his response. A light flashed from the raised part of the church with the table—Ian had called it the *sacristy*—before fading into a soft, warm yellow that filled the room, eliminating the strands of colour. Ian stood over the tall candlestick, the light flickering over his face.

"There is a box of wax candles, and other provisions." Ian reached down, then hoisted a box onto the table he'd called an *altar*. "These are not basics." From the box, he pulled out plush toys, small models of old-world planes and cars, a white ball the size of an apple with wandering red seams. "These are for children."

Cadlen had had plush animals when he was younger. There was a blue one with white ears and buttons for eyes. His mother had told him his name was Norman. He hadn't thought of Norman for a long time. The stuffed bear probably didn't survive when the Inn blew up.

Unable to get comfortable, Cadlen stretched and made his way up the aisle, climbing the steps until he could see inside the box on the altar. Ian offered him the stuffed bear. He didn't take it.

"Maybe you're too old for a stuffie, Cad." Robbie stepped beside him. "But it might make a pillow, at least."

Cadlen narrowed his eyes and pursed his lips. It came back to him how Norman used to sleep next to him. He'd fall asleep with the bear nestled in his arms against his chest, only to find it face down, leg flopped awkwardly on the floor in the morning. He used to imagine the bear living a secret life while he slept, going on adventures, rushing to get home before Cadlen opened his eyes. He couldn't remember the day Norman left on his last adventure.

Ian held the bear in his hands as if he were holding a live explosive. Cadlen couldn't imagine Ranger Man holding a child's toy, and Ian Null doing the same was just as unlikely. He took the stuffie from Ian's hands, instantly relieving him of the burden.

"It kind of looks like your old bear, Cad. What was his name? Marvin?"

"It was Norman. *I* had Marvin." Lorrie sat up, disgruntled from his lack of comfort. "How about everyone quiet down a bit. I haven't had a full night's sleep since Ling locked us in a crate."

Cadlen brought the bear back to his bench. *Pews*, Ian had called them. It was a strange word. Spreading out the padding, he tucked the bear under his head and pulled both covers up to his shoulders. Lorrie muttered some more, and Ian and Robbie spoke in hushed tones up on the sacristy. The faint candle light was still flickering when he fell asleep.

Norm. In honour of of his lost bear. *His name is Norm.*

Carrion

Saturday, 7 July AC 0245
Moab
Cadlen Sheppard

The church was about six hours in their rearview when Cadlen sipped the last drops of water from his canteen. At the rear of the line, two jugs dangled from Robbie's over-stuffed hiking pack, so the party wouldn't dehydrate for a while. The promise of fresh water deeper inside Moab was reassuring even if his tongue was drier than before he knew they were so close to the city. He must have convinced himself he wasn't so thirsty before.

More houses lined the sides of the streets as Ian Null guided the party through a maze of gridded blocks, not unlike the lay of Capston's downtown, except that they were more spaced apart. As they passed, some were clearly unoccupied; short crops of feathery grass grew taller in front of some, while others had been clearly groomed in recent weeks. Some were boarded shut, just like the windows on the church. Cadlen squinted as the high sun began to crest. A slight breeze cooled his skin and birds wheeled overhead. Tiny, flying insects stole quick bites whenever the breeze lulled. Ian had given Cadlen and his brothers a small bottle with a pungent, oily liquid to rub on their exposed skin. It kept the bugs away, for the most part. Some of them were very persistent in their attack.

"Lotta birds," Lorrie muttered, dragging every step as though he'd already walked fifty kilometers. "That has to be a good sign, right?"

Ian pressed on, his handheld level with his eyes. Cadlen walked alongside him, noting every stumbled step, every shaky sip from his canteen, every laboured breath. He'd told him he was fine. Cadlen didn't believe him.

"Sometimes."

"I mean, birds are smart, aren't they? They'd only hang around where it's safe?"

Ian let his arm and handheld dangle at his side. "Yes. They also hang around where there is food." He reached into his rucksack and retrieved his binoculars, aiming them further up the street. Cadlen and his brothers came to a halt with him.

"Those birds, they're bigger." Robbie unhooked one of the spare water bottles and refilled his canteen.

Ian nodded. "Ravens." Cadlen pursed his lips. They'd seen the large black birds before, but not in numbers like this. Above him, black spots peppered the white-blue sky. Ian looked ahead through his distance glasses again. "There are many in Moab. The Ansati revere them."

"Nice. What do you think of 'em?" Lorrie grabbed the water jug from Robbie to fill his own bottle.

"Where I come from, they are harbingers."

"How about in words we all can understand?"

"They are often known as signs of dying."

Lorrie almost choked on his last gulp. "Great. More death."

Ian lowered his binoculars and pointed ahead. Cadlen studied his face. Ian held a grim disposition in the best of times. Something in his eyes looked more worried than usual. He offered Cadlen the binoculars without shifting his gaze.

Through the lenses, Cadlen saw the outline of a crumpled shape lying at the junction of the main street ahead of them and the front walkway to a house. Instead of a tended lawn, several rows of plants with different leaves and stalks covered the space between the home and the street. It reminded him of the Hanging Gardens, only smaller and overgrown. He counted three black birds picking at the fallen body.

Without any further instruction or comment, Ian marched toward the grizzly scene. Within minutes, Cadlen could see with his naked eyes that the shape was of an adult, facedown on the stone walkway, facing the street as though he were leaving the house before he'd fallen. A heavy cloak covered him, hood over his head and bunched to one side.

The carrion birds had been picking at his abdomen for some time. As the party came within a few meters, the smell of decomposition filled Cadlen's nostrils.

Ian stepped forward, and Cadlen tugged his sleeve. Don't touch dead things, he'd told them only a few days ago.

"It is fine." Ian nodded, as though he'd heard his inner thoughts. "This man was not taken by red tide." He motioned for Lorrie.

"What do we do with him?" Lorrie waved his hands in sweeping arcs, but the carrion birds were undeterred.

"Behind the house, there should be a storage shed. Find shovels, gloves, something to cover the body."

Lorrie dropped his pack and jogged through the garden and behind the house. A few minutes later, he returned with Ian's list filled. Three shovels, a bunched-up plastic sheet, and several pairs of earth-hued canvas gloves, all in a hand-barrow Lorrie pushed through the weeds. Ian instructed Lorrie to spread out the sheet next to the decaying body. Cadlen's eyes watered from the smell.

As Ian knelt at the head of the fallen man, the ravens squawked and fluttered a safe distance away. With a firm grip of his shoulders, Ian turned the body onto its back. Cadlen winced at the sight of his face. Shielded from the birds, his face was spared their assault. Still, the image was no less gruesome. The man had had a beard in life, but patches of it had fallen off. His mouth was frozen open, teeth missing from his gums. The skin itself was sunken, pallid. Ian crouched impossibly close, tilting his head as he examined the dead man's face.

"What happened to his eyes? Do they dry up like that after… you know?" Lorrie knelt beside Ian, a rag wrapped around his nose and mouth.

Ian shook his head. "No, this is not what happens." Cadlen refused to close his own eyes for fear he'd see his mother, his father, and the man they'd found and burned in that cabin. As he knelt closer, Robbie gripped his shoulder.

"Not so close, Cad. Let Ian take care of this."

Cadlen jerked his shoulder from his brother's hand. Something about this body was different. Closer examination revealed a low buzzing of insects from the open wounds in his chest and abdomen, making his undershirt ripple.

"The eyes are gone."

Gone?

"What do you mean… the ravens?" Lorrie scrunched his brow.

Ian sat back on his heel, teetering before he balanced himself. Cadlen watched the beaded sweat leak down his temples. "No. They were removed. By his killer."

Cadlen insisted on shoveling. Ian drove the tip of the spade-shaped blade into the earth behind the victim's home. He managed three shovelfuls before dropping to a knee. Robbie and Lorrie looked at each other. Their guide had been so steadfast in the weeks they'd known him. Clearly, they had caught on to his deteriorating health. Cadlen, spared the labour by the older Sheppard brothers, gripped his hand around the wooden handle.

At first, Ian refused to let it go. "I am hungry, that's all. When we finish digging the grave, I will rest."

Cadlen moved so his face was directly in front of Ian's. Words weren't necessary. They rarely were.

Up close, Ian's eyes were sickly yellow. Tiny veins streaked them like cracked, bloody glass. As he breathed, his lips trembled. "Dig as deep as this handle is long."

Cadlen blinked. The shovel was heavier once Ian had let go. He turned to his brothers, and without a word between them, they dug until the grave was as deep as Ian had instructed, and wide enough that the dead man could lie straight and flat. It comforted Cadlen to know that he wasn't going to be crumpled up.

Ian insisted on moving the body. Lorrie insisted on helping, so long as he could lift the feet. The eyeless sockets really spooked him. Cadlen wasn't sure what to feel. Without eyes, it would be impossible to see.

Of course, it was impossible to see once he'd died, but for some reason, he hoped that the man hadn't had to see his killer, how he'd been stabbed first in the back, then slashed across the belly, just below the ribs. That's how Ian had described the crime. He and Lorrie slid the body onto the sheet, and together they lifted him from the ground, drooping like he was in a hammock. After they lowered the body into the grave, Robbie began to cover him with dirt. Filling the hole took far less time than digging.

Cadlen shoveled the last of the dirt. For a lingering moment, the four stood over the grave, eyes to the ground, silent as the dead. Ian reached into his pocket and produced a shiny silver pendant, its chain dangling around his shaking hand. Kneeling at the edge of the fresh dirt, he placed the pendant about where the heart would be. Cadlen narrowed his eyes. It was the Ansati symbol, familiar to him from graffiti, news reports, and rumours. In the center, where the arms crossed the center stave, he spotted an engraving that had gathered enough dirt to look like a thread.

XL

The letters didn't mean anything to him. Ian stayed on his knee, bending his neck as though to offer a silent prayer—that's what they did for the fallen in all the Ranger Man episodes he'd seen. What someone was supposed to say in times like that was anyone's guess.

"Should we say something?" Lorrie was first to break the silence. "Maybe some kind words for... Mr. Ansati? We don't even know his name."

"His name was Simon." Ian uttered the words under his breath. "*Brother* Simon."

"Simon? How do you know?"

Ian reached into the pocket he'd stashed the pendant. This time, he pulled out a paper letter, sealed with a burgundy, stamped wax seal. He passed the letter to Cadlen, and the brothers crowded around to examine it. The seal contained the same XL logo. On the obverse, "Brother Simon" was written in beautiful, curved writing, as though the hand that guided the pen flowed like water. Mud stains from Ian's hands smeared the paper, already yellowed and wrinkled.

"Should we open it?" Lorrie asked out loud what Cadlen was also thinking.

Ian took the letter back and tucked it into his pocket. "The contents are not for our eyes."

"Who, then? Somebody with 'XL' for initials? I don't even know any names that start with X."

Ian turned and started for the front of the house. "Brother Simon will have left food in his pantry. Robbie, I am told you are a good cook."

Lorrie laughed. "Good cook? Who in hell told you that?"

Cadlen smiled. As far as he was concerned, Robbie was a good cook, maybe even as good as his mother had been.

Soup

Every building they'd stayed in overnight had been run down, abandoned, and derelict. By the time they'd stayed in the old church, Cadlen had determined that sleeping under the stars was better. It smelled better. The must and mold in the outdoors still held a freshness, a richness. Indoors, it was dry, stifling, unsettling. His eyes itched more frequently. He sneezed. He woke with headaches that only subsided when the door was flung open and the outdoor air cleansed his airways.

This house, though—Simon's house—was different. As soon as he crossed the threshold into the main living area, Cadlen sensed the complete opposite of their previous shelters. There was a scent, sweet and rich as though flowers were growing indoors. The evening's last rays of light seeped in through the partially drawn curtains, allowing enough light for him to take in his surroundings. From the outside, the house looked just like all the others in the neighbourhood—a triangular peak with a window blinking like an eye from a dormer, powder blue horizontal polymer siding wrapping the entire structure, speckled with black spots where the sun shone the least. Windows with gridded panes, framed with permanently-opened shutters. A screen door creaked on its hinge outside a stronger, solid one. A brass-ringed door knocker would have been rapped by guests coming to call. Cadlen wondered if Simon's killer had used it.

But inside, the living space couldn't have looked any different. Along the far wall, a plush sofa was draped with several blankets and a pillow. Simon must have spent many nights sleeping there. The rest of the room's contents offered an explanation. A fireplace on the left adjacent wall was dead, a half-burned log the last remains of Simon's last fire. The rest of the room's walls were concealed behind bookshelves, crammed tight with vertically arranged spines, and where available, even more volumes were shoved flat. The floor space was no less full. Wood and polymer tote bins and boxes with trinkets, from figurines to photographs, tools to toys, littered most of the floor. All of this *stuff*—it couldn't all have been Simon's, could it?

At the center of it all, however, appeared to be the focus of Simon's work. A sturdy office-type desk with a straight-backed, wicker-bound chair was stacked high on most of its surface with even more books, loose papers, files, and photographs. Cadlen crept over to the work space and leafed through the photos. No two had the same faces. Most were faded to the point the people in them looked like ghosts. Maybe they were.

One book was opened on the desk, indicating the final words Simon likely ever read. Cadlen sat on the chair, creaking as the legs dragged on the wooden slatted floor. It was uncomfortable. If anyone was going to sit at this desk intent on reading for hours and hours, it would have been impossible to be so comfortable they'd get drowsy. A brass candle holder with a ring wide enough for an adult finger to fit held a half-melted cream-coloured candle, its drippings pooled around the base.

Cadlen narrowed his eyes in the dimming dusken light and tried to read the words, tiny in a fancy font on sickly yellow pages. The words were in a language he didn't understand:

Lux semper super nos effunditur ; in latitudine oceani et latitudine oculi.

With no success interpreting any words in the first paragraph, Cadlen closed the book carefully. The front cover was deep burgundy, the inset lettering in a soft gold.

Chronicles of the Ansati

☥

The familiar Ansati symbol occupied the center of the cover in the same golden print. Cadlen pursed his lips. This was a sacred text. Simon must have consulted this book daily, maybe more than once. If he were still alive, maybe he'd be sitting in this exact spot, reading those ancient words and finding some sort of meaning, some sort of comfort.

The words made no sense to Cadlen. It likely wouldn't have mattered if they were in English.

"The house is safe, Cad." Robbie poked his head into the living area from the adjacent kitchen. "And we have enough food here to stay for weeks if we wanted! Barley soup sound good?"

It sounded amazing. Cad enthusiastically nodded and Robbie retreated back into the kitchen. He could hear his oldest brother talking and Null occasionally responding. But Lorrie was unusually absent. He hadn't seen him come inside after the burial of Simon's corpse. Maybe he was still outside.

Shrugging his shoulders, Cadlen stood, scraping the chair again, before leaving to explore the other rooms on the ground floor. Down the short hallway, he passed a restroom before two bedrooms, one of which had a window that looked into the backyard. A bed, trimmed immaculately with unblemished blanket and pillow was flanked with two small tables, each with a pair of drawers and adorned with matching lamps. There was no wall switch. Maybe they were lit with matches. Cadlen wished he knew how to light the room, as the sun set on the far side of the house, and no natural light found its way inside at this hour. Save from the backyard where the rising moon offered enough light for him to find his way.

Gently moving the curtain aside with a finger, Cadlen peered outside, to find Lorrie kneeling at Simon's grave, his head lowered.

Cadlen watched his brother tremble, as though he were crying. He couldn't remember ever seeing him cry. He hadn't at their parents' funerals. He hadn't when he found out about the inn being blown up. He hadn't when Crystal left. He might not even be crying now. But something told Cadlen that maybe burying Simon was his breaking point. That somehow this slain stranger had managed to do what nothing and no one ever could.

He had made him show emotions other than anger.

Cadlen let the curtain fall back into place. Examining one of the lamps more closely, he found a small dial that clicked when he turned it. A soft light blinked to life, and the dust on its bulb cooked for a few minutes. Cadlen sat on the edge of the bed and opened the top drawer. His eyes widened when he saw its contents.

A sketch book! It's been forever! The pad could have been rigged with a trap, and Cadlen would have fallen for it. He snatched it from the end table and opened it as if it were one of Simon's many books in his living room. It was empty, save for some torn pages near the front. The new first page had some scuffing, so he turned it to the next, whiter and cleaner. He always started with the second page. The first would always scuff against the cover, smudging his work. Now, if only he could find something to draw with…

The second drawer answered his prayer. Inside, he found a box with several wooden drawing pencils, and even a green and yellow box with coloured varieties. He was used to the more modern, ever-sharp pencils from home, but these would do just fine. It was better than scratching shapes in the dirt with a stick.

Footsteps crept in the hallway. Cadlen panicked—maybe he should have asked before snooping around in the bedrooms. He crammed the sketch pad and pencils into the top drawer and shoved it closed just as Ian opened the door.

"Robbie has made supper. He sent me to find you." Ian looked around the room, wrinkling his forehead at Cadlen's obviously suspicious composure. Still, he didn't question him. "Have you seen your brother?"

Cadlen pointed over to the window. Ian nodded.

"Go eat, Cadlen. Robbie is indeed a good cook."

Cadlen stood and rushed from the room as though he were fleeing a crime scene. Ian stayed in the room, peering out the window. Maybe Ian would beckon him. Cadlen didn't want the task. He may have never seen his brother cry before, but he didn't want to, either.

Robbie's barley soup was so tasty, Cadlen had nearly scarfed down an entire bowl before Ian and Lorrie came into the kitchen. All four hunched shoulder to shoulder around a small kitchen table. The Sheppard brothers ate until they were full, and Lorrie ate some more. Ian managed to finish half of the bowl Robbie had served him, and it was clear that he laboured to swallow those last few mouthfuls. Cadlen noticed that he ate less every meal, often skipping them. They weren't lacking in food; Ian had successfully taught Lorrie and Robbie how to snare rabbits and prepare dried meat strips for long marches. This meal, it was different. He might have been buried in the backyard, but Simon still provided for the weary travelers. Cadlen wiped some broth from his lower lip, and wished he could have met him.

He avoided looking directly at Lorrie. In a sweeping glance, he could tell he'd been crying. His eyes were red and puffy. No one said a word about Simon, about the labour of preparing his final resting place, about shoveling the last load of mud and laying his pendant as a marker.

"We will stay the night here. Lorrie, Cadlen, you can sleep in the beds. Robbie, the sofa." Ian looked into the soup, stirring it slowly as if he was mustering the ability to finish it.

"You should have one of the beds," Lorrie said. "We know you're sick. You should get a solid sleep for once."

Ian forced a spoonful. "There is a lounge chair near the fireplace. That will do for me."

"Well, I won't say no to a clean mattress." Lorrie slurped the last of his soup. "I wonder if Simon had anything decent to read..." Cadlen tried his best not to smirk. For better or worse, Lorrie always met trepidation with humour, even if it was misplaced.

Ian attempted to help clean the kitchen, but Robbie forced him to retreat into the living room. Two hours had passed during their meal, and it was the first time Cadlen remembered sitting at a table with family. *Family.* He wondered if Crystal might one day sit at the table with them again. If she would meet Ian Null.

He didn't have to fight over the bedroom with the drawing supplies. Lorrie probably chose the bedroom the farthest from Simon's grave. In any case, he slipped into the room after the kitchen was tidied and Robbie and Ian settled into their respective sleeping arrangements. One last time, he peeked outside as the moonlight bathed the backyard in an eerie glow. A glint of light sparkled from Simon's pendant.

Cadlen propped a pillow so he could sit upright in the bed, Norm tucked against him so he could draw in the soft lamp light. He selected a 3H lead, leaving the colours in the drawer for now. Opening the sketch pad, he noticed writing on the inside of the cover. It hadn't been there before, unless he had skipped it in his excitement.

You have a gift, Cadlen. Draw what you see.
Ian

He should have known. Ian Null never missed anything. Only, how could he really know if he had a gift? Cadlen smiled, and began to trace an outline of a person—a man, walking confidently, backpack over one shoulder, long hair and piercing eyes, ready to take on anything. Anyone.

It could have been Ranger Man.

He drew half the night. Robbie's soup may have nourished their bellies. But Cadlen's art was the soup his spirit had been missing, for too many days to count.

A Bridge to Cross

Saturday, 7 July AC 0245
Moab
Lorrie Sheppard

Julia and Robert died of the same underlying cause, but Lorrie experienced each death differently. He had always had a bipolar relationship with his mother. On one hand, she was the law and order of the household. On the other, a free spirit trying too hard to stay young. Cheering too loudly at longboard meets. Butchering young people's slang. Regaling tall tales from the Hyacynthe Youth Retreats. As a young boy, Lorrie relished in her stories. By the time she'd fallen ill, he'd heard them all, and had begun to notice cracks in the narrative. He remembered the night he finally told her he didn't need bedtime stories anymore. When he sat on the wrong side of the protective glass, as Julia Sheppard gasped through breathing tubes, he wished he could hear just one more.

And then there was his father. As much as Lorrie loved to chide Robbie for trying and failing to be the renaissance man Robert had been, he knew his father was more a master of none than a jack of anything. He worked hard—that was without question. While he usually succeeded in the end, the path to success was fraught with hurdles and bad luck. As a young boy, Lorrie loved helping his father, even if that help was mainly moral support. He remembered the day when the lobby needed new carpet. It was all a ten-year-old could manage to drag the big love-seat out of the way so they could rip up the mustard-yellow shag, stained almost brown where guests walked the most. Only a few hours, Robert had assured him. Laying carpet, it couldn't have been difficult. By the fourth hour, after mis-cuts and mis-measurements, Lorrie had scrunched himself into a corner, eyes down to avoid the look in his father's eyes. At the time, he had interpreted the tears in his eyes as a sign of disappointment, or failure. It was only when Robert Sheppard was laying in that same hospital bed, quarantined behind that same protective glass, that he understood. His father had that same look in his water-puddle eyes.

Without words, Robert said it all. *I never wanted to let you down, Lorrie. Never.*

Kneeling in the grass, Lorrie still looked downward, as if his mother's or his father's eyes would be looking back at him from Brother Simon's grave. His brothers and Ian Null had left him there for the warmth of the house behind him. He was hungry enough to eat whatever was still in the pantry, tired enough to sleep on any bug-ridden mattress. And still, he couldn't leave. Not yet.

Lorrie closed his eyes. Were Julia and Robert cold inside their plots? Was Simon any warmer with two meters of soil insulating him from the world above that had so cruelly ended him? Did Simon know his killer? Surely, the killer feared something in his eyes. Why else would he have plucked them out?

A wave of anger washed over Lorrie. Without eyes, how else can you cry? As his own watered and itched from sweat and dirt, he wished he could put them out. He wished he'd been born without them. That way, he would never have had to see the death in his parents' final gazes. And Simon—a man Lorrie had never met, never had a chance to distrust or dislike—was robbed of the most basic of humanities. Was he alive when the killer had stolen his eyes? Was he dead before the final blow?

A searing pain flashed between his temples and his mouth tasted of metal. Lorrie howled an ungodly cry that would surely have embarrassed him if anyone had been there to hear it. The sobbing wavered in a discordant tone, crackling his voice as though he were still ten. His whole body shook in a way he had never experienced before. Not when Julia died. Not when Robert died. Not when Crystal left. Not when the Inn exploded.

Only when the pangs subsided did he realize he wasn't alone.

Somehow he knew who it was without even looking up.

"Leave me alone, Ian."

"Supper is ready. I was sent to——"

"To what—cheer me up? Rescue me?"

Ian didn't answer, which infuriated Lorrie even more.

"I don't give two shits about this guy." The lie was harder to say out loud than he'd expected. "I mean, I'm sorry he died. It's just…"

"You know death. You have seen it before." Ian's bedside manner was terrible.

"I watched my mother die a painful death. And a few months later, I got to do it all over again with Dad." Lorrie rubbed his eyes, but it only made them more itchy. "Red tide, it was dormant inside of them for who knows how long? And just like that, it came back." He snapped his fingers.

"You never grieved them." Ian stepped forward until he was next to Lorrie. "You have carried all of this on your own."

"And I plan to keep it that way. Not a word, Ian. Please."

Ian crouched. "You have my word."

The pair remained motionless for a long minute. Lorrie's headache receded and his eyes began to clear. In his corrected sight, the Reaper—Ansati pendant glistened in the moonlight.

"Any idea what that 'XL' means?"

"They are old symbols," Ian answered. "It means 'forty'. Brother Simon was an important person."

Important? Isn't everyone? "So, what's so important about forty?"

"The Ansati are governed by a council of forty Brothers and Sisters. They are what they call the Catholic Forty."

"What does *catholic* mean?" *Leave it to the Ansati to have mysterious words in their names.*

Ian shifted his weight. "It means 'all-encompassing'. It is the view of the Ansati that all belief is one."

Simon was a member of the Catholic Forty. "If he was one of them, where are the other thirty-nine?"

Ian reached over Simon's grave and grasped a handful of the fresh dirt, squishing it in his fingers. "I fear they are dead." He turned for the first time and looked directly at Lorrie. "All of them."

All forty—dead? "How? Who would do this to them?"

Ian dropped the dirt and looked back to Simon's pendant. "I don't know." Lorrie noticed that Ian used a contraction instead of his usual mechanical speech pattern. "You and your brothers must stay here."

"What do you mean, stay *here*? I thought you were going to bring us to Ozarck!" The pulsing headache behind his temples crept back. "You can't just bring us all this way just to leave us in a dead priest's house!"

"Leave if you wish. You are not prisoners." Ian lost balance and teetered on one knee.

"And what about you, Ian Null? Where are *you* going?"

"You knew your mother."

"What does that have to do with anything?"

"I did not." Ian drew a deep breath and hoisted himself to his feet. "She lies in the Ossuary of Moab. Before I leave, I need to see her."

"What do you mean, she's in the—what is that—the *Ossuary?*" *More weird words.*

This time, Ian didn't answer. He turned on his heel and made for the front of Simon's house. "We all must reconcile with the dead. It is a bridge we all cross."

Lorrie waited until he heard the door open, then close, before standing. He couldn't blame Ian for only trying. How could someone so rigid, so automatic, be so understanding? Lorrie's stomach rumbled. He'd never admit as much, but Robbie was a decent cook. Just like Julia Sheppard was a great storyteller, and Robert Sheppard was a good handyman. Maybe it wasn't too late to see eye to eye with Robbie. Maybe that bridge hadn't burned yet.

The Hand of Restraint

Sunday, 8 March AD 2544
Village of Jude
Tirel Desantos

The loudest explosion yet rocked enough to shake the room and cause the electronic gear of the medics to short out. The shouting and screaming amid gunfire drew closer. The masked medics began to panic.

"We need to leave *now*, ma'am! Do we take him or leave him?"

The woman's face was stern, the nostrils of her hawkish nose flared as she sighed in resignation.

"Get him a canteen of fresh water." One of the medics tossed a circular canteen with an elbow strap. She tilted his head back and poured a mouthful of cool liquid into his parched mouth. The water leaked over Tirel's lips down his chin as he nearly choked on the forced drink. Within seconds the water nourished him. He didn't care if it was the tainted. It wasn't tea, and it was going to keep him alive, at least for the time being.

Another explosion, and another wave of running and shouting.

"Take him or leave him? Jennings, we need to go now!"

The woman named Jennings secured the cover on the canteen and placed it at the boy's side. The gun shots were getting closer. Her medics had already packed their gear and were beginning to file out.

"Leave him," she answered, her face hardened. Tirel looked into her eyes. He reached his hand out for her to grasp it, to take him with them, to find his mother, to guard him from whomever was moving into the village with guns and bombs.

Jennings did not take his hand.

She stood, turned her gaze from the cot and barked at her medics to flee. Tirel found his voice at last as she reached the doorway.

"My mother…"

Jennings paused for a moment, but she didn't turn around. She slipped out the doorway, pulling it closed behind her. The lock clicked shut as a loud boom echoed the complex, hailing the arrival of the invaders.

After several minutes of shouting, guns firing, and other muffled commotion, the door handle rattled as someone tried to force it open. Tirel tried to remember the prayers his father had insisted he learn.

The light… pours over us… always…

He couldn't lie to himself. No sacred incantation would deliver him from whatever evil was about to charge through the doorway. Instead, he surrendered himself to the moment, succumbing to the belief that a shot to the temple would be the only deliverance guaranteed to free him from everything. His mother was gone. His freedom was gone. He was surely dying from poisoned water anyway.

Tirel silently begged for the door to crash open so the assailant on the other side could just finish it already.

When the door finally burst off its hinges, Tirel was disappointed to see that the man wasn't carrying a gun. Instead, the officer in green fatigues carried a backpack. He did not wear a mask. He kept his hair pulled back in a neat ponytail.

"I'm not going to hurt you, son," he said softly as the commotion behind him began to recede. "We're going to help you get well."

There was no solace in the soldier's words. Just the same oppressors in different disguises. Tirel had swapped the prison of his family home with that of the whole community. He was tired of prisons.

"Sir, two more on the second floor. The rest are processed in the courtyard."

The soldier nodded to the officer behind him. "One here, he looks dehydrated and malnourished. I'd say no more than eleven or twelve years."

Two more officers wearing the same deep forest green fatigues entered the room where only minutes before masked, sterile, white lab-coated medics fretted and fussed over him. While the medical team was quick to leave him behind, these army soldiers were keen to take him with them. He wasn't a human being any longer. He was collateral in an armed conflict he didn't understand. Before he could process what was happening, the soldiers had fastened his arms snugly behind his back and hoisted him over the shoulders of one of the burly men, feet forward so he couldn't see the direction they would take.

Tirel left the medical facility a free prisoner. The Motherland force that had come to liberate the city, had been waging a long battle on the outskirts of Jude. The elders were all too eager for Heartsburg's scientific delegation to come in. To find and destroy any evidence that New Inland had knowingly allowed their chemical discharge to pollute the water table, in exchange for better food, water, and technology as a bribe for their silence.

It did not take him long to learn the truth. As a ward to His Eminence, Tirel began to learn all about the towering monster of New Inland that loomed over the land, casting its oppressive shroud on anyone who dared exist in spite of it.

All those years later, and Tirel was still not free. So long as the structure remained strong, it would continue to oppress the outsiders. It would exert its law upon everyone.

With nothing left to lose, Tirel Desantos dreamed of a day when he would look into Jennings Marribel's eyes once again. This time, he would have the words, and he would cram them down her throat.

Domingo, 8 julio NE 267
Chapel of St. Jude
Colonel Tirel Desantos

The Reaper had left, but the silhouette of Paolo Desantos, dressed in his finest uniform, trim and proud, remained behind the altar. Tirel couldn't look in his son's eyes without an agonizing pang ripping him in half.

De Léon was a fool to think these petty attacks would accomplish anything, Father.

"Santiago De Léon *is* a fool. Incompetent. Fraudulent." Tirel spat the words.

He is incapable of deciding what is right and what is wrong.

"He is family, son. More of a father to me than Luther."

He is the hand of restraint.

Tirel's eyes watered. He had swapped the prison of Jude for the prison of De Léon. He was tired of prisons.

Sleepwalker

January, AC 0241
City Hospital, Capston, New Inland
Cadlen Sheppard

It was beautiful. Light more brilliant than I've ever seen…"

Cadlen held his father's hand even though the doctors had warned him against it. Even with the quarantine barrier between them, where the red sickness had no chance of infecting him, he insisted on reaching into the vulcanized gloves, to touch his dying father's frail hand. Robert Sheppard's energy was waning quickly now. He barely squeezed his gloved hand for fear of snapping his father's fingers.

Robert turned, his face sunken and sallow. "I felt the weight of my body disappear. I was floating in the ocean, looking down. Schools of fish… seagrass in the current. And when I remembered I was breathing under water, I gulped—that's when I saw the flash of light, you see…"

Cadlen had no idea what his father was trying to tell him. Lately, in the agonizing degradation of the illness, he'd muttered incoherent stories. His own childhood. Friends long lost, relatives long forgotten. It's like he's sleepwalking, Lorrie had said. He'd snap awake, and suddenly he remembered his children, his dead wife, his disease.

Robbie, Crystal, and Lorrie tried in varying degrees, but none had Cadlen's patience. They spent too much time talking to listen.

"Everything was wavy… out of focus… but the colours, they were perfect." Cadlen rested the rubber glove over his father's hand, wrinkled and spotted as if he were twenty years older.

"When you're up above, everything below is so beautiful… When it's time, son, look long and hard. While you can…"

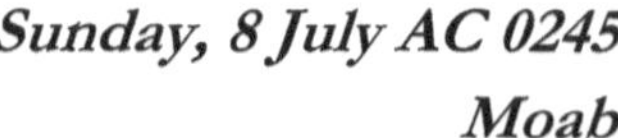

Sunday, 8 July AC 0245
Moab

Cadlen woke with his sketch pad still open on his lap, still half sitting against propped pillows. The house was silent. The image of his father trying to talk to him through his respirator mask, through a quarantine curtain, through hallucinations—it never really left him. His brothers and sister had always told him that his memory of detail was a gift. He wished he could explain that that gift came with a curse. Remembering everything meant remembering *everything*. Even the stuff he wished he couldn't.

Quietly, so as not to wake anyone, Cadlen crept out of the bed. Barefoot, his toes crossed the floor softly, down the hallway, past the heavy breathing of Lorrie in the opposite bedroom, past the kitchen that still smelled of Robbie's soup. Into the living room piled high with unsorted and unread books, boxes of artifacts, and piles of photographs. On the couch, Robbie slumbered under a heavy blanket, face toward the back cushions. Robbie deserved the rest. He worked hard to fill in the void left by his mother and father. No one was left to parent him.

Ian Null was nowhere to be seen.

Cadlen looked around the room, lips tight as he pondered. In the early days, Ian often left to hunt, or check traps, or to bathe, or to just be alone. He always came back.

But that was before he had become so sick.

Warning bells went off in Cadlen's mind. Here, in Moab, in Brother Simon's house, they needed nothing. There was no need to source food or water. There were rooms for privacy, soft beds for resting. A large easy chair near the fireplace was draped with messy blankets—he'd at least started to relax, but for some reason he'd left.

Cadlen narrowed his eyes and retreated to his bedroom. He opened the sketch pad to the message he'd scrawled inside the cover. *You have a gift, Cadlen. Draw what you see. Ian.*

It was a farewell message, written the only way Ian Null knew how. Cadlen's stomach felt hollow. Ian had struck out on his own sometime in the night, maybe even while he was still awake drawing what he "saw". He was sick. Worse with every passing hour. And he had no medicine.

There was only one thing to do.

Cadlen packed his things into his backpack. He filled his canteen with fresh water. He took a ration of soup from the refrigerator. With any luck, he wouldn't need more than that. Ian wouldn't be moving very fast in his state. When he caught up to him, he would find the right words to convince him to stop his mission, at least until he recovered. He had done so much for them. It was time someone looked after *him*.

In the streets of Moab, everything looked the same in the moonlight. All the houses looked the same. Some were different colours, some had gardens, some tall grass, some shrubs, but their basic shapes were identical, as if they were planned that way. Block after block, Cadlen walked softly along the cobblestoned streets, listening carefully as he always did for any hints of someone walking. Crickets and birds creaked all around him. But no signs of anyone else.

An hour later, the first shuffles of feet broke the stillness of the earliest morning light. Cadlen left the open street, creeping along the hedge of one of the cloned houses. With enough concentration, he could determine the direction from which the walking emanated. It was uneven, arrhythmic, almost pained. It had to be Ian.

Until it wasn't.

In the dawning light, a figure shuffled into view from an adjacent street, past one of the houses. It was more than a block away. Cadlen knelt low behind the hedge and peered at the ghostly figure drifting across the street. It was a slender person—possibly a woman. She was covered in a long veil, concealing her face and upper body completely. As she stumbled, Cadlen heard a low moan, wavering with every troubled step. A chill fell over him as she continued her sleepwalking. Within earshot, Cadlen heard her words.

"I see you… I still see you…"

Was she talking to him? Cadlen held his breath. The shape of the ghostly specter drifted on, moaning, muttering, her voice soft and broken. She continued past the intersection and up the next street, between houses, aimless. When her movements and her voice had faded completely, Cadlen stood and left the safety of the hedge.

Moab kept its ghosts. Some of them were still alive.

In the distance, a tall tower pointed skyward. Panning across the city skyline, Cadlen saw another pointed spire, only this one looked familiar. The steeple, Ian had called the pointed peak of the church they'd spent the night two days ago. Finding him would be like finding one grain of sand on a long beach. This church was as good a place as any to look.

As Above

Sunday, 8 July AC 0245
Moab
Cadlen Sheppard

The heavy doors closed, darkening the inside of the church. Cadlen rubbed his eyes. The sun hung low in the west, and the last speckles of colour shone through the fancy glass windows. In the smaller church where they'd spent the night, he'd noticed the shards of coloured glass. The windows had been long boarded up. Here, they were not only intact, but they glistened like brand new.

Everything inside this church was clean. It was a living space, maintained by the Ansati until very recently.

From the top of the aisle, Cadlen glared in awe at the openness of the sanctuary. The high-vaulted ceilings arched down over the chamber like an umbrella, each spoke disappearing behind two levels of deep burgundy hand-crafted wood railings. The main sanctuary sloped down to a raised platform, just like in the small church where they'd slept. The altar, draped with a long, white fabric looked small from the top of the aisle. On the rear wall, tall brass pipes reached up like antennas, the organ they once belonged to nestled in a booth just beneath them. Cadlen closed his eyes and imagined the sound it made. It would fill the room with enough sound to drive out any darkness that dared remain.

As the darkness overtook the last rays of coloured light, Cadlen searched for any switch or control buttons. Maybe the Ansati used candles instead of electricity. Simon's house had electrical switches, but the remnants of long-burned wax sticks suggested he preferred the softer, natural light. Either way, he had to find something to light up the room if he was going to explore a little longer.

Before the shadows fully draped over him, he spied a series of small levers, all pointing downward. He'd seen these kinds of switches in

Simon's house. Flicking the first upward, soft potted lights above him came to life. He switched the rest, one by one, until all the lights inside the church came to life, bathing him in a radiant yellow-white glow. He adjusted his backpack strap on his shoulder. Taking a deep breath, he stepped forward, gravity, or something else pulling him down the aisle in the direction of the altar on its stage.

Cadlen turned and gazed up at the balcony circling the sanctuary in a second level. Two sets of spiral stairs corkscrewed from the rear corners, poking through the second level, giving access to the rows of seating. His stomach churned at the thought of sitting so high, looking down over the pews on the main floor. There was barely any railing to prevent a long fall if he were to stumble. Why would anyone choose to sit there?

When you're up above, everything is so much more beautiful down below, son. When it's time, look long and hard while you can…

Robert Sheppard knew what he was saying. Cadlen gulped and ascended the aisle until he reached the left stair. He inhaled. Resting his hand on the curved handrail, he followed the velvet-lined steps, one by one, around and around. At the top, he let go his breath slowly through his thin lips. He chose the pew closest to the half-rail, closest to falling over if he were to trip. Every step was fueled by controlled breaths, slowed enough that a dozen heartbeats passed in between. He could have sworn he was being guided by hand.

Cadlen set his pack on the pew and leaned hard into the back rest. After a few more deep breaths, he realized that as long as he didn't look directly beneath him, he could adjust to the height. For many long minutes, he did nothing except look around the church. One of the switches he'd flipped had turned on the hanging ceiling fans. From his vantage point, everything unfolded beneath him like a holographic projection. He counted the pews, the candles, the pillars, and the statues of robed men and women. Proportion and line, scale and texture. All of it blossomed behind his eyes, so vividly that when he closed them, he saw it all down to the tiniest engraving and smudge.

Opening the flap of his backpack, he pulled out his sketch pad and pencils. Opening the cover, he lingered for a moment over Ian Null's message.

You have a gift, Cadlen. Draw what you see.

Robert Sheppard never met Ian Null. If they had, Cadlen believed they would have been friends. His father had taught him to open his eyes. Ian had taught him to capture what he saw.

With light strokes, Cadlen laid out the dimensions of the sanctuary from his point of view on the balcony. As hours passed, the scene in front of him came to life on his page, first in black and white and grey, then with rich colours. He imagined the forms of patrons in their seats. Mothers and their children. Itinerants and servers in blanketed robes and sashes. Men with long beards. Women in gowns, shawled, veiled. A priest seated at the high chair behind the altar, reading from the chronicles of the Ansati as the choir sang and the organ pipes echoed across all of Moab.

Robbie's voice startled him.

"That's incredible, Cad." His oldest brother moved the scattered pencils aside and sat next to him. He'd been so focused on his drawing, he hadn't heard him enter the church, climb the steps. "Next time, though, don't leave without telling us where you're going."

Through the coloured windows, the first streaks of morning light had reappeared. Cadlen yawned.

"Let's get back to the house. Looks like you haven't slept."

Cadlen nodded. "Ian?"

Robbie shook his head. "I thought you'd be with him. No, no sign." He helped Cadlen pack up his pencils. With one last look, Cadlen stared down into the sanctuary. For a second, he thought he was floating.

Josiah's Tower

Sunday, 8 July AC 0245
Moab
Lorrie Sheppard

He'd had this dream before. The one where he was doing tricks with his street deck, even though he hadn't used it in years. The old Hang Twelve always needed new bearings. It listed left no matter how often he tightened them. Still, he loved doing kick flips and coasting the bowls at the local skate park. A crowd of kids had gathered, Warren Connelly among them. As usual, Lorrie was talking himself up, and soon he had to prove himself against kids who were older and more skilled. Gathering enough momentum, he coasted up the side of the bowl, launching himself vertically, defying gravity and all reasonable expectation.

That's where everything shifted.

He flipped the deck, but his feet never reconnected. Beneath him, instead of the concave skating bowl, there was nothing for hundreds of meters. Lorrie plummeted, as if he'd skated straight off the Hanging Gardens. The city of Capston raced upward to meet him. That was when he jolted awake, in a pool of sweat.

This time, his voice crackled as he spasmed in Brother Simon's spare bed. Through the east-facing window, he could tell the sun had risen. Still, the house was as quiet as midnight. Something seemed off.

"Cad, you awake yet?" Lorrie rapped on the door opposite his with enough force to push it open a hand width. The rising sun blinded him when he pushed it all the way, and when he regained his sight, he saw an empty, unmade bed and none of Cadlen's belongings.

Cadlen wasn't in the kitchen either. Or the living room. Nor was anyone else.

"*Robbie!*" His first instinct was to holler, but it made little sense given the house was small and he'd checked every room. A quick glance told him that someone had slept on the big chair near the fireplace, and someone else slept on the sofa. Robbie's pack was still here, but there was no sign of Ian Null's.

Lorrie burst through the front door, the brightness again blinding him. Before he'd re-adjusted, Robbie's voice echoed off the vacant houses that lined the street.

"*Cad! Ian!*" He couldn't have been more than a block away. Rubbing his eyes, Lorrie saw the shape of his brother pacing in the street. He hadn't noticed before that Robbie's beard was coming in, sad patches uneven beneath his jawline. His hair was pressed flat on one side—classic Robbie bed-head.

"Where are they?" Lorrie shouted. "*Robbie!*"

"I don't know! They were both gone when I woke up." Lorrie's oldest brother cupped his eyes above his brows, scanning up and down the streets for any sign of movement.

Both of them. Could they have left together? Or one at a time? Who followed who? Cadlen wouldn't have struck off on his own. He had no reason. But Ian Null certainly did.

"Null took him!" Lorrie blurted his theory. "The guy's sick—getting worse all the time, and he doesn't think we know. He wants to go find his mother, but he can't do it alone. So, he brings Cad—and you *know* he'd do anything for the guy!"

"Hold on, Lor. There has to be some explanation."

"Oh sure, like they went for a cup of java. Wake up, Robbie! Null was going to leave us sooner or later. You know how much a kid Cad's age goes for with the traders?"

Robbie spun around. "Stop it, Lorrie. We don't know anything yet."

Leave it to Robbie to defend a stranger over his own family. "Maybe you don't but I know that this guy has spent the last two weeks convincing you and Cad that he's our guardian angel or some shit!"

"And *you've* spent the last two weeks taking everything he's given us, and you *still* can't give him the benefit of the doubt!" Robbie's eyes were wide, fierce. Half of it was out of fear for Cadlen's well-being. The other half, though.

"Sorry for looking out for my family!"

"Since when did you look out for *your family*, Lor? Fill me in—I was too busy running the Inn, and feeding you and Warren!" Robbie barked, a mean sarcasm darkening every word.

"Since I'm the only one with the sense to—"

Robbie swung an open hand, slapping Lorrie's face hard enough for his neck to buckle. "Enough, Lorrie! Enough of your attitude!"

The sting caused his cheek to numb. Lorrie tasted blood. Every ounce of him wanted to strike back, but his hands hung like wet rags. Never in his life had his brother laid a finger on him. Incredulous, he cradled his cheeks with his hands and glared back at him. Robbie's eyes glistened, tears not yet rolling welled in the corners.

"You know what? You're right, Lorrie. I'm no father! I'm barely a brother!" Robbie's breathing was uneven and he shook as if he were about to collapse. The pain in Lorrie's cheek dissipated, replaced by the heaviness of guilt in his gut.

"Stop, Robbie. I'm sorry, okay?"

He'd hoped it was enough. Never before had he seen his brother so close to a complete breakdown. Not when their parents fell ill. Or when Crystal left. Not even when they were reunited at Holt Tower after the Inn was blown to bits.

But it didn't change the fact that Cadlen was missing, and Ian Null had probably taken him along. "Alright, let's say Ian left alone—Cadlen might have noticed and went after him."

Robbie wiped his eyes before the tears could leak. "Maybe so. But they couldn't have gotten too far. You said yourself, Ian's sick. He could hardly lift the shovel."

"So, what do we do?" A realization fell over Lorrie. Less than twenty-four hours ago, they'd buried a slain Ansati monk in his own backyard. *Someone* had killed him. And the killer might still be out there. Granted, even a lame Ian Null would be tough to kill. But Cadlen, he was still a kid. Unwilling or unable to talk. Would he even be able to cry for help? *Could* he?

Robbie pressed his flat palms together. "Okay. There's a chance they haven't *left*-left. I'll go a couple blocks, see if there's any trace of them. But you should wait at Simon's, in case they come back."

"We shouldn't split up."

Robbie snarled, still raw on emotion. "Just stay at the damn house, Lorrie! For *once*, just agree with me!" His eyes burned. Robbie needed this one. And he was probably right, anyway.

"I'll stay at the house—but if you're not back by sundown…"

The sun began its dusken descent, and Robbie hadn't returned. Lorrie paced the hallway, sat outside Simon's grave, ate second and third helpings of barley soup, and even tried to read one of the hundreds of books the Ansati had stacked around the living room. Most of them were non-fiction, biographical accounts of families, towns, famous people. The written words were longer than he was used to. Most of them had a musty smell, and he sneezed upon opening a few of the older titles. The big book splayed open on his desk was something else, completely. It had the Ansati cross on the front and words in a different language for a title in fancy gold script. The first few hundred pages were in arranged verses like endless poetry. Most of it was gibberish.

Then there was a section that was written like a fictional story. Much easier to follow than the verses that preceded it, the story told the tale of a distant land, in which a great tower was built by generations of families. One day, it was learned that after all those years and decades, the tower was built with deliberate flaws. Some guy named Josiah learned of it, but when he tried to explain it to others, no one would listen. One day, the whole thing was going to collapse, and there was nothing he could do to stop it.

Reading had always fatigued Lorrie, so after an hour he closed the book and resumed pacing. Faced with yet another meal of barley soup, good as it was, he remembered that he still had smoked meat strips in his pack. Unfastening the flaps, he dug in only to scratch his hand against something metallic.

"Son of a bitch!" Lorrie yanked his hand, a thin line of blood leaking along his index finger. He was careful to sheath his knives. Sucking the blood, he opened the mouth of the pack and peered inside.

His eyes bulged. *This changes everything.*

Ian Null had left, and he'd brought all his gear with him. Except for his handheld. The key, he'd called it more than once. The ugly, half-finished machine had proved invaluable the past two weeks. He'd used it as a motion sensor, a map, a database, he'd even used it to remotely access other electronics.

There's no way he'd leave this without a good reason. Moreover, he'd deliberately crept into his room while he slept, hidden it inside his pack, and left without a word. No instructions. No warnings. No rules. It didn't make any sense.

Except that Ian Null did *nothing* without reasons. Lorrie had never in his life met anyone so deliberate. He held the device in his hand. Ian had to have left on his own. He was dying, and he probably decided that it was best to leave his best tool with the Sheppards if he weren't to live much longer.

Cadlen must have gone after him.

Lorrie changed into thicker pants and a long-sleeved shirt. He filled his canteen and unsheathed his longest knife. The barley soup would still be good in the fridge when they came home—together. Three Sheppard brothers, with or without Ian Null.

Spectres

20 November, 0242

Dear Robbie,

I'm sorry I'm so late writing back. There's something about this place that makes time slow, and before you know it months have passed! Must be the salt water in the air. It's been almost two years and I'm still not used to it. Makes my hair coarse, and I think it's even gotten lighter.

Second year quarterlies are coming soon—couple weeks from now. I'll be finished them by the time the Allens get this letter to you, I bet. Monsieur Laurent told me it usually takes three or four weeks for anything to get through. Have you heard any more about the embargo? Monsieur doesn't say much about it, though he probably knows more than he's letting on. I swear, Robbie, there's no one in Hyacynthe who he doesn't know!

Druna is finally settling in. The girl is something else! First semester was rough for her. I think she failed two of the five compulsories, but she swears she passed them all. I don't know how you can pass anything when you're at the Marais five nights a week. She's cut it back to Tuesday night and weekends. That right there tells me she needed to settle down. That, or she's broke. As long as she pays her share.

Mireil and I try to get out once in a while, but I just can't bring myself to spend the money, you know? Here I am, away from you and the boys, and all I can do is send some tutoring money every six months. And Laurent is generous with the pay—I overheard one of the tutors and she only gets half what I get. If anyone found out, they'd ship me back to New Inland in a minute! Wouldn't be so bad, though.

I loved Cad's pictures! He is getting so good—he knows how to shade so well, it's like the people jump right off the page. He could draw a smile on Lorrie once in a while, though! I know, it's not like he'd actually smile, but it would be a nice change. I miss them both. I know Lorrie's still mad at me, and you know what? I don't blame him one bit. Sometimes I wish I'd just stayed, took on a loan and went to Heartsburg instead. Or maybe I should have worked a year, helped you out at the Inn. But on the other hand, I don't know how you do it, Robbie. I was only there a few weeks after dad died, and I could feel their ghosts everywhere. But I'll tell you a secret. I still feel them here.

Last time you wrote, you told me that you didn't think you were doing a good job. Well let me tell you, big brother, you're doing a wonderful job! Business will come around. And Lorrie will grow up eventually! But don't give up on Cadlen . He might not talk, but he listens to everything. He's so smart. And he has a huge heart. But you really should get his hair cut more often—pretty soon he won't be able to see what he's drawing!! Just teasing.

And for the last time, NO, there is no boyfriend. I can't relate to most of the Hyacynthien boys (note that I said boys, not men!) Besides, I'd have to find one Druna hasn't been on a date with yet.

Anyway, that's all for now. Monsieur says that he may be able to arrange another correspondence in a few months. If so, I'll try to send a little more money. Please give Lorrie and Cadlen hugs for me, if they let you!

Love,

Crys

PS: Mireil would die if she knew I told you, but she thinks you're handsome (her words!)

Sunday, 8 July AC 0245

Moab

Robbie Sheppard

Every decision was dangerous. Strike out further into Moab, where the buildings were closer together and taller, and the greater the risk of coming across a straggler still in the city, even if Ian believed it was empty. Not to mention the possibility of brigands and traders. Worse, he'd almost certainly find more dead bodies. Robbie tried his best to keep a brave face whenever they encountered one. He wasn't fooling anyone. There was a reason Ian had designated the task of field dressing their kills to Lorrie. The blood was just too much.

If he stayed in place, he would become a target. To brigands and traders, of course. But the circling carrion birds overhead lingered a little too close for his liking. More than once he could have sworn he heard trotting dogs, and he could feel their eyes even if they were out of sight. Packs of wild dogs yipped in the twilight shadows out in the wilderness. Within Moab, it was notably quieter, but the silence was unsettling all the same.

Leave, and run into murderers. Stay, and be easy prey. *It's just like running the Sheppard Inn...*

Ultimately, the decision wasn't difficult. Robbie picked a direction and started to walk. Staying put is exactly what Lorrie would expect him to do. It's what he always did.

Robbie marched up the long avenue, keeping Simon's house in a familiar location when it was time to backtrack. Weaving between different blocks would be akin to walking in circles in the woods. Ian had taught them how to keep track of landmarks, how to pick a destination point and never look away from it, walking in straight lines from one point to the next. After an hour and only a few deviations from the main road, the houses all looked the same. If not for the open sky above, he could have been in a derelict side of Capston. He wasn't sure which was safer.

Far ahead, a tall, spindly tower rose about the buildings. Further still, the faint outline of a massive stadium hid in the spectral haze of the afternoon horizon. Ian had told them he intended to seek out a place he called the Ossuary, but he had never described it. The idea of aiming for these huge landmarks presented their own potential dangers. Surrounding them, taller downtown buildings, just like in Capston around Holt Tower, huddled like sentinels. If anyone was lying in wait, it would be there. Maybe Ian was heading for the downtown core. Maybe Cadlen was with him. Maybe he wasn't, and he was wandering just like him. Robbie almost called his mute brother's name.

Don't yell, idiot! Robbie cursed himself. Any chance of keeping away from people who would harm him would be gone if he started yelling. Cad hadn't just wandered up the wrong aisle in a supermarket.

The low moaning from up ahead was all he needed to keep as silent as death. The deep, female voice took him by surprise. He hadn't heard any footsteps, no closing doors, no clattering on the cobbled stone. Just a low, dissonant caterwaul, pained and afraid. If Robbie was still a young child, he'd have been convinced that a ghost was coming after him. Adult Robbie tried his best to rationalize what he heard. At times, it sounded as though she were uttering words, but they were too jumbled and distant to discern. Side-stepping the paved roadway, he moved softly along the grassy shoulder toward the sound.

Turning the corner of another block, the voice sounded like it was moving away from him. He wondered if whoever it was knew he was following, and she was more afraid of him. Rounding a second corner, her form came into view. Stumbling right up the middle of the street, a lithe, hooded woman moved step after pained step, her low moan cascading louder in the echo of empty houses.

"*...I see... I see... you... I see you...*"

She couldn't be talking to him. Robbie had yet to see her face, let alone be within a stone's throw of the woman. Was she even aware of him? Maybe she was reliving something?

What if the "you" she had seen was Cadlen?

Any chance of finding a clue to his little brother's whereabouts was worth a shot.

"Hello!" Robbie cleared his throat and called out to her. She didn't stop walking. She didn't stop mumbling.

"I see you... I see you..." The timbre of her voice was older, older than his mother's voice when he'd last heard it.

"Who do you see?" Robbie closed within a hundred meters. The woman moaned louder and quickened her step.

"I know you... I KNOW you..." Panic laced her voice. *Impossible.*

"We've never met, Miss. Are you lost?"

"I know you. I see you..."

"I'm looking for my brother. Have you seen *him?*"

The woman stopped walking. Her moan faded into a close-lipped hum and she teetered from side to side.

"The quiet one..." Her voice crackled as though she were speaking over a radio. Quiet—it had to be Cadlen.

"A boy, about this tall." He held his hand out at Cadlen's estimated height, about a hundred and fifty centimeters. It did no good; the woman stared away from him. They were within a few steps now. "He's about your height, give or take..."

The woman hummed some more. "The quiet one... He is safe..."

Robbie felt a gush of relief. "That's fantastic—thank you! Can you bring me to him?"

The woman didn't answer. She recommenced stumbling, one shaking step after another, crisscrossing to keep from listing to one side. "Safe... Safe... Quiet one... I see you... I know you..." It sounded like she was about to cry.

Robbie almost started to cry. He was going to bring his little brother home. Lorrie would see. And Crys would be proud.

One, Two, Three

Monday, 9 July AC 0245
Ap-Oz Research Facility
Cal Merrick

Cal Merrick couldn't wait to set foot on the Ap-Oz landing platform. Travel by Tan-Ro was nerve-wracking in the best of times. The loss of one of the flying transports didn't help. Overcast with brisk winds over the Appalachian range, the ride was unsettling. From high above, New Inland still visible behind them, he looked down at the mottled colours of the outside wilderness. Beneath the drab green and brown, thousands of outsiders scurried about like ants.

Somewhere down there, three Capston DefCorps officers could be alive or dead. Either way, they had to be found.

Cal made for the crow's nest without hesitation. The landing guards told him Steven would be there, as usual. At least he wasn't holed up in his quarters. That was a good sign.

Steven Reekan leaned over the northern guard rail, gazing in the direction of New Inland. He turned when the door shut. "Simmons?"

Cal nodded. "He's unloading the cargo. And if you're nice, maybe he'll bring you a cup of java!"

Steven laughed—another good sign. "Bless! Any more of this tea piss and I'll turn into a houseplant."

"Thinking of putting down some roots, are you?"

"Don't push it." His temperament shifted into a serious tone. "What's the word from Brien?"

The communication lines between New Inland and Ap-Oz weren't secure enough for any meaningful conversations. Cal thought it best that they meet in person, and since Steven wasn't leaving the mountain fort, the only option was to go to him.

"So, Pax Brien was able to convince the DHC to allow us access to

Capston funds—but with conditions."

Steven sighed. "Of course. But I'll take it."

"First, all transactions need to be approved."

"Let me guess—Kendall?"

Cal nodded. "When I spoke with Pax, he was very agreeable. He offered a budget for you to continue the search outside for the missing DefCorps officers."

"Which is fair—DefCorps is under DHC administration, so they'd have a vested interest if there are interlopers. Bad look for the whole sector."

"Pretty much what Pax said," Cal replied. "Kendall agrees, too. But the budget is… well, modest, let's say." He handed Steven his handheld with the numbers on the screen. Steven's eyes widened.

"You're not kidding. No five-star meals for you folks on this one. Anything else?"

So far, so good. Steven was taking the news well enough. "The downside is what you gain in funding, you lack in personnel."

Steven huffed and turned back to the rail, draping his arms over the edge. "Let me guess again—five?" A standard dispatch on a search and rescue mission should have no less than ten. *This isn't going to go well.*

"Two."

Steven hung his head. "You and Simmons. That's all?"

"It wasn't going to be Shonn, but Ling cleared him. You'll need a forensics lead, and I can't do it alone."

"You two aren't the problem, Merrick. How do they expect two forensic officers to find three missing men—*out there?*"

He wasn't wrong. Cal and Shonn had plenty of experience in the outside world, which helped their pitch. Ozarck had on and off agreements with La Cumbre, and with a few calls, Cal figured he could reconnect with some prior acquaintances. But that was all unofficial. Ozarck wouldn't risk trade with New Inland by openly dealing with outsider organizations, even if New Inland did the same from time to time. Hyacynthe had paid a steep price for making similar decisions.

"First thing we do is trace the last point of contact. That's easy enough. We know they were in the area of the open pit mine lake where the Tan-Ro went down. From there, we'll have a better lay of the land."

"You have all the tracking equipment you need," Steven said. "Percival's downstairs at QM. Send him your wishlist. And one last thing, Cal."

This went much better than he'd expected. "Name it."

"Tell Simmons I want that java yesterday. Milk, no sugar."

The Tan-Ro brought Cal and Shonn only as far as the foothills. Ap-Oz provided a shuttle with a nuke-cell fully charged. They could cover a lot of ground. Shonn secured La Cumbre and Rust credit in case they needed to barter. That'll appear in the books as petty cash, Shonn assured him. They weren't going to get receipts out here. And they weren't going to buy souvenirs. For transmission, the quartermaster Percival issued them both short-wave and quantum accelerometric radio. Enough field rations and clothing in the style of locals, mostly tunic shirts that tied rather than zipped, khaki trousers with pockets and rope-twist belts.

Shonn Simmons fretted with the waistband and belt of his pants. "I don't know how they walk around in these. Damn uncomfortable!"

Cal laughed. He would have missed his partner's humour. "Use your DefCorps belt, just let the tunic hang over it. And don't lift your arms too high or they'll see it!"

The shuttle wound through thin brush in the direction of the bearing on their monitor. Five kilometers out from the last confirmed location of the three missing DefCorps officers: Raijen Croft, Stirling Leander, and Augie Pembroke. Cal knew Pembroke well. He had joined the team at Ap-Oz before Steven Reekan had taken over the lease. Croft and Leander sounded familiar, but he couldn't place the names to faces in his mind. Leander—that could have been a Heartsburg name, like Shore and Jennings. Many Heartsburgers kept their reversed given and family names, so maybe *Leander* went by *Stirling*. Raijen, that was a common enough given name in Ozarck. Oddly enough, he couldn't recall ever having met him.

It wasn't so odd at all if the name was a cover.

The monitor flashed, and the signatures of three people appeared in an orange-red blotch. They were huddled together, stationary. Probably eating, given it was 1400 hours. La Cumbre often ate later than noon. Cal slowed the shuttle and tapped the monitor, expanding the scope. Three men, by the look of it. Unlikely they'd stumbled onto their missing men, but worth a look.

The shuttle emerged from the brush, and the three orange-red splotches were on their feet, weapons drawn. Cal parked the rig and Shonn waved a white rag out his door. It was a universal signal of non-aggression, but that didn't mean their quarry would abide.

The leader of the band was well-groomed, but his clothes were worn from outside exposure. He was likely La Cumbre. Cal opened his door.

"Cal Merrick, Ap-Oz. I worked with Lonzo Ashburn." Hopefully, Lonzo was still in favour with La Cumbre.

The leader lowered his sidearm. "Lonzo? What's his drink?"

Trick question. "Water. He never liked the bottle."

The La Cumbre agent nodded and motioned for his men to ease. "It's a wonder the man's still alive, from the water table this far south. What brings you out here, Cal Merrick?"

The agent introduced himself as Win Stoke, a natural-born outsider with deep connection inside Ozarck's trade sector. He only referred to his men as Two and Three. The less information that passed from lips to ears in the outside the better. Shonn attempted humour by asking Stoke if the others called him One. No one laughed except Cal.

"We're looking for three officers. New Inland DefCorps uniforms, only two of them aren't who they claim."

Stoke took a long drink from his leather canteen, droplets of whiskey leaking down his chin. "I don't know about your two fakers, but we buried a DefCorps body not far from here." Two and Three both nodded. "No ID on him, but he's your man, unless you have more of 'em wandering around out here."

"Not so far as we know," Shonn answered, trying to make up for his poorly-landed quip. "We'd like to see the body. We're forensics."

"I can save you some trouble—single shot to the back of the head. Your man didn't know what hit him."

"All the same, we need to check him. Bring the body home for his family."

Stoke nodded to Two and Three. "We'll bring you to him. But there's a matter of settling accounts."

"We have La Cumbre credit. I'm sure we can work something out."

Before Cal could open his waist pouch, a rustling of bushes interrupted the transaction. Two and Three spun in the direction of the noise. Stumbling from foliage, two men in only their underwear tripped into the clearing. Both were scratched across their chests and backs, dotted with red and black spots—black for the latched ticks, and red for the bites. One tried to call out, only his voice failed him.

"Who in sweet fuck are you two?" Stoke aimed his sidearm at the nearest.

Cal and Shonn exchanged glances. This was an interesting turn of events.

"Look at them, they're not about to hurt anyone." Shonn reached into the shuttle and retrieved his scanning kit. "Let me have a look. I have a hunch." The leader of the pitiful, nearly-naked wanderers fell to a knee. Shonn approached him, offering his canteen. The man snatched it from his hands and splashed it on his face, letting the water cascade over him. Shonn winked to Cal.

"Do we have our officers, Shonn?"

Cal's partner smiled. "Not sure, but we definitely have Kayewati. Nice ink you have here, fella!"

Two stepped forward and raised his gun. "Kayewati?"

Stoke raised a hand. "Hold, Two. Merrick, what's your business with Kayewati?"

"If these two are who we think they are, they killed our other officer—the guy you buried back there." Cal wasn't sure why the La Cumbre agents were so concerned.

"'Fess up, now. Croft? Leander? Or do I call you Stirling?"

The man nodded in affirmation of *Stirling*. He gasped his words as though he only had a few breaths left.

"H-h-he's alive… He didn't die…"

Shonn raised an eyebrow. "Well, if you don't *die*, you're usually still *alive*."

Before Cal could ask anything else, Three raised his gun and fired two shots, one into the chest of each Kayewati.

"WHOA!! What are you *doing?*" Cal charged at the La Cumbre sideman, raising his own gun. "We had a deal, here!"

Stoke was cold. "Except that changed when we found out your quarry were Kayewati. La Cumbre has a shoot-on-sight standing order. They could have been Le_Renard agents."

"I don't give a shit if he's Le_Renard himself—you cost us big time, Stoke! Lonzo wouldn't have been so reckless!" Cal raged. Any chance of getting answers was snuffed out. Three smirked. Cal wanted to wipe the grin off his ugly outsider face.

"Sorry for the trouble. We'll reduce our asking price." Stoke offered an open hand. Cal couldn't believe he was about to renegotiate with these murderers.

Cal and Stoke settled for half the original offer, and they agreed to bring them to Pembroke's body. Schonn scanned the second man, just to be sure. Both were Kayewati, although their true identities were lost through the bullet holes in their chests. Cal kept the safety off on his sidearm—the La Cumbre agents weren't to be trusted.

Stoke turned and motioned for Two and Three to follow. "Half a click this way. And by the way, Lonzo would have shot him quicker than Three."

Q&A

Monday, 9 July AC 0245
Farbend Trading Camp
Crystal Sheppard

If only she had a handheld that was capable of determining geographic location in relation to Ozarck. Crystal's device was a cheaper model—the only one she could afford at the time. Ironically, the wealth that had fallen into her lap that existed as data within her device's circuitry could have bought a dozen state-of-the-art models, with plenty to spare. As the coach trundled deeper into the mid-south, they encountered many wanderers. None of them could accurately explain how close or far they were from the southern federation. Hamm would gaze at the sky, squinting as he calculated its position compared to who knew what. Crystal believed that he wanted to offer something useful. Something *smart*. He often commented, through the corner of a half-full mouth or between gulps of flat ale, that he wasn't very smart. She didn't disagree, but she kept it to herself.

The coach driver never bothered Crystal or Hamm for more money after the incident with the Hyacynthien creep. On the fourth day, the youth who'd stolen the sidearm during that incident left sometime in the night. Who he was, where he came from, where he was going— four days on the lam with him, and Crystal knew nothing more. He was perfectly anonymous. He had to be. For whatever his reasons, he already knew in his short time on this earth that he needed to be simply nobody. Nothing.

Null and void.

Ian Null had been no different. He'd arrived impossibly late, dressed in clothing still creased from the packaging, with an obviously false name, for a prescription filled by Dr. Doherty. And just as quickly, he was gone—but not before making her rich for a few minutes of work and a missed shuttle ride. Even Hamm wasn't aware of exactly how much Rust credit she carried. He and Duncam had bolted from Hewer and Jamiss before Hewer had converted the Hyacynthien money. Without taking a single unit. No money could bring back Jamiss.

Five days removed from the harrowing encounter with Laurent's bounty hunters, the coach converged upon a makeshift settlement deep in the thick back roads past the foothills of the Smokeys. At his latest estimation, Hamm predicted they were only a few days out from Ozarck. He'd predicted the same the last few days. Crystal wasn't convinced they'd arrive before the first snowfall, if snow even fell at this latitude.

The clearing was grown in with tall rushes, matted down from passing settlers. The coach driver explained that there were traders from up north that had moved in recent weeks, and that they were well-connected with traders from the plains through Carroway. Better still, they were Rust traders, so Crystal's credit held some value. It might be their last chance to refill their canteens for some time, as they were dangerously close to the red line, south of which water tables weren't always clean. She knew that she'd need to restock on antivirals and other inhibitors. Still shaken from her near-assault, Crystal peered out of a seam in the coach canvas at the hastily erected village.

Like in Carroway, children played and adults shared the work, only this time the tasks were more difficult. Men and women alike carried massive loads of everything from sticks to sides of meat to water barrels balanced on their heads, steadied with both, one, or no hands. Horses dragged felled timber and men see-sawed long blades hewing them to length and width. Semi-permanent huts and open-faced shelters offered tradable commodities from meats, foraged vegetables and mushrooms, tools, and even electronics. From one building, metallurgy was on display. In another, the sharp lightning of welding sparks twinkled as a tinkerer reconstructed small electronic devices. *Maybe she could install a global positioning application…*

"I could go for some of those wild mushrooms, it'd go good with our chops." Hamm's mouth watered to the point drool was leaking. Crystal laughed as he teetered over to the produce vendors. The sun was high in the sky. The driver indicated he was staying at the settlement for the afternoon, that it was too hot for his horses, and that they'd make way after supper. It was for the best. The coach was stifling hot when the sun was at its highest, and trail dust still found its way inside. With any luck, the new village had a place to wash, and shade for a rest. Hewer had once told her that road weariness was real. She hadn't believed him.

Drawing the hood of her shawl up over her tied-back, knotted hair, Crystal approached the tinkerer. The older woman hunched over her counter, a makeshift workstation with boxes of loose parts, wires, and tiny tools. She reminded her of the vegetable vendor from Carroway, except younger. Under the wide, circular welding goggles, her face was tanned a deep brown, white lines where her wrinkles hadn't had the same sun exposure. Her hair appeared to have been once blond, except wiry grey streaks were quickly overtaking her natural hue. Her hands and lower arms were scratched from both new and old wounds. She looked old in appearance, while the old lady from Carroway was old all over. At least that's how Crystal reasoned it.

"Good afternoon." Crystal stayed a few meters back from the counter and shielded her eyes from the welding sparks. The tinkerer didn't look up. "Our driver tells me you trade in Rust. I'm looking for handheld upgrades."

"You and ev'ryone else." The tinkerer muttered, zeroing in on a small circuit in an opened device with yellow casings. "Sensors? Geiger? What'you want?"

"I was wondering if it were possible—"

"Out with it. Got no time."

"Sorry. I need a digital map of the area."

"GPS. That's what y'want." Crystal had heard the term before, but couldn't remember what exactly it meant. Fortunately, the tinkerer gave her a layperson's description. "Global positioning satellite. 'Cept there's no satellites up there. So we have to go on QA. It'll cost ya."

"Money isn't an issue."

The tinkerer stopped welding and looked up, lifting her goggles to her forehead. Her eyes were yellow and red-streaked and huge baggy puffs occupied her lids. Crystal's eyes widened. She was sick. Probably radiation exposure.

"Fifty thousand. Up front. Still int'rested?" She set her welding gun on the table and shifted in her seat.

"Twenty-five, and I help you with your radiation poisoning."

The tinkerer nearly fell off her stool. "Thirty, and you better know your stuff."

Crystal transfered the Rust credit to the tinkerer's account, listed under the singular name "Aynslie". Aynslie estimated that she could have it ready by morning, or before sunset for another thousand. Crystal replied that morning was fine, and set off to find an apothecary in the settlement with the right combinations of iodine and inhibitors to offer her some comfort. By suppertime, she'd rounded up enough from three different vendors to treat her sickness, at least in the short-term. Whether or not cancer would rear itself years from now was anyone's guess.

Hamm fried up some wild boar chops smothered in butter sauce and fresh mushrooms. From the corner of her eye, Crystal watched Aynslie assembling a small chip that would fit right inside her handheld. With any luck, they'd be able to find their way to Ozarck and her brothers without roaming in circles.

Morning came early. The nomadic Farbend folk stirred before the sun rose, and Crystal emerged from the back of the coach with sleep in her eyes and knots in her hair. She made her way into the thicker foliage to a stream no more than ankle-deep, alongside a mother and her two toddler children. Cupping her hands, she splashed water on her face. The cold woke her fully. Maybe upstream she might find a deeper pool for a more thorough, full-body scrub. The thought of the Hyacynthe officer leering at her before Hamm and the sleeping teen had leaped to her defense quashed any idea of removing her clothing within any distance of anyone else.

Not out here, anyway.

She walked back to the clearing of the camp, dew droplets wetting her trouser legs halfway to the knees. The afternoon sun would dry them, like it did every day. Crystal peered over to Aynslie's station. As though she'd worked through the night, the tinkerer hunched over the device, goggles reflecting tiny sparks as she put the final touches on the handheld.

"All done." Aynslie continued to pick at the device. It didn't look all done.

"Is it hard to use?" New applications rarely gave her any trouble. But this QA thing—quantum accelerometer, Aynslie had explained—it might as well have been magic. Sure, she could learn which tabs to tap, but how it all worked… Crystal understood viruses, how to identify them, treat the symptoms, ease the pain. But how or why the virus did what it did, that was still uncertain among even the most learned virologists. One needn't look any further than red tide.

Aynslie turned off her welding gun and moved her goggles to her forehead. Sweat and round creases ringed her eyes. "All you need to know is that QA runs hot. Need to keep it cool—lots of airflow. But the tabs, no, they're easy. Should be for a domer like yerself."

Domer. That was new. "Why do you think I'm a domer?"

Aynslie pressed the outer casing on Crystal's handheld until it clicked. "'Cause you talk like one. Besides, Hamm told me."

"You know Hamm?"

Aynslie nodded. "Been trading with Hewer and his lot for ages. Heard you tried to help his boy."

Jamiss. Whether the youth had red tide like his father had suspected, he'd suffered intense radiation exposure. How long he'd wandered in the brush was anyone's guess. Crystal figured he'd have had to been exposed up close and for more than a few minutes. Anyone who'd endured that would surely face the same fate, unless they had some means of flushing the toxins from their body. Even then…

"There was nothing I could do. Or anyone. Too much radiation."

"That's why we're here. If that Null fella hadn't warned us, I'd be dead too, and you'd be shit out of luck."

Null? "Say that again?"

Aynslie flipped the handheld on its front and wiped her finger smudges. "Ian Null, he came stumbling into Farbend, looked half-dead himself. Before we left, I gave him supplies, 'n he used his little machine to send off a warning to go way 'round the accident. We was expecting Hewer. Looks like you lucked out there, too."

Crystal couldn't even process the details. The name *Ian Null* rang over and over. She saw the prescription and order slip, his eyes, his neatly tied hair, his trim, fresh wardrobe. His air of mystery.

His generosity. His kindness.

Somehow, she knew she'd hear that name again, far-fetched as it may have been.

"Ian Null—he sent the warning?"

Aynslie nodded. "Clearly, since you're here and not dead."

"What happened to him? I mean, after… Did he say where he was going?"

"Nope. Only that he was leaving. Not a man of many words, that guy."

No kidding. When they'd last spoken, Ian Null had seemed awkward about his choice of words. Not so much that he was hiding anything, but in whether the right words came to his lips. As though he rarely spoke. To anyone.

Crystal leaned onto the counter as though she'd lost her balance. Ian Null had made her wealthy with the touch of a tab. He'd haunted her ever since, and evidently saved her life without knowing it. Every time she paid Rust credit, he was saving her all over again.

And he may very well be dying.

Aynslie passed Crystal the finished product. It was heavier in her hand. "I'll show you how to bring up maps. There's a trick to it—"

Before she could finish her thought, Aynslie turned as the radio transmitter behind the counter and out of view crackled with feedback. A voice broke in and out of the static, unintelligible warbles punctuating the bustling of Farbend business. The tinkerer rolled her eyes and turned to the radio, twisting a reception dial. "Never mind, missy. Y'get all sorts of signals comin' in round here. Good reception, I'd say."

Crystal tapped the new tab that brought up a screen with multiple options for maps—topographical, thematic, even old-world political boundaries with names she couldn't pronounce. A finger tap on the thematic tab brought her to a host of possibilities, not the least of which indicated radiation contamination. A wide swath known colloquially as 'the seam' stroked across the continental mid-west as though a comet had struck the earth, intense around its impact, trailing in uneven and interrupted streaks north-east. She couldn't yet figure out how to situate herself in this region, though Hamm's Geiger readings suggested they weren't yet close enough to worry. Still, anyone with prior exposure to radiation would be wise to steer clear of the seam at all cost.

"Anybody… any… need… repeat—help…"

As Aynslie adjusted the dial, the voice transmitting over the radio signal sharpened. Discernible words began to form crude sentences. It sounded like a young man in distress, but the nature of his call was impossible to decipher. "Y'get distress calls all the time. Half of 'em are usually fake. I used to cry wolf, m'self. Easy money."

Something nagged in Crystal's mind. The voice on the other end wasn't a fraudster. There was too much urgency in the tone. She leaned in closer.

"…oh-ah… all dead… dying… empty except… please…" The caller was painting a bleak picture, whoever he was. "Anybody… ans… city… mo-ah…"

"Moab." Aynslie perked up. "I think he's in Moab."

Crystal thumbed the tabs of her new application, but nowhere by that name appeared. "Where is Moab? Is it far?"

Aynslie nodded. "Bit of a trek, but deep in the seam. That's where the Ansati live. They been on the road, in daylight the past few weeks."

The transmission crackled and for an instant, the message cleared. "We're in the Ansati city Moab. Everyone is dead. Our guide is dying, needs medicine. Anybody out there—"

It was enough. Crystal only needed a few sentences to determine who was transmitting the distress call. Her heart fell into the pit of her abdomen.

Lorrie… How in the hell did you end up in Moab?

Crystal grabbed Aynslie's dirty sleeve. "Please, another thousand if you can show me how to work this right now!"

Ladders

Monday, 9 July AC 0245
Moab
Lorrie Sheppard

The tower was further than Lorrie had anticipated. The afternoon sun punished him for his miscalculation. He'd drank more than half of his water and still the tower loomed several blocks ahead. Looming beyond it, a stadium that could rival anything in any of New Inland's five cities dominated Moab's horizon. Clusters of taller high-rises crowned the immediate blocks surrounding what was surely the archive, and Ian Null's destination. The city was empty, he'd said. Lorrie didn't believe it. Moab boasted hundreds—maybe even thousands in its capacity. They couldn't have all left, could they? How would they know to leave? How would they all *agree* to just leave? The Ansati were getting weirder with every passing day.

Then again, Simon was slaughtered outside of his own home. He'd been struck in the back before his killer finished him with a slash across the abdomen. Before or after his eyes had been gouged out? Lorrie took another drink, sloshing it around his mouth.

Afternoon became evening when the base of the tower finally came into sight. He stood under its shadow, gazing up to its pinnacle. At ground level, it was wide—wider than the area of Simon's house by a fair bit. Something so tall had to have a strong foundation, he reasoned. As far up as he could see without squinting in the waning sun, Lorrie saw no windows of any kind, only huge brick patterns, divided at every story, narrowing the higher it stretched. At the top, a tall spindle like an antenna pierced the sky, peaked with a cross-shaped symbol that resembled Simon's pendant.

At the doors, Lorrie examined the frame for any access panel. Nothing electronic was visible, and the doors themselves, steel and without handles or knobs, remained airtight.

"Why am I even here?" Lorrie slumped to the grass next to the door and opened his rucksack. Chewing on the last strips of cured meat from the journey. He wished he'd brought along some of Robbie's barley soup.

Robbie. Where *was* he? And Cadlen? And Ian? It was as if they'd each fallen one by one into a bottomless pit. All four could circulate through the streets of Moab for weeks without seeing one another. It was foolhardy for any of them strike out on their own.

"And here I am—just as stupid as the others." The cured meat made him thirsty. Down to the last quarter of his canteen, Lorrie sighed. He could walk back to Simon's house, assuming he remembered the way. He could press on toward the stadium. Or, he could find shelter in any one of the closest buildings. None of them appeared to be houses—rather, old shops from businesses long shuttered. The image of the old hotel where he and Warren had overheard the Motherland terrorists came into his mind.

Warren. He'd blocked his best friend from his thoughts ever since the Tan-Ro copter fell out of the sky. Had Clara Connelly not made such a fuss, Warren would have been with them. If he'd survived, that is.

He hadn't spoken with Warren before they'd left. Lorrie had tried to find him, to explain the ruckus that led to the Sheppards being evicted from Holt Tower. What had led to all of *this*. Surviving an aerial crash, getting lost in the outside world, meeting Ian Null. No closer to home, no closer to Ap-Oz. No closer to Crystal.

"It's *my* fault." Lorrie uttered the words out loud for the first time. He had always known he was to blame. If he'd only taken the shuttle to the meet instead of illegally riding the highway, he and Warren would never have hidden in that abandoned hotel. They would never have become targets for the terrorists. The Connellys would have been as anonymous as anyone, free to live their unhappy lives, but at least *safe*.

He wished Warren was with him. Adventures were always better with his oldest friend. Maybe it was because he followed Lorrie no matter what. A hollow realization overtook him—Warren was far away, just like everyone else. Crystal was up north, probably unaware that her brothers were missing. His brothers, they'd wandered off in this cemetery of a city. Warren, he was still on the 92nd level of Holt Tower, keeping his father company while Clara entertained Jason Holt's advances.

"I'm sorry, Warren. I wish I could just tell you. I'm sorry…"

So, just tell him! Lorrie looked up. The highest radio tower for hundreds of kilometers offered the chance—if he could somehow get inside it. His eyes widened.

Digging into his rucksack, Lorrie retrieved Ian Null's handheld device. He'd watched the stranger use it to remotely access electronics before. The old shuttle he'd commandeered. Ian had used it to detect movement, search old maps, analyse plants, and water sources. Lorrie looked down at the screen. With the touch of a thumb, it flashed to life.

Multiple tabs appeared as options on the menu screen. But one rang in his mind.

<BRIDGE>

We all must reconcile with the dead. It is a bridge we all cross. They were Ian's parting words, spoken as Lorrie knelt at Simon's grave. It didn't mean any more than its surface meaning. As he gazed at the open tab, he started to wonder.

"You *mean*t for me to use this, didn't you?" Such a valuable tool for anyone to just abandon, let alone stuff in a teenager's rucksack. Ian Null was mysterious, but if nothing else, he was meticulous. Ian did nothing without a reason. Tapping the <bridge> tab, a series of prompts led to an outline of the closest electronic panel—the doors of the tower. With only a tap, the doors clanged and inched open. Lorrie felt a burst of energy as he sprang to his feet. This was his opportunity. The handheld could open doors. It could probably activate the radio atop the tower.

Finally, a chance to make things right. He would send a distress signal. Maybe Ap-Oz would hear it.

Maybe he could contact New Inland. Holt Tower. As he pulled open the metal doors, he began to think about what he would say to his best friend. He'd *have* to listen.

Inside the tower, Lorrie stood in awe of the geometrical patterns and symbols that adorned the inside chambers. To his relief, he found running water in a small kitchen that was empty of any foods. Filling his canteen, he took a long drink before investigating the lay of the ground floor. Finding a lift elevator, he delightedly used the <bridge> tab again, forcing its doors to open and shut, then rise upwards floor by floor. When it came to a halt, he held his breath as the doors slid open. He was disappointed to find that the lift ended about halfway to the antenna, and there were no visible control panels in sight for him to hack into with Ian's device. The junk key, he'd called it. It was far from junk, that's for sure.

The only option to reach the highest level of the tower was to climb a narrow, steel-runged ladder. It reached high above him, ringed with circular steel guards wide enough for a hefty man to climb and not fall outwards if he lost his grip. Inside the cylindrical shaft, Lorrie couldn't maneuver with his rucksack. He took the junk key, clipped his canteen to his belt, and began the arduous ascent. Every fifty steps or so, he leaned into the guard rings, wedged enough that he wouldn't fall without first ripping off a limb or two. He kept the key in his pocket, fastened closed for fear of dropping it. He needed it for at least one more job.

One hundred fifty steps later, Lorrie reached upward into the darkness and a searing pain ripped through the palm of his right hand. One of the rungs must have had a jagged edge. Recoiling, Lorrie fell straight downward four or five steps before his left leg caught one of the guards, grinding him to a halt, but not before his head rapped against the steel, nearly blacking him out.

"Son of a *fucking*…" Lorrie cradled his injured hand. With a gentle touch, he felt blood coursing from the wound. Flexing his palm as best he could, the wound was open enough that he felt the skin parted. There were clean bandages below in his rucksack. But he knew that if he climbed back down, he wouldn't likely have the energy to try again. At least not right away. He looked up into the blackness. Somewhere up above, there was a platform with a control panel that would allow him to send a radio signal. Somewhere up above, Lorrie had a chance to make things right.

With his good hand, he ripped a scrap of fabric from his shirt, just as he'd done after the Tan-Ro crash. Wrapping it tight around his wounded palm, he figured the bleeding would at least slow while he continued climbing. A quick drink from the canteen, and he continued his ascent, using only his left hand to pull. Aware of potential sharp edges now, he took his time to verify that each rung was safe. It took him twice the time, but eventually, a thin light in the shape of a circle came into view, just above the final rung.

He didn't need the junk key to open it. Light from the setting eastern sky greeted him as he flopped onto the platform. All around, panes of plexiglass allowed him a breathtaking view of the surrounding area. The stadium, so massive from the ground, looked much smaller from up high. Lorrie sat up, examining his wound for the first time. He didn't dare remove the rag; it was already soaked through, but appeared to have stopped bleeding, at least for the time being. It ached, pulsing with his heartbeat. Sooner rather than later, he knew it needed to be treated properly or infection would surely set in.

But that could wait. He was finished with ladders, at least for tonight.

Sanctum Occultus

Monday, 9 July AC 0245
Moab
Ian Null

Ian hadn't made it out of sight of Simon's home before dropping to his knees and wretching onto the cobbled stone. As long as he was far enough that the Sheppard brothers weren't wakened. The last thing he needed was for them to follow him.

The convulsions drained him of his breath. Closing his eyes, he willed himself to calm, his heart rate to slow, his muscles to stop spasming. After half a minute, he drew half a breath and wiped the sweat from his forehead. Short, staccato breaths eventually filled his lungs, and he opened his eyes. The splash of vomit was mostly the colour of Robbie's barley soup, only streaks of blood curdled between the undigested bits. Ian pulled back his hair, tying it in a short ponytail. The midnight breeze was cool on his pale face.

Before standing, Ian retrieved one of the portions of soup he'd prepared for his departure. Raising the container to his lips, he sloshed a mouthful, forcing himself to swallow. His stomach tried its best to send it back, but Ian kept his mouth shut tight, forcing himself to swallow again and again the broth until he'd triumphed over his digestive system. The nutrient-rich soup would go a long way to keeping his energy for the last day of travel.

At least, until he'd reached the *Sanctum Occultus*. One way or another, the journey was leading to this.

Satisfied that he wouldn't vomit, Ian stood and continued on his way through the night toward the heart of the city of Moab. In the light of the moon, he has able to travel without lanterns or the guidance of his key. The key was of little further use to him, anyway.

The suburb of Moab maintained spacious plots for the small houses the Ansati had built over generations in the same style, quaint but functional. Passing each house, Ian watched for any signs of occupancy. All of them were dark, either from sleep, death, or flight. He came across more bodies—men, women, and children, all killed in the same manner. All eyes were removed, except for the children, who were all finished with one thrust into the heart. The sight of murdered children nearly caused Ian to vomit, but he forced himself to keep the contents of his stomach down.

Andreas, you are a demon…

Ian's greatest regret was his inability to offer any of them a proper burial like he and the Sheppards had done for Brother Simon. He had neither the energy nor the time. 0300 hours, by his estimation, and he spotted in the distance the shape of a tall tower and a large, domed structure not unlike New Inland. Parched with thirst, he knelt to the roadway and sipped from his canteen. Ian tasted blood from his cracked lip and the sour aftertaste of soup and bile. He listened. Shuffling feet from dogs or cats, insects creaking, and birds cooing. No human feet, no human movements. Ian sighed. The Sheppards weren't following, at least not yet. He was certain that Cadlen would try to follow him and prayed that his brothers kept him in Simon's house. They had food, water, shelter, medicine.

And he didn't realize it yet, but Lorrie had the key to their survival.

A shuffling of feet caused Ian to focus. The night sky had yet to give way to early morning light, but with that of the moon, he was able to make out basic shapes within a hundred meters from his position. Spying from house to house, down streets and into bushes, he tried to locate the source. Whoever it was, they were ahead of him, so it couldn't have been one of the Sheppard boys. Ian continued walking, keeping his steps light to hear further sounds. To be sure, he kept his sidearm in hand. If it was Andreas lurking in the shadows, he was bringing a machete and a hunter's knife. It wouldn't be enough for Ian's gun.

An hour passed with no further sounds of feet apart from his own, dragging more and more. By about 0400 hours, he'd noted how heavy his boots were on his feet. By 0500 hours, as light streaked through the darkness and the *Sanctum Occultus* loomed ahead, he could barely lift his feet. *Close enough.* Dropping his pack, he untied the laces and kicked free the boots. He didn't need them anymore. His unburdened feet breathed in the morning air as he flexed his toes. One more mouthful of water, and he set his sight on the entrance of the old-world stadium.

Long before the Ansati occupied the city they rechristened Moab, the structure was a place of leisure, entertainment, and sport. *L'Estadio Real* in Motherland served the same purpose. Ian closed his eyes and remembered the day of his promotion. He'd watched from behind a curtain while the military parade circled the stadium floor. He'd listened to the throngs of spectators cheering. He'd scowled as his father delivered his poisoned address—all in the name of Paolo Desantos. He'd reached into his pocket and covered his eyes with wide sunglasses, mirrored on the outside so no one could detect his true feelings.

And when he walked onto the stage, the sun came out and he felt ten degrees warmer in less than ten seconds. In front of him, the crowd chirped like a nest of chicks by the thousands, mouths open for the worm. And from the gathered wards up front, Andreas had thrust into the open air the silver *crux ansata* pendant that glistened in the sun, penetrating his shielded retina. The memory always ended at that point. Ian opened his eyes.

The sun was rising. In front of him, Ian gazed at the front entry of the *Sanctum.* One time, it had many, glass-paned doors to allow crowds to enter in great numbers safely. All had been bricked in save for one, a vestibule entrance with two heavy doors, each adorned with the Ansati symbol. Reaching into one of his cargo pants pockets, he pulled out a pendant just like the one Andreas had that day. In his hands, the pendant was cool and smooth. Brother Simon couldn't do much more for him, but he could offer a way inside.

In the right side of the doors, Ian found a narrow slit in a panel with electronic components and a small, polymer light that glowed red. Shaking, he raised the pendant and inserted the stave until the light turned green. The double doors clicked. The Junquer's key could have done it. But any pendant belonging to a member of the Catholic Forty would do the trick just as easily.

Listening one last time for anyone tracking him, Ian took another sip of water, only to throw up violently. *So much for keeping the nutrients down.*

Man of Action

Shonn Simmons examined the body of Augie Pembroke. Stoke was correct. He'd been shot in the back at close range, dying instantly. The scanner showed no sign of a Kayewati stamp. He was one of theirs. It always hurt worse when it was one of their own.

Cal Merrick piloted the shuttle on through the dense brush, directionless in a sense. One case was closed. Pembroke had been betrayed and slaughtered by the Kayewati sleeper agents he'd trusted. As fate would have it, the interlopers had fared no better. Cal cursed the La Cumbre agents who'd decided to kill them first and ask questions never. Their permanent silence ensured that the second case may never close.

What became of the Sheppard brothers?

Cal opened all scanning frequencies to one kilometer, the farthest he could stretch them. He and Shonn decided on a south by southwest bearing, bringing them deeper into La Cumbre territory and closer to the Ozarck Federation dome.

Away from the more level area around the open pit mine lake, Cal steered the shuttle into the Appalachian foothills, rising in blisters, the taller peaks looming in the distance. Somewhere in that misty horizon, Steven Reekan was leaning over a crow's nest railing. From the higher ground, Cal could send a clear transmission, unsecured, but direct. His ears popped.

"Whoa, feel that?" Shonn called from the rear cargo bay. His ears must have popped as well.

"Don't suppose you have any chewing gum—

"…oh-ah… all dead… dying… empty except… please…anybody… ans… city… mo-ah…"

The radio crackled, and the words of a male voice cut in and out of the static. Cal slowed the shuttle until it came to a soft stop. "Hold it, Shonn. Picking up something, here." He tapped on the datapad until the frequency settings appeared on the screen. Adjusting them as though he were trimming a table's legs to make it level, the transmission cleared.

"We're in the Ansati city Moab. Everyone is dead. Our guide is dying, needs medicine. Anybody out there—"

The signal cut. Frantically, Cal reconfigured the frequency until the same message reemerged. It appeared to be on a loop. The broadcaster didn't identify himself. But there were other ways to identify voices.

"Think we can ID the voice?" Shonn crawled into the cab, taking his seat alongside Cal.

"If it's a voice from our database, we should." Realistically, any voice from an outsider wouldn't be identifiable. A distress signal emanating from Moab was certainly unusual. Cal had never seen the fabled Reaper city. It appeared on maps within a wide swath of radiation-contaminated land called the seam. It's very existence was only speculation.

"I think I have it." Shonn manipulated his datapad, and a name flashed across his screen.

<Laurent Sheppard>

"That's the middle Sheppard kid! They call him Lorrie for short. Double check that." Cal opened the navigation tab on the datapad. The eastern edge of the seam lay one hundred and ninety kilometers west. If Lorrie Sheppard was in Moab, let alone alive, he needed help immediately. Especially if, as he'd relayed, everyone else was dead.

Everything he'd disliked about the teenager dissipated. He'd been through too much.

"Get Reekan—we need air transport!"

Two hours later, the Tandem-Rotor helicopter descended out of the sky, touching down on the grass-covered hillside Cal had directed it. Twin blades whirring in a slow blur, the transport doors slid open and Mayor Reekan hopped to the ground. He was in full operational fatigues, for the first time in ages. This was not Steven Reekan, the politician. This was Steven Reekan, the charismatic soldier who'd recruited Cal and Shonn from Ap-Oz. This was the man of action who'd as of late been reduced to a shell of himself. Finally, some good news—or at least, a starting point. Steven's eyes were wide. His stride was long.

"Anything about Robbie or Cadlen?"

Cal shook his head. "Only Lorrie's message, and it's on loop. Shonn figures there was limited power wherever he was transmitting, so the message autosaved and went into a loop. For all we know, he might be still talking."

"QM rigged me up with heat sig scanns up to half a kilometer. If Moab is as empty as he says, we should be able to find anyone still alive down there." Steven threw an arm over Cal's shoulder. "Sorry about Pembroke. Hard worker, terrible loss. At least the bastards that killed him are dead."

"I wish we could have got some answers before Three shot him."

"Three? It took three of them to kill a Kayewati?"

Cal rolled his eyes. "Never mind. I'll explain it later."

The Great Wheel

Monday, 9 July AC 0245
Sanctum Occultus, Moab
Ian Null

He'd expected total darkness. The Junquer's key would have been useful for navigating his way around the vastness of the Sanctum Occultus, but his lantern would have to do the trick. Once inside, the heavy doors drew closed behind him as though by an unseen, divine hand. Null dropped his pack and shed his long-sleeved outer shirt, dropping it to the floor. It was difficult to judge the climate; he sweat profusely in the wake of emptying the contents of his stomach moment before.

His lantern gave enough light to show the surrounding vestibule. In the old times, this space had served as the gate, where guests were greeted by attending staff eager to scan their admission tickets and direct them to their seats. Did Ansati attendants do the same? Given the city of Moab was situated inside a pocket of clean earth surrounded by radiation, it was unlikely they received many tourists.

Peering to where a counter might once have been, Null held his lantern higher. Mounted on the wall, an enormous wheel hung in prominent view. It appeared to have been carved from wood. The outer ring was adorned in symbols, many of which meant nothing to him. The center of the wheel also contained symbols—this time, familiar ones. A stack of books. A roman column. A compass rose. Anyone who had studied even a cursory course in old-world symbology could figure out what those meant.

At the center, the axle of the wheel, one symbol stared back at him.

The empty recess of the skull's eyes nearly caused him to throw up again. Null had seen many faces without eyes in the final leg of his journey. Wasn't it natural for an Ansati to imagine every face without eyes, when the flesh was gone and only the bones remained? The Ossuary, located at the center of the facility, as indicated by the symbol on the wheel, would be populated with countless skeletal remains. Not one would have their eyes intact.

Around the outer ring, Null spied intermittent symbols that likely indicated each room's purpose. A music note. Likely an archive for all things to do with music. A needle and thread. Clothing, perhaps? Or maybe where the Ansati fabricated their trappings. Did they use electronic machines to make textiles, or massive weaving looms like the days of old?

What the blueprint wheel didn't indicate was how to make way from the outer concourse loop to the inner spaces. Those cavernous areas that once hosted athletes and performers, now dedicated to archives, libraries, and maps. There had to be access somewhere. Maybe every room had a hidden stair, or ladders, or a lift. One way or another, it was going to be an exercise in trial and error.

Think, Null. Paolo's voice prodded him. *The Forty would surely have a meeting place.* While Null's body was weakening, the survivalist instinct of Paolo Desantos urged him, refused to let his mind give in. He was right. The Catholic Forty would definitely have a chamber or a hall in which they conferred, dined together.

Raising his brow, he looked to the highest arc of the wheel. The symbol might as well have been a neon sign.

The chalice could have meant many things. But the XL that adorned it gave it away, at least to someone who understood the ancient Roman numeral system. Null had his destination, unfortunately the farthest he could walk in the concourse. With any luck, the Catholic Forty's meeting hall would have nutrients, possibly even medicine. *Do you think medicine can help you now?*

Circling the Sanctum Occultus would have taken a healthy Ian Null about twenty minutes. More than an hour later, he found a far-less obvious single door, over which the chalice logo stared down. Tugging the brass handle, it didn't budge. *You shouldn't have left the key with the teenager.* It was the lingering essence of Paolo that still disliked Lorrie Sheppard, even if Null had come to understand him in their time together. So much that he'd left the Junquer key in his pack before departing in the night. He hadn't told him. He hadn't told anyone. He didn't even understand himself why he'd chosen Lorrie to wield the device. *It's because you're a fool, Ian Null.*

No.

It was because neither Robbie nor Cadlen needed it.

Keep telling yourself that, coward.

Pushing Paolo's voice back into his subconscious, Null inspected the frame of the door. Unlike previous entryways, there didn't appear to be any electronics locking the door shut. The key wouldn't have made a difference. Null smirked at the irony. A door like this needed a different key.

The one in your pocket, fool.

Simon's pendant might work. It made sense—only a member of the Forty should have access. Inserting the lower stave of the pendant into a thin slot next to the handle and latch, the door clicked.

Before he took even one step inside, the smell nearly doubled him over. The ventilation must be shut off, Null reasoned. The entire stadium could have been powered down manually, or the backup fuel reserves had exhausted and it went dark all alone. He wrapped a torn rag from a spare shirt and wrapped it around his nose.

In the light of his lantern, he panned around a room adorned with several plush chaises and sofas. Paintings in patterned frames covered most of the wall space. To his left, a cold and dead fireplace yawned. Null imagined it ablaze, a snug warmth filling the room while the Ansati elders rested. Instead, it was cold and pungent. It didn't take long for Null to find the source.

Slumped on one of sofas was a dead Ansati, robe splayed open revealing gaping shot holes crawling with insect larvae. As expected, the eyes were removed. Upon closer inspection, a trail of blood led from another door at the rear of the room to the monk's final resting place. Null stopped only long enough to draw the cloak closed over the abdominal gun wounds. The second door wasn't latched, so Simon's key wasn't needed. He tucked it back into his pocket and instead drew his sidearm.

Beyond the second door, Null encountered a different rotten odour. The banquet hall opened in front of him, ceiling fans dead like those in the church they'd visited earlier. Statues occupied the four corners of the room, and all four couldn't have looked more different from each other. In one, a hooded woman crying red tears. Another, a horrifying figure with a goat's head, three fingers raised on one hand and holding a scepter in the other. An obese man sitting cross-legged, some smug grin across his fat face. And a wooden totem of a man with hard features, crowned with a long headdress of feathers. All four faced the center of the room and the long banquet table, still set for a mighty feast: Roast meats, bowls of fruit, containers with sauces and dressings, vegetables, stews, decanters with wine, shakers with seasonings. Silverware and plates at almost half the forty seats, most still heaped with a last meal for whomever had sat to eat. At the far end of the table, a broader chair with higher armrests and curving woodwork trim was drawn back from when its occupant had stood to leave.

You know who sat there. Remember? You left him to die.

"I treated as best I could." Null countered the voice of Paolo out loud. Brother Raël was the eldest of the Forty. He would have sat at the far side. Stumbling, Null passed the seats one by one, the stench of decay seeping in the spaces between his rag and his stubbled face. By the time he reached Raël's throne, Null's equilibrium wavered. He slumped into the old man's chair, looking down the length of the banquet. For an instant, he saw the Catholic Forty alive, peaceful, seated across from each other with knives and forks in hand. Candles lit. Drinks poured. Laughter shared.

He blinked, and all of that was gone. No Brothers or Sisters. No laughter. Only the mocking gaze of four statues from four corners of the world, offering nothing but indifference. They did nothing as Andreas slaughtered them at their most vulnerable—as they sat to eat together. From the evidence of blood spatter the length of the table, he had entered the room and opened fire quickly. The Brothers and Sisters wouldn't have been armed. Even if they were, they stood little chance.

Yet Raël survived. Long enough to convince you to come to this terrible place. And for what, Ian Null?

"To find my mother, *that* is what," Null seethed through gritted teeth. The old man had shown him nothing but kindness when they met in the cabin. In his waning strength, he had managed to convince Ian Null that Paolo Desantos was inextricable, inexorable. And that it wasn't a bad thing.

But that it would only make sense when he knew his history. All of it.

Null took another drink from his canteen. Somewhere in this room there would be another exit, possibly a stair that would lead into the center of the great wheel, into the heart of the Sanctum Occultus.

The belly of this beast.

88MHz

Monday, 9 July AC 0245
Minaret Tower, Moab
Lorrie Sheppard

High above Moab, Lorrie panned a full 360 degrees. Most of the city crouched in lush green foliage. Its caretakers allowed tall trees to grow and stretch, their branches joined like clasped hands. The old city core was dim from both the distance and the drab colours of steel and stone. He wasn't as high as the Hanging Gardens were to Capston. From the vast levels of agricultural engineering, the ground below was impossible to see with the naked eye, at least in any detail. Atop the radio tower, Lorrie would be able to spot someone walking in the immediate block. Except no one passed through. He closed his eyes and imagined looking through a seeing glass down on Capston, except the city was dead—devoid of the citizens, flora, anything that lived and breathed.

"Okay, let's see…" Lorrie mumbled to break the silence as he capped his canteen. The radio transmission room was circular, windows forming the upper half of the round walls. Half of the circumference was occupied by a series of control panels filled with dials, buttons, and levers. It resembled the cockpit of the Tan-Ro, only Captain Ferrer wasn't sitting in front of it. Lorrie hadn't thought about the lost pilot since before Ian Null had found him and his brothers. For the first time, it sank in that the pilot was dead, unlikely to ever be found. The thought jarred him to action.

Opening Ian's handheld, Lorrie thumbed the <BRIDGE> tab. Lights blinked, and the full schematics of the control panel replicated on his screen. Multiple options presented.

```
<MIN.P.A>
<RADIO>
<Q.ACCEL>
<ALERT>
```

The panel labeled as <ALERT> blinked. Tapping the access tab, Lorrie increased the scale so he could read the status bar. He didn't expect to understand any of it.

```
[Moab City Evacuation Alert. Activated 19 June.
                XL.BR.RAËL]
```

The dates weren't New Inland standard, so Lorrie couldn't determine how long ago the evacuation had been activated. What he could determine, however, was the person responsible. XL. Ian had explained that the letters were old numbers, that it was used to identify the Catholic Forty, the senior-most council of Ansati elders. BR. That had to stand for Brother, like Brother Simon. He didn't know how many of the Catholic Forty were Brothers, or if there were any women among their ranks. Were they Sisters? Did the killer slaughter them as viciously? Did they have children?

RAËL. It must have been his name. Her name? Whoever it was, they had access to the control tower, either remotely or up close. Lorrie saw no evidence anyone had been in the radio room recently. In any case, Raël activated an evacuation alert to the occupants of Moab. They either fled or were killed. Did the tower emit a siren? Or did the Ansati receive a signal on their personal devices? Either way, the evacuation alert had ended.

The alert served no further purpose, so Lorrie backed out of the tab and refocused on the other options. <RADIO> expanded at the touch of a finger.

```
[88MHz. VHF. Frequency Modulation. Air. Ground]
```

Lorrie didn't know much about radio frequency, but he knew that

New Inland communication standards were served over quantum accelerometer. As long as the two parties were connected, they could communicate anywhere across the continent instantaneously. Hyacynthe had severed the quantum connection with New Inland as part of its embargo, leaving Lorrie and his brothers with illegal correspondence through the Allens as the only means to contact Crystal. Maybe there was another way, after all. Maybe old radio waves could have kept them in contact.

"Okay, but what's the range of this old thing?" Lorrie flipped through a series of sub-tabs, but the further he tapped, the more confusing the information. He retreated to the <Q.ACCEL> tab, only for it to be a dead end. The quantum accelerometer was offline, and even Ian Null's fancy machine couldn't establish a remote connection. Returning to the <RADIO> tab, he tapped it to life, and the panel lights blinked welcoming green.

Through Ian's handheld, Lorrie tapped the frequency adjustor. 88 megahertz was the highest setting. Next, he pressed the activation button for the microphone. A small, mesh-covered hole crackled as though it were cracking its finger joints. A small red light blinked beneath the message screen.

[Transmission Open]

Shit, what do I say? Lorrie's mind raced. Who was he calling? How much time did he have? Should he identify himself?

[10. 9. 8…]

"We're in the Ansati city Moab. Everyone is dead. Our guide is dying, needs medicine. Anybody out there look for the high tower. Over."

[Transmission closed]

Lorrie couldn't tell if all of his message recorded. Tapping again and again on the <RADIO> tab, the application had frozen. If only he had prepared a script. Receding back to the main schematic window, Lorrie tapped the small broadcast icon.

[Radio Broadcast Loop. Activated 9 July. NULL]

The message was sent. The only thing Lorrie could do was wait. He slumped to the floor against the panel as the pain in his injured hand pulsed with his heartbeat. It didn't hurt while he had a mission to fulfill. Now, he had nothing but time to think about the likelihood of infection if he didn't get it cleaned. Shaking his canteen with his healthy hand, the last slosh of water would barely be a mouthful, let alone enough to clean his wound. The thought of climbing back down made him dizzy since he'd looked out the radio room windows.

Guess I'm staying put. He found the last strips of meat he and Ian had cured in the wild. It didn't help that there was leftover stew in Brother Simon's refrigerator. A quick search of the room yielded no rations, not even a stale crust of bread. Lorrie nibbled a corner of dried meat. *The rest might have to last a while.*

Lorrie managed to make the dried meat last two days. On the second day, he mustered the courage to unwrap the torn fabric that had been holding his sliced hand closed. Carefully peeling it back, he reopened the deep cut. It was deep red, crusted with yellow and white scabbing and leaking pus.

Drink the last of the water or clean the cut? Outside, grey clouds stretched across the sky. Rain would be welcome, but it might cause trouble for his looping transmission, still blinking on Ian's device. It didn't matter, because no rain fell. Worst case scenario, he'd piss in the empty canteen and… His stomach churned at the thought of using his own urine for either sustenance or for treating the wound. He fell asleep on the second night dreading having to decide the next morning.

He didn't have to.

Lorrie woke to the spattering of rain on the windows. A thin ladder reached through the ceiling of the radio room outside to the antennae.

He climbed, pushing open a smaller circular hatch. A rush of cold wind and rain poured over him, drenching his hair in minutes. Opening his mouth wide, Lorrie let the water rain over his face, stinging his eyes, following the crease of his mouth, collecting in a mouthful before he swallowed. His dry lips cracked and the metallic taste of blood mixed with the bitter, cool precipitation. Propping himself with his armpit, he unwound the bandage and let the water roll down the wound. He winced as it soaked the crusted scab, softening the infected tissue.

The thrumming of helicopter blades approaching distracted him from the pain. Lorrie laughed as the twin-bladed craft descended into view, floodlight beaming through the rain. For better or worse, at least he didn't have to climb back down.

Desiccation

Monday, 9 July AC 0245
Sanctum Occultus, Moab
Ian Null

Ian Null watched the decaying feast spread upon the Catholic Forty banquet table. In the days since the massacre, there was no one to clean the uneaten food. Without climate control, the meats had drawn flies, and within days, their planted larvae wriggled on the rancid flesh. In a feverish dream, Ian watched the natural decomposition in augmented speed. The flies buzzed louder. The maggots writhed like rippling waves. The leafy vegetables wilted and twisted, changing colour and emitting noxious odours. Simply turning his head caused a half-second delay while his consciousness caught up. Everything in front of him was animated as though it were a holographic projection.

Fever dreams had begun within days of Ian's exposure to the leaking nuke-cell. He'd shed his clothing and immersed himself in the nearest stream. He'd swapped out his Motherland-issue rucksack, keeping only the indispensable items. Even then, he wiped everything down and discarded the rag. And he began the regimen of Radiogardasse immediately. Ian gave himself the best chance of staving off radiation poisoning.

He knew it could all be for naught. Jamiss had endured significantly worse exposure, and he probably didn't know to cleanse himself as quickly as possible. When they'd last spoken, Ian Null lied to him. He'd kept the medicine to himself, for the long journey ahead. If symptoms didn't present, he could make it through the seam with plenty left for any unforeseen events.

Being tied to a derelict thrasher's nuke-cell by bumbling brigands was about as unforeseen as anyone could guess.

In the aftermath of his stop at Farbend, his memories became hallucinations. It usually happened when it was quiet, when he had time alone with his thoughts, with the antagonizing voice of Paolo Desantos inserting himself into his decision-making. The lines blurred between Paolo as a construct of his subconsciousness, and Paolo as a separate being entirely, non-corporeal. Paolo chided him constantly. Early on, Ian could suppress him. But it was getting more and more difficult.

And what was more troubling was Paolo was often right.

How fitting—Ian Null, Lord of Decay! I propose a toast…

Ian gripped a goblet half-full of wine. Fruit flies dispersed in a cloud of black specks. He was thirsty, but not that thirsty. Further up the table, a bottle still corked stood above the serving platters like a minaret. It was likely the only unspoiled food or drink in the room.

Sloshing the wine onto the floor, he reached for the bottle. The cork only popped after he latched his teeth onto it, twisting until brittle bits chipped off and stuck to his lips. He spilled about half a goblet's worth before filling the drinking vessel. Two long gulps burned in his throat and leaked over his partially bearded chin. His eyelids fluttered, and for a moment, the wine had become blood, rust-tinged and bitter. The fluid languished in the pit of his stomach, coagulating and leaking its alcohol into his veins.

Gathering second-wind energy, Ian hoisted himself out of Brother Raël's chair. Around him, in the light of his lantern, what appeared to be wine sloshed stains were in fact blood, or the remnant of blood after the bodies were dragged away. All trails led to a rear wall with the bust of some historical figure he didn't recognize. Tirel Desantos had secret passages beneath his quarters that led under the earth and outside of Motherland. Often they were accessed by a hidden lever or knob.

Ian placed a sticky hand on the face of the bust, covering its eyes and nose. With a twist, a door clicked and the wall panel swung outward. Most likely, a Catholic Forty pendant would be needed to reenter from the other side. Double checking his pocket for Simon's *crux ansata*, he stepped into the darkness and nearly toppled over a thin, iron handrail. The lantern showed him that the fall would have been a long one.

The spiral stair wound like a corkscrew downward, into a cavernous darkness even his lamp had trouble illuminating. Every bare-footed step peeled from the blood trail like removing an adhesive bandage. Seventeen seats, not including Raël's, had shown evidence of a killing. By the spatter range, they'd been shot. All of them except Rael, who had suffered only slashing wounds when he'd stumbled into Ian's refuge. For reasons unknown, Andreas had shown restraint with the eldest of the Forty.

Someone had laboured to drag all of the slain down a spiral staircase at least three stories. Raël couldn't have done it alone. Andreas couldn't have had a change of heart. Once outside the Sanctum Occultus, he'd left his victims where they'd fallen. Ian held the center pole as he wound down the stairs, fighting off vertigo as he reached the floor of the lowest level. The room was vast. Scanning around him, he spotted a fountain-shaped oil diffuser. Flicking the briquette lighter, the lamp burst to life, bathing the area in softer light. All around him, arched openings like mouths greeted treadmills. Ranked columns of cut firewood partitioned the room into small cubicles for each furnace. A lingering sweet smoke laced the decay that filled the chamber. He didn't need to look far for the source.

Seventeen bodies were lain side by side, supine, hands crossed gently upon their torsos, concealing most of the gun wounds. Of the seventeen, ten were men and seven women. All had hoods drawn, cradling their lifeless heads. Faces expressionless, save for one characteristic that left Ian puzzled.

All seventeen still had their eyes.

Andreas would have plucked the eyes. What about it, Null? Figure that one out.

"Raël." Who else could have done it? The bodies were moved from the banquet hall down into the chamber where the Ansati burned bodies. Not burned—*desiccated*. Before a body could be interred in the Ossuary, it had to be treated. Ian stumbled over to one of the columns of piled wood. By the sweetness, it could have been birch, maybe a fruit wood of some sort that was plentiful in the area. These weren't furnaces at all. They were drying kilns for desiccating the dead.

Ian pulled the half-drank bottle of wine and gulped a mouthful. He gazed over the bodies of the Catholic Forty, peaceful in their dead repose. His head swam, and in a blink, the Ansati corpses became Motherland sappers in an old barn in the lake region. Yael was dead. Paolo had to decide what to do with the dying soldiers, teeming with red tide.

There was no other way. They were dead men walking.

"You killed them."

We killed them.

"*I* killed them."

Semantics.

Ian tilted the bottle upside down and poured its contents down his gullet. The bottle fell to the cement floor, shattering around his blood-sticky bare feet. How fitting if he were to just lay down beside the monks, clasping his hands above his navel and closing his eyes one last time.

Lay down and die if you must. Reaching the west coast was a foolish plan, anyway.

"I have a job to do." Ian stepped across the shards of wine bottle glass towards another door adorned with the skull and bones logo he'd seen on the great wheel. The Desiccatorium wheeled around him.

The Ossuary.

Karina Desantos.

"Mother."

One Law

Monday, 9 July AC 0245
Farbend Trading Camp
Crystal Sheppard

Crystal paced in tight circles, hoping the puzzle pieces swirling in her head would fall into place, or at least in a way that made sense. In less than five minutes, the trader woman Aynslie had revealed to her two equally astonishing bits of news. Ian Null had passed through the region, and in dire health. Lorrie was in Moab, and sending off a distress signal. Ozarck, be damned. She had a new destination.

"Let me get this straight. You want to go *to* Moab?" Hamm stood out of arm's reach of her. "You saw the Reapers on the move. If *they* don't want to stay there—"

"Then why is my *brother* there, Hamm?" Crystal's voice shrieked. She wasn't doing nearly as well keeping herself together as she'd hoped. "If Moab is so damned dangerous that the Ansati had to leave, why would anyone want to go at all, unless they were forced to?" Where Lorrie went, likely Robbie and Cadlen followed.

"You don't even know if that is your brother! Besides, aren't they supposed to be in Ozarck?"

"I should have been there weeks ago, and here I am!" The magna-rail would have delivered her to Ozarck in a day. From the moment she was kidnapped, it was one new twist after another. She could have traveled to and from Ozarck half a dozen times if things just went as planned. If she'd learned anything in the outside world, it was to not count on anything. Or anyone.

Hamm crossed his arms. "Well, I think it's stupid to go there."

"And I didn't ask you." Crystal stormed over to the shuttle. The driver was preparing to leave the makeshift Farbend camp. Her gear was already packed except for the spare medicines and food rations she bought from Aynslie. She couldn't buy and Radiogardasse. But if she could travel by coach, and the driver kept the cab and cabin closed, they could pass through a seam relatively unexposed.

Crystal rapped on the window until the coach driver rolled it down. "How much to get me through the seam to Moab?" He laughed at her request.

"More than you can afford."

"Oh yeah?" Crystal opened her handheld and keyed into her Rust bank account. The five-figure offer made the driver's eyes nearly burst.

"If you can give me 10% in La Cumbre credit, you have a drive, lady."

Crystal played with the numbers. "Done. We leave in five."

"Engine's already warm…" The coach driver rolled up the window. Hamm had arrived next to her during the negotiations.

"Listen. You can buy your way to Moab, but the Reapers—they ain't interested in your money. And neither is the radiation."

Crystal knew he was speaking the truth. But it was his truth. Not hers. "You're a good man, Hamm. But this is where our paths separate." She opened the rear hatch of the coach and climbed inside. The stowaway who'd help fend off the brigands had left as soon as they'd pulled into Farbend. She hadn't even asked him his name. It didn't matter.

"There's only one law in this world—in *any* world. Survive, whatever the cost."

Hamm nodded. He raised an open hand as she closed the door.

The journey through the seam was the least eventful of her journey, by far. It was also the loneliest. She huddled in the centre of the cargo bay, replaying everything that had happened since she found out the Sheppard Family Inn had been blown to bits. She was the last to know, it seemed. Even Monsieur Laurent, her most trusted benefactor had been dishonest. He had proven to be no better than anyone she'd met in her travels since.

Hamm, Duncam, Hewer.

Aynslie.

Ian Null.

What part did he have to play in all of this? Handsome yet awkward stranger buys medicine for treating radiation exposure. Pays her an exorbitant amount of money—enough to more than make up for the lost Sheppard Inn. But that was all a stretch. How could Ian Null have known who she was…

Unless he was the one who blew up the inn. And in some show of conscience, he tried to make it right with money. Crystal laughed. The irony wasn't lost on her.

It was Ian Null who'd warned Aynslie and the Farbend traders to get away from the radiation leak. The one that had killed Hewer's son, Jamiss. Again, how would he have known…

Unless he was there when it happened. And if he was, he'd need more than the supply of Radiogardasse he'd bought at Lacraie. He'd need urgent medical attention. Did he think he'd find it in Moab—a city smack in the middle of a seam?

Lorrie had said their guide was dying and needed medicine. Ian Null couldn't have found her brothers on the outside, right? Captain Ling had assured Laurent that she was moving them to Ap-Oz, safe from whoever was looking for them…

Unless something changed. Unless they hit roadblocks just like me. Robbie, Lorrie, and Cadlen—and maybe the Connelly family—were in the wilderness, trying to find their way home, or maybe to Ozarck. Maybe they were expecting to meet her there. Something had to have happened that caused them to need a guide. And who other than someone who knew who they were?

Ian Null hadn't found the Sheppard siblings by accident.

Unless it was an accident. Pure chance. He showed empathy the night we met at Lacraie. He would do the same for my brothers, wouldn't he?

An intercom crackled, interrupting her cycling thoughts. "Passed through the seam; we're in clean land now. Moab's only a few hours."

Crystal stretched out her legs and cracked her finger knuckles. She was going to find Lorrie, and Robbie and Cad. She was going to find Ian Null. And if he's still alive, he would answer all her questions.

We Lay in the Same Grave

Sábado, 9 abril, NE 237
Royal Sanctuary, Motherland
Paolo Desantos

Paolo kept his back as straight as a four-year old could on the hard, wooden bench. He hated this place. The Royal Sanctuary was not a place just any Motherlander could pray—only Eminence De Léon, or those he deemed worthy.

Paolo's father had explained that it was an honour that His Eminence had taken the Desantos family under his wing, like *La Golondriña* had adopted the free people from the mother land so many years ago. In truth, his father spent more time in De Léon's court than he did with his wife and son. Mother had to take care of the household alone. And heavy with child, it was difficult. Young Paolo did as best he could, of course, sweeping the floors, cleaning the kitchen, and feeding the animals. And when Father returned, the joyful character seen by Motherland next to His Eminence became something else. At best, he was sullen, withdrawn, and mean in his sideways remarks.

The first time he'd attended a service in the Royal Sanctuary, Paolo was confused. Old men in draperies and sashes spoke in riddles, and sometimes in the old tongue, which Paolo only learned piecemeal from his mother. Father had never learned the language. His Eminence didn't seem to mind—Paolo didn't know if even the sovereign of Motherland knew it. Regardless, it was common enough that any amount of time in the streets was bound to blend into the spoken tongue.

The ritual involved a lot of standing and sitting. Repeating words, even if you didn't understand them. The faith had nothing to do with understanding, anyway. Father only dragged his family to the Sanctuary for the optics.

On his first visit, one of the priests hollered loudly before lowering his voice in a key that penetrated his chest and made his ears ring. In an effort to block out the sound, Paolo cupped his hands over his ears, only for his father to yank them away, planting them firmly at his side. Father's eyes pierced him in silent fury. After they returned home, his father's open hand across his bare buttocks left a stinging that remained numb for days. As he laid in bed on his belly, Paolo decided that it was a terrible place, and that he would only set foot inside when absolutely necessary.

There was no more necessary time to return than for the funeral of his mother.

Only his father was permitted to sit on the nearest bench to the casket. It had been built of wood from Karina Desantos's *spiritus arbor*, a tree planted upon her birth in the Spirit Gardens just beyond Motherland's walls. The tradition held that parents planted a special tree in the Gardens to celebrate the arrival of a newborn, and that the child would grow with it, watering and nurturing their spiritual twin throughout their life. And when they approached death, the wood was harvested and crafted into the final burial casket, so the two could lie together in the same grave for eternity. Paolo took no comfort in this.

Sitting behind his father in the second bench, Eminence De Léon sat next to him in his thick, royal robes and other accoutrements. He smelled of several perfumes in a pungent mix. His Eminence draped an arm over his shoulder in an attempt at offering the comfort his father could not. He wheezed, smacking his dry lips and mumbling incoherently. At least it was quiet.

"Rem…arkable woman, your mother," De Léon drawled. His words often stretched as though he temporarily forgot how to finish them. "Kindest sssoul."

Paolo already knew that. Tirel Desantos knelt on the bench ahead of him, bowed low enough that it appeared as though his head disappeared. In times of sorrow, Father was especially volatile. De Léon must have known it. He never came down from his balcony seating for anything.

"And the infant… sssuch a losssss…" Paolo had tried to forget about the stillborn child whose birth caused his mother's death. He'd grown to resent the forthcoming baby. All it had done was add an extra burden on his mother, and when it took her life, Father cursed the lifeless fetus. He wouldn't even allow for a funeral service. You don't honour murderers, he'd said.

The memory was riddled with inconsistencies. At first, De Léon was wearing a garish purple and blue mottled costume. But the colour changed to blue mixed with pale yellow. Memories from so young in life were bound to distort, to fade.

They were bound to lie.

In one instant, Paolo heard Tirel sobbing in agony. In the next, the mournful howl of the priest belting a terrible psalm. In another, he couldn't picture Tirel at all, only the casket, impossibly high for him to even see if there was a body inside. Maybe she wasn't dead after all. Maybe it was all a horrible ruse. Maybe she would come back someday.

Tuesday, 10 July AC 0245
Sanctum Occultus, Moab
Ian Null

Shaking his head, Ian Null pressed on, into the vast open space the Ansati called the Ossuary. He found another oil diffuser of the same design as that in the Desiccatorium. Setting it alight, the Ossuary burst to life with rich burgundies and natural wooden and earthen hues. The ceilings vaulted high above, arched in intricate symmetry. Tall stacks of marbled drawers formed aisles, and ladders mounted to rails with wheels allowed for caretakers and visitors alike to access the plots. They numbered in the thousands—tens of thousands, maybe. The cavern beneath the ancient stadium likely stretched well beyond its above-ground form. The remains of so many dead people were preserved by the cleansing fire and smoke, then placed in plots with whatever belongings the Ansati saw fit to preserve. It wasn't enough to keep photographs, or to write about them—although they did as much. The remains *themselves* were considered sacred, and were treated as such.

Ian's head bobbed as though his neck were a spring. His reflexes were slower than ever. It could have been the wine. It was probably the radiation sickness. *Not far now, Ian.*

Staggering, he made his way to the center of the chamber. Wide tables with chairs, and an office-styled work area with a wall of machines formed the fulcrum of the facility. Here is where an attending archivist would normally be working. There was no one. Anywhere.

As he slumped on the countertop, it occurred to him he'd made a terrible mistake. In leaving the key with Lorrie Sheppard, he'd left behind his best chance of tapping into the database. Eyeing the rows and rows of plots, he had no idea how he was going to find Karina Desantos among the skeletons of so many.

Worse, upon closer examination, the boxes were labeled in Roman numerals, just like the Catholic Forty used to inscribe their pendant keys.

You could read the numerals to ten thousand at one time.

"No, *you* could."

Enough! When will you realize that I am not the one you are fleeing?

Ian shook his head and fell off the edge of the counter, striking his temple against the corner of the nearest studying table. His vision blurred like a video streaming white noise. When he focused, a woman stood above him, veil over her head, moaning. He'd seen her in the streets after he'd left the Sheppards behind.

Like you left Motherland behind. Your family. Your heritage…

"Tirel Desantos… He is no longer my father…"

The shape of the veiled woman rippled and faded. There was no woman. In the absence of the spectre, Ian noticed splotches of blood on the tiled floor. They could have been footprints. *Ghosts do not leave prints.*

Ian pulled himself to his feet, his legs wobbling. Following the uneven blood stains, he found an aisle occupied by the dead body of an Ansati woman, eyeless and slumped against a drawer.

MCMLXXXV

The drawer was partially open. Ian gripped his fingers over the top, pulling backward. It was heavier than his conscience. Peering inside, a careful arrangement of clean, white bones lay on a velvet lining. A wooden box, deep mahogany and smoky, bore an engraving.

Karina Desantos

Ian reeled at his mother's name and collapsed to the floor next to the dead Ansati. A heaving wave of vomit erupted from his cracked lips; blood and bile mixed with sour wine spilled all over him. He reached for the pills Crystal Sheppard had sold him. They were in his rucksack, left behind in the concourse... or maybe the banquet hall. It didn't matter. It was too late.

Paolo...

A voice he barely remembered sang like *La Golondriña* in the spring. Through his slitted eyes, the Ansati woman had changed shape, and Karina Desantos knelt over him. Her smile warmed his cold body.

Paolo. You don't have to run anymore, my son.

"Don't have to... run... Mother..."

Rest, Paolo. You're forgiven.

"I... I'm sorry..."

Karina Desantos touched her tiny hand on his cheek. *You were just a boy. Just a boy...*

Ian Null. Paolo Desantos. One and the same. He closed his eyes, waiting for Paolo's voice to retort. Nothing. When he opened them, his mother was gone, and the body of the Syballine Sister, eyeless and lifeless, made no sound, no movement, nothing.

Submitting to the poisoning, Paolo's arms fell limp, and his head rested against the side of Karina Desantos's plot. There was nothing more to learn. Brother Raël must have known he was dying, and that he was simply providing him the way home to the family of whom he'd been robbed at such a young age. Perhaps he would lay in the same grave, forever in his mother's arms. The thought covered him in peace.

Ian! Ian Null! Please, wake up! Ian!
He could have sworn it was the voice of Crystal Sheppard.

Sunflower

Wednesday, 11 July AC 0245
Moab
Crystal Sheppard

This is as far as I go." The coach driver stopped driving at the sight of a dead body, flayed and face down on the outskirts of Moab. He wouldn't leave the cab. Crystal slung her bag over her shoulder and leaped from the open mouth of the cargo hold. She couldn't blame him. If traveling into the forbidden city of the Reapers wasn't unsettling enough, coming across a dead one laying in the road would. Crystal stared at the robed victim. Her heart sank. She'd seen plenty of death in the outside world. It was almost becoming routine.

Thanking him with a quick La Cumbre credit transfer, the coach turned and retreated quicker than it had arrived. Dust whirled in its wake, and when it settled, Crystal took in the silence of the farthest reaches of the fabled Ansati territory. Far in the distance, a city core reached above the hazy horizon. Swaths of green intermingled with houses, eerily uniform in design and arrangement. A road stretched forward, swallowed by an outer suburb. She had a long walk ahead.

Unique to this area, however, was a wide stretch of farmed land grown tall with leafy green, spiked buds reaching from the top of the stalks. As she moved further along the dusty road, more and more patches of the tall plants splotched the land around houses, roads, and other cultivated plots. Up close, she was certain they were sunflowers not yet in bloom. She closed her eyes and images of the robust crop plants shone like a million suns. The public garden in Hyacynthe had a modest patch of them, and ingredients were harvested for all sorts of medicinal purposes in Lacraie. She'd even seen them in the Hanging Gardens when she was a young girl. They were a hardy species. Evidently the Ansati recognized their worth. In a matter of weeks, the fields of green would blossom into yellow for kilometers.

As the afternoon bled into early evening, Crystal had passed two more bodies in the streets that had gone from dirt to stone. Urban blocks spread like spider webs in all directions. The rumours were true. Moab was empty—at least it appeared to be. No faces peeked through curtains. No one was working in their gardens, moving goods in carts, or playing with dogs or children. Not even that eerie feeling of unseen eyes following her.

She chose the nearest house after her stomach rumbled. At the top of the front step, she nearly knocked. Old Crystal would have been embarrassed to knock at a stranger's door. Today, she placed her ear to the door, and with no sounds from inside, she opened it and stepped inside. One of the dead bodies she'd found might have been the owner. Maybe it was the Ansati that had drifted through Carroway. Maybe it didn't matter.

To her relief, the kitchen was still stocked with preserves and non-perishables. With everything available, she could have prepared a feast. Robbie would have been impressed. Crystal served herself a jar of pickles, sweet and tangy, likely harvested from the proprietor's own crops. It tasted fresher than the prepackaged food from the domes. Everything in the outside world tasted different, as if all food manufactured in the cities had been skimmed of some magical ingredient.

Using one of Hewer's tricks, she took a glass-paned picture and dropped it on the floor inside the doorway. With the heel of her boot, she ground the shards into smaller flakes, spreading them in a wide, thin radius. If anyone entered while she was sleeping, the steps on broken glass would alert her. She slept well with the insurance of her rudimentary perimeter alarm.

Crystal woke before dawn. The broken glass remained untouched. Even if no one was coming back, she couldn't leave the mess behind. After sweeping up the larger pieces, she gathered some more preserve jars and a second water canteen. Light in the eastern sky began to bleed through the dark blue. She had a lot of ground to cover.

She passed dozens of houses just like the one that had sheltered and nourished her. Birds with long wingspans whirled, likely hunting for small prey, or possibly finding more dead bodies in Moab's abandoned streets. She crept off the open roads, keeping closer to gardens and hedges in case someone was looking for her. Laurent was still looking for her. The thought of the Hyacynthien officers who'd tried to have their way with her still wandering around made her shudder. The overcast skies didn't help.

The shuffling of feet from somewhere up the street didn't either.

You can't hurt me if I see you first. Crystal glided across the lawns of houses, peering around the corner. Staggering up the street, a woman covered in a thick veil and robe paid her no mind. Crystal watched her teeter before correcting herself, and move directionless, one foot in front of the other. A breeze had picked up, so she couldn't tell if the woman was making any sound. Whenever she drifted too close to the edge of the street, she altered her trajectory, remaining on the cobbled stone. Whoever she was, she made no effort to hide. She might not even have been aware of Crystal's presence.

"I see you... I see you...," the woman murmured and Crystal's heart skipped. She stood from her crouch, moving in measured steps closer to the ghostly figure. If she'd seen her by now, and had not run or called for help, maybe the woman wasn't a threat.

Everything out here is a threat.

Crystal kept about twenty meters between herself and her quarry for several blocks. The woman kept moving, slowly and steadily, turning corners and changing directions as if she had a digital map guiding her. She continued murmuring, "I see you... I see you..." She couldn't have been talking about Crystal. Not once had she turned her head.

"I see you too," Crystal called out to the woman. She didn't stop walking. Quickening her pace, Crystal closed to within a few paces. "Are you hurt?"

The veiled woman finally came to a stop, teetering in place. She didn't reply.

"I'm looking for my brothers. Have you seen them?"

"I see you… I see you…"

Crystal huffed. "You can't see anything through your veil. *Madame*, please. Have you seen—"

"The quiet one…"

Quiet. It had to be Cadlen. "My little brother, yes—he's very quiet. Where is he?"

The woman murmured unintelligibly. The clouds overhead were darkening quickly and in the distance, thunder rumbled. "I don't have time! Please! My *brothers!*" Crystal stepped within arm's reach and grasped her frail arm. With little force, she turned the veiled woman. Beneath the veil, her face was wrapped from her head down to just above her mouth. *She's blind.*

"Brothers… *brothers…*" Behind the fabric, her lips trembled, split and scabbed. "I see you… *I know you… Brothers…*"

Crystal dropped her bag and opened the flaps, searching for her medical kit. Whoever this woman was, she was in poor health and not in her right mind. Brothers. Was she just echoing her own words? Or was she talking about her *Ansati Brothers?* Perhaps the slaughter of her kin had reduced her to a traumatic state of shock. Was *anything* of consequence passing through her mind?

In the minutes she spent digging through her kit of bandages and ointments, the woman had wandered startlingly fast up the street, uttering nothing further. Her gait had quickened and straightened, no longer staggering, as though she'd woken from a trance and panicked.

"Wait! I can help you! I can treat your injuries!" The woman whisked away, turning a corner and disappearing like a phantom. Crystal's eyes watered. She'd offered her services to Aynslie and the Farbend traders. But she hadn't been able to save Hewer's boy, Jamiss. Everything was a coin toss, a blind choice, a shot in the dark. Some you win, and some you lose. The outside world was as beautiful as it was ugly. Maybe one day, Crystal would be reduced to wandering aimlessly, blind and insane, drifting across the land like so many other ghosts, invisible to all who chose not to see.

The first drops of rain spattered the stone streets, and Crystal clutched the medical kit in her fingers, gazing in the direction the veiled woman had fled. In the distance, a high tower stood guard over a domed stadium in the heart of Moab. The thrumming of helicopter blades sputtered. Crystal wiped the rain and tears from her eyes.

Lorrie had sent a radio signal. The tower sprouted a tall antenna, like a solitary sunflower stalk without a floret. Only her brother's distress call had radiated from it like rays of sun. The rotary humming intensified, and in a crack of thunder and flash of lightning, the craft descended, pouring a white floodlight over her. The blind woman must have heard it first. And her reaction was to run.

As the craft lowered, the twin blades whipped and whirled the rain on her face like a cyclone.

Reborn

How about I make lentil soup this time?" Robbie dug through the pantry and retrieved a jar of beans, sealed tight and dry. "Unless you want more barley—I think there's still leftover…" The house was so much quieter without Lorrie. Somehow he knew he'd come back to Simon's house and Lorrie wouldn't be there. Since when had Lorrie ever followed instructions?

Cadlen sat at the small kitchen table, pencil in hand, narrowing his focus on the tiniest of details of the church where Robbie had found him. In the empty city at night, the glow of coloured windows shone like a beacon to him. No one trying to hide would have turned on the church lights. Maybe the veiled woman was there. It turned out that Cadlen had found his way there, turned on the lights, and began to draw everything he saw, from the intricate patterns in the wood paneling, to the mottled panes of glass, to the altar and its adornments. And when those details were finished, he drew worshipers, unnamed patrons of all ages, as if he were staring at them from another moment in time.

"Your picture looks amazing, Cad." Robbie added the beans to the boiling broth. "But why the church?"

Cadlen shrugged his shoulders. It was the same answer as every other time Robbie asked him about his art.

"Well, I think Brother Simon would have loved it, too." In the brief time he'd spent in Moab, Robbie had admired the Ansati appreciation of art and culture. And the longer he stayed in Simon's house, the more he felt as though he'd known him. He must have been a kind person. Attentive, learned, patient. He would have been in awe of Cadlen's skill. Robbie hoped that Simon would have been happy to have provided the brothers food and shelter. If only the rest of the world understood Ansati charity.

They hadn't lifted their spoons for the first taste of lentil soup when that familiar Tan-Ro twin blade rush filled the air outside. Cadlen pursed his lips and narrowed his eyes as though it made him hear more clearly. Robbie dropped the spoon into the bowl, splashing broth onto the table.

"Get to the bedroom, Cad." There was no telling whether the approaching aircraft was a friend or a foe. Tan-Ro transports were signature Capston craft. But who was piloting it?

Cadlen shook his head and ran into the living room.

"You know, I expect that from Lorrie—not you!" Robbie followed, rounding the corner into the living room still piled high in Simon's collections. He couldn't argue with him. Whoever had touched down in the street outside likely knew they were inside. Hiding wouldn't have made any difference. All they could hope was that whoever was about to come through the door weren't the same people who had tried to kill them in the first place.

The door swung open. A gust of wind from the twin blades gushed into the house, blowing pictures and papers around the living room. The familiar face of Captain Shore, hidden behind thick goggles and headgear over his ears, greeted them with a smile of relief.

"Word has it there's leftover soup!"

Robbie laughed. "Fresh batch on the stove, too!" He grasped the Capston Captain's hand. "If you like lentils, that is."

"Only *you* could find the worst ingredients…" Lorrie stepped around Shore and smiled. "But I'm sure it's the best in the neighbourhood."

Robbie looked at his younger brother. They'd been apart for less than a day, but the look in his eye made it seem like a year. Robbie swallowed his regrets and opened his arms. Lorrie fell into them in the biggest hug they'd ever shared.

"I'm sorry, Lor."

"Forget it. I'm sorry too." Lorrie pulled one hand away, bandaged from his fingertips to his wrist.

"*Damn*, what happened?"

Lorrie held the gauze-wrapped hand up palm first. "Cut it up pretty good. Hurt like you wouldn't believe. But I'll be okay."

Cadlen rushed into the circle and wrapped his arms around Captain Shore.

"How do you do, Cadlen?" Shore rustled his thick hair.

"Don't worry about *me*, Cad!" Lorrie retorted. Cadlen released his grip on Shore and turned to face his brother. The two smiled at each other—another first. Cadlen brushed his fingers over the gauze.

"Clean as can be. I had the best possible care."

As if on cue, Lorrie turned to the front door. A woman with wavy, messed hair and dirty outsider clothes stepped into view. She carried a small travel pack on her shoulder and a cautious look on her face.

"Robbie… Cad…" Crystal's eyes widened and she dropped her bag to the floor with a thud. Cadlen ran to his sister. Next to her, he'd grown a lot in the four years since they'd last seen each other. Robbie's heart ached and he steadied himself against Simon's work desk.

"You're so *big*! And this hair—Robbie, I *told* you, get it cut!" Crystal buried her youngest brother's face into her shoulder, cradling the back of his head like she was cuddling a newborn. Robbie looked to each of his three siblings, all in the same place for the first time in four years. All three older, all three reborn.

Three more men entered the house as the Tan-Ro engines whined and decelerated. Robbie recognized two of them as forensics officers from news footage of the Sheppard Inn attack. The third he'd met before in Holt Tower. He was decked from head to toe in heavy combat fatigues. His usually stern face showed an expression of relief.

"Good to see you, Robbie." Steven Reekan pulled off his goggles. "Now, where's that soup I keep hearing about?"

Nullify

☥

Inside the barn, light hid in corners, timid and terrified. Rancid corpses and manure and stale hay. There was no more suitable place for Yael to commit his crime. In the shadows of light's abandonment, the girl had lost all will to fight. She cried a low, mournful dirge. Yael ripped away her clothing, her thin armour. In the absence of light, nothing remained between them. He didn't even have to touch her—a part of her that had been hers alone was already gone. The light in her eyes extinguished. Paolo Desantos searched for her light, but it was nowhere to be found. Yael descended upon her like cancer.

With the squeeze of a trigger, the cancer was eradicated, but the damage it caused remained. The girl didn't even try to cover herself. Paolo shrouded her with her torn clothes as if this pitiful act could bring back anything she'd lost. He opened his mouth, but words didn't come. In the girl's eyes he saw open holes, like freshly dug graves. She clambered backwards, as if Paolo were just the next Yael, ready to finish what had begun. By survival instinct alone, she held the torn shirt against her breasts, scrambled to her feet like a bloody, newborn fawn, and fled, naked as she came into the world.

She will never forget his face. If only he could have seen hers.

In the baking sun, where the light exposed everything, Paolo Desantos crept behind dilapidated buildings waiting for the right person, who arrived in the form of an orphaned private called Wrengel. A ward, just like Paolo's father. Promised the world, but given fairy-tales. Stories about how his father had been killed on the job, and that Paolo Desantos was to blame. Forced to work hard labour in Allentown, he drew the short straw once again. With every swing of his pick, his hatred swelled, waiting for the perfect opportunity to present itself.

It did, in the round, red form of an apple. The fruit was so tempting, the hand that offered it meant nothing.

Instead of squeezing a trigger, Paolo murdered Wrengel with eloquence, with carefully sequenced rhetoric. The apple was not poisoned. The poetry that heralded it delivered the dose. Wrengel died wearing his killer's uniform. In death, he wouldn't be remembered. No one even noticed he was missing.

The tinkerer who scurried underground in his lair, festering with boils and carved in scars, spent his final days and years seething over the injustices of the surface world. Paolo pinched his nose to keep out the stench of living rot. There is usually an underlying smell of nature in the decaying process. Not in this place. The putrefaction in Junquer's lair reeked of an unnatural contamination of the body and of the spirit. Even rats avoided this place. And in his final words, he spoke of his desire to be consumed by the filth, to be interred beneath his life's work, where no one would ever find him or remember him. As if his very existence was the greatest profanity.

Paolo Desantos nullified the living dead man as the first step in nullifying himself.

So why did it hurt so much when he left Jamiss to die? The chiding voice of Paolo Desantos in the back of Ian Null's mind urged him to euthanize the boy before he turned into the Junquer, a walking corpse with peeling skin and misanthropy in his heart. But he couldn't do it. Not because it was right, but because Paolo told him he should. Instead, he watched the terrified boy with gravestone eyes scurry into the bushes as though he'd been violated at gunpoint in a dark, decay-ridden barn.

Only this time, Ian Null would never forget his face, or his name. He imagined Jamiss in Paolo's uniform, standing at attention, so proud of his country and his title. Pitifully unaware of the lies that propped up his fantasy.

And then, interrupting his first full sleep in years, Raël of the Ansati stumbled upon him, wheezing and spitting blood, holding closed slash wounds as if they had any chance of healing back together. The old priest spoke in riddles, with foolish optimism and childlike naivety. He thought he could convince Ian Null that Paolo Desantos still lived. That he was a good man, no less. That he'd been swinging the pick axe at the rubble for as long as he could remember, and that he'd only needed the right apple to be offered to him. That kind words are sometimes just that. For a sliver of a second, Ian Null wanted to end Raël's life before even one more poisoned word was uttered.

He could not.

Only this time, it felt right. Staying his hand and sparing the old man changed something in him. He'd been offered a purpose. Fleeing to the west coast was never a purpose, only an excuse. Raël gave him no answers. He offered instead a means to find them.

That means led to the final resting place of Karina Desantos, a mother he knew only by secondary memories and inferences. But not before confronting more ghosts from Paolo Desantos's terrible wake.

The Sheppard brothers were only sketches when he gazed upon Cadlen's portrait in the lobby of the Inn. In that moment, the family was together, alive. Julia and Robert were dead, but they lived on in the picture, in the rendering of a young child, behind whose eyes they still lived in some manner. If only he could remember Karina in her youthful beauty forever, not just in the distorted, faded snapshot of a young boy poisoned by his father's cruelty.

The Sheppards represented all the good that remained in this world. Ian Null realized he had to do what he could to preserve it. So they wouldn't decay. To keep the Yaels away, and the poisoned fruit from their lips. To shelter them from both the unforgiving light and the blanket of darkness.

Maybe Junquer had given him his new name on purpose. Paolo Desantos— subtracter, cleaner, nullifier.

Null.

☥

Wednesday, 11 July AC 0245
Sanctum Occultus, Moab
Ian Null

Ian! Ian Null!

"Please wake up, Ian!"

His eyes strained under the weight of his lids. Light seeped in the slit and the tangle of his lashes. The smell of decay assaulted his senses, bringing tears to his stinging eyes and befouling his nostrils. Staring down at his pathetic carcass, Crystal Sheppard placed her soft hands on his cheeks. She stared directly into his eyes. Hers were a soft blue, pure water on a peaceful bay. Wisps of hair tumbled alongside her cheek. Her voice pleaded for him to summon the strength to stay alive, just for a little while. His eyes opened wide for the first time in memory; he nodded as much as his neck allowed.

He stayed alert long enough for Steven Reekan's officers to administer the intravenous line, cover his mouth and nose with a breathing apparatus, and arrange him on a flat spinal board. As the officers called Simmons and Merrick hoisted him off the Ossuary floor,

he could have sworn that the veiled woman he'd mistaken for his long-
dead mother watched.

Homecoming

Domingo, 9 agosto NE 233
Chapel of St. Jude
Tirel Desantos

As the months stretched into years, Tirel succeeded in learning how to subdue his red episodes for all the right people at the right times. His Eminence befriended him, holding him high among the other wards. It was a weakness too good to be true. He learned that so long as he showed the foolish young ruler unwavering loyalty, he was easily influenced. Wards were seldom granted the freedoms Tirel enjoyed, such as the ability to leave the city walls unaccompanied. Eventually he found his way back to the ruins of Jude. Fallow fields, visibly ruined by the poisoned water table, sprouted jagged, dried branches instead of lush greens. Rocks blighted the land. Even the sound of wildlife had muted. *This place is dead, and so it shall remain.*

Only one sign of the former settlement remained.

Beyond the barren earth, still standing despite the wiping away of the village years before, stood the chapel of Jude, visibly showing its age yet soldiering on in a small thicket of trees that appeared to have adapted to the poisoned earth. In truth, the thicket was along the frontier of non-polluted land, beyond which the untamed forest still thrived. Jude was a polio scar, an anomaly in an ecosystem too stubborn to die.

Tirel pulled open the wide doors, stepping inside a memory as much as a monument. The scent of the burned and decayed spirit trees greeted him like a hard punch to his jaw. Slamming shut the doors, he fled, the darkness rising too quickly for him to temper it with any feeble attempt at reason. It took weeks for him to build the courage to return.

And when he did, it was with a jerry can of petrol and red intent.

Dowsing the room with fuel he had stolen from the reserve tanks, Tirel was proud of how he had learned to tame his rage. His new life in Motherland was little different from his childhood in Jude, except he was older and wise enough to manipulate his situation. Whenever another ward curried favour from His Eminence, Tirel learned how to discredit them without blow-back. And in extreme cases, he killed them himself, leaving clues that brigands from nearby towns were the culprits. The Reapers did the cleanup for free. He'd built himself a promising future. The chapel was the last remaining thread that allowed his memory of life before Motherland to dangle.

"I think you've used more than enough, don't you?"

Tirel spun to see a man wearing a simple tunic not dissimilar to the style of dress worn in Motherland, standing in the shadow behind the farthest pews next to a covered wooden font.

"Who are you?" Tirel fumbled in his pouch for matches.

"You've grown," the man replied. "Much taller than I expected."

Tirel flipped the flap over the sulfur tip, pinching the match hard against the rough ignition strip. "I'm going to burn it down." He slowly rubbed the match head between the cardboard. "Then it will all be gone."

The strange man in the shadow shook his head. "Tirel, nothing is ever *really* gone."

"It is *all* gone! My mother, my father, all of Jude!"

He snapped his fingers and the packet of matches ignited in a quick flash, the smell of burned sulfur mixing with the petrol fumes. It was no empty threat. The man didn't flinch.

"You miss your mother."

"My mother left me."

"She left because she feared you."

The flame burned hot and fast. The sweet smell of his cooking flesh mixed with the fumes. Tirel pinched his fingers tight, ignoring the pain as the red episode spread like a cancer from his abdomen.

"She left, and she is *never* coming back!" Tirel's adolescent voice crackled through his shrieks.

"You don't know that."

"Do *you?*"

The man frowned, lowering his gaze. "I don't, no."

The tears rolling from his eyes might have been caused by the flame. It could have been the stranger's unwelcome news.

"If you burn this place, how would your mother ever hope to find you?"

The words stunned him, so much that the pain roared into his blackened, blistering fingers. "*Where is my mother?*"

The man lifted the cover of the font, swishing the stale water with his fingers.

"You should clean that burn." He lifted a handful of water, dribbling it back into the concave vessel. "This water will work wonders, if you let it."

Tirel dropped the dead matchbook to the floor. There was no burst of flame. He was good at death.

The man stepped out of the shadows, his face obscured by a modest growth of beard, deep brown and trim. The light from the broken windowpanes glinted in his light, hazel-coloured eyes.

"She is safe," he answered. "From you."

"*Reaper!* You kidnapped her!"

"She's no captive. But I cannot, and I will not speak for her, of course. Brothers do not speak for Syballine Sisters."

It sure felt like he was speaking for her. "Why hasn't she come back for me?" The last shards of his youthful voice vanished.

"You reside in shadow. You wear it like a cloak. It was from that darkness you murdered your father."

"*He deserved to die.* And I would do it again." Tirel collapsed to his knees, howling into his open hands as the darkness took complete control. His tears stung the open burns. When he looked up, the man was standing above him.

"Burn it down if you must," he said. "But you will regret it."

Tirel didn't know what to say. He slumped sideways, his shoulder propping him off the floor against the pew.

"You may never see your mother again, Tirel. But if ever there is a chance, you risk losing it in the flames."

The man turned and walked to the double doors, leaving Tirel crumpled on the chapel floor next to the trampled soot mark of the burned matches.

"Who are you?" Tirel yelled, his agonizing voice echoing through the sanctuary.

The man stopped at the doors and answered without turning.

"I am Raël," he said before the doors shut. Tirel lay on the floor, ashamed of his own weakness as he kicked at the darkness like a newborn. After his tantrum subsided, he hobbled over to the wooden font, looking into the still water that reflected his tormented image. Forsaking the healing waters, he heaved the pedestal across the floor. The chapel would not burn today. But one day, it would, and he swore to himself that he alone would strike the match.

Tirel would not see Raël again for many years.

The next day, as the medic tended to the infected burns on his right hand, a girl in the same room was being treated for some respiratory illness. She asked him how he burned his hand. Tirel saw the deep blue in her eyes and was instantly disarmed. All the red that simmered within him, extinguished. A warm ray of light poured through the window, bathing him in a sensation completely foreign to him.

"I'm Karina." She smiled, showing an empathy he had never known. As the doctor applied salves and wrapped his injury, he explained that he was trying to burn the remains of an old chapel he had found in the forest so the Reapers would stay away. It was a partial truth, but more than he'd ever confessed to anyone.

"Did you do it?"

"No," he sighed. "No point, it's far from here anyway."

Karina smiled again. "Maybe you can show it to me…"

Sunday, 15 July AC 0245
Chapel of St. Jude
Colonel Tirel Desantos

You see, Father, Andreas was right.

Tirel spent most of his days in the front pew. Waiting. He'd waited for years, decades—a lifetime in this hallowed building. He'd dreaded the services when he was a boy. He'd tried to burn it as a young man. He'd returned to it every year out of a sense of duty, a promise to a ghost long dead by now. Hazel never came back.

"You see, Colonel, I was right." In the throne, Andreas leaned forward, clutching a small wooden box.

"You warned me of Raël." The Reaper reemerged in his life over the years, for no other reason than to remind him that his mother would not return while he remained bathed in red. He was there when he wed Karina. He was there when Paolo was born. He was there when Karina died in childbirth.

And one day, a new Reaper appeared. Andreas spoke differently than the others. He understood the red inside of him. He viewed it as an asset rather than a disease. *Andreas was right, after all.*

"Raël is dead. I struck the blow, and I left him with his eyes to see the death of his world. The Catholic Forty had to be eliminated, just as your Council of Regents."

Tirel inhaled through his flared nostrils. The cleansing of Motherland's leadership freed him in a way he'd only felt once before, on the day Paolo had been born. Only upon Karina's death did the red seep back.

Andreas stood, lifting the wooden box. "Raël can no longer restrain anyone." He stepped off the sacristy and in front of the colonel, placing the box into his hands. "You shall wait no longer."

The box was light. Polished wood shone in the flickering of the candlelight. Tirel looked up, his eyes meeting Andreas's. For an instant, Paolo's face smiled back at him, nodding as if to say *open it*.

Carefully lifting the lid, Tirel stared inside at an arrangement of clean white bones. Bejeweled rings, an envelope of letters, and some glossy, faded photographs surrounded Hazel's remains. Andreas folded his hands and bowed, then returned behind the altar.

All these years, and he couldn't find the words. She had finally come back for him. Tirel's eyes remained dry.

"I regret nothing, Mother."

Mea Culpa

Saturday, 14 July AC 0245
Sanctum Occultus, Moab
Crystal Sheppard

If we don't get him to Lacraie now, we're going to lose him!" Crystal's heart raced as she followed Merrick and Simmons up the long, winding spiral stairs. The Capstonian forensic officers had only basic first aid. If Ian had only suffered a broken arm, they'd have been able to set the bone. But significant radiation exposure, over two weeks ago… Crystal didn't like his odds. By all rights he should have died already. Likely his earliest doses of medicine stemmed the contamination.

Within hours, Reekan's backup summoned from the Ap-Oz base arrived. The doctors on site were able to administer intravenous lines to rehydrate him. They'd scanned his platelets, white blood cell count, and bone marrow damage. Reekan made the call to Ozarck's Chair for specific medicines needed to stabilize Ian Null's depleted immune system. As soon as the spinal board had reached the main level of the stadium, he was encased in a polymer-infused bubble. The slightest infection could have killed him in minutes. Again, something about him defied all the odds. Crystal stared through the semi-opaque bubble at Ian Null, eyes closed but lids twitching, arms at rest yet still coursing with adrenaline, fingers flexing.

All his money, he'd given to her. And none of it made a difference here on the precipice of life and death. She pitied him.

Rain spattered on the bubble as Merrick and Simmons whisked him into the waiting Tan-Ro. A second copter had already lifted off, her brothers on board, en route to Ap-Oz, their original destination. As the cargo doors slammed shut and the transport teetered off the ground, Crystal gazed out the port-side window. She could have sworn the veiled woman was waving to them as they lifted into the blustery sky above Moab.

Ap-Oz reminded her of Lacraie. The hallways were stark and lifeless, only here they were darker grey as opposed to Lacraie's sterile white. Personnel scurried from room to room, up and down corridors. Once inside the hospital wing, Crystal barked the required layout of a treatment space. Complete decontamination scan. Polymer partition between patient and non-medical observers. All medics required full contamination suits and breathing apparatus. And as soon as the medicine arrived from Ozarck, he needed to start the regimen yesterday. Crystal donned her plastic suit and pulled the mask over her face. Her commands echoed in a sharp tone as though she were speaking through a megaphone. Reekan's people followed her every command.

Once he was cleaned, restrained to his bed, and hooked up to the monitors and medicine lines, Ian Null lying still, submitted to the procedure. Crystal sat next to the electrocardiogram as its lines peaked and fell in a slow, steady rhythm. He looked nothing like the image in her mind, from when they met in Lacraie. There, his hair was tied back neatly. Here, it was loose, curled and wavy, knotted and streaked with wisps of grey. Then, a clean-shaven face showed his strong cheekbones and jawline. Now, despite days of growth, his face had sunken from the dehydration. His fresh-off-the-loom clothes had been replaced with outsider wear—dirty, stained, and ripped.

"I don't know what to say to you, Ian Null. Or do I call you Paolo Desantos? Who *are* you?"

Crystal sat straight on the stool. Ian's chest moved up and down. The breathing mask fogged from his respiration. "I don't know what to say. You saved my brothers' lives. But the only reason they needed to be saved was because of you in the first place! Our *home*..." Never had she thought that when she walked out the front door of the Sheppard Inn that she'd never see it again.

"You saved them. I don't know your story. I feel like you wanted to tell me when you came for your prescription. You gave me enough money to…" *To make up for destroying the Inn.* "You gave it to a stranger, just like that." She tried to snap her fingers inside her plastic gloves. "And you were nothing but kind to my brothers."

Crystal stood and looked at the monitor. Ian—Paolo's life dangled by a power cord plugged in the wall. One quick tug and he'd be gone in minutes. Crystal Sheppard was not a doctor. She was not bound to any oaths to keep him alive. The law of the outside world dictated that you reaped what you sowed. Two weeks in the outside world had completely changed her. She closed her fingers around the cord.

Perhaps two weeks in the outside world had changed *Paolo*, too.

"Thank you." Crystal let go of the cord. Ian's left eye leaked a single tear.

Saturday, 14 July AC 0245
Ap-Oz Research Facility

By the third day, Ian had shown remarkable resiliency. True to his stubborn nature, he'd tried to wriggle from his restraints the second he'd gathered enough strength to test the bonds. Crystal smirked at the scowl on his face. Robbie and Lorrie had each described a very different person from their time with him. According to her big brother, Ian Null was stoic, calm, like a finely-tuned machine. Yet, he had shown compassion for them, learning to slow his pace when they needed to catch up. Taking the time to teach them survival skills. Enduring Lorrie with patience that had to be superhuman. And according to Lorrie, he was stubborn, impenetrable, iron-willed, and incapable of admitting weakness. Crystal told him that those qualities were a lot like his own. Lorrie didn't appreciate the observation.

His eyes opened, and he scanned the room constantly. Crystal understood—in the outside world, you had to be aware of everything. Alertness kept you alive. It's an instinct you can't just turn off. The medics confirmed that his platelets were recovering, and that his white blood cell count was improving in no small part due to the biosynth technology available at Ap-Oz. The repair to his bone marrow would take time, and several rounds of biosynth infusion directly into the spine. Ian Null nodded every time a course of treatment was explained to him. Crystal held his hand when the needle entered his spinal column. Even in a weakened state, his grip nearly broke her fingers. He relaxed the grip when he realized how much pressure he was applying. The experimental treatment made him sleep longer and deeper. He wasn't awake to notice Cadlen on the other side of the plastic barrier. Crystal's baby brother spent most of his time watching, sketching in his book. When Ian had left them at Simon's house, Cad had ventured out on his own to find him. The mysterious "Ranger Man" had made an impact on him.

Wednesday, 18 July AC 0245
Ap-Oz Research Facility

"I will not try to escape. Take off the restraints, please." Ian had begun to speak on Monday, first with whispers, then broken words as his vocal cords readjusted. Breathing tubes in his nostrils replaced the respirator. Fresh linens for his old, ratty clothes. A shave, hair trim, and salves to heal the nicks and cuts, slowly diminishing the scar tissue. Dr. Jarren had returned over the weekend, and upon inspection of the deep scars across his back, he suggested that biosynth may be able to cover them. Ian appeared indifferent. Crystal nearly cried when she saw the whipping scars. No wonder he was so detached.

Ian Null touched his feet to the floor for the first time at 1400 hours on Wednesday. Crystal and Shonn Simmons steadied his arms as he curled his abdomen, sat up and moved his legs over the side of the bed. Only one intravenous line remained in his hand, and the monitors read healthy numbers. The ECG had been unplugged for two days.

"I will not stand up," Ian promised. Simmons smiled and stepped back. Crystal sat on her stool, leaving him to support himself of his own strength. The yellowing in his eyes had receded significantly. He was able to lift a cup to his lips and drink without shaking or spilling. The doctors had begun reintroducing him to solid foods, although he grimaced at the blended, pale green goop. Lorrie, on one of his rare visits, held a piece of dried meat to the plastic curtain. Crystal scolded him for taunting him. Lorrie argued that he was dangling a carrot, that one day soon he'd be able to chew the meat just like they used to on the outside.

Steven Reekan arrived, dressed in his own polymer suit. He entered the quarantined side of the room and Simmons left. Crystal insisted on staying. The mayor didn't argue with her.

"What do I call you? Ian? Paolo?"

"Null is fine." Ian clasped his hands in his lap.

"I have questions if you're able to answer."

Ian nodded.

"Motherland is responsible for five civilian attacks in Capston, is that correct?"

"No. Only four."

"Which four?"

Ian reached for his cup of water and took a sip. "The first four. I am responsible for the fifth."

Crystal swallowed. The fifth, the Sheppard Family Inn. Ian set the cup back on the end table.

"It was the desire of Colonel Desantos to attack a different target. I chose the Sheppard Inn."

Steven looked grim. "And why is that?"

"I was assigned a Kayewati partner who would report directly to the colonel. When it was learned that Lorrie and his friend had overheard us, Grant decided they had to be silenced."

"Well, you didn't exactly get the job done."

Ian turned to Steven. "I was given an opportunity to save many lives. The original target would have devastated your city."

"And what was that original target?"

Before Ian could answer, the door opened, and a second figure appeared in a polymer suit. His voice echoed.

"Holt Tower."

Steven snapped toward the man on the other side of the barrier. "About time you got here! Phil Fox, I'd like you to meet Ian Null, also known as Paolo Desantos of Motherland."

Crystal had never seen the former mayor in person. He was less imposing than Steven, but he wielded a quiet confidence, nonetheless.

"Steven, as solicitor, I have to advise you that Mr. Null doesn't have to answer any questions without legal representation."

Ian waved his hand. "I will tell you all you need to know. Holt Tower is still in jeopardy."

"May I?" Phil gestured to the zipper. Crystal nodded. The quarantine measures were nearly finished since his platelets and white blood cells had recovered. Phil climbed inside and closed the barrier behind him.

"You faked your own death so you could defect from Motherland—from your father. You chose the Sheppard Inn for two reasons. One, to kill Grant in a way that wouldn't appear suspicious. Second, as a means to demonstrate to the colonel that you were intent on pursuing Lorrie and Warren as witnesses. And you accomplished this with no other casualties."

Steven's eyes widened. "How do you know all of this?"

Phil and Ian's eyes met. "Slava Allen sends his regards." Ian nodded.

"You met with the Allens? Marribel'll have a field day over this one!"

Phil smiled. "She's not impressed. Huh! Nor is the rest of the council. But that's for later." He turned again to Ian. "Your father will attack Holt Tower, won't he?"

"After me, he will turn to Captain Tomás Alvara. He has been training sleeper agents. He will lead the mission personally, as I was to."

Ian trembled at the last statement.

Crystal took his hand. Despite his best efforts, Ian Null suffered the same emotions as anyone. Maybe, if he were in full health, he'd be able to hold himself together. The man who'd entered the dispensary had shown an awkwardness. Now, with all eyes on him, symptoms of his past trauma revealed themselves in flinches of muscle memory and nervous reaction. She'd seen similar in all three of her brothers, each in their own way.

"We've already investigated DefCorps. Any agents without verifiable credentials have either vanished or were rounded up. Are there any names we should be checking for?"

For the first time, Ian closed his fingers over Crystal's. "I am sorry for everything, Crystal." He turned his gaze back to Phil and Steven. "Florian Willis. That is Tomás Alvara's pseudonym."

Steven nodded. "One more thing, Mr. Null. Eminence De Léon is dead, and the Council of Regents are nowhere to be found. Sources tell us the colonel has staged a coup, and that he is scarcely seen in the city."

Ian let go of Crystal. Placing his hands firmly against the mattress, he pushed, lifting himself to his feet. He stood about the same height as Phil, but several inches shorter than Steven. Still, standing straight, he looked taller than both.

"I know where you will find him."

The Botanists

*M*ove on Holt Tower now. Easy for him to say.

If Colonel Desantos ever spent any time on the details of the plan, he'd realize that since the Grant debacle, their safe house in the 300-block had been compromised. The components for the explosives had taken months to import, bit by bit so as not to raise any hackles through DefCorps. Even with planted agents. But after Leander Stirling sabotaged the Tan-Ro carrying the Sheppard brothers, Captain Ling tightened up. Tomás didn't have any more boots on the ground in the Defense Corps. So, he had to start over, and building false identities took time to do properly. With the traffic coming and going from New Inland, it would be nearly impossible to scrutinize everyone. And with new names in the system, they'd have no red flags to watch for. What might once have taken a week needed four.

Commuters coursed through the Arterial Causeway bow to stern, only a whisper of space between each shuttle at peak traffic. The causeway formed a wide circle around the central pillar that marked the center of the New Inland dome, rising like an elevator into the stratosphere. Within, DefCorps offices occupied much of the support structure, air traffic platforms jutted out high above ground level. Higher than Tomás could see, the DHC rotunda crowned the central column, ringed with the immense and sprawling Hanging Gardens and sky mirrors. His head swirled at the thought of standing so high.

Tomás glanced at his handheld. 0900 hours, and as he'd hoped, the log jam of traffic began to thin. Through his dashboard radio, the news reported a minor delay at Capston's border post. *No kidding.* The actions of lesser agents and officers had led to higher security measures leading in or out of Capston. He cursed Paolo under his breath.

In the passenger seat, Hastings Benjamin twiddled his fingers. "Boy, am I ever ready for a long nap!"

And I wish you were napping now… The agent had mastered his story. All he needed to do was relax and try not to draw unnecessary attention. The shuttle inched closer to the processing window. Tomás didn't answer him. They were too close for the sensors not to pick up on their conversation.

At the window, a hefty man in a DefCorps uniform pushing hard against its buttons leaned forward. "Good morning, sir, and thank you for your patience." There was a brief pause.

"No trouble at all," Tomás replied. An awkward second elapsed. He turned to face the scanning screen just beneath the window. A quick, red light swept over his face. He should have done it automatically.

"Sorry, it's been a long shift."

"Tell me about it! Name, age, and home city, please." The officer peered down at his datapad. The results of the scan had to match what Tomás was about to say.

"Florian Willis. 37, New Mills." he said. "We're AgriCorps, been on a field study of coniferous trees."

"Ah, that's why you smell like pine!" The big man laughed. Tomás scrunched his nose. The agent reeked of body odour. Hastings Benjamin twitched, his forehead wrinkling in confusion. The officer barely contained his laughter.

"I'm just kidding, I can't smell you at all!"

Tomás feigned laughter. Chit-chat annoyed him. "Of course not! I was wondering if they added new sensors."

"Anything to declare, Mr. Willis? Pinecones, or what?"

"No sir, just two tired botanists ready for some rest."

"Indeed. Manifest says you're going to Capston, I see. The Regal?"

A second DefCorps guard shuffled in the background. She had short-trimmed hair, and the big man dwarfed her.

"We have rooms reserved at the Regal. The Holt is a bit out of my price range, unfortunately."

"You'll have all you need at the Regal." The female guard sat next to him. "Meeting your family, are you?"

Red flags waved in Tomás's mind. He'd prepared for this scenario. John Gry knew Florian Willis had no children—he'd read as much on the retinal scan readout. Tomás leaned closer to the window, fully aware of Gry's test.

"My wife is meeting me."

"That sounds lovely! Apologies, it's your partner here who has kids."

Hastings spoke up. "My daughter, Macie, just turned nine this past week."

The officer smiled. "Send my regards, Mister... Hastings! Yes! Your manifest checks out. On your way, then!"

Hastings Benjamin nodded in approval. *He did well.* Tomás smiled as the shuttle lurched forward. For a second, he thought the two DefCorps officers glanced at each other. Tomás had recognized both John Gry and Kenzy Wall, senior officers in Reekan's police service. Survivors of an explosion in Allentown. Reekan had posted two of his best at the window—they were clearly looking for someone. *Best skip the Regal altogether, in case they're setting a trap.*

Artemis Select

19 July AC 0245
Holt Tower, Caspton
Lieutenant-Colonel Tomás Alvara

Tomás marveled in the frivolity of Holt Tower's accented rooms. A faux waterfall trickled in the far corner from the double-wide bed adorned with a plush duvet over fine-woven Empress Veil linens. Jason Holt had promised him the best. Tomás was used to Elbi Garcia personally serving him drinks, but he hadn't expected the infamously rich owner of Holt Tower to tend bar in his own lounge. Holt came from old-world money. Still, continuing success required hard work. Clearly, he wasn't a lazy man.

He keyed the control panel touchscreen to dim the lights and augment the water sounds. He chose not to dispense a fine "natural woodland" scent. He didn't miss the smell of the forest. The pungent rot held no sentiment, only memories of rigorous training in the deep bush north of Motherland. His home city smelled of culture. The aroma of street vendor carts and their produce and meats, the crispness of hewed hay, and the faint wisps of fireplace smoke curling through the streets. The control pad couldn't reproduce any of these.

Tomás understood most of the technology inside the domes. The television screens didn't differ much from similar devices in most homes in Motherland, though the New Inland network offered choice of broadcast, higher resolution to the point the images appeared so lifelike as to discomfort him. Spectres, facsimiles of the natural world, devoid of soul.

He keyed in a selection of traditional folk music—soft guitar strings and husky-voiced singers, sweeping brushes on cymbals and light-timbre drums, soulful women backing the chorus. As he lay back into the pillows, clasping his fingers behind his head, he imagined local entertainers with hand-crafted guitars and banjos, upside-down baskets and barrels and bean-filled maracas. The music of Motherland was rich, of the earth, and for those who lived within it. He hated the clangour of metallic horns and brass tubes. Machine-generated noise pierced the brain. The replication was so lifelike. Almost relaxing.

The control panel glowed blue. A nondescript generated voice proclaimed that room service had arrived with a special delivery courtesy of Jason Holt. When Alvara did not reply, the voice indicated that the delivery was a bottle of Artemis Select. Former mayor Phil Fox's favourite, he'd mused. When Tomás had ordered the potent liqueur, Holt had told him that the next shipment wasn't due for a few weeks. He must have found a bottle, after all. To be certain there was no ruse in play, he keyed the pad to activate the camera. Indeed, a uniformed man with a pressed white shirt, black apron draped over pleated trousers, and shiny shoes held a bottle of the elusive liqueur, patiently waiting for the door to unlock.

Pulling open the door, Alvara greeted the server.

"Mr. Holt is very kind." Tomás inspected the green bottle. "Quality service."

"Mr. Holt apologizes for the delay," the server replied. "He wanted me to tell you that he checked after you left, just to be sure. Fortunately, we can accommodate your tastes this evening."

As the server turned to leave, Tomás noticed the scent of forest floor wafting throughout the room, notably stronger than the setting he'd keyed earlier. Upon further scrutiny, the fountain no longer trickled.

"Now that you mention it, the climate settings seem to be in error," Tomás mused, scanning around the room for anything else out of place.

The server wrinkled his nose. "This isn't the fragrance you requested? That's odd. I'll send for technical assistance right away."

"I'm sure it's nothing," Tomás replied. "Maybe I confused the settings on the device."

"Ah." The server nodded. "Could be. I can take a look if you like."

The server's neatly trimmed hair revealed a high forehead above his hazel eyes. His clean-shaven face resembled a freshly polished mannequin head.

It's half-past ten. He's too clean-shaven for this hour.

"Oh, that's fine. I don't want to impose this late in your shift."

The server smiled. "No trouble at all. I just came on shift at nine. Can I look?"

Tomás sighed, gesturing into the room with his right hand, cradling the Artemis Select with the other. The fresh-faced server immediately made for the control pad on the nightstand while Tomás kept his annoyance to himself.

The server toggled through menus with his thumbs, and deftly maneuvered through the systems as his eyes widened and narrowed, occasionally muttering to himself. The smell intensified. Tomás grew impatient.

"Is there anything you can do about that woodland rot?" he asked with an air of ill temperament.

"Mm-hmm, just be a moment or so," the man answered without looking up. "I kind of like it, myself. But hey, it's your room."

Within a few seconds, the waterfall roared to life, startling Tomás. The server apologized and turned the volume from a roar to a gentle trickle. The music, muted before, blasted back at full volume to the crashing of cymbals and electric guitars. Once again, the man turned the volume down nearly to zero, sheepishly grinning back at him.

"I imagine you're not a fan of the heavier stuff either?"

Tomás glared without answering.

After a few more awkward minutes, the rotten smell began to dissipate. The server asked if he could supplant it with a light whiff of lilac to help cancel out the pungency of the forest. Tomás nodded, relieved that the situation appeared to be under control. Finally, the server proved useful.

"There you go. I've reset your music selection to your previous selection. Very nice choice there. Folk music is under-appreciated around here!"

"Indeed." Tomás cracked his knuckles. "Where I'm from, it's very popular. It reminds me of my youth."

The server stood, returning the pad to the small table. "That's really interesting! I've been to Sascota plenty of times. I thought they were more into that western style, more pianos and all that."

Sascota?

"I never told you I was from Sascota." *Where did he get that idea?*

The man never missed a beat. "I was going by your accent, but sorry, I shouldn't have assumed." He began to make his way to the door, but stopped about halfway, turning back to him with a quizzical look.

"You know who *does* like that folk style though? The Motherlanders. I mean, everyone there loves that stuff. You know what they say, where do you go for a concert in Motherland? The kitchen!"

Tomás narrowed his brows. This was no server. The sidearm in his travel bag did him no good across the room. The sooner this man left, the better. "Yes, well, I will take your word on that. I have never been."

The server laughed. "Couldn't imagine you had! It'd be awful hard to live there with all that outdoor stink, I imagine!"

"And thanks to you, my good sir, I don't have to endure it here either," Tomás huffed. "Now if you will excuse me."

"Of course, of course," the man apologized as he backed toward the doorway. "Sorry, it's been quiet around here these past few months. With all of the terrorist attacks and all, business has dried up—I'm sure Mr. Holt told you as much."

"Send my regards." Alvara cut him off and motioned to the door. "Now, I'd like to rest and enjoy my Artemis."

As he reached the doorway, the man spun around. Tomás groaned. *This guy might yet talk himself to death.*

"Oh, one more thing, is the television to your liking? Figure I should ask while I'm here."

"It's *fine*. Now if you please—"

"Have you turned it on? Maybe we should check just to be sure. Those climate settings reset for some reason. I'd hate to have the monitor switch on to some other guests changing, or some nature program on…"

Brushing past him, the server made his way across the bedroom once again, this time keying the control pad with his right-hand fingers as he cradled the device in his left. Tomás moved silently to his travel bag. While the server occupied himself with the television controls, he pulled out the polymer pistol he'd successfully smuggled. He hadn't raised it before the blank grey screen flashed to life.

"Ah, here we go! Anything you want to watch?"

The default setting showed a menu with options. Channel 21 brought them to a local sports broadcast, cyclists looping the wide track of the Velodrome, which was in this very tower in the lower levels, the server informed him. He flashed through the channels, from entertainment to news to information commercials, stopping at a news broadcast with a wide red band scrolling along the bottom quarter of the screen.

"Ooh, something's up!" the server exclaimed.

"I'm not concerned about local matters…" Tomás clicked the safety button and raised the pistol. On the television screen, the news anchor introduced footage of an armed force storming into the city streets of an outside city. Motherland militia engaged the forces while smoke and fire erupted from De Léon's palace. The footage rolled into a surrender and streams of militiamen filing out of the courtyard in pairs, hands behind their heads in submission. An unseen reporter thrust a microphone towards a high-ranking officer turned away from the camera.

"Major, if you could give us an update," the reporter muttered.

Turning to face the camera, Major Wall glared while her troops continued to secure the background chaos.

"Yes, as you can see here, the resistance was strong, but we've been able to limit casualties on both sides." Wall wiped dirt and soot off her cheek as another familiar face moved into the shot. Tomás lowered the gun. He could feel his face reddening.

"Mayor Reekan, it is well known that New Inland's jurisdiction outside of the structure is limited, yet here you are with a DefCorps deployment from all five cities. The DHC has obviously approved of your incursion into Motherland?"

Reekan nodded. "Chair Marribel signed the decree herself."

"Major Wall mentioned the Motherland chain of command was broken?"

"Right, well, we've learned that Eminence Santiago De Léon was murdered some time ago, along with the Council of Regents. Colonel Desantos executed a coup and has kept the news from the citizens. The colonel has fled the city, but we're in pursuit."

"And the lieutenants?"

"Lieutenant-Colonel Tomás Alvara has been apprehended in a sweep within New Inland, along with six cohorts. One of them even tried to jump from the Hanging Gardens, but those nets are there for a reason!"

Tomás felt his life seeping from him as he sat quietly at the foot of his bed, resting the pistol in his lap.

The server just stared at the monitor, dumbfounded. "How about that now!" He switched off the screen and set the pad back on the nightstand. "Never thought they'd catch those guys." He glanced at the pistol, then back to Tomás.

"I suppose it wouldn't do me any good to flee," Alvara sighed. Regimented footfall filled the corridor and shadows draped across the open door.

The server smiled, sitting on the easy chair across from the defeated lieutenant. "I don't have to worry about any cyanide tablets in your teeth, right? You'd have swallowed them by now."

Tomás shook his head. It was a coward's death. If Reekan found Magister Solanis, he'd know that Tomás had executed the regents. He'd face execution on the same gallows where the colonel had humiliated the Reaper all those weeks ago. Tomás imagined his body swinging lifeless from the noose while scavengers picked him clean. If he cooperated with Reekan, he'd never see the light of day outside—but he'd survive the retribution of Motherland.

The man leaned forward on his elbows. "We're going to find the colonel, but we want to take him alive. Maybe you can help us out with that."

"I wish to seek asylum." Tomás gulped. *I can't go back now.*

"I'm sure Solicitor Fox is willing to listen."

Lieutenant-Colonel Tomás Alvara breathed deeply. A calmness fell over him for the first time in memory. "I'm ready when you are, Captain Shore."

The server laughed and peeled off the soft polymer face covering. Tomás *knew* he looked too clean. "When did you realize?"

Tomás stood as two armed soldiers entered the room, rifles drawn. "I have my ways, as you have yours."

The two guards seized Tomás, securing restraints around his wrists. Somehow, he was freer now than ever.

"Thank Holt for his courtesy." The guards led him from the room. "And tell Fox he has good taste."

The Bomber

Friday, 6 July AC 0245
DHC Rotunda, New Inland
Solicitor Phil Fox

Phil hadn't missed the rigid pod seats in the DHC rotunda. The silence, once comforting, offered only a stifling, sterile feeling after so many weeks back at Spruce Grove. As the pages flitted into the chamber, preparing their respective cities' delegate pods with fresh water and datapad access, the slow rustling of activity sounded more and more like the natural world of the Jackson Homestead. Closing his eyes, he smelled the fresh-split firewood, the curling wisps of fireplace smoke, the salt borne on the sea breeze off the bay. One of two outcomes awaited the closed-door council session. He may never see the port of Gasperro again. Or, he may be banished there permanently. Phil smiled at Melinna as she topped his java cup and he took a sip. In the next sixty minutes, he'd have his answer, one way or the other.

Pax Brien took the mayor's seat next to him. They exchanged pleasantries as the pages set up the Capston 1st Representative's datapad and poured him a tall glass of water. Miss Kendall occupied the guest delegate seat just behind them, her datapad perched on her lap for rapid note-taking. Phil understood why Kendall had voted against Steven in his hearing. He'd become too emotionally invested— equally good and bad for his position and circumstances. Still, an emotionally compromised mayor muddies the water, and Kendall knew well that Steven would ultimately serve a greater purpose from Ap-Oz for the time being. She was right. And because Reekan hadn't put up a challenge, he knew she was right, too.

But things had changed—very quickly. Phil shared the content of his address with Brien. The AgriCorps chief sat in bewildered silence as Phil laid out the details of Walpurgis's intelligence. Phil stopped short of confessing a connection with Le_Renard. The only other person in New Inland who knew that secret sat behind him, and she wasn't saying anything.

As Phil and Brien caught up, the rest of the DHC arrived, taking their respective seats in their city pods that formed a circle beneath the high viewing gallery, muted and opaque. At exactly 0900 hours, Chair Marribel lowered her gavel.

"I bring this special session of the Domestic High Council to order. As per our agenda, I wish to welcome back Solicitor Phil Fox to the Capston delegation. You've been missed!" A smattering of applause circulated the room. Phil nodded.

"Let the record show that I am still owed time on my approved leave of absence, which I will fulfill at a later date." The delegates chuckled. Phil could feel Kendall's glare in his back.

"Noted, my friend." Marribel squinted at her datapad screen, eying the itemized agenda. "You've petitioned the council for the opportunity to share updates on Capston's leadership. You are allotted twenty minutes, followed by standard question time in our current order. The floor is yours, Solicitor."

Phil glanced over his shoulder. Karyn Kendall wasn't glaring. She nodded as if to say, "Here's your chance." Phil exhaled and cleared his throat.

"Madam Chair and delegates of the DHC, I thank you for your time in this unscheduled sitting. I am grateful for your diligence and your dedication to your cities and the federation." With that out of the way, Phil glanced at his prompting notes and continued.

"My successor as mayor, Steven Reekan, faced a censure vote, in which the council voted 6-4 for his suspension from the DHC as 1st representative of Capston. Representative Pax Brien has assumed the role as 1st in his absence, and has done an admirable job. Karyn Kendall has served as interim solicitor during my leave, and as I had no doubt, has also represented Capston with dignity on the council, and has indeed kept the city running in both mine and Mayor Reekan's absences. I would thank the council for welcoming them in these battlefield promotions.

"The charges levied against Mayor Reekan were indeed serious. They contravened the charter of the Federation of New Inland. As solicitor, I understand fully the gravity of the charges and their consequences to Capston and New Inland alike. And while I respect the votes cast against Mayor Reekan, my vote, had I been present, would have likely been the same as Miss Kendall. I would have voted to censure Steven Reekan."

Phil noted the murmurings of approval from the Heartsburg and Preston pods. As Miss Kendall had pointed out in their earlier debriefing, Mayor Phil Fox had voted onside with Marribel 85% of the time, while his second Pax Brien had voted only 72%. Jennings had missed having Phil as an ally in his absence, Kendall had observed.

"On Thursday, 28 June AC 0245, I received information that would have changed my mind." The chamber fell silent. The light chatter among the anti-Reekan delegates ceased.

"I received an electronic file from a Kayewati information trader and smuggler known only as Walpurgis."

Representative Easton interrupted. "Solicitor, apologies, but you're telling us that you've had correspondence with a Kayewati?"

"I am telling you, Blythe, that I have the floor and you will hold your questions until I have concluded." Phil glowered at the Preston 2nd Representative. Easton appeared taken aback by Phil's directness, but she acquiesced as he resumed his report.

"The Kayewati Walpurgis gathered intelligence from inside Capston concerning a Motherland plan to carry out a significant assault on the city's most prominent structure, Holt Tower. The reason this attack hadn't taken place is because two teenaged boys also overheard the terrorists planning, which led to the attack on the Sheppard Family Inn instead. That attack cost only one life—that of one of the two perpetrators, another Kayewati agent hired by Motherland."

Phil paused and took a drink of his sufficiently cooled java. The page, Melinna, moved to top off his cup. Phil held out his hand and she sat back in her seat.

"In the communication, Walpurgis attached audio files that corroborate his information. Coupled with data received by Mayor Reekan from his mission into Allentown, it is irrefutable that Motherland state-sponsored these attacks on Capston, with intent to expand further into all four other cities once the economic hub had been struck. Delegates—this is not a Caspton fight. It is a New Inland fight."

Finishing his java, he raised his hand and Melinna rushed over to fill his cup. Delegates murmured in their pods before Phil continued.

"Upon reception of this news, I immediately contacted Miss Kendall. In the communication, it was disclosed that the Allen Consortium had also been forwarded this information. I initiated contact with the Allens, specifically the agent who had done business with Walpurgis. During our meeting, I was able to negotiate further intelligence as to the survivor of the Sheppard Inn attack. Mr. Allen confirmed to me that Motherland Lieutenant-Colonel Paolo Desantos was the perpetrator, and that he deliberately set off the explosions while his partner, a Kayewati named Ennis Grant, was killed in the blast. This was indeed a targeted killing."

Phil panned around the room. He could have guessed the litany of questions brewing in his peers' heads. "Paolo Desantos paid an Allen agent to hack into the Holt Tower closed-circuit network. The goal was to cause the police services to move the Sheppard and Connelly families out of the tower. This was done to cause panic, and for as many people to leave the tower as possible. You see, Paolo Desantos had a plan of his own—he orchestrated the explosion in Allentown's north end to fake his own death. He paid the Allens to change the records so that a low-ranking Motherland officer would be identified as him. He did this in an attempt to defect from the leadership of his father, Colonel Tirel Desantos, a known megalomaniac and usurper of Motherland from its sovereign and regents."

Phil sat back. "I yield my time for questions."

Chair Marribel's microphone crackled. "You've provided us with a lot to chew on, solicitor. If the council pleases, I would like to invoke the Chair's privilege to intercede in questioning."

The delegates from Arcadia and Preston buzzed while their pages scanned for confirmation of the legality of Marribel's interruption of procedure.

"Solicitor Fox, you have revealed to the DHC that you received correspondence from a Kayewati source. Have you been in contact with this individual in the past?"

"No."

"Since?"

"No. Walpurgis is believed to be deceased."

Marribel nodded. "You have also stated that you have made contact with the Allen Consortium in Allentown. You are aware that this contravenes the charter, yet you still did so."

"That's correct, yes."

"Phil, you know that admitting as much requires a vote of censure, don't you?"

Phil inhaled, his chest heaving and his shoulders squared. "I will accept a censure hearing. But, only if the other delegates do as well. I'm aware of the contacts made by all five cities with the Allens." Phil locked eyes with Marribel. She glared back at him with the most hostile look he'd ever seen from the veteran politician. He knew about her illegal plant imports, and more. She knew he knew.

"Since all five cities have opened business with the Allens, I have proposed to the Consortium that I will petition the DHC to debate normalizing relations with them as reciprocation for their generous cooperation in Capston matters."

Blythe Easton exploded. "This is treason! Madam Chair, I move to—

"And I move to censure Representative Easton for interrupting me again!" Phil shouted across the chamber. "Shut off your mic, Blythe, and wait your turn!"

"Order!" Marribel slammed her gavel. "Solicitor Fox, I may not have much time left as Chair. But I promise you one thing—the DHC will never recognize normalized relations with an outsider criminal ring! You spoke on behalf of the council without consent."

Mayor Sylla Pierre of Preston buzzed for permission to speak. "Madam Chair, as you know, I voted to censure Mayor Reekan. However, Solicitor Fox has received shocking information—Kayewati agents are inside New Inland, moving freely through the five cities. The Allens have offered to turn evidence against the perpetrators in exchange for respectful cooperation. Jennings, this changes everything."

Marribel cleared her throat. "Yes, everything! It weakens our position in the Hyacynthe embargo. If threatens our standing with our trading partners in Sascota, Ozarck, and Arctica."

"Then perhaps it was inevitable?" Mayor Salter of Arcadia buzzed. Phil watched the rigid formality fracture while Jennings Marribel squirmed. "We have overwhelming evidence from both Mayor Reekan and Solicitor Fox. If New Inland can unite to confront the perpetrators, we must plan accordingly."

"As Chief of DefCorps, I propose a vote to pursue Colonel Desantos and Motherland." Mayor Pierre turned to Marribel. "I propose that the DHC also vote against normalizing with the Allens at this time as a compromise for consensus military mobilization."

Miss Kendall leaned in between Phil and Pax. "You sure know how to drop bombs of your own, don't you?" The chamber was in complete disarray. Melinna slunk low in her seat, unsure where to look or what to do.

Phil smiled. "Wait till I tell them about Jackson Auto."

The Spirit Tree

Monday, 23 July AC 0245
Chapel of St. Jude
Steven Reekan

The siege took Motherland's armed forces by surprise. Mayor Pierre's eager involvement took Steven by even more surprise. The mayor of Preston had received him with a warmness he'd never felt in his brief tenure in the DHC. The morning he walked into her office in the Rotunda complex, Sylla Pierre had offered him a firm hand. She was taller than he'd realized. Her normally restrained hair draped her broad shoulders as they exchanged pleasantries. Finally, a peer recognized him. But all that had to wait.

Phil had already caught him up back in Ap-Oz while they lingered over Ian Null's recovery from near-fatal radiation sickness. They had plenty of time to compare notes. Between them, they deduced that Motherland's leadership had been severed. Colonel Desantos and his lieutenant-colonel Alvara had murdered Eminence De Léon. Next, they purged the Council of Regents so no one would object to the coup. Reports of mounting chaos in the streets of the old city reached the ears of Shore's intelligence chain—low food stores, lack of sanitation, all in parallel with unsafe drinking water. And no visible sign of the usurper, who was reportedly still deep in mourning over his son's evident assassination. If only he knew…

Once the DHC voted in favour of a coordinated DefCorps incursion into the city, things moved quickly. Even Heartsburg contributed to the effort, albeit in a support role, which came as no surprise to Steven. For the first time in her tenure as DHC Chair, Jennings Marribel had landed on the losing end of a binding vote. It must have killed her to read aloud the results.

With common cause and newfound camaraderie, Steven and Pierre planned the siege into the early hours with their top officials. They moved on the city at the same time Shore closed the loop on Tomás Alvara—detected by Gry and Wall and tracked to the Holt Tower where he presumably planned to detonate nuke-cell charges in his suite. They would have exploded with enough force to sever the structural integrity, leading either to a complete collapse, or rendering the tower crippled enough to be deconstructed. The radiation leak that would have followed, however, may have been the greatest strike. The contamination would have rendered Capston uninhabitable. It would have spread into the Hanging Gardens above. It would have likely seeped into the Foundry level below. Colonel Desantos's ultimate plan was inconceivably devastating. In light of all this, breaking a few DHC rules seemed petty in hindsight to Sylla Pierre, and most of the representatives.

Motherland suffered more than a hundred casualties before Steven's forces discovered that Magister Solanis of the Council of Regents had survived the purge. Imprisoned and in isolation, Steven learned of him from a surrendering officer, himself dismayed at the upending of his city's leadership. The ancient regent shuddered when Steven's troops burst into his cell, huddled in a corner with only stale bread and unsafe water for sustenance. The Magister, the ranking official in Desantos's absence, ordered the surrender of the city, provided New Inland agreed to pull back their troops beyond the city walls. The people needed peace. Steven agreed to the reasonable request.

His attention turned to Desantos. If not for Ian Null's cooperation, he might have escaped into the vast underworld of the outside. Neither Steven nor Phil had gleaned his whereabouts. But the former Paolo Desantos knew of a small church west of Motherland where his father traveled for a pilgrimage of sorts. The long-gone village of Jude had been young Tirel Desantos's childhood home when their water table became contaminated. Orphaned in the disarray of a Motherland incursion, he had been taken in by Eminence De Léon, but the colonel never forgot his roots, where his family once gathered to worship old gods in the company of old ghosts. Advanced scouts confirmed that he was inside the sole standing building of Jude, remaining still in the dimly lit sanctuary. Steven and Sylla agreed to move in a wide sweep around the church, allowing no chance for escape. At the top of the stairs, Steven opened the front doors, sidearm drawn. A faint light from inside greeted him.

"Come in, Mayor. The service is about to begin." In the front-most row of wooden benches, the colonel knelt facing the altar, piled high with stripped, twisted branches of wood. Steven winced at the odor of petrol throughout the church.

"Colonel Tirel Desantos, by the authority of Magister Solanis, and the Domestic High Council of New Inland, I arrest you."

The colonel chuckled. "Solanis has no jurisdiction here. Nor does New Inland. Believe me, Mayor Reekan, Marribel abandoned all responsibility here decades ago."

"If you're talking about the town well, we know about that." Steven crept inside, flanked by a cadre of officers aimed at the madman on his knees. "Your people deserved better."

"Better? No, they did not. Jude was a pitiful town! Its people were weak, cowardly. They fled without looking back. No, Steven Reekan, I don't grieve my hometown. In fact, I had it burned to the ground."

"Except for this church?"

Desantos rose, hands high to keep Steven's officers from opening fire. As he slowly turned, Steven noticed a fire-starting briquette tucked in his right palm. The situation had worsened. By the overwhelming fumes of spilled petrol, he estimated that the whole place could go up in seconds if the maniacal colonel flicked his fingers. He was grateful Sylla waited outside. Her lack of military training would have been a detriment.

"I made a vow a long time ago to an old, foolish man that I would not burn the chapel until my mother returned to me." Desantos motioned with his head behind him to the altar piled with sticks. "Do you know what *spiritis arbor* is, Steven?"

"No, I'm not familiar." Steven considered outsider rituals and beliefs nonsensical, infantile in their esoteric beliefs.

"It is a beautiful tradition. Upon birth, every Motherlander is celebrated with a tree planted in the sacred grounds—the spirit tree. We grow together. When we die, wood from our *spiritis arbor* is harvested for the funerary rites. We are laid to rest in caskets built from our trees. In a way, it's like our trees embrace us as we slip into the afterlife."

Steven couldn't help appreciating the tradition. It made sense for a people so attached to nature to envelop themselves in it when they die. He imagined Trahearn Reekan's ashes, stuffed into a small urn and stored in a family plot, away from light and love. Motherland's devotion to the land was admirable.

"My mother, she left me behind when I was a small boy. Raël told me that she would return one day. And she has come home." Desantos gestured to the altar. "Hazel Desantos was not born of Motherland, so she has no *spiritis arbor* for her pyre. But…"

The colonel froze in his thoughts. Steven inched closer, about a third of the way up the aisle. Desantos mentioned Raël. The name held no significance to him.

"*…my son* was born under *La Golondriña.*" The colonel's voice broke, agony in every syllable. "How fitting for him to provide solace to his grandmother. He would have been proud."

From the shadows behind the altar, movement caught Steven's eye. The forward-flanked officers raised their rifles. Steven raised a hand. "Easy, easy." The heat scan from outside had indicated two bodies inside the structure. *This is going to get interesting…*

"You do not speak for me, Colonel." Ian Null stood next to the officiant's chair, looking down at the piled wood. "My spirit tree is felled. But I am not."

Colonel Desantos's eyes widened and he burst into laughter. "Very good, Andreas! Leave it to you to appear in my final hour! Here you come again to blur fantasy and reality! And to think I almost believed Paolo lived through *you*!"

"Face me, father." Ian Null's hair hung around his cheeks, his eyes glowing in the faint light. Still weakened from his recovery, he rested a hand on the back of the chair for balance. "Andreas is not here."

Steven watched as the colonel turned, hands still raised. The laughter distorted into mournful sobbing as he shook, lowering his hands. Steven kept an eye on the right hand holding the briquette. Motioning his cadre forward, Steven strode in soft, long steps forward to close ground on the colonel.

"No further, Reekan." Ian Null raised his own sidearm, aiming directly at his father, shaking in a blubbering mess. "This is between us."

"Ian, please—

"*Ian!* Yes! This cannot be Paolo. My son would not abandon me! Who are *you, Ian?*"

Lowering his weapon, Ian glowered at the colonel. "I am Paolo Desantos of Motherland."

Colonel Desantos stopped moaning and shaking. Steven couldn't see his face, but he imagined how it had changed from grief to disbelief.

"Andreas warned me you would turn against me. Against your *people*. I never would have believed it."

"*You* created Paolo Desantos, father. I grew to despise who you made me to be." Steven thought he heard his voice tremble. "I meant to walk away from Paolo Desantos forever. But Raël convinced me to wait."

"Raël! That old fool! I should have killed him!"

"He is likely dead by now. By Andreas's hand."

"Yes! Raël and his kin are gone, wiped from the earth! Dead as history, and soon forgotten."

The exchange between the two made little sense to Steven. His cadre fanned out around the pews forming an arc, all barrels set on the colonel. If this conversation continued much longer…

"Why have you returned, Ian?"

"To reclaim my name. I am *Paolo.*"

"Liar! You return to kill me!"

"No. I am not you. And you are not Luther Desantos."

Tirel flicked the briquette and a flame danced above his thumb. "If you are not like me, you'll watch me burn the chapel with all of us inside. Or, you stop me and fulfill your name."

Paolo Desantos raised the sidearm. He didn't say anything.

"When you kill me, son, promise me one thing. Bring home your mother's remains."

The shot from Paolo's sidearm echoed in Steven's ears. In a matter of seconds, Colonel Tirel Desantos crumpled over the wooden backrest. The officers barked as they converged on the fallen man. The briquette tumbled from his hand, its flame extinguished before it bounced off the dirty floor. Paolo lowered his sidearm and sat in the chair, gazing into the piled spirit wood as a second cadre of officers poured inside from the sacristy.

"Don't restrain him!" Steven hollered as his officers seized Paolo by the shoulders.

The DefCorps officers moved the body up the aisle and out of the chapel. Sylla Pierre conferred with Steven, agreeing to return the body of the colonel to Magister Solanis. As the officers finished photographing the scene, Steven sat on the bench behind the pooled blood. All around him, the sanctuary quieted. He closed his eyes and imagined the chapel filled to capacity with hopeful worshipers, music filling the air and prayers ascending to the heavens in their minds. The rancid petrol became sweet incense, and the light bathed everyone in a peace that couldn't be found anywhere else. Young Tirel Desantos sat between his parents, among his own, as it should always have been.

Paolo Desantos remained stoic in the officiant's chair. The service had concluded.

Celebration Day

Saturday, 25 August AC 0245
Site of Sheppard Family Inn, Capston
Lorrie Sheppard

So long as I live, I'll never complain about cleaning my room again."

The destruction hadn't looked as devastating in the rapid video flashes the day the Allens hacked into Holt Tower's closed-circuit television. Seeing the ruins of the fully-leveled Sheppard Family Inn felt to Lorrie as though he were looking at a phantom limb—an arm he had lost, but could still feel. The small mounds of debris organized in reclaimable material resembled scar tissue, rippled and sealing off the wound. The separating crew had long quit for the day. The heavy machinery slept, cordoned off from vandals and gawkers.

Life in the neighbourhood had slowly come back to life while Lorrie and his brothers were away. Traffic circulation coursed again throughout the veined streets like a fresh blood transfusion. Commerce couldn't be delayed. Meanwhile, the demolition and rendering of a small family business had all the time in the world. Life goes on. Within the walls of Capston, the living never suffered the ghosts of the past.

Except these ghosts came home, with no castle left to haunt.

Lorrie tugged at the armrest of the chair he recognized from the foyer. Cadlen spent hours nestled into the cushions, drawing and colouring. With the slightest tug, the arm tore from the backrest, the cracked and splayed plastic crumbling in his fingers.

"They can render the plastic into polymers, right?" Lorrie called over his shoulder.

"I think so?" Robbie continued sorting through the smaller debris the separators had salvaged from the living quarters. Very little survived the explosion. Most of the Sheppard siblings' belongings were replaceable. Still, on the off chance some mementos waited in the soot, they kept poking around.

"Robbie! Look!" Jutted from charred debris, the twisted handlebars of a racing bike caught Lorrie's eye. Robbie squinted. Instead of bounding over to see his old racer, he sauntered, as if he were afraid to confront it again. Only the front half of the frame remained. The rest was either still buried, or already salvaged by the separators.

Robbie sighed. "I dunno, this might take a while to make race-ready." Lorrie couldn't help but laugh.

"As soon as we find the ratchet set…" Robbie brushed soot off the frame and the hand-brake line fell loose. "Didn't they find the 10mm wrench, though?"

Lorrie kept digging. "Of course they would. The only wrench you couldn't find for years, and it took the whole damned building collapsing for it to be found. Wonder if I'll find all those missing socks!"

"From what, that one time you did your own laundry?"

The catharsis of sifting through the debris lightened the brothers' spirits. Lorrie hadn't felt this care-free since before his parents had passed. His cheeks were sore from the unnatural smiling.

Robbie came across the bent lock-box from the office, cracked open in one corner but otherwise intact. Inside, his father's gold wedding band winked in the dimming artificial twilight.

"Think you'll ever wear that?" Lorrie remembered it on his father's ring finger, before Robert Sheppard's hands had swollen in his last weeks. Of the three Sheppard boys, Robbie was most likely to marry one day. Who could endure his own sarcasm? And poor Cadlen, would he ever actually *speak* to anyone let alone propose?

"Who knows? But if the love bug hits you first, I'm happy to let you have it."

Lorrie smiled. Love and happy endings weren't natural story arcs for the Sheppard family. His attention shifted to the narrow, shiny band his mother once wore, ensconced with a sparkling clear gem.

"Maybe Crys'll wear Mom's ring someday. Or maybe you'll slip that on Mireil's finger…" Crystal's flatmates from Hyacynthe had been granted permission to travel to New Inland despite the continuing embargo. Likely Laurent had made it happen, and more likely through private channels. Both Mireil and Druna stayed, their quarterly exams finished. Druna fell completely for the glamour of Holt Tower, which softened the blow of flunking her term.

"I was waiting for you to say something like that and ruin the moment," Robbie snarled. He'd spent a lot of time getting to know Mireil despite Crystal's observation that any romance between them would be weird. Still, Crys didn't try too hard to discourage the budding relationship. And Mireil was in no hurry to move back to Hyacynthe.

"A little defensive, there? Relax, she's a good girl."

Robbie smiled. "I'm glad she meets your approval."

"Anyway, it was good of Laurent to let Crys write her quarterlies later."

"You know, I don't think she was in any hurry to leave." Robbie picked through the singed papers from the lock box. "She kept telling me how much you and Cad have grown."

"Speaking of our sister, wasn't she supposed to meet us here?"

"Been here and left already," Robbie answered. "Said something about going back to Holt Tower with Warren and Cad. Holt's having that swanky party tonight." Jason Holt couldn't help himself. The terrorists had been caught. Business was booming again. The guest list for the celebration included dignitaries from the DHC, business leaders, and Capston's police force. Jason had insisted the Sheppards, Connellys, and their closest friends would be guests of honour. He likely carried guilt over his role in their debacle.

The only notable name not on Holt's guest-list was Ian Null. After he left Ap-Oz, none of the Sheppards had seen him again. Standing in the ruins of Ian Null's doing, Lorrie chose not to think about him. Robbie didn't mention his name. Still, Cadlen missed him—he'd drawn multiple pictures featuring the Ranger Man. And Crystal had formed a bond with him while he healed from his sickness.

Lorrie scrunched his forehead. "That's an about-face. She was all for going through the junk."

Robbie continued to wade through the debris. "Druna convinced her to go. But I think she's holding on to a lot of guilt. From being away so long."

Lorrie's fingers came upon a broken picture frame. The photo inside had burned. "I did her no favours, that's for sure."

Robbie put his hand on Lorrie's shoulder. "She knows, Lor. She knows."

"Everything's *different* now, Robbie. Once we rebuild, it'll be completely new. No rooms we shared with Mom and Dad. Yeah, we got Crys back, but *I* feel different." Lorrie rubbed his healed palm. The infection had itched during the rigorous treatment at Ap-Oz for his wounds. The doctors had cleaned flakes of rusted metal from the layers of his skin, each a tiny poison-tipped lancet injecting bacteria into his system. The scar tissue formed peaks for the valleys of his life lines. The sensation in his touch tingled. It never completely went away.

A low rumble emanated from the downtown core. Lorrie and Robbie turned in time to see a flash of light from about halfway up Holt Tower.

400-Block Offices, Capston
Karyn Kendall

"You had the air set on 'ocean breeze' before you left. I assumed you'd had enough of that for a while?" Karyn leaned over the datapad that controlled the climate of Phil's old office. He'd finally accepted a suite on the 93rd level of Holt Tower—maybe the surest sign of how much he'd changed on his trip to the Jackson Homestead.

"It's like you know me." Phil took his coat from the hook behind the door. "But this is your pad, now. I already miss it, believe it or not."

Karyn wasn't sure if he missed the office or the Homestead. "I can sprinkle in some chum bucket aroma for good measure."

"I'll never see it again, you know." Phil paused in the door frame.

Karyn stopped working. He'd been talking about Spruce Grove, whose ownership had been transferred to Slava Allen.

Karyn changed the topic. "Aren't you going to go over to Holt's?"

"I'm not feeling very festive. I might make an appearance, but I'd just as soon go to bed."

"Figured as much." She reached under the desk and retrieved a wrapped liquor bottle, bow-tied at the neck with a cheap ribbon. "Pharos is delivering again. Holt told me he's counting on your patronage."

Phil laughed. "I think he's doing okay. The shindig he's throwing tonight's all the proof you need of that. Huh!" In his time with his father, Phil had picked up some of Emmanuel Jackson's most annoying quirks.

Karyn had declined the invitation to Holt's "shindig". She'd spent enough time with the DHC in the last few months. Appointed to a standing committee tasked with inquiring into the claims Tirel Desantos had made about New Inland's role in the contamination of Jude's well, she saw the worst in her peers. None more so than Jennings Marribel. She'd been expected at Holt's party. That was enough to keep Karyn away.

"Well, thanks for the aquavit. I'll be on my way—sooner I make my appearance, the sooner I can hit the hay." Phil tucked the bottle inside his jacket. "Try not to work too late. The couch isn't so comfortable. Trust me!"

Karyn smiled and Phil shut the door behind him. The windows set at five dimmed to seven at the touch of her finger. Setting the datapad on Phil's old desk, she leaned forward on her elbows. She'd always wanted to see Gasperro's wharf and seaside shops. Spruce Grove's crop fields and the last standing petrol garage. Burnside-on-the hill. The piers in the strait and the long sand dunes up the coast. He'd told her stories so vivid, she could picture them. But he'd wagered it all to save Capston. Her mentor, puttering across town in an ugly all-terrain buggy with a tacky logo painted on the hood, was the most selfless person she'd ever known.

Karyn felt the low reverberation in her abdomen an instant before the thunder crack split the artificial sky outside the dimmed office window. The flash of light caught the corner of her left eye, instinctively whipping her head toward Holt Tower. She imagined the screams of commuters, gazing and pointing upward as they cupped their eyes, mouths round and toothless, bulging eyes with narrowed pupils.

About half-way up Holt Tower, a burst of smoke billowed from a gaping crater, as flames jabbed at the early evening sky. Debris fell in slow motion like snow from the vantage point of the office window. She shrieked, drowning out the imagined terror of the ants who scurried as fast as they could from the epicenter.

A horrible, dissonant groan of heaving metal girders pierced her eardrums like nails. The sky lift protruding to the Hanging Gardens twisted, as though from some invisible hand, until it snapped like dry kindling. A long segment of the connected walkway swung like a pendulum and the spindly elevator tumbled to the streets below, disappearing into the rapidly expanding smoke and dust cloud, now engulfing the entire block and coursing through the maze of streets.

Karyn pressed her hands and face against the window, peering into the streets for any sign of Phil's buggy. Somewhere in the swath of toxic smoke, he had to be there. Her thoughts snapped to the gathered guests in Jason Holt's bar. There would be music, food, drink, laughter. Steven Reekan and his staff. The mayors and representatives of the council.

The Sheppards. Tears rolled down her cheeks.

The upper half of the tower gave way under the weakened support, toppling down to the streets, teeming with innocent people, stunned and too slow to escape the destruction that was supposed to have ended.

5 km North of New Inland
Paolo Desantos

The words his father said rang like a broken bell. *Stop me and fulfill your name.* Paolo Desantos left New Inland in his wake by long strides. His energy had never fully returned to the levels before his exposure to the leaked nuke-cell, and the weeks of deterioration before he'd been rescued in the Ossuary. And no matter how he justified shooting his father dead with one cold shot between his bulging eyes, the image simmered like a Dakota hole fire that never fully extinguished.

Yael.

Junquer.

Tirel.

Awful human beings, all of them. Each executed by Paolo Desantos without even flinching. Ian Null would never have had the courage to do it. Ian Null let Jamiss walk away to die slowly. He'd patched Raël's wounds, only delaying the inevitable. All along, Paolo's true self had pleaded with Ian Null, only to be suppressed by the most unlikely of sources. The Sheppard family.

Robbie had shown him what family really was.

Crystal had shown him compassion the likes he'd never known.

Lorrie had shown him courage.

And Cadlen…

All he'd wanted was to see the young man again. To thank him for believing in him when no one else did. Getting into New Inland wasn't difficult. Finding the Sheppards without raising alarms was nearly impossible.

Nearly.

At least he was able to see Crystal one last time. To say goodbye, and to thank her for her forgiveness.

Paolo's rucksack shifted with each stride. Behind him, the towering dome of New Inland watched him travel through the thinner woods of the old buffer zone. Threshers like the one that nearly killed him with radiation once crawled over this land, keeping trees from reclaiming the old-world nature. The machines were silent now. Their terrible work was not forgotten by the people who lived in fear of the giant superstructure.

Rising in pitch, the thrumming of Tan-Ro blades approached from behind him. At first, Paolo paid it no mind. New Inland transportation buzzed frequently in this area. He continued marching until the wind from the transports blew his hair free from his restraining tie. Fluttering in front of his face, Paolo pulled back his hair and turned to face the trio of DefCorps Tan-Ro copters descending, uniformed officers pouring from their open bay doors. Paolo dropped his rucksack at his feet as John Gry emerged, rifle drawn. Red laser dots peppered his chest and face.

Raising his hands to the twilight sky, Paolo waited to see if the big man was an Ian Null or a Paolo Desantos.

Epilogue: A Time to Regret

Monday, 16 July AC 0245
Moab
Syballine Sister Esparánza

I know you. *I know you…*"

When the city emptied, Sister Esparánza had been alone, shut inside her cottage so no one could witness her shame. When she hadn't called upon her brothers and sisters in the Catholic Forty, Brother Simon came to her door. She did not open it. Andreas had warned her—tell anyone of our visit, and they will all suffer. She'd seen it in his eyes. He had spoken the truth, a horrible, horrible truth.

She knew how to tend to her wounds. She had attained the mantle of Syballine Sister for her wisdom in natural sciences. Jars upon jars of salves, dried herbs, and syrupy medicines lined her pantry. Esparánza counted from the left of each row until she found the precise jars she needed. She'd learned how to find her way around every corner of her small cottage. Up and down every row of sunflowers in her greenhouses. How many lefts and rights, and even how many minutes to walk from her plot near the western outskirts of Moab to the Sanctum Occultus. Before you see the Light, you must learn how to navigate through the darkness. The Chronicles of the Ansati said so.

When the alarm had sounded, she hid in her bedroom when her neighbours came to check on her. She scrawled a note and left it on her dining table.

I have left. Save yourselves. Esparánza

She had no intention of leaving Moab. Someone had to stay. She would make her way to the Sanctum. If she was near the end of her life, she would lay down in the Desiccatorium. Someone would come back.

Someone would clean the remaining flesh from her bones. Someone would process her life and place what remained in her plot next to her beloved childhood friend, as she'd requested when they Reclaimed her remains.

After three days, Esparánza heard no more commotion outside. The sirens continued for several days, warning the Ansati to stay away. Radiation contaminated the city, Brother Raël had broadcast.

But she knew. It was a lie. A well-intentioned lie, but no less deceitful. Esparánza knew what had happened. Andreas was holding on by the barest of threads. It was only a matter of time before he was totally consumed by the red deep inside him.

She wandered the streets of Moab, veiled and bandaged, counting her steps until she reached the doors of the Sanctum. She cried out as she hammered her frail fists against the locked entrance. No one came. Night fell and she slept where she lay, in the middle of a street, against a fence post, beneath trees. Without sustenance, she weakened. Where there was once blackness, she began to see vivid swirls of colour. Shapes twisting and shifting. The lay of the ground spread out in front of her.

When footsteps tapped up and down the streets behind her, she listened. There was no point fleeing. Andreas had long left the city. Yes, she was safer here. The steps were distinct. First, a grown man, staggering under the burden of some serious impediment. The next, a younger boy, cautiously keeping his distance. She kept near him until he found the church. Once inside, he would be safe there. Another boy, older than the first, but creeping with a false sense of bravery. Another adult man, only younger, looking for his little brother. He is safe, she tried to say, but the words trembled between her cracked lips.

And the young woman...

She'd tried to help Sister Esparánza. There was no helping her. She was looking for her brothers too. Brothers. *Brothers...* The word carried a different meaning to Esparánza. The young woman wouldn't understand.

You're blind, she'd exclaimed. *No, girl. I see far more than anyone should.* She heard the approaching flying machines first and fled up and down streets and around corners to get away from them.

One day, after silence had fallen over Moab again, another pair of feet approached. These were the steps of a small child—a girl.

"Sister Esparánza?"

The Ansati had come home. Esparánza stopped. The girl took her thin, veined hand into her own. "Let me take you home, Sister. You need medicine."

"I see you. *I see you…*" The cadence and the timbre of her voice triggered memories long suppressed. The girl walked slowly, steadying her every step of the way back to her cottage. The sounds of the Ansati returning to their homes, praying over the bodies of the fallen, the return of wildlife. The rustling of the tall sunflower stalks—they'd have bloomed by now. Light over dark.

"Thank you, Karina." Esparánza saw the shape of her dear friend around the little girl who had guided her home. Her voice, her touch. Her sorrow.

"I'm not Karina, Sister. I'm Estelle." The girl placed a cup of hot tea in Esparánza's shaking hands. The cup was lumpy, as if formed by young hands. She knew whose cup it was. She shook enough to slosh the hot liquid over her fingers.

"*I know you…*" She couldn't cry. But if she could, she'd have dampened her bandages with her tears. "I'm sorry, Karina. I should have looked after your son. I'm sorry…"

Appendix I
Characters (Dramatis Personae)

Note: Characters are presumed alive as of the events of Tuesday, 3 April AC 0245 (the fourth terrorist attack in Capston, as depicted in the *Exiles* chapter "The New Normal") unless otherwise indicated as deceased (d.).

The Sheppard Family and Associates:

Robbie Sheppard – Eldest son of Julia and Robert Sheppard; legal guardian of his three siblings Crystal, Lorrie, and Cadlen.

Crystal Sheppard – Daughter of Julia and Robert Sheppard; student of nuclear medicine at Lacraie Research Facility, Hyacynthe.

Laurent (Lorrie) Sheppard – Third Sheppard sibling; competitive longboard racer.

Cadlen Sheppard – Youngest Sheppard sibling; selective mute; talented artist.

Robert Sheppard (d.) – Owner of Sheppard Family Inn; met his wife Julia on a youth retreat in Hyacynthe. Father of Robbie, Crystal, Lorrie, and Cadlen.

Julia Sheppard (d.) – Owner of Sheppard Family Inn; met her husband Robert on a youth retreat in Hyacynthe. Mother of Robbie, Crystal, Lorrie, and Cadlen.

Warren Connelly – Lorrie Sheppard's best friend and fellow longboarder.

Charles Connelly – Warren Connelly's father; husband of Clara.

Clara Connelly – Warren Connelly's mother; wife of Charles.

Willits – Employee of the Sheppard Family Inn

Monsieur Laurent – Elderly benefactor of the Sheppard family. Governor of Hyacynthe Medical College; highly influential figure in Hyacynthien politics.

Mireil – Crystal Sheppard's flatmate and best friend; serious student.

Druna – Crystal Sheppard's second flatmate; enjoys Hyacynthien nightlife.

Chérie – Supervisor at Lacraie

Associates of Phil Fox and Emmanuel Jackson:

Phil Fox – Former mayor of Capston, born near Gasperro, biological son of Emmanuel Jackson; raised by adoptive parents Lucas and Elsa Fox of Sascota.

Emmanuel Jackson – Mechanic and businessman of Gasperro; owner of Jackson Homestead and Jackson Auto service station in Spruce Grove.

Albert Schiff - Resident of Gasperro; adopted as a child by Bernard Schiff. Caretaker of Jackson Homestead.

Bernard Schiff (d.) – Adoptive father of Albert, uncle of Phil Fox. Close confidante to Emmanuel Jackson.

Elsa Fox (née Schiff) (d.) – Sister of Bernard Schiff of Gasperro; adoptive mother of Phil Fox. Died from complications of red tide.

Lucas Fox (d.) – Husband of Elsa Fox and adoptive father of Phil Fox. Magna-rail coach driver, killed on the job by outsider brigands at Badlands Junction.

Fisher (The Lighthouse Keeper) – Former Kayewati national; secret liaison between Le_Renard and Kayewat.

Walpurgis – Kayewati agent employed by Le_Renard. Overhears plans for terrorist attacks in Capston; presumed murdered in Kayewat by an unknown assailant.

Claw_Finger (CF) – Kayewati agent employed by Le_Renard and friend of Walpurgis; presumed murdered by an unknown assailant.

Associates of Steven Reekan:

Steven Reekan – Embattled mayor of Capston and Chief of Capston Police and Security Services. Lease holder of Ap-Oz Facility. Son of a Foundry worker.

Trahearn Reekan (d.) – Father of Steven Reekan, lifelong Foundry worker, died of lung cancer.

Dianna Langley – Estranged mother of Steven Reekan and ex-wife of Trahearn. Presumed alive; known to work in the Hanging Gardens of New Inland.

Shore Hayward – Lieutenant; second in command of Capston Police and Security.

Kenzy Wall – Major in Capston Police and Security; friend of Lt. Shore.

Ender Ling – Captain of Capston Police; third in command.

John Gry – Captain in Capston Security; field officer, member of Steven's executive.

Kyle Jarren – Doctor of biotechnology; Ozarckian national granted Capston citizenship by Phil Fox. Supervisor of research division of Ap-Oz.

Francis Ferrer – Captain and pilot, Capston Security.

Cal Merrick – Forensic scientist and Capston Security officer.

Shon Simmons – Forensic scientist and Capston Security officer.

Jason Holt – Wealthy businessman; owner of Holt Tower and all its services.

New Inland Domestic High Council and personnel:

Jennings Marribel – Mayor of Heartsburg and New Inland DHC Chair. Longtime politician, former medical researcher.

Cooper Fellows – 2nd Representative of Heartsburg and New Inland Chief of Treasury.

Jeffres Marsh – Mayor of New Mills and New Inland Chief Solicitor.

Shal Adem – 2nd Representative of New Mills and New Inland Chief of Aquaculture.

Harus Salter – Mayor of Arcadia and New Inland Chief of Public Health.

Wynn David – 2nd Representative of Arcadia and New Inland Chief of Energy.

Sylla Pierre – Mayor of Preston and New Inland Chief of Defense Corps/DefCorps.

Blythe Easton – 2nd Representative of Preston and New Inland Chief of Foreign Affairs.

Pax Brien – Interim 2nd Representative of Capston and New Inland Chief of Agriculture.

Melinna – Capston student page.

The Ansati:

Brother Raël – Elder of the Ansati Catholic Forty.

Brother Simon – Member of the Ansati Catholic Forty and mentor to Brother Andreas. Senior archivist and researcher.

Brother Andreas – Ansati; rescued from red tide-stricken village of

Haven as a child by Simon. Antagonist to Tirel Desantos, banished to Kayewat before returning to the Ansati at Moab.

Sister Mora – Syballine Sister of the Ansati and archivist in Sanctum Occultus Ossuary.

Sister Esparánza – Syballine Sister of the Ansati; horticulturalist and herbologist.

Sister Hazel (*see* Hazel Desantos) – Estranged mother of Tirel Desantos and Syballine Sister of the Ansati.

Sister Estelle – Young Ansati girl.

Sister Ave Maria – Syballine Sister of the Ansati and archivist of the High Reclamation.

The Free City of Motherland:

Tirel Desantos – Colonel of Motherland armed forces. As a child, murdered his father; abandoned by his mother. Adopted as a ward by Eminence De Leon. Father of Paolo Desantos.

Karina Desantos (née Bianchi) (d.) – Wife of Tirel and mother of Paolo. Deceased during the birth of her second child.

Paolo Desantos – Lieutenant-Colonel of Motherland; son of Tirel and Karina.

Tomás Alvara (aka Florian Willis) – Captain in Motherland armed forces; promoted to Lieutenant-Colonel upon the death of Paolo Desantos.

Yael (d.) – Commander in Motherland armed forces; killed by Paolo during an excursion to source clean water.

Mott Wrengel – Orphaned private in Motherland armed forces.

Hastings Benjamin – Pseudonym; Motherland agent

Halston Rivers –Pseudonym; Motherland agent

Abrams Livingston – Pseudonym; Motherland agent

Creighton Anthony – Pseudonym; Motherland agent

Russ Cedric – Pseudonym; Motherland agent

Gerardi Phelps – Pseudonym; Motherland agent

Grant/Ennis Grant – Kayewati agent, former employee of Le_Renard_Subtil.

Eminence Santiago De Leon – Sovereign ruler of Motherland.

Magister Solanis – Senior Magister of the Motherland Council of Regents.

Mariana – Housekeeper
Tonia - Housekeeper
Elbie Garcia – Dive bar owner and operator in Motherland.
Baylor Zayne – Clandestine Motherland agent in Capston.
Jeremie Beth – Clandestine Motherland agent in Capston.
Kjell Sundland – Clandestine Motherland agent in Capston.

Outsiders:
Ian Null – Traveler in the outside world. Running from his past, determined to reach the continental west coast.
Slava Allen – Allen agent; nearing retirement.
Junquer – Reclusive tinkerer and manufacturer of high-end electronic equipment.
Elms – Outsider brigand and trader.
Berglund (Berg) – Outsider brigand and trader.
Jamiss – Young adult outsider and brigand trader.
Hewer – Outsider and brigand trader, father of Jamiss.
Duncam – Outsider and brigand trader.
Hamm – Outsider and brigand trader.
Anlee – Outsider and Farbend trader. Skilled at tinkering and repair work.
Mayor Harp (d.) – Mayor of Haven; deceased from red tide.
Chair Enstrom – Chair of Ozarck Federation High Council.
Lonzo Ashburn – Ozarck security officer.
Stoke – La Cumbre agent.
Two – La Cumbre agent, subordinate to Stoke.
Three – La Cumbre agent, subordinate to Stoke.
Leander Stirling – Kayewati interloper in New Inland DefCorps.
Raijen Croft – Kayewati interloper in New Inland DefCorps.
Augie Pembroke – New Inland DefCorps officer; dispatched outside.

Appendix II
Locations

Domed Federations on the Continent:

New Inland – Located in the foothills of the northeastern Appalachian Mountains. Constructed from reclaimed old-world cities of the North-Eastern seaboard, New Inland consists of five cities: New Mills, Preston, Arcadia, Heartsburg, and Capston. These cities share administration of the Hanging Gardens agricultural level, the Foundry industrial sublevel, and the Arterial Causeway. New Inland has trade relations with all continental domes except for Hyacynthe and Kayewat.

Hyacynthe – Straddling the St. Lawrence Seaway, Hyacynthe is constructed from reclaimed urban sprawls north of the Great Lake region. It boasts a robust fishery and agricultural sector, administering multiple smaller installations outside of its dome, notably the Lacraie Nuclear Medical Research Facility. Hyacynthe maintains more relaxed restrictions with the outside world, which partly led to its trade embargo with New Inland. It has no formal relations with Kayewat.

Arctica – Located south of Great Slave Lake, Arctica is the largest by size and population on the continent. Largely self-sufficient, Arctica maintains formal trade relations with all domes except Kayewat, though informal trade occurs with them. All continental dome trade with the far east moves through Arctica, exerting influence along the west coast as far south as the Red Line.

Sascota – Situated in the Midwestern plains, Sascota is unique among domes for its shorter, wider construction. Largely self-sufficient, Sascota boasts strong institutions in law, education, and medicine. Predominantly constructed from mining materials, it is naturally protected from outside invasion or attack due to its vast, arid land. Sascota has no formal trade relations with Kayewat.

Ozarck – Nestled in the old-world Ozark region, the Ozarck Federation is closest to the Red Line. Known for research and development in all fields of science, Ozarck holds several outside installations, notably the Appalachian-Ozarck Research Facility (Ap-Oz). Ozarckians experience more health-related issues due to their southerly location and prevalence of tropical illness, yet boast stronger resilience against red tide than other continental domes. Ozarck maintains no formal trade relation with Kayewat.

Kayewat – A rogue-state federated dome located in the far north on old-world Baffin Island. Originally a refuge for fugitives after the collapse of the old world, Kayewat was constructed equally from reclaimed materials and natural resources. It has no formal relations with other domes due to its policy of openness to all fugitives. Kayewati citizens have the right to choose their own name, stylized with underscores between words. They engage in both formal and informal trade with various outsider businesses and communities.

Notable City States, Communities, and Locations on the Continent:

Motherland – Established by refugees from the southern continental isthmus, Motherland is north and west of New Inland. The walled city fought a brutal war against a coalition of five cities which would confederate and construct New Inland. Motherland exudes major influence in the region, governed by a birthright sovereign and a Council of Regents.

Allentown – Site of a protracted military campaign between New Inland federated cities and Motherland, Allentown is now an exclusion zone occupied by the Allen Consortium, descendants of the original citizens.

Jude – A defunct village south-southwest of Motherland, razed to the ground during a heated conflict between rival armed forces.

Haven – A defunct community along the Hudson River, ravaged by red tide. Orphaned children of Haven were trafficked, with Brother Simon discovering a young child named Andreas.

Farbend – An outsider trading post west of New Inland, hub of commerce chiefly controlled by brigands and syndicates.

Carroway – An outsider town south and west of New Inland, known for robust agricultural trade and harboring brigands.

Inland Open-Pit Mine Lake – Kilometers-wide gutted open-pit mine filled with water, becoming a vast, artificial lake.

The Red Line – A line of demarcation separating the northern safer land from the southern more dangerous region prone to tropical diseases.

Seams – Swaths of land contaminated by radiation, rendering vast areas poisoned.

Lake Region – Land south of the cluster of great freshwater lakes, known for its abundance of freshwater and small settlements.

Badlands – Arid and dusty flat land stretching into the Midwest, crisscrossed by magna-rail lines and known for lawlessness.

Sheol – A cavern deep beneath the surface, considered a sacred site to the Ansati.

Moab – City of the Ansati, concealed inside a radiated swath of land. The city maintains large structures to archive human history, with the Sanctum Occultus serving as its central archive and government house.

Badlands Junction – A confluence of magna-rail lines administered and patrolled by security forces from several domed federations. Despite the armed presence, the outpost is virtually lawless.

La Bermude – An affluent island community in the Atlantic Ocean southeast of the Hudson Harbour, serving as a gateway to travel further east across the ocean.

Sable – A crescent-shaped sandbar in the north Atlantic, known for its hardy population of horses.

Gasperro – A small seaside village nestled in the Baie of Green, hub of trade in its region.

Spruce Grove/The Grove – A settlement north of Gasperro, mainly farmland with Jackson Auto Services as the sole surviving business.

Burnside-on-the-hill – Hillside cemetery overlooking the Baie of Green and Gasperro.

Ebbequit Strait – Body of water separating Ebbequit Island from the mainland, known for dangerous maritime travel.

Massiemi Bay – Home to several settlements from the open water of Ebbequit Strait, inland, and up the Massiemi River.

Bas-Etang – An island north of Gasperro, serving as a trading post with direct links to the St. Lawrence Seaway.

The Avalon – A bustling trading town on an island east of Ebbequit, known for its deep port and ideal trading conditions.

Appendix III
Outsider Organizations

Allen Consortium – Operating beneath the streets of the old-world city of Allentown, the Allen Consortium trades currency, information, and goods between outside communities and domes. Generations of Allens have built a network of underground offices and passages from old bomb shelters and catacombs. Agents, publicly identified as Mister (Mr.) or Madam (Mme.) Allen, remain anonymous in an encrypted database. With continent-wide influence, the Allen Consortium excels in technology and infiltration of domed federation databases. They have formalized trade with other outsider businesses like Rust and La Cumbre, maintaining off-the-record dealings with domes except for Kayewat.

Rust – A clandestine trading consortium operating continent-wide, Rust specializes in salvaging, trading physical goods, currency, and information. Employing brigands on term jobs, Rust's organizational structure remains elusive; contacting agents without personal connections is challenging.

La Cumbre – Primarily influential in Red Line regions and Ozarck, La Cumbre, like Rust, lacks a physical base. Known for no-nonsense field agents, they primarily trade in medical ingredients, drugs, and contraband technology. Connected with the Open Sky consortium in the west, La Cumbre maintains trade relations with other consortiums.

Open Sky – Predominantly operating in the west with networks spanning the continent, Open Sky maintains contacts in badlands, mountains, and coastal townships. Partnering with La Cumbre, they maintain a low profile along the east coast, remaining elusive to outsiders.

Le_Renard_Subtil – A notorious crime boss based in Kayewat, Le_Renard's extensive network spans the continent. Operating through agents on renewable contracts sworn to secrecy, he avoids permanent settlements outside of Kayewat, preferring mobility.

Appendix IV
Calendars & Chronological Systems

Federated domes each use their own calendar. All domes and most outsider communities use the Gregorian calendar of days, weeks, and months. All domes except Kayewat label "year one" based on the year of federation of their respective dome, backdated to 1 January. Kayewat maintains the old-world calendar, as do the Ansati. Most outsider organizations use the calendar of their trading partners or business clients during transactions but follow the old-world calendar internally.

Federation/State	Calendar	Old-World Year 1*	Present Narrative**
Old World	Gregorian (*Anno Domini*)	AD 1	AD 2590
New Inland	AC (*Anno Coniuctionis*)	AD 2345	AC 0245
Hyacynthe	NU (*Nouvelle unification*)	AD 2359	231 NU
Arctica	AC (*After completion*)	AD 2470	120 AC/AR
Sascota	AC (*After completion*)	AD 2277	0313 AC/SC
Ozarck	AC (*After completion*)	AD 2309	281 AC/OZ
Kayewat	KW (*Kayewati Gregorian*)	AD 1	KW 2590
Motherland	NE (*Nuestro año de eminencia*)	AD 2323	NE 267

* Indicates the Gregorian calendar year in which each respective federation/state began their own calendar/year one.

**The present-day narrative in the story is a historical retelling by Sister Ave Maria.

Appendix V
Terminology

Ansati – Religious order of outsiders who preserve history
Anties – Antibiotic medicine
Aquavit – Strong alcoholic beverage, green-tinted
Biosynth – Biological synthetic technology designed to cover or alter skin
Brigands – Outsider criminals
Brother – Adult male Ansati
Council of Regents – A form of senate in Motherland
Crux Ansata – Ankh cross, symbol of the Ansati
Credit – General term for money
Dome – Superstructure designed to cover and protect cities in the Reclamation Age
Domestic High Council (DHC) – Governing body of New Inland
Domer – Outsider term for anyone from a domed federation
Datapad – Larger than a handheld, designed for work rather than daily tasks
Eminence – Royal title of the sovereign of Motherland
Flowers – New Kayewati immigrants
Foundry – Industrial sector of New Inland, located in sub-levels
Handheld – Personal electronic device that is used for multiple daily tasks and functions
Java - Coffee
La Golondriña – Sparrow, national symbol of Motherland.
Magister – Chief of the Council of Regents
Magna-Rail – High-speed rail transportation that links domes.
Nuclear Cell/Nuke Cell – Nuclear fusion-based power source
Old-World – Civilization before the collapse that ushered in the Reclamation Age
Ossuary – Archival hall where the Ansati store human remains, possessions
Outsiders – Term for anyone not from a dome
Petrol – Gasoline, or fuel produced from petroleum
Reaper (See **Ansati**)
Red tide – Potent respiratory disease, causes delirium in extreme cases

Reclamation – Age of dome construction, from Old-World salvaged materials

Rotunda – Official parliament of the DHC in New Inland

Seam – Irradiated areas, resulted from nuke cell leaks and ruptures

Shuttle – Standard automobile, used for simple transportation

Sister – Female Ansati

Sister (Syballine) – Sister who has attained a high degree of illumination

Sleeve – Biosynthetic covering designed to conceal Kayewati stamps from detection

Spiritis Arbor – "Spirit tree" planted and harvested for Motherland rites

Stamp – Tattoo made of a concoction of inks, required for all citizens of Kayewat.

Tan-Ro – Tandem-rotor helicopter cargo transports used by Capston.

Velo – Racing bicycle

Velodrome – Racing facility for competitive cycling.

Acknowledgements

It's been two years since I published *Exiles*. I intended to have *One Law* ready in eighteen months, but life tends to get in the way. This book, the second of three in the *Chronicles of the Reclamation*, is a two-act story. It changed significantly after I completed *Exiles*, but definitely for the better. It may have taken me a while, but I can only tell my characters' stories if I take the time to listen to them. And did they ever have a lot to say!

I have so many people I would like to acknowledge. First and foremost, my family: My parents Joan and John LeBlanc; sisters Marcie and Brianne their spouses Alan and Dave; my nephews Rohan, Piersen, Alexandre, and Leo; my fiancée and partner in crime Christina Jones; my sons Kieran and Colby. I love you all more than I could ever express.

Thank you to the staff and students at Stanley Consolidated School who have supported me from the very beginning; the SCS Writer's Workshop for continuing to amaze me with their imagination, creativity, and silliness; Tim Sarty and the Stanley Community Library; Julian Christie and the McAdam Public Library; my author friends Em Whelley, Angela Van Liempt, and Kim Doucette; and everyone who purchased, borrowed, or read *Exiles*—thank you so much for your support!

Brandon J. LeBlanc lives in Penniac, New Brunswick (Canada), and teaches in the nearby village of Stanley. *One Law* is his second novel, and the second of three in the *Chronicles of the Reclamation* series.